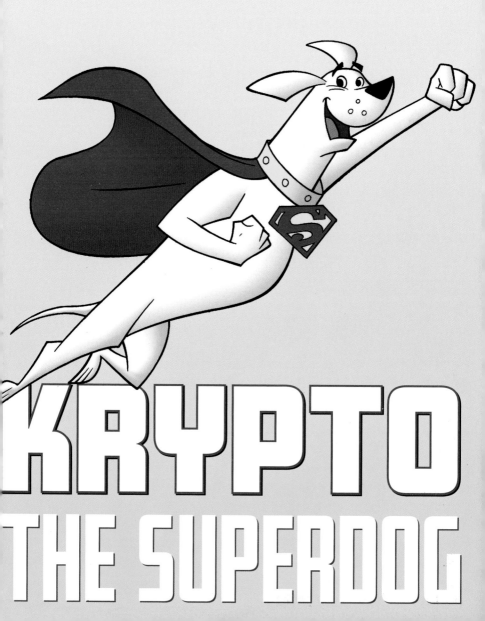

KRYPTO
THE SUPERDOG

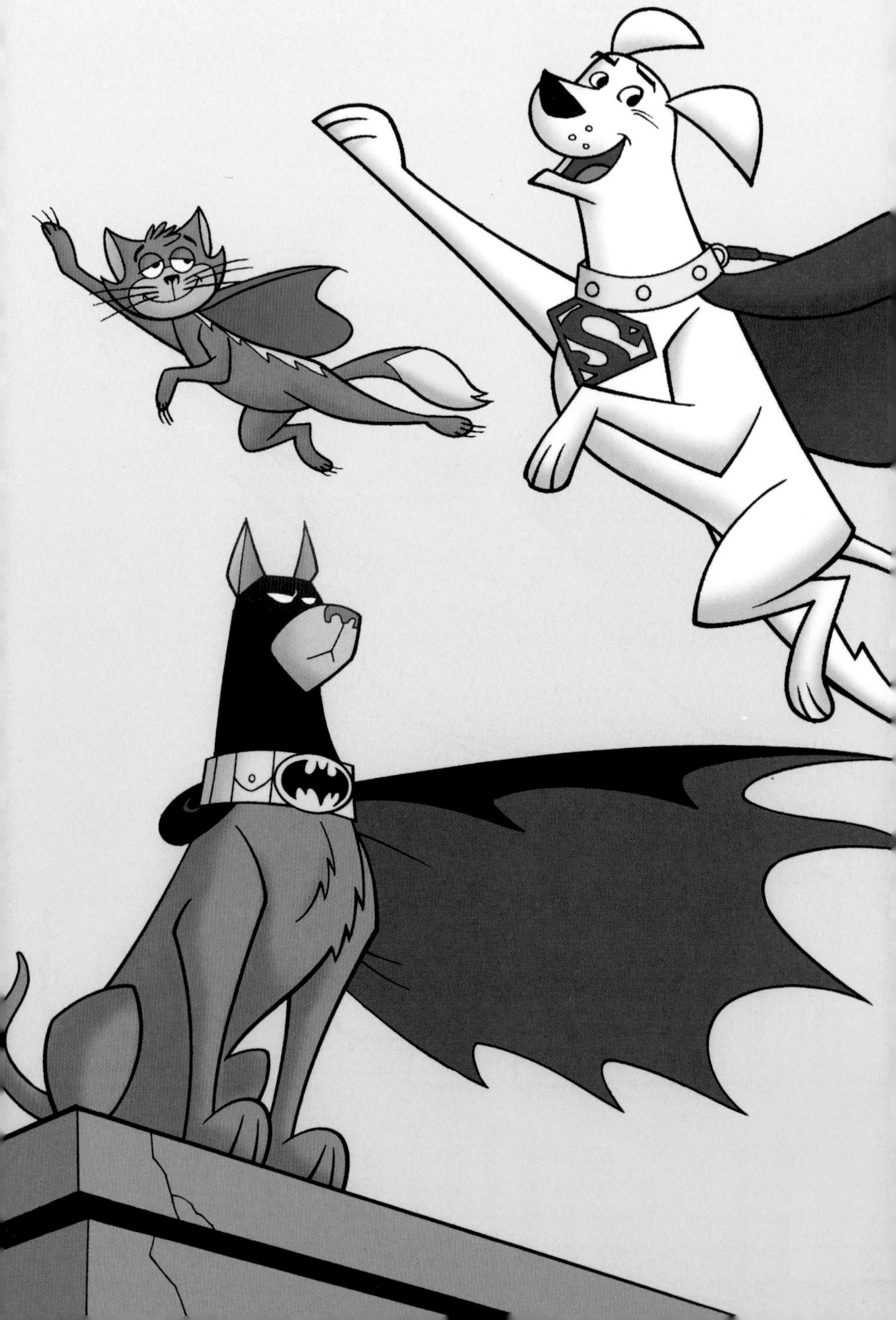

JESSE LEON McCANN
writer

JEFF ALBRECHT
AL NICKERSON
inkers

MIN S. KU
SCOTT COHN
pencillers

DAVID TANGUAY
colorist and letterer

SCOTT JERALDS
collection and series cover artist

SUPERMAN created by JERRY SIEGEL and JOE SHUSTER
By special arrangement with the Jerry Siegel family

KRYPTO
THE SUPERDOG

JOAN HILTY
Editor - Original Series
RACHEL GLUCKSTERN
Assistant Editor - Original Series
ALEX GALER
Editor - Collected Edition
STEVE COOK
Design Director - Books
AMIE BROCKWAY-METCALF
Publication Design
CHRISTY SAWYER
Publication Production

MARIE JAVINS
Editor-in-Chief, DC Comics

DANIEL CHERRY III
Senior VP - General Manager
JIM LEE
Publisher & Chief Creative Officer
JOEN CHOE
VP - Global Brand & Creative Services
DON FALLETTI
VP - Manufacturing Operations & Workflow Management
LAWRENCE GANEM
VP - Talent Services
ALISON GILL
Senior VP - Manufacturing & Operations
NICK J. NAPOLITANO
VP - Manufacturing Administration & Design
NANCY SPEARS
VP - Revenue

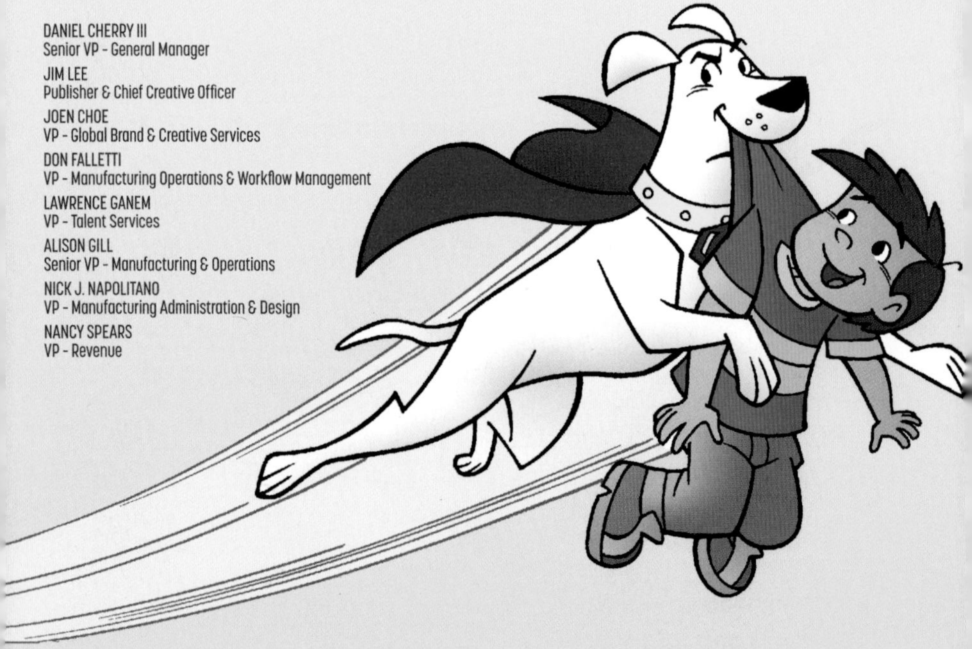

KRYPTO THE SUPERDOG

DC Comics, 2900 West Alameda Ave., Burbank, CA 91505
Printed by Worzalla, Stevens Point, WI, USA. 4/23/21. First Printing.
ISBN: 978-1-77950-927-7

Library of Congress Cataloging-in-Publication Data is available.

MIX
Paper from responsible sources
FSC® C002589

CONTENTS

KRYPTO

KRYPTO

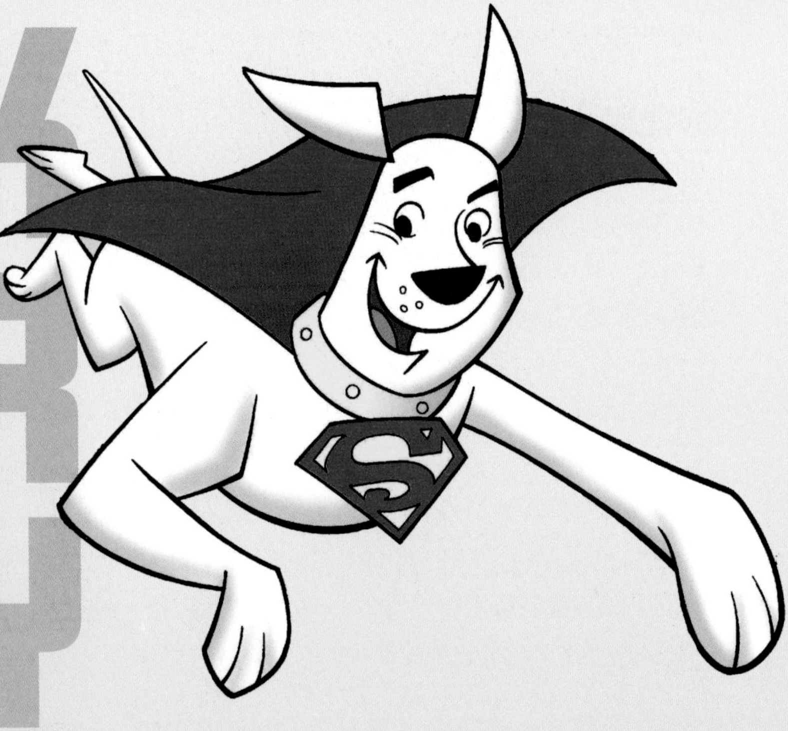

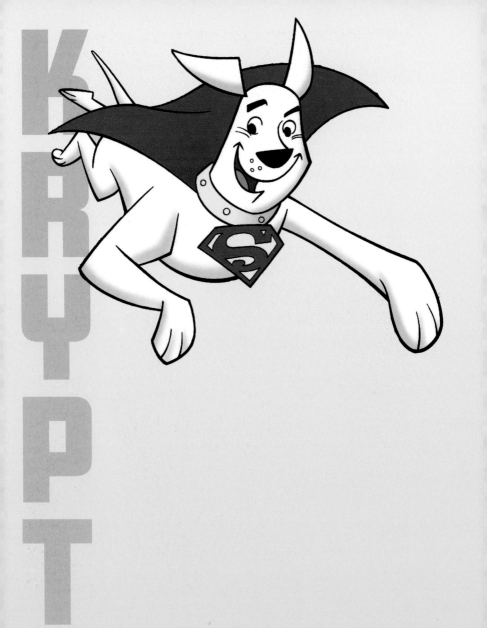

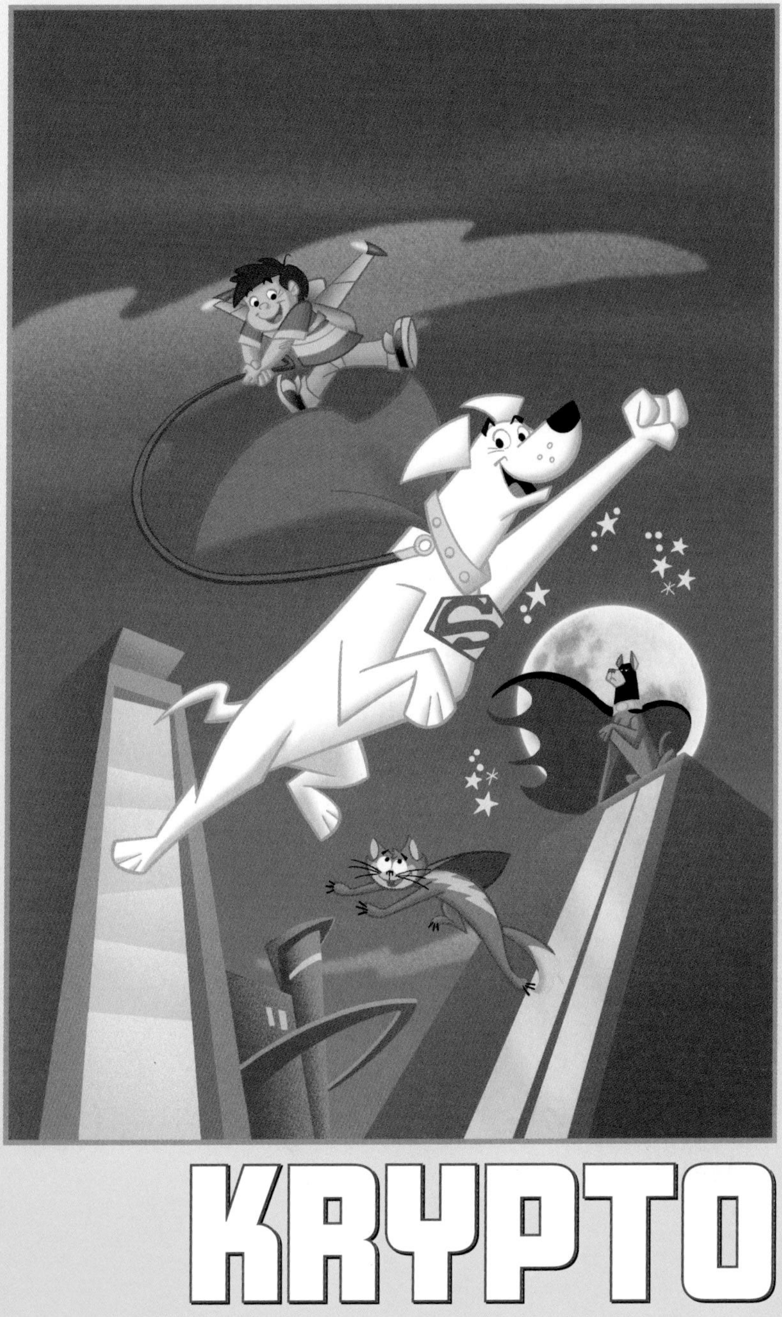

KRYPTO
THE SUPERDOG

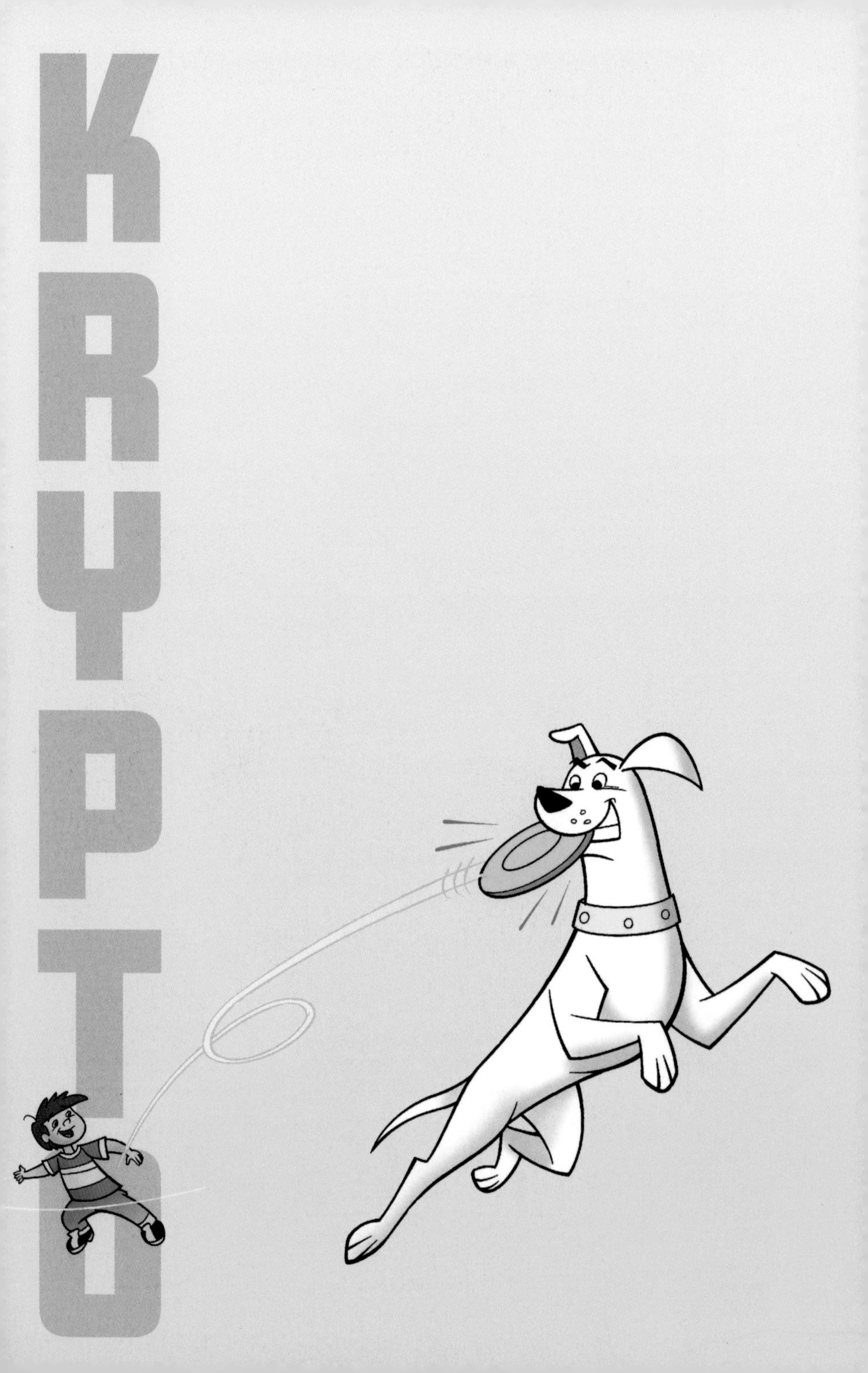
KRYPTO

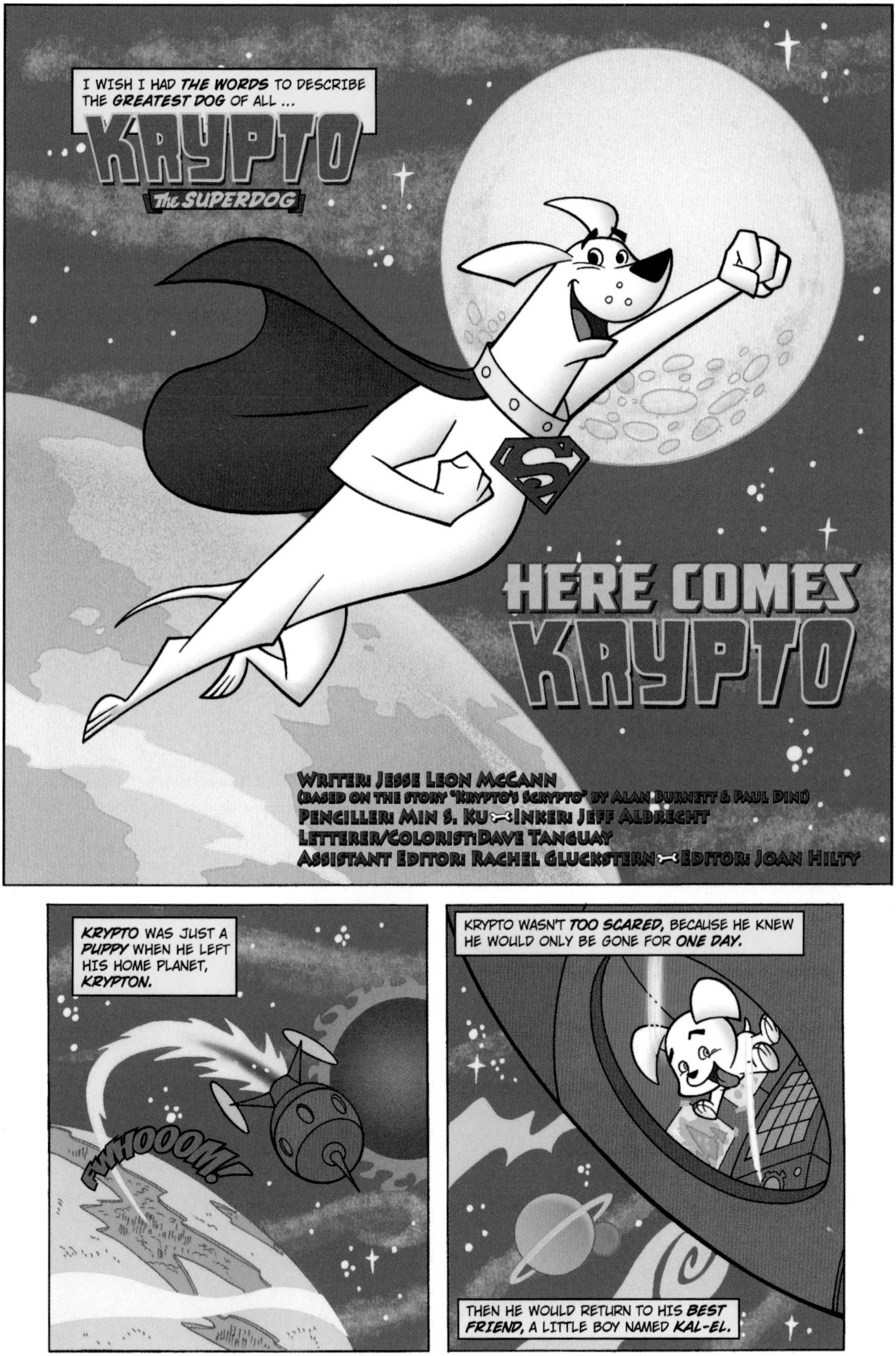
I WISH I HAD THE WORDS TO DESCRIBE THE GREATEST DOG OF ALL ...
KRYPTO
The SUPERDOG
HERE COMES KRYPTO
Writer: Jesse Leon McCann
(based on the story "Krypto's Scrypto" by Alan Burnett & Paul Dini)
Penciller: Min S. Ku Inker: Jeff Albrecht
Letterer/Colorist: Dave Tanguay
Assistant Editor: Rachel Gluckstern Editor: Joan Hilty
KRYPTO WAS JUST A PUPPY WHEN HE LEFT HIS HOME PLANET, KRYPTON.
FWHOOOM!
KRYPTO WASN'T TOO SCARED, BECAUSE HE KNEW HE WOULD ONLY BE GONE FOR ONE DAY.
THEN HE WOULD RETURN TO HIS BEST FRIEND, A LITTLE BOY NAMED KAL-EL.

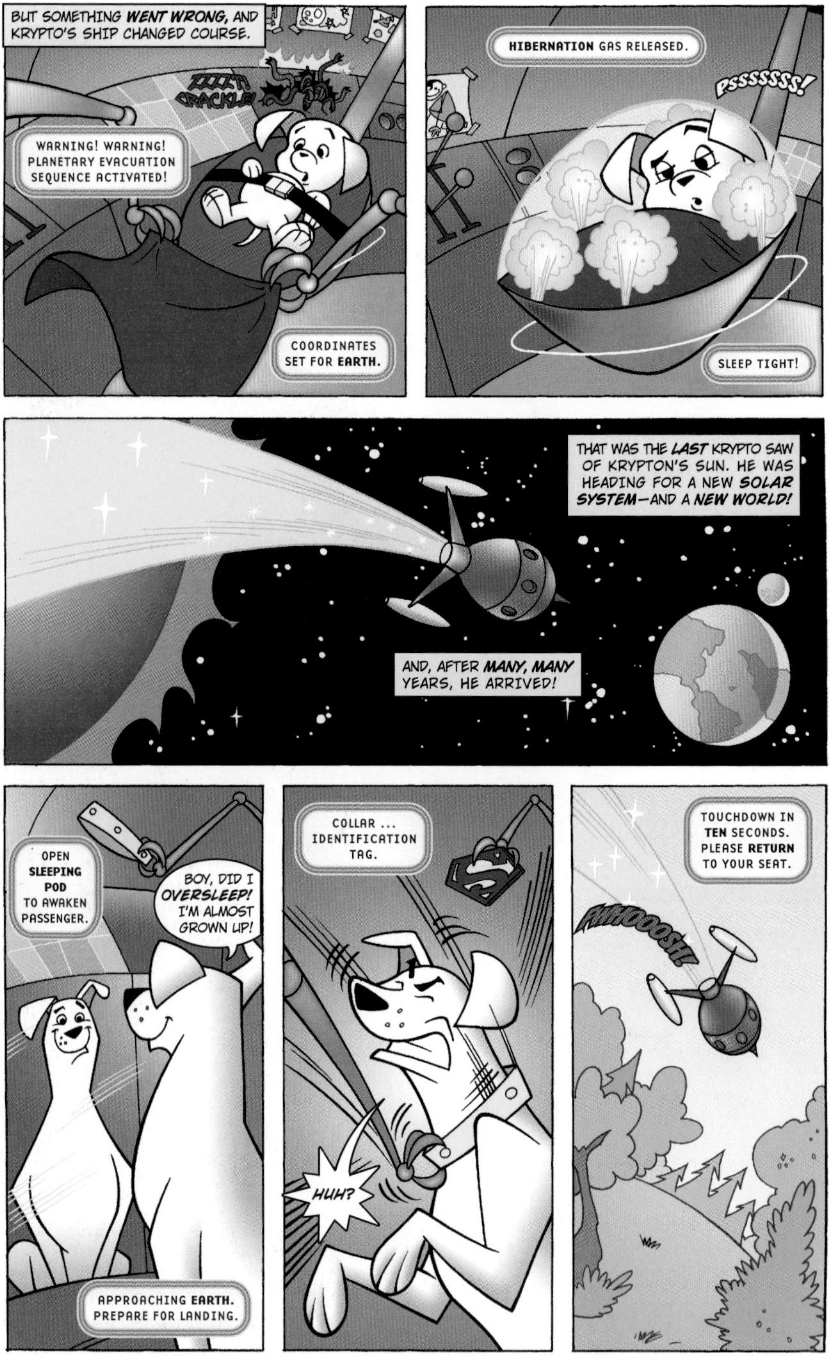

BUT SOMETHING **WENT WRONG,** AND KRYPTO'S SHIP CHANGED COURSE.
ZZZZT! CRACKLE!
WARNING! WARNING! PLANETARY EVACUATION SEQUENCE ACTIVATED!
COORDINATES SET FOR **EARTH.**
HIBERNATION GAS RELEASED.
PSSSSSSS!
SLEEP TIGHT!
THAT WAS THE ***LAST*** KRYPTO SAW OF KRYPTON'S SUN. HE WAS HEADING FOR A NEW ***SOLAR SYSTEM***—AND A ***NEW WORLD!***
AND, AFTER ***MANY, MANY*** YEARS, HE ARRIVED!
OPEN **SLEEPING POD** TO AWAKEN PASSENGER.
BOY, DID I ***OVERSLEEP!*** I'M ALMOST GROWN UP!
APPROACHING **EARTH.** PREPARE FOR LANDING.
COLLAR ... IDENTIFICATION TAG.
HUH?
TOUCHDOWN IN **TEN** SECONDS. PLEASE **RETURN** TO YOUR SEAT.
FWHOOOSH!

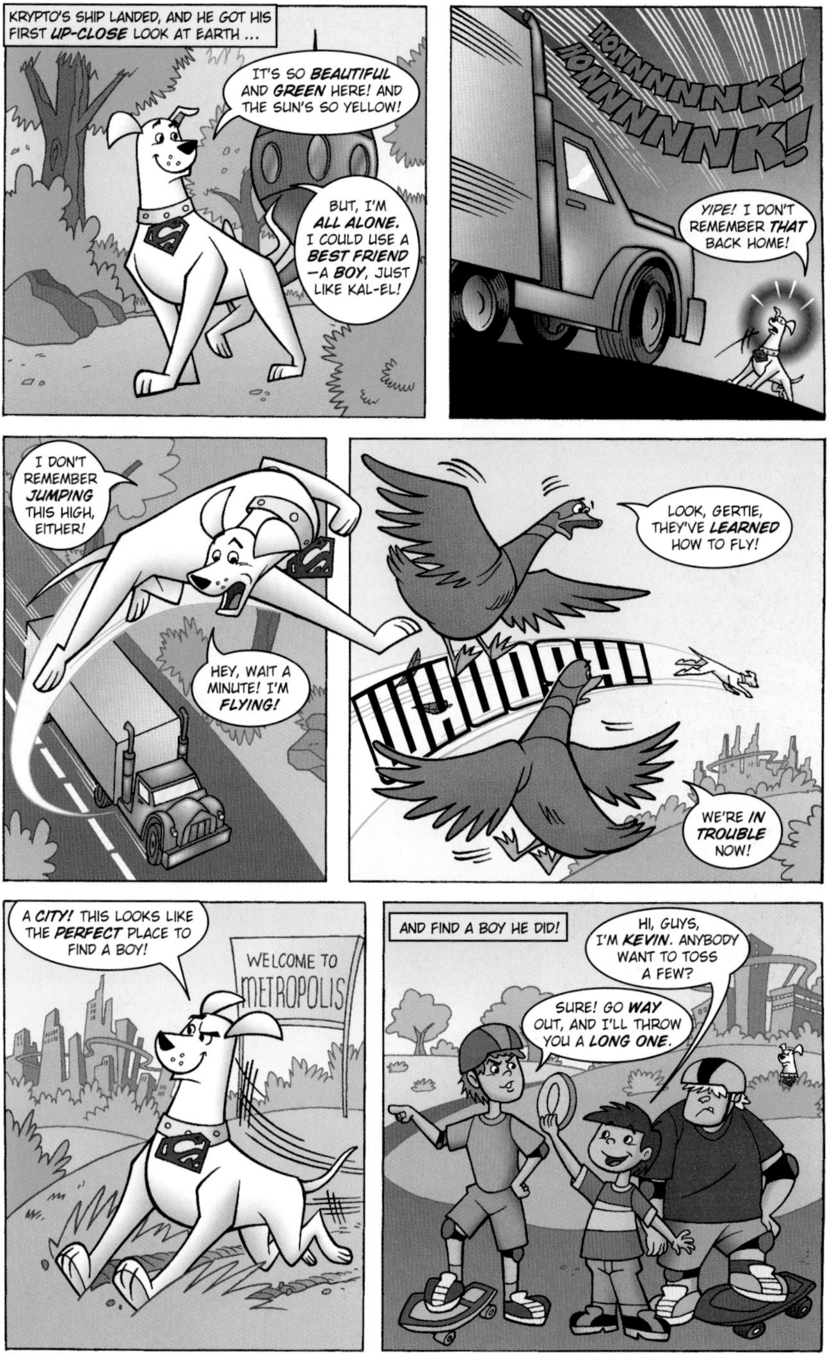
KRYPTO'S SHIP LANDED, AND HE GOT HIS FIRST UP-CLOSE LOOK AT EARTH ...
IT'S SO BEAUTIFUL AND GREEN HERE! AND THE SUN'S SO YELLOW!
BUT, I'M ALL ALONE. I COULD USE A BEST FRIEND —A BOY, JUST LIKE KAL-EL!
HONNNNNNK! HONNNNNNNK!
YIPE! I DON'T REMEMBER THAT BACK HOME!
I DON'T REMEMBER JUMPING THIS HIGH, EITHER!
HEY, WAIT A MINUTE! I'M FLYING!
LOOK, GERTIE, THEY'VE LEARNED HOW TO FLY!
WE'RE IN TROUBLE NOW!
A CITY! THIS LOOKS LIKE THE PERFECT PLACE TO FIND A BOY!
WELCOME TO METROPOLIS
AND FIND A BOY HE DID!
HI, GUYS, I'M KEVIN. ANYBODY WANT TO TOSS A FEW?
SURE! GO WAY OUT, AND I'LL THROW YOU A LONG ONE.

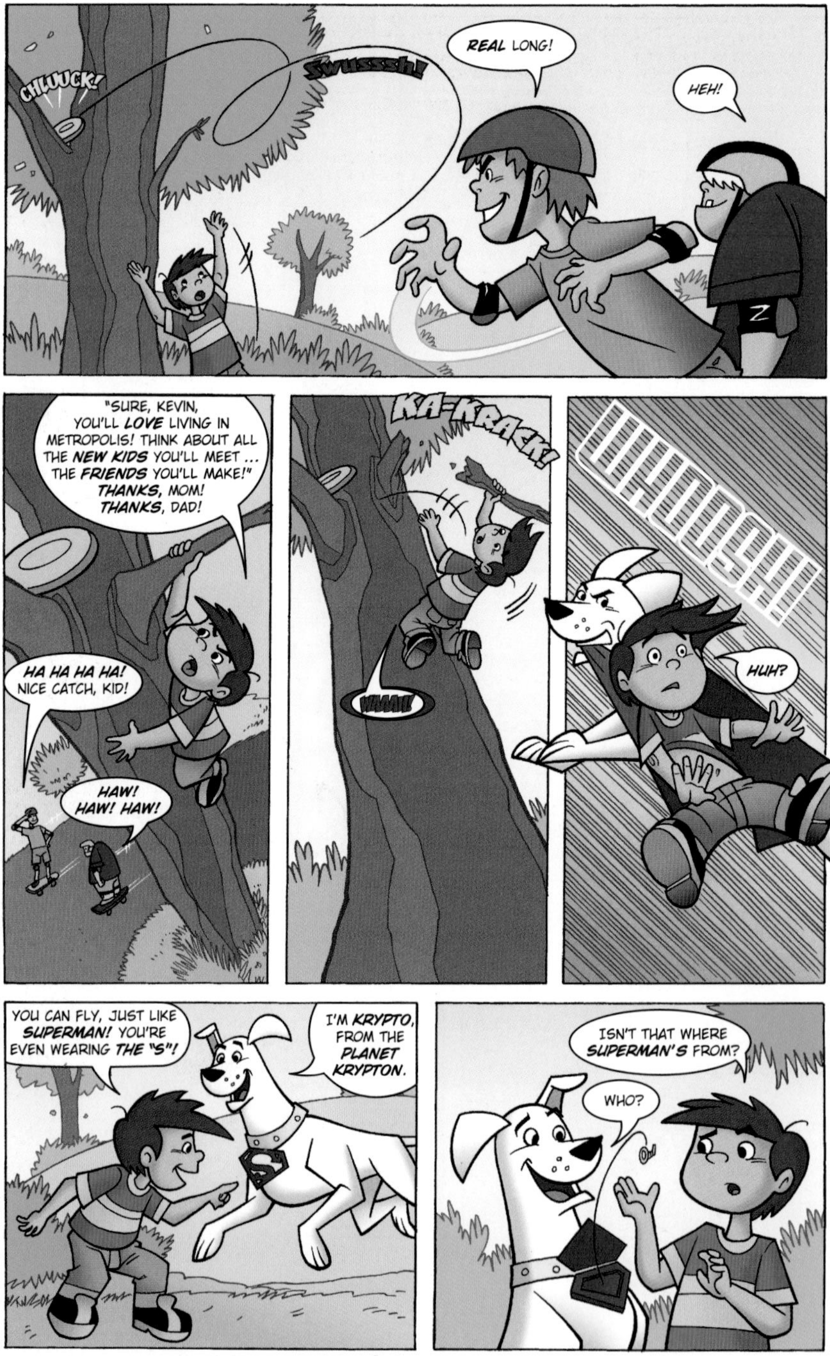
CHUUCK!
SWUSSSH!
REAL LONG!
HEH!
"SURE, KEVIN, YOU'LL LOVE LIVING IN METROPOLIS! THINK ABOUT ALL THE NEW KIDS YOU'LL MEET ... THE FRIENDS YOU'LL MAKE!" THANKS, MOM! THANKS, DAD!
HA HA HA HA! NICE CATCH, KID!
HAW! HAW! HAW!
KA-KRACK!
WAAAH!
HUH?
YOU CAN FLY, JUST LIKE SUPERMAN! YOU'RE EVEN WEARING THE "S"!
I'M KRYPTO, FROM THE PLANET KRYPTON.
ISN'T THAT WHERE SUPERMAN'S FROM?
WHO?

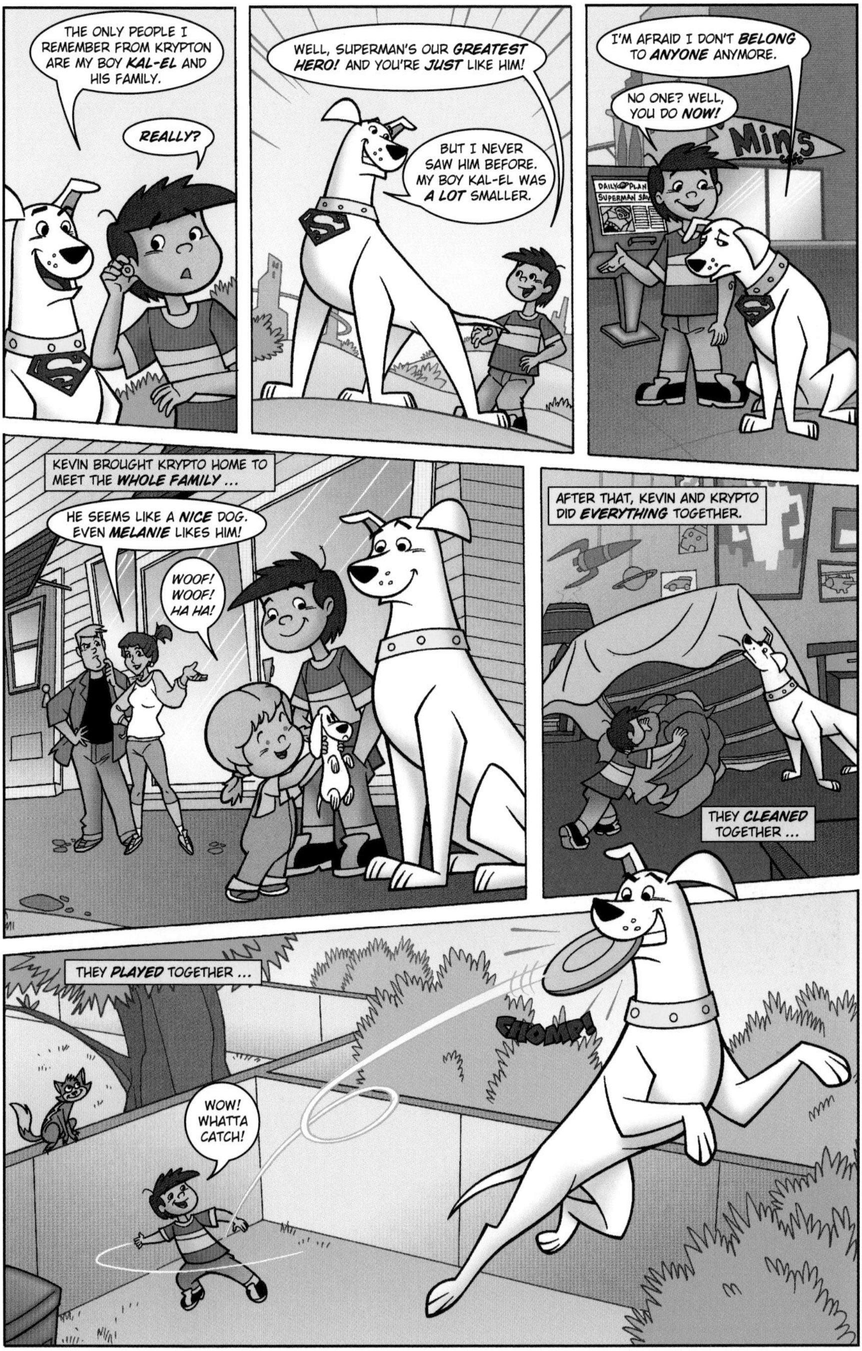
THE ONLY PEOPLE I REMEMBER FROM KRYPTON ARE MY BOY KAL-EL AND HIS FAMILY.
REALLY?
WELL, SUPERMAN'S OUR GREATEST HERO! AND YOU'RE JUST LIKE HIM!
BUT I NEVER SAW HIM BEFORE. MY BOY KAL-EL WAS A LOT SMALLER.
I'M AFRAID I DON'T BELONG TO ANYONE ANYMORE.
NO ONE? WELL, YOU DO NOW!
KEVIN BROUGHT KRYPTO HOME TO MEET THE WHOLE FAMILY ...
HE SEEMS LIKE A NICE DOG. EVEN MELANIE LIKES HIM!
WOOF! WOOF! HA HA!
AFTER THAT, KEVIN AND KRYPTO DID EVERYTHING TOGETHER.
THEY CLEANED TOGETHER ...
THEY PLAYED TOGETHER ...
CHOMP!
WOW! WHATTA CATCH!

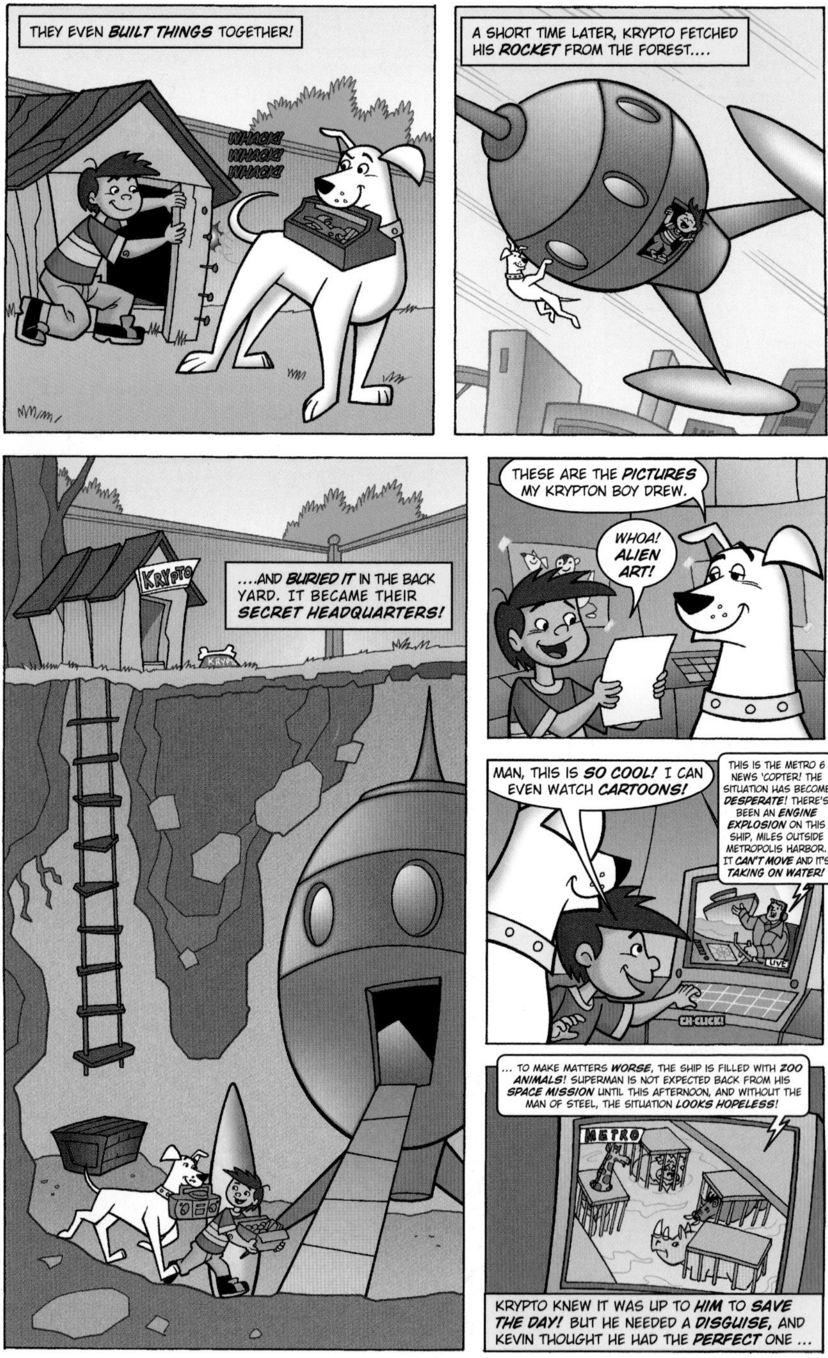

THEY EVEN BUILT THINGS TOGETHER!
WHACK! WHACK! WHACK!
A SHORT TIME LATER, KRYPTO FETCHED HIS ROCKET FROM THE FOREST....
....AND BURIED IT IN THE BACK YARD. IT BECAME THEIR SECRET HEADQUARTERS!
KRYPTO
THESE ARE THE PICTURES MY KRYPTON BOY DREW.
WHOA! ALIEN ART!
MAN, THIS IS SO COOL! I CAN EVEN WATCH CARTOONS!
THIS IS THE METRO 6 NEWS 'COPTER! THE SITUATION HAS BECOME DESPERATE! THERE'S BEEN AN ENGINE EXPLOSION ON THIS SHIP, MILES OUTSIDE METROPOLIS HARBOR. IT CAN'T MOVE AND IT'S TAKING ON WATER!
LIVE
CH-CLICK!
... TO MAKE MATTERS WORSE, THE SHIP IS FILLED WITH ZOO ANIMALS! SUPERMAN IS NOT EXPECTED BACK FROM HIS SPACE MISSION UNTIL THIS AFTERNOON, AND WITHOUT THE MAN OF STEEL, THE SITUATION LOOKS HOPELESS!
METRO
KRYPTO KNEW IT WAS UP TO HIM TO SAVE THE DAY! BUT HE NEEDED A DISGUISE, AND KEVIN THOUGHT HE HAD THE PERFECT ONE ...

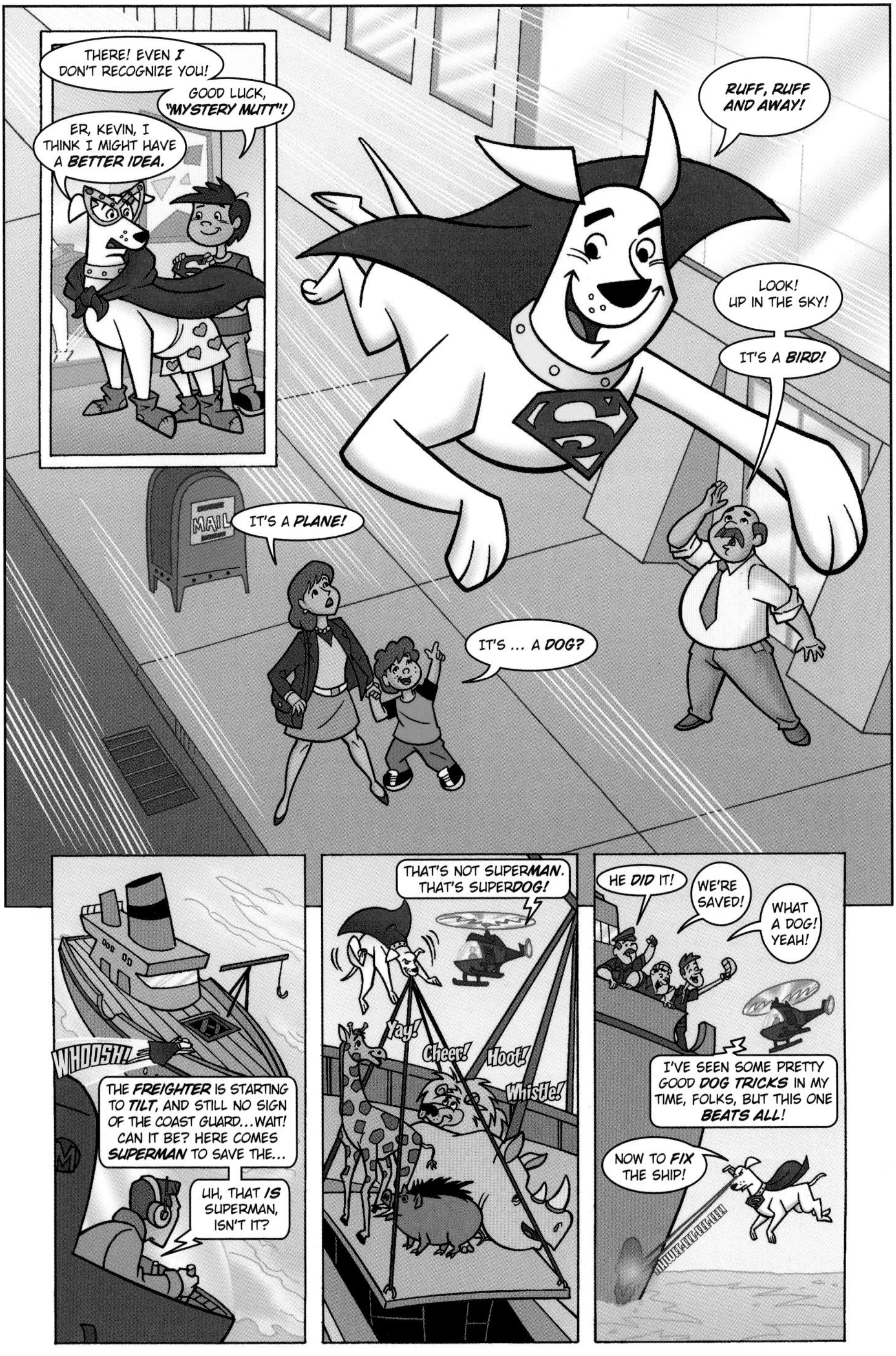
THERE! EVEN I DON'T RECOGNIZE YOU!
GOOD LUCK, "MYSTERY MUTT"!
ER, KEVIN, I THINK I MIGHT HAVE A BETTER IDEA.
RUFF, RUFF AND AWAY!
LOOK! UP IN THE SKY!
IT'S A BIRD!
MAIL
IT'S A PLANE!
IT'S ... A DOG?
WHOOSH!
THE FREIGHTER IS STARTING TO TILT, AND STILL NO SIGN OF THE COAST GUARD...WAIT! CAN IT BE? HERE COMES SUPERMAN TO SAVE THE...
UH, THAT IS SUPERMAN, ISN'T IT?
THAT'S NOT SUPERMAN. THAT'S SUPERDOG!
Yay!
Cheer!
Hoot!
Whistle!
HE DID IT!
WE'RE SAVED!
WHAT A DOG! YEAH!
I'VE SEEN SOME PRETTY GOOD DOG TRICKS IN MY TIME, FOLKS, BUT THIS ONE BEATS ALL!
NOW TO FIX THE SHIP!

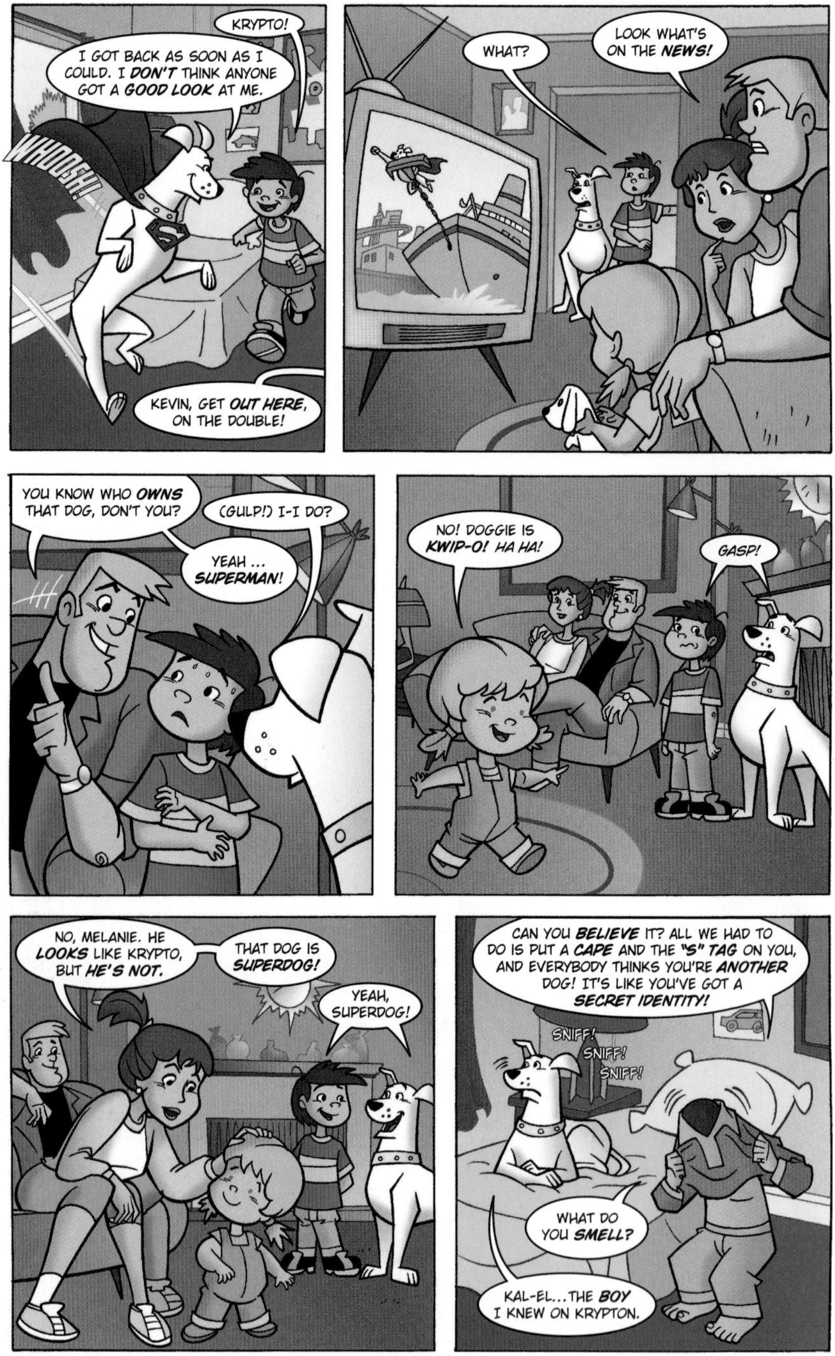
KRYPTO!
I GOT BACK AS SOON AS I COULD. I DON'T THINK ANYONE GOT A GOOD LOOK AT ME.
WHOOSH!
KEVIN, GET OUT HERE, ON THE DOUBLE!
WHAT?
LOOK WHAT'S ON THE NEWS!
YOU KNOW WHO OWNS THAT DOG, DON'T YOU?
(GULP!) I-I DO?
YEAH ... SUPERMAN!
NO! DOGGIE IS KWIP-O! HA HA!
GASP!
NO, MELANIE. HE LOOKS LIKE KRYPTO, BUT HE'S NOT.
THAT DOG IS SUPERDOG!
YEAH, SUPERDOG!
CAN YOU BELIEVE IT? ALL WE HAD TO DO IS PUT A CAPE AND THE "S" TAG ON YOU, AND EVERYBODY THINKS YOU'RE ANOTHER DOG! IT'S LIKE YOU'VE GOT A SECRET IDENTITY!
SNIFF! SNIFF! SNIFF!
WHAT DO YOU SMELL?
KAL-EL...THE BOY I KNEW ON KRYPTON.

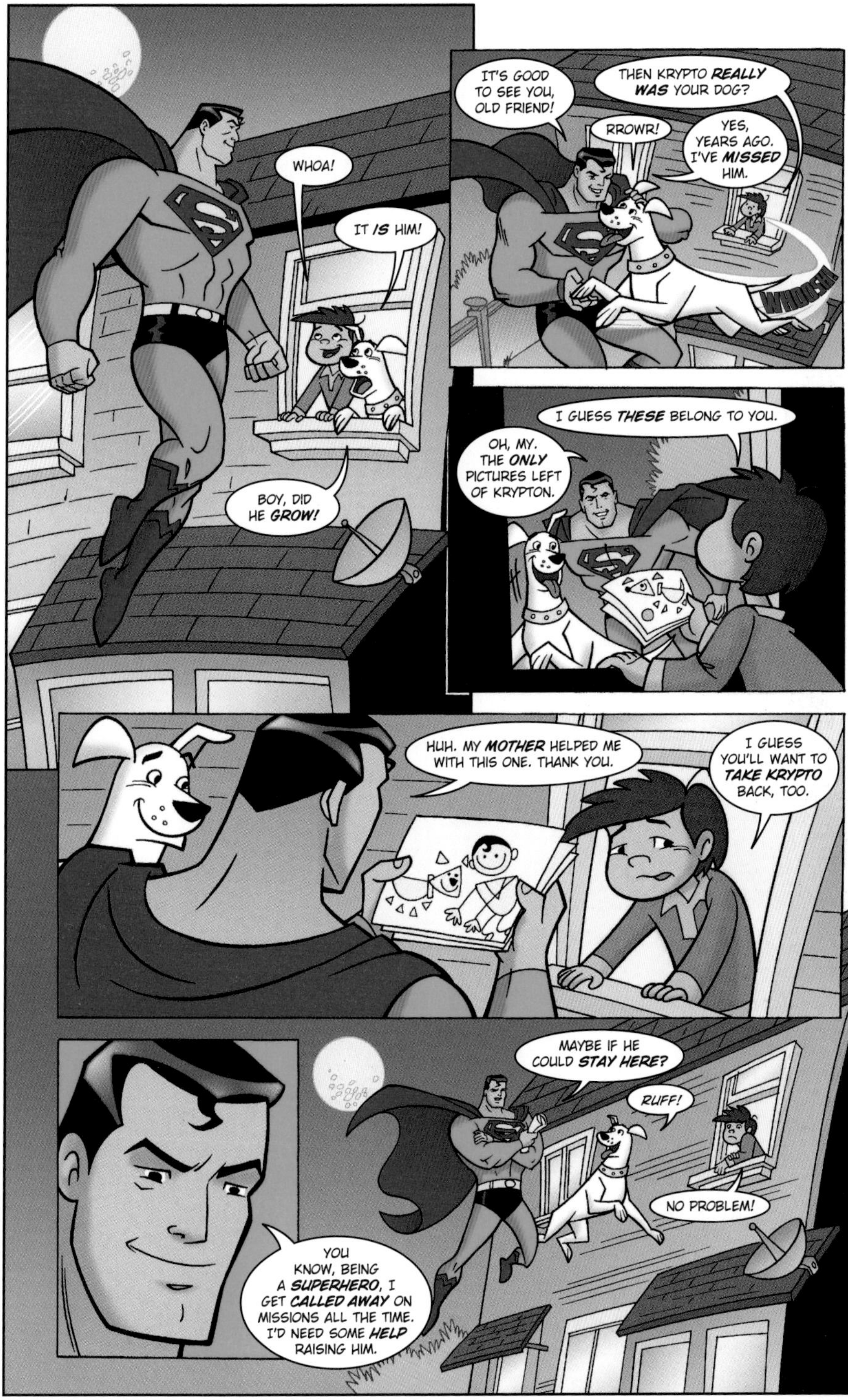
WHOA!
IT IS HIM!
BOY, DID HE GROW!
IT'S GOOD TO SEE YOU, OLD FRIEND!
THEN KRYPTO REALLY WAS YOUR DOG?
RROWR!
YES, YEARS AGO. I'VE MISSED HIM.
I GUESS THESE BELONG TO YOU.
OH, MY. THE ONLY PICTURES LEFT OF KRYPTON.
HUH. MY MOTHER HELPED ME WITH THIS ONE. THANK YOU.
I GUESS YOU'LL WANT TO TAKE KRYPTO BACK, TOO.
YOU KNOW, BEING A SUPERHERO, I GET CALLED AWAY ON MISSIONS ALL THE TIME. I'D NEED SOME HELP RAISING HIM.
MAYBE IF HE COULD STAY HERE?
RUFF!
NO PROBLEM!

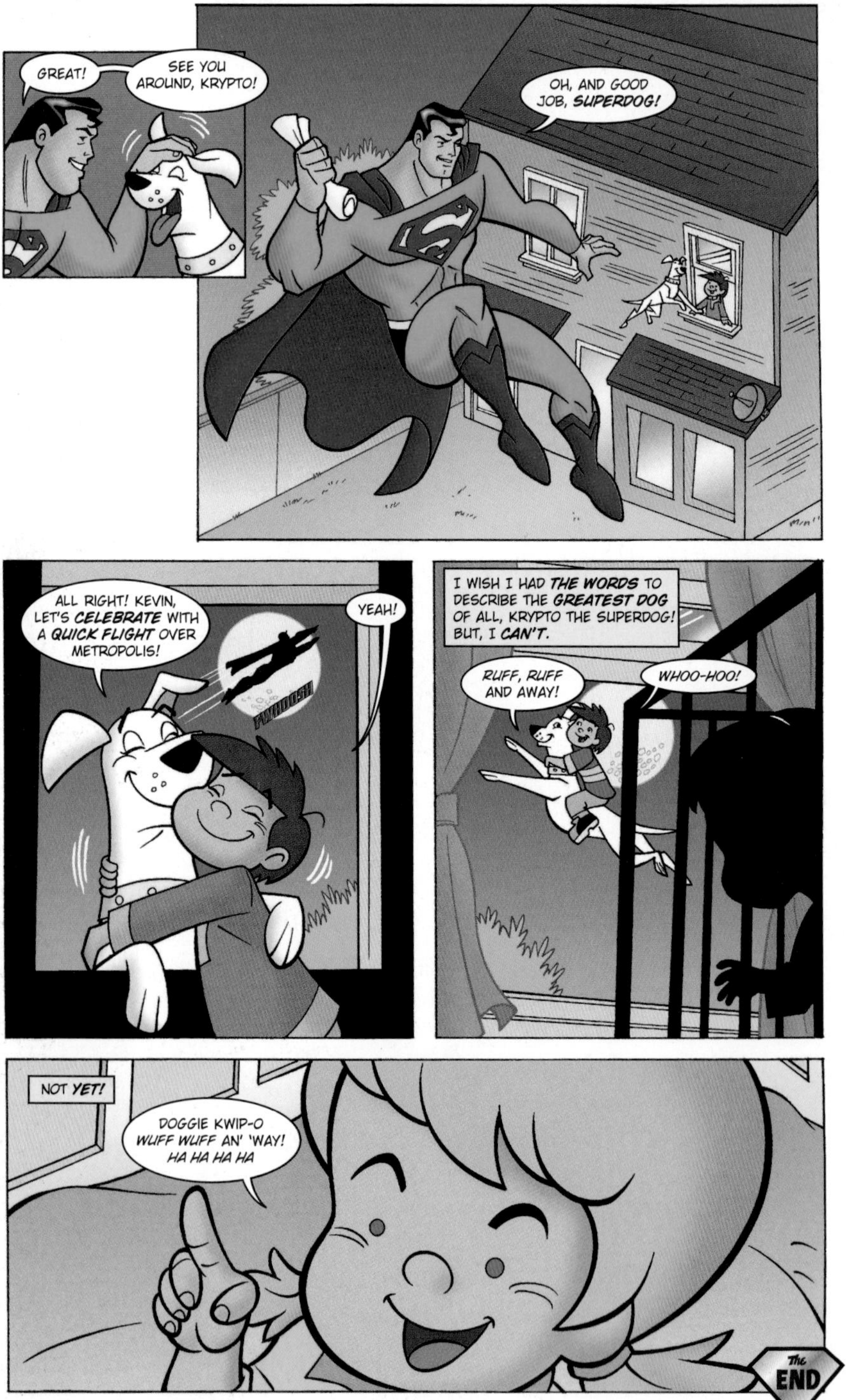
GREAT!
SEE YOU AROUND, KRYPTO!
OH, AND GOOD JOB, SUPERDOG!
ALL RIGHT! KEVIN, LET'S CELEBRATE WITH A QUICK FLIGHT OVER METROPOLIS!
YEAH!
FWOOSH
I WISH I HAD THE WORDS TO DESCRIBE THE GREATEST DOG OF ALL, KRYPTO THE SUPERDOG! BUT, I CAN'T.
RUFF, RUFF AND AWAY!
WHOO-HOO!
NOT YET!
DOGGIE KWIP-O WUFF WUFF AN' 'WAY! HA HA HA HA
The END

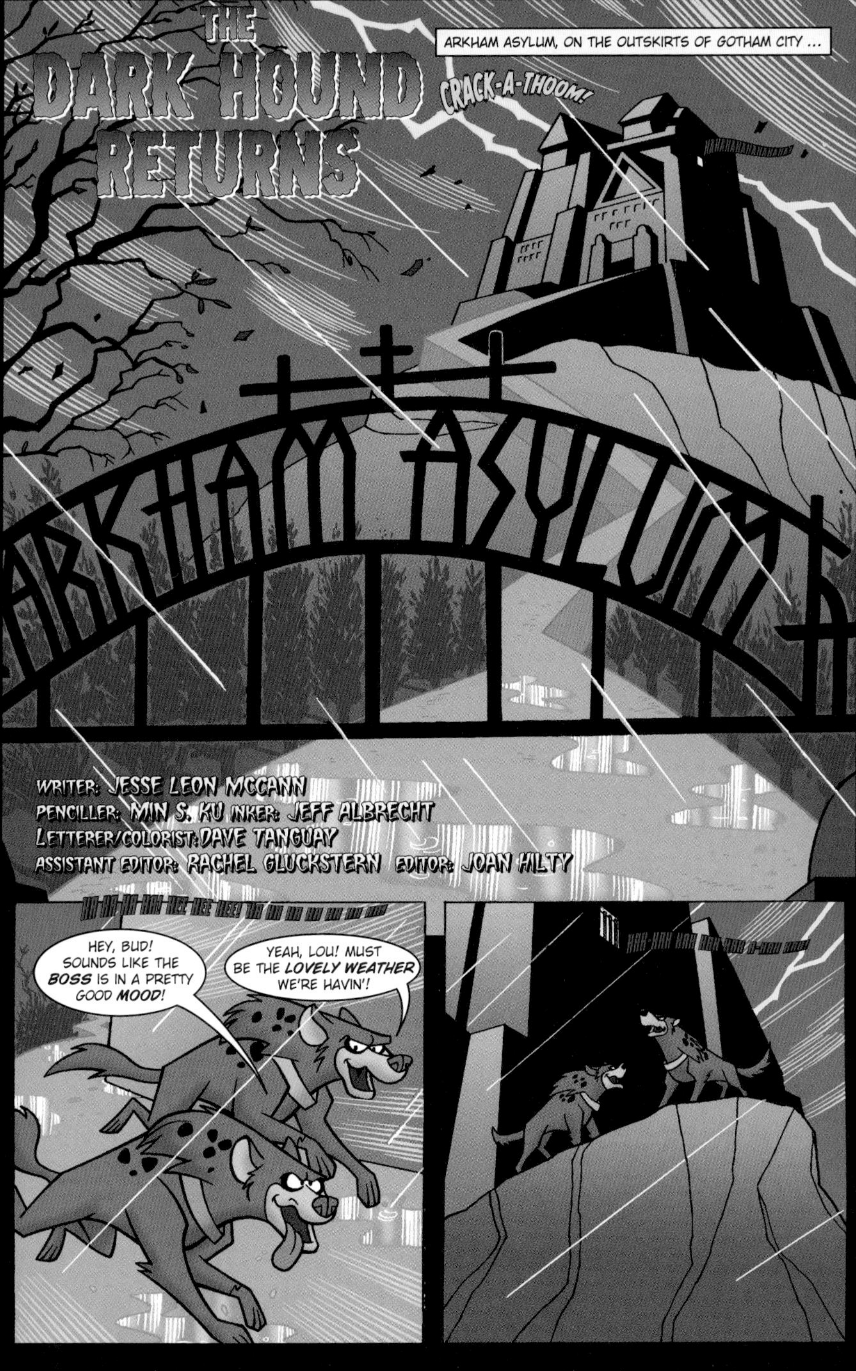
THE DARK HOUND RETURNS
ARKHAM ASYLUM, ON THE OUTSKIRTS OF GOTHAM CITY ...
CRACK-A-THOOM!
ARKHAM ASYLUM
WRITER: JESSE LEON MCCANN
PENCILLER: MIN S. KU INKER: JEFF ALBRECHT
LETTERER/COLORIST: DAVE TANGUAY
ASSISTANT EDITOR: RACHEL GLUCKSTERN EDITOR: JOAN HILTY
HA-HA-HA-HA! HEE HEE HEE!
HEY, BUD! SOUNDS LIKE THE BOSS IS IN A PRETTY GOOD MOOD!
YEAH, LOU! MUST BE THE LOVELY WEATHER WE'RE HAVIN'!
HAH-HAH HAH HAH HAH A-HAH HAH!

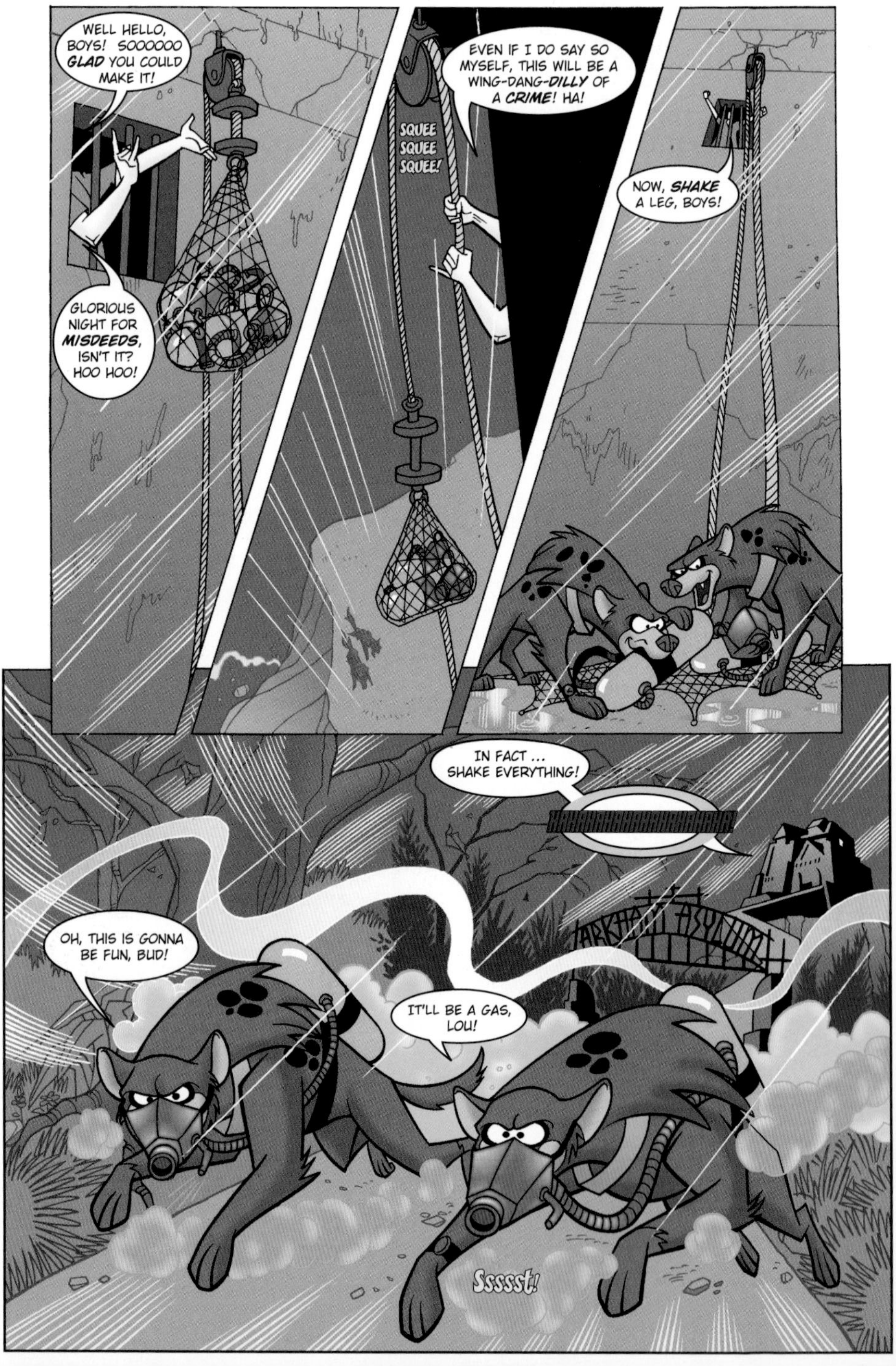
WELL HELLO, BOYS! SOOOOOO GLAD YOU COULD MAKE IT!
GLORIOUS NIGHT FOR MISDEEDS, ISN'T IT? HOO HOO!
EVEN IF I DO SAY SO MYSELF, THIS WILL BE A WING-DANG-DILLY OF A CRIME! HA!
SQUEE SQUEE SQUEE!
NOW, SHAKE A LEG, BOYS!
IN FACT ... SHAKE EVERYTHING!
ARKHAM ASYLUM
OH, THIS IS GONNA BE FUN, BUD!
IT'LL BE A GAS, LOU!
Ssssst!

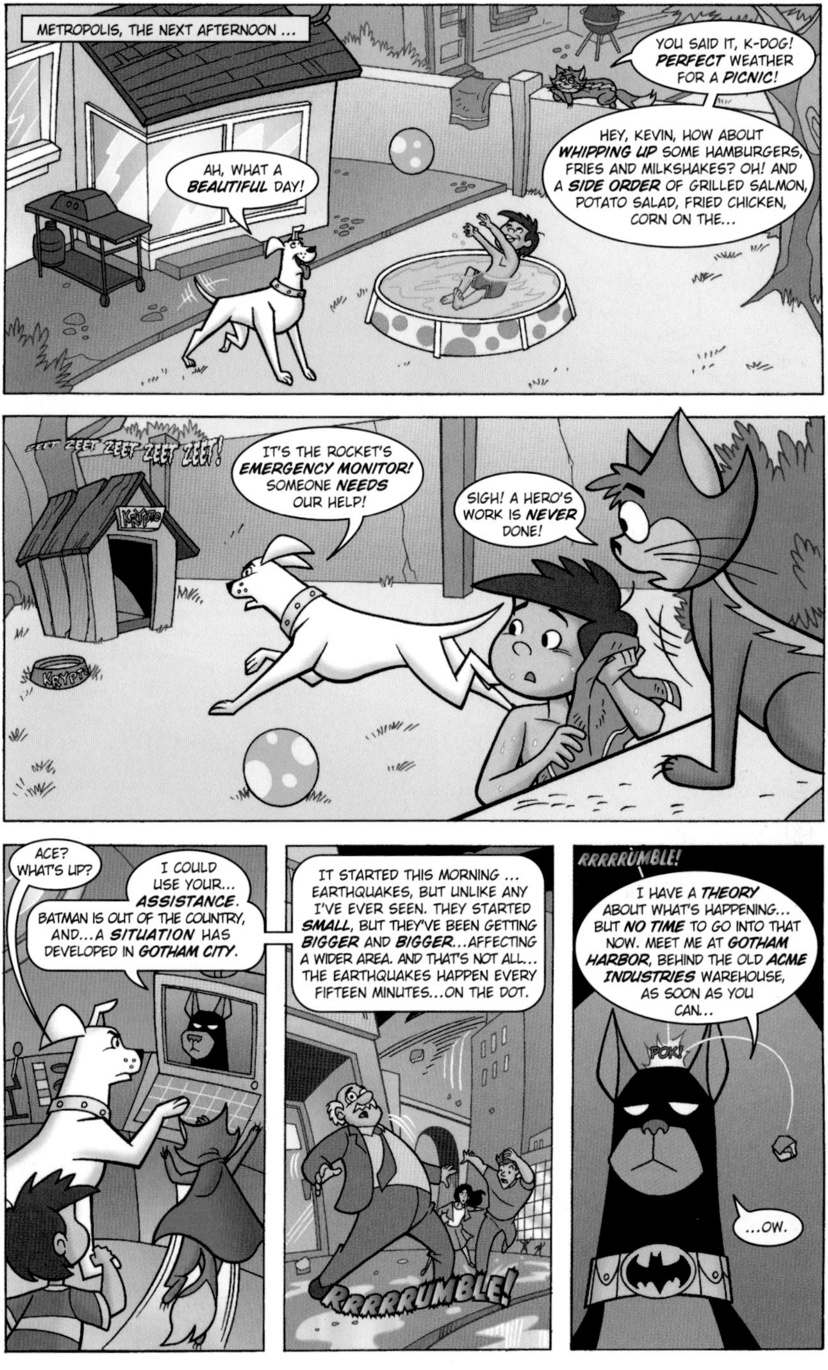
METROPOLIS, THE NEXT AFTERNOON ...
AH, WHAT A BEAUTIFUL DAY!
YOU SAID IT, K-DOG! PERFECT WEATHER FOR A PICNIC!
HEY, KEVIN, HOW ABOUT WHIPPING UP SOME HAMBURGERS, FRIES AND MILKSHAKES? OH! AND A SIDE ORDER OF GRILLED SALMON, POTATO SALAD, FRIED CHICKEN, CORN ON THE...
ZEET ZEET ZEET ZEET ZEET!
KRYPTO
IT'S THE ROCKET'S EMERGENCY MONITOR! SOMEONE NEEDS OUR HELP!
SIGH! A HERO'S WORK IS NEVER DONE!
KRYPTO
ACE? WHAT'S UP?
I COULD USE YOUR... ASSISTANCE. BATMAN IS OUT OF THE COUNTRY, AND...A SITUATION HAS DEVELOPED IN GOTHAM CITY.
IT STARTED THIS MORNING ... EARTHQUAKES, BUT UNLIKE ANY I'VE EVER SEEN. THEY STARTED SMALL, BUT THEY'VE BEEN GETTING BIGGER AND BIGGER...AFFECTING A WIDER AREA. AND THAT'S NOT ALL... THE EARTHQUAKES HAPPEN EVERY FIFTEEN MINUTES...ON THE DOT.
RRRRRUMBLE!
RRRRRUMBLE!
I HAVE A THEORY ABOUT WHAT'S HAPPENING... BUT NO TIME TO GO INTO THAT NOW. MEET ME AT GOTHAM HARBOR, BEHIND THE OLD ACME INDUSTRIES WAREHOUSE, AS SOON AS YOU CAN...
POK!
...OW.

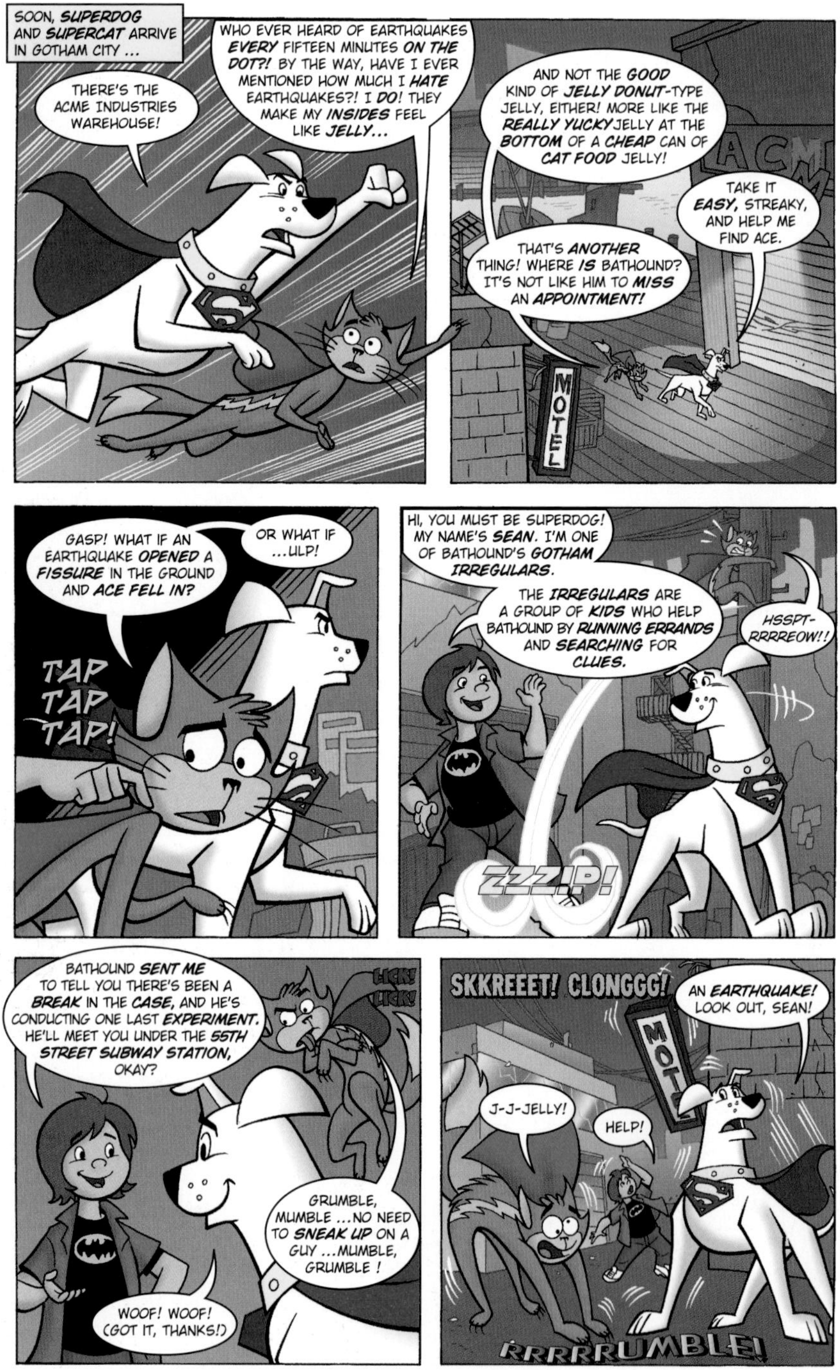
SOON, SUPERDOG AND SUPERCAT ARRIVE IN GOTHAM CITY ...
THERE'S THE ACME INDUSTRIES WAREHOUSE!
WHO EVER HEARD OF EARTHQUAKES EVERY FIFTEEN MINUTES ON THE DOT?! BY THE WAY, HAVE I EVER MENTIONED HOW MUCH I HATE EARTHQUAKES?! I DO! THEY MAKE MY INSIDES FEEL LIKE JELLY...
AND NOT THE GOOD KIND OF JELLY DONUT-TYPE JELLY, EITHER! MORE LIKE THE REALLY YUCKY JELLY AT THE BOTTOM OF A CHEAP CAN OF CAT FOOD JELLY!
TAKE IT EASY, STREAKY, AND HELP ME FIND ACE.
THAT'S ANOTHER THING! WHERE IS BATHOUND? IT'S NOT LIKE HIM TO MISS AN APPOINTMENT!
MOTEL
GASP! WHAT IF AN EARTHQUAKE OPENED A FISSURE IN THE GROUND AND ACE FELL IN?
OR WHAT IF ...ULP!
TAP TAP TAP!
HI, YOU MUST BE SUPERDOG! MY NAME'S SEAN. I'M ONE OF BATHOUND'S GOTHAM IRREGULARS.
THE IRREGULARS ARE A GROUP OF KIDS WHO HELP BATHOUND BY RUNNING ERRANDS AND SEARCHING FOR CLUES.
HSSPT-RRRREOW!!
ZZZIP!
BATHOUND SENT ME TO TELL YOU THERE'S BEEN A BREAK IN THE CASE, AND HE'S CONDUCTING ONE LAST EXPERIMENT. HE'LL MEET YOU UNDER THE 55TH STREET SUBWAY STATION, OKAY?
LICK! LICK!
GRUMBLE, MUMBLE ...NO NEED TO SNEAK UP ON A GUY ...MUMBLE, GRUMBLE !
WOOF! WOOF! (GOT IT, THANKS!)
SKKREEET! CLONGGG!
AN EARTHQUAKE! LOOK OUT, SEAN!
J-J-JELLY!
HELP!
RRRRRUMBLE!

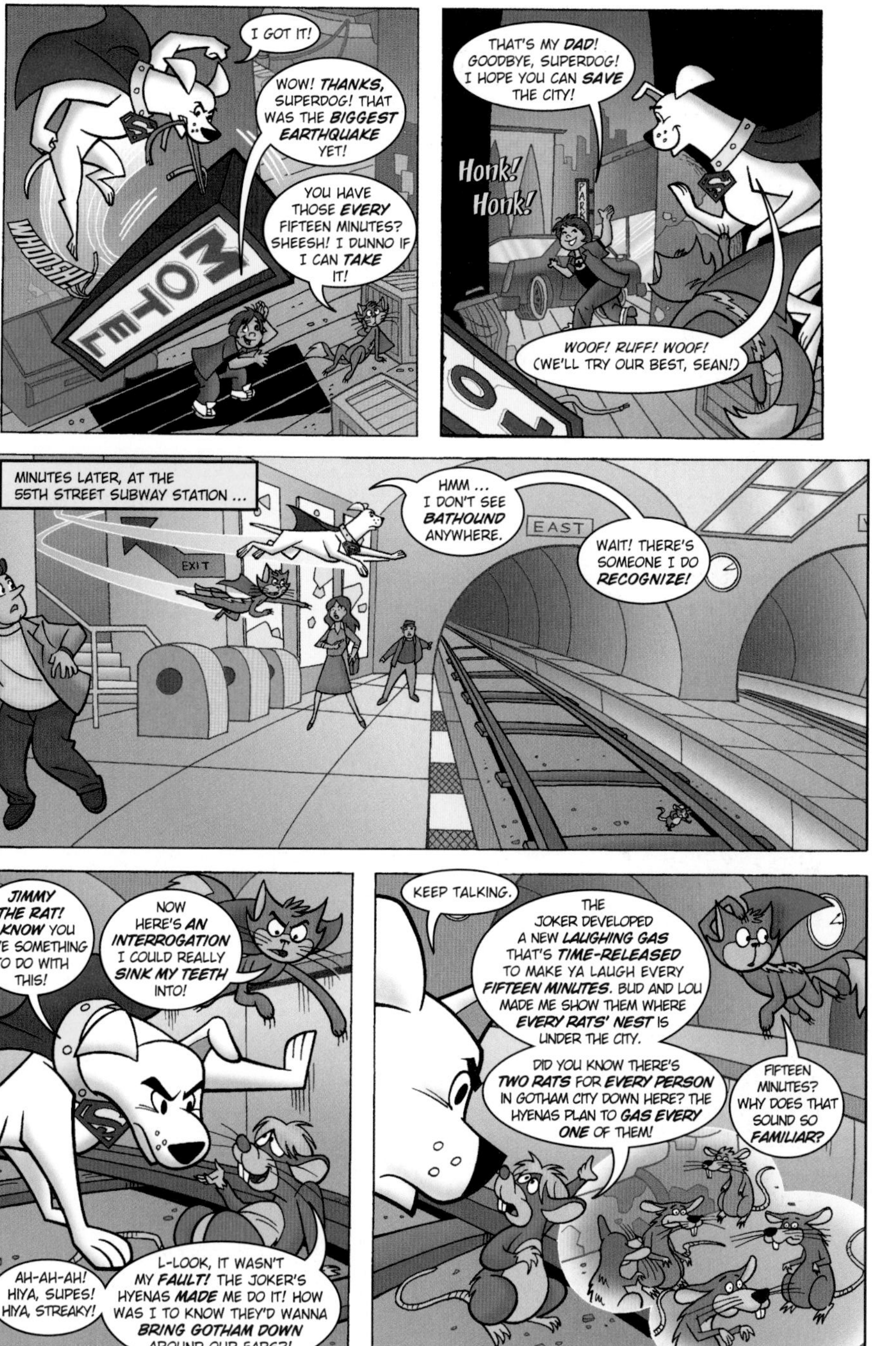
I GOT IT!
WOW! THANKS, SUPERDOG! THAT WAS THE BIGGEST EARTHQUAKE YET!
YOU HAVE THOSE EVERY FIFTEEN MINUTES? SHEESH! I DUNNO IF I CAN TAKE IT!
WHOOSH!
MOTEL
THAT'S MY DAD! GOODBYE, SUPERDOG! I HOPE YOU CAN SAVE THE CITY!
Honk! Honk!
WOOF! RUFF! WOOF! (WE'LL TRY OUR BEST, SEAN!)
MINUTES LATER, AT THE 55TH STREET SUBWAY STATION ...
HMM ... I DON'T SEE BATHOUND ANYWHERE.
EAST
EXIT
WAIT! THERE'S SOMEONE I DO RECOGNIZE!
JIMMY THE RAT! I KNOW YOU HAVE SOMETHING TO DO WITH THIS!
NOW HERE'S AN INTERROGATION I COULD REALLY SINK MY TEETH INTO!
AH-AH-AH! HIYA, SUPES! HIYA, STREAKY!
L-LOOK, IT WASN'T MY FAULT! THE JOKER'S HYENAS MADE ME DO IT! HOW WAS I TO KNOW THEY'D WANNA BRING GOTHAM DOWN AROUND OUR EARS?!
KEEP TALKING.
THE JOKER DEVELOPED A NEW LAUGHING GAS THAT'S TIME-RELEASED TO MAKE YA LAUGH EVERY FIFTEEN MINUTES. BUD AND LOU MADE ME SHOW THEM WHERE EVERY RATS' NEST IS UNDER THE CITY.
DID YOU KNOW THERE'S TWO RATS FOR EVERY PERSON IN GOTHAM CITY DOWN HERE? THE HYENAS PLAN TO GAS EVERY ONE OF THEM!
FIFTEEN MINUTES? WHY DOES THAT SOUND SO FAMILIAR?

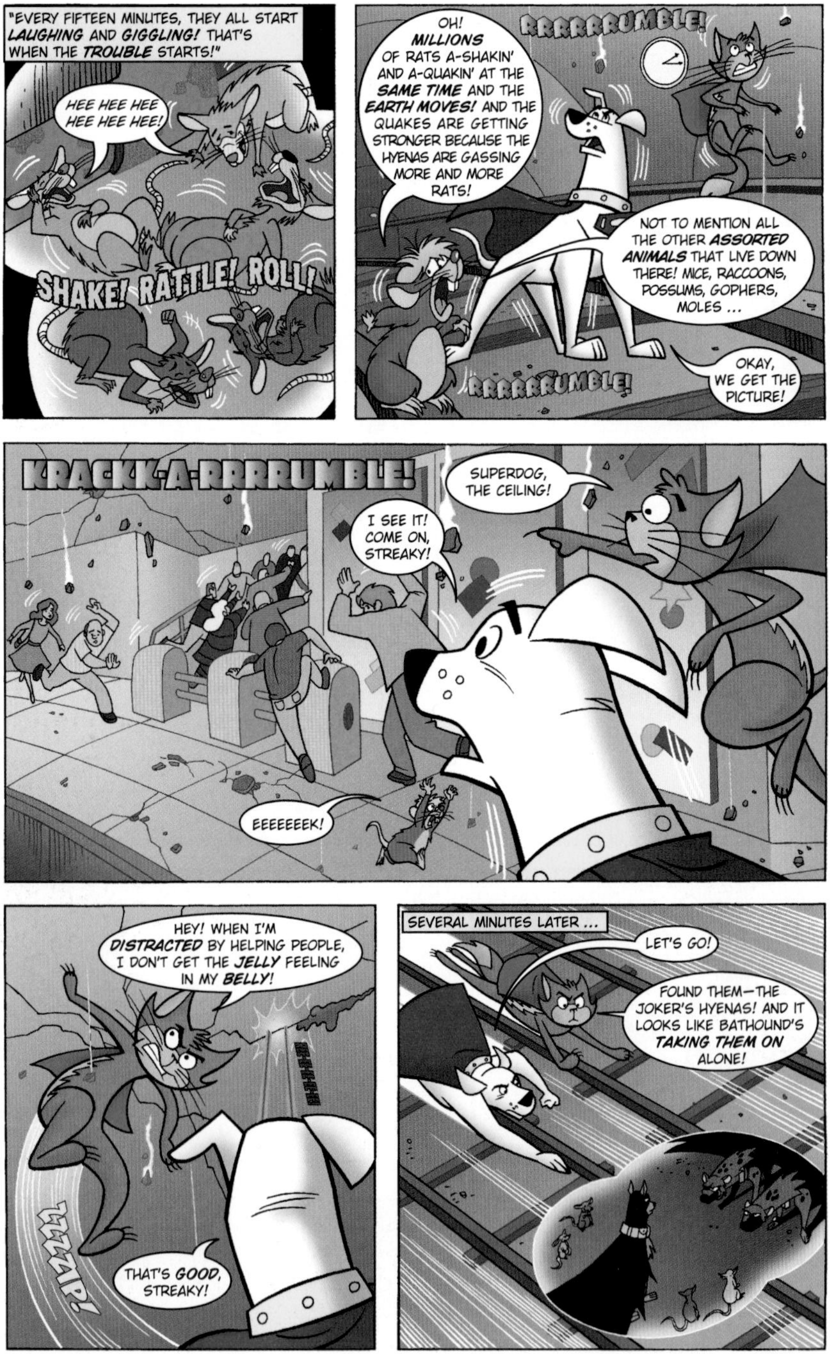
"EVERY FIFTEEN MINUTES, THEY ALL START LAUGHING AND GIGGLING! THAT'S WHEN THE TROUBLE STARTS!"
HEE HEE HEE HEE HEE HEE!
SHAKE! RATTLE! ROLL!
RRRRRRUMBLE!
OH! MILLIONS OF RATS A-SHAKIN' AND A-QUAKIN' AT THE SAME TIME AND THE EARTH MOVES! AND THE QUAKES ARE GETTING STRONGER BECAUSE THE HYENAS ARE GASSING MORE AND MORE RATS!
NOT TO MENTION ALL THE OTHER ASSORTED ANIMALS THAT LIVE DOWN THERE! MICE, RACCOONS, POSSUMS, GOPHERS, MOLES ...
RRRRRRUMBLE!
OKAY, WE GET THE PICTURE!
KRACKK-A-RRRRUMBLE!
SUPERDOG, THE CEILING!
I SEE IT! COME ON, STREAKY!
EEEEEEEK!
HEY! WHEN I'M DISTRACTED BY HELPING PEOPLE, I DON'T GET THE JELLY FEELING IN MY BELLY!
ZZZZIP!
THAT'S GOOD, STREAKY!
SEVERAL MINUTES LATER ...
LET'S GO!
FOUND THEM—THE JOKER'S HYENAS! AND IT LOOKS LIKE BATHOUND'S TAKING THEM ON ALONE!

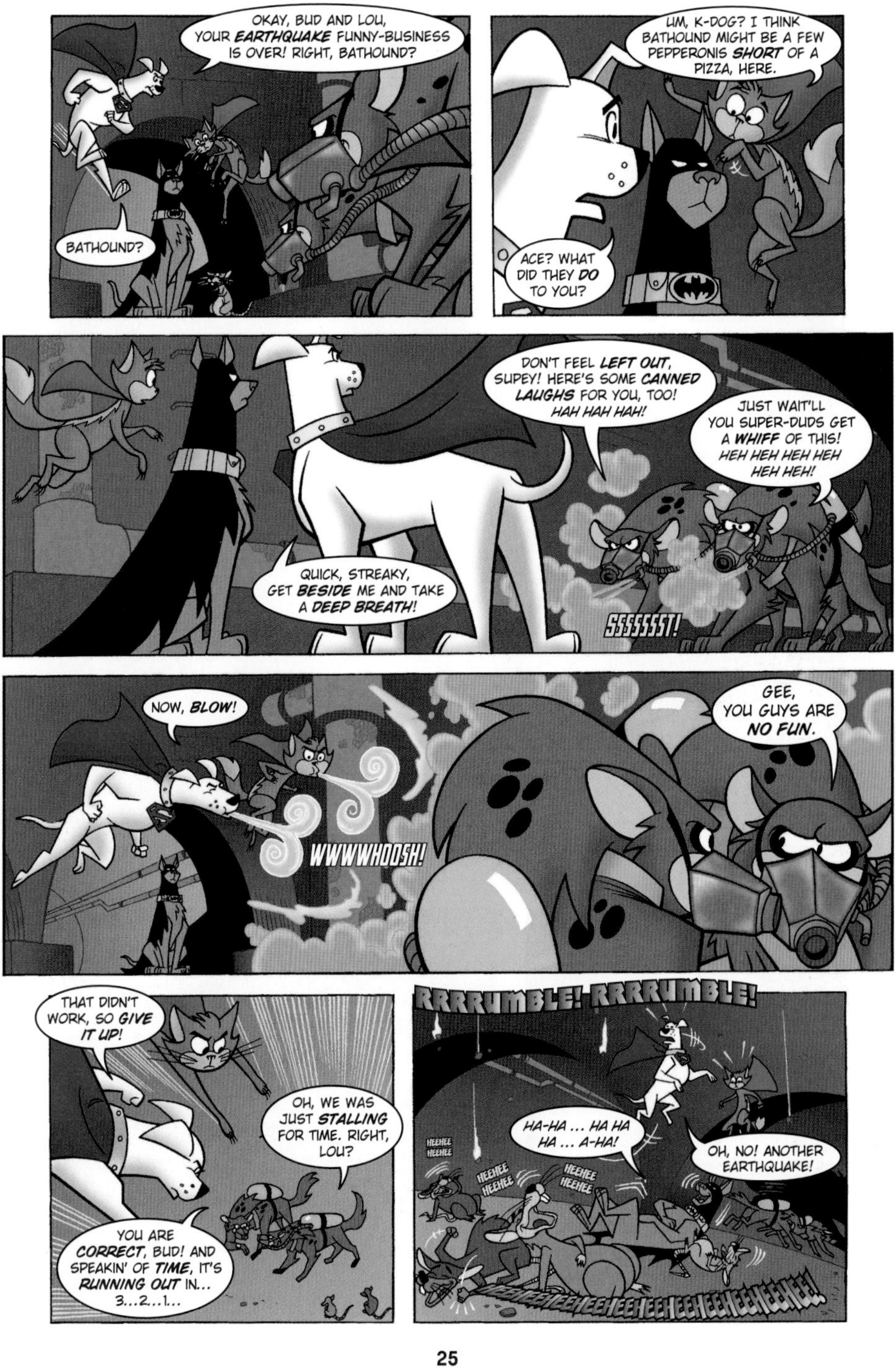
OKAY, BUD AND LOU, YOUR EARTHQUAKE FUNNY-BUSINESS IS OVER! RIGHT, BATHOUND?
BATHOUND?
UM, K-DOG? I THINK BATHOUND MIGHT BE A FEW PEPPERONIS SHORT OF A PIZZA, HERE.
ACE? WHAT DID THEY DO TO YOU?
DON'T FEEL LEFT OUT, SUPEY! HERE'S SOME CANNED LAUGHS FOR YOU, TOO! HAH HAH HAH!
JUST WAIT'LL YOU SUPER-DUDS GET A WHIFF OF THIS! HEH HEH HEH HEH HEH HEH!
QUICK, STREAKY, GET BESIDE ME AND TAKE A DEEP BREATH!
SSSSSSST!
NOW, BLOW!
WWWWHOOSH!
GEE, YOU GUYS ARE NO FUN.
THAT DIDN'T WORK, SO GIVE IT UP!
OH, WE WAS JUST STALLING FOR TIME. RIGHT, LOU?
YOU ARE CORRECT, BUD! AND SPEAKIN' OF TIME, IT'S RUNNING OUT IN... 3...2...1...
RRRRUMBLE! RRRRUMBLE!
HA-HA ... HA HA HA ... A-HA!
OH, NO! ANOTHER EARTHQUAKE!
HEEHEE HEEHEE
HEEHEE HEEHEE
HEEHEE HEEHEE

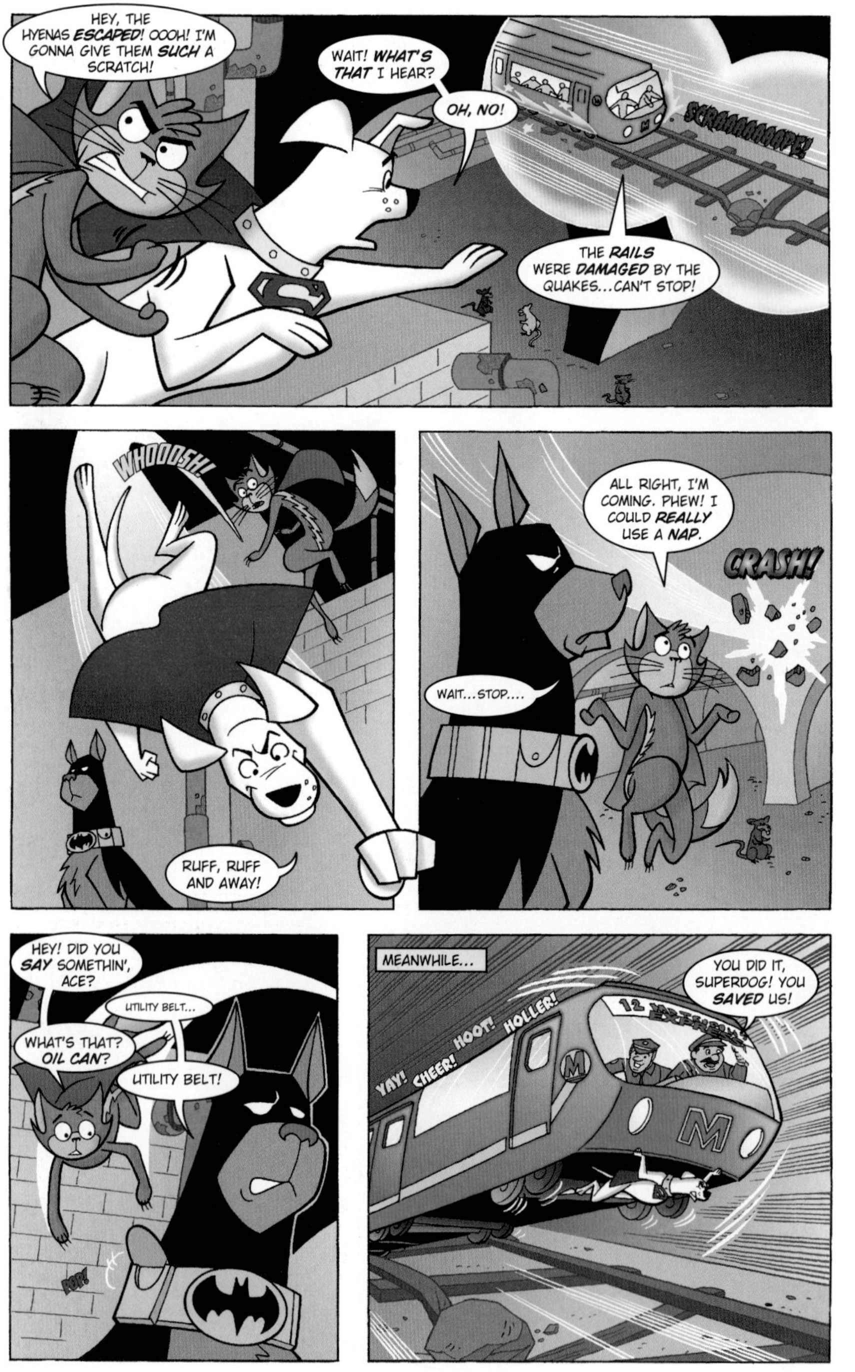
HEY, THE HYENAS ESCAPED! OOOH! I'M GONNA GIVE THEM SUCH A SCRATCH!
WAIT! WHAT'S THAT I HEAR?
OH, NO!
SCRAAAAAAAPE!
THE RAILS WERE DAMAGED BY THE QUAKES...CAN'T STOP!
WHOOOSH!
RUFF, RUFF AND AWAY!
ALL RIGHT, I'M COMING. PHEW! I COULD REALLY USE A NAP.
CRASH!
WAIT...STOP....
HEY! DID YOU SAY SOMETHIN', ACE?
UTILITY BELT...
WHAT'S THAT? OIL CAN?
UTILITY BELT!
POP!
MEANWHILE...
YOU DID IT, SUPERDOG! YOU SAVED US!
YAY! CHEER! HOOT! HOLLER!

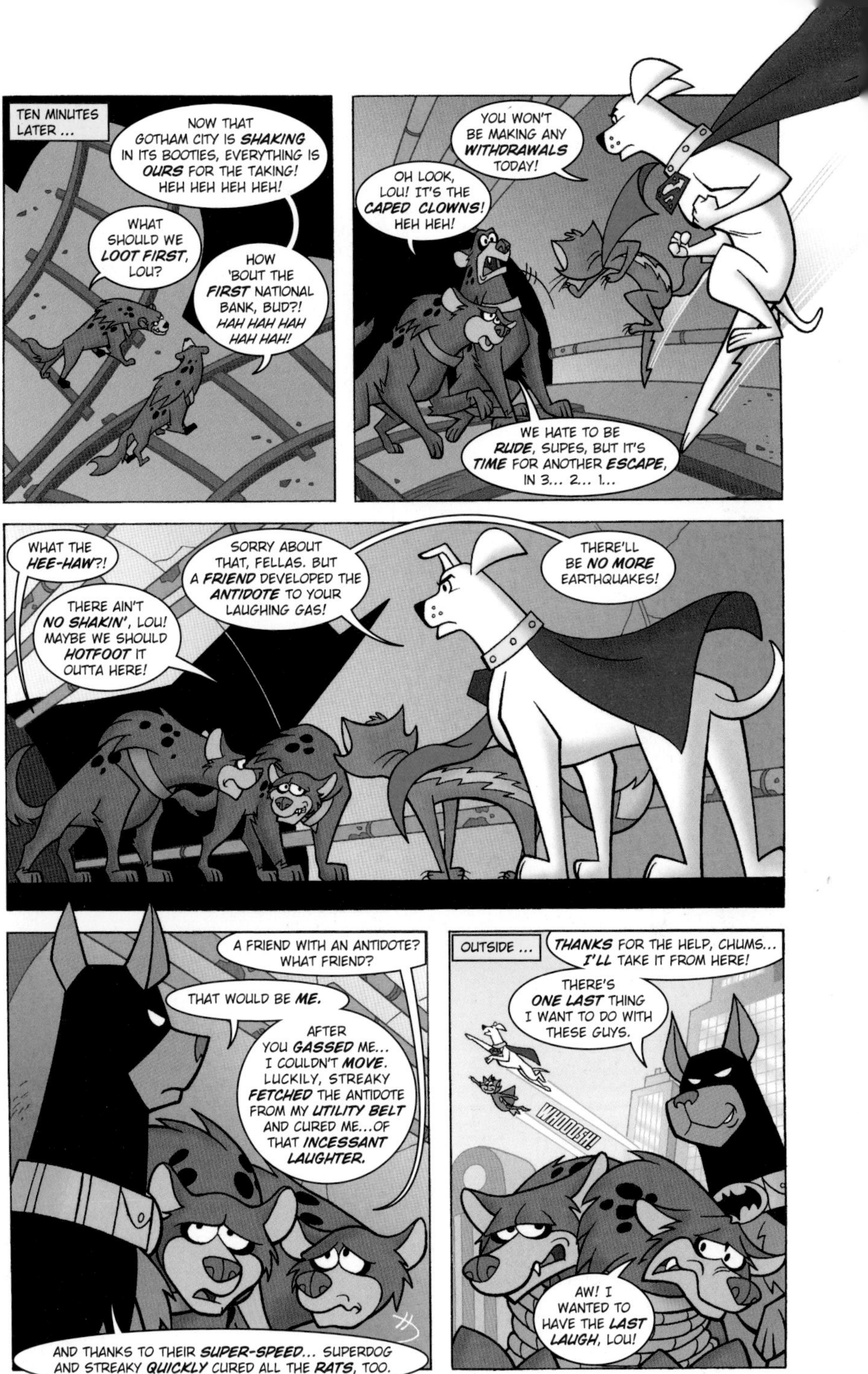
TEN MINUTES LATER ...
NOW THAT GOTHAM CITY IS SHAKING IN ITS BOOTIES, EVERYTHING IS OURS FOR THE TAKING! HEH HEH HEH HEH!
WHAT SHOULD WE LOOT FIRST, LOU?
HOW 'BOUT THE FIRST NATIONAL BANK, BUD?! HAH HAH HAH HAH HAH!
YOU WON'T BE MAKING ANY WITHDRAWALS TODAY!
OH LOOK, LOU! IT'S THE CAPED CLOWNS! HEH HEH!
WE HATE TO BE RUDE, SUPES, BUT IT'S TIME FOR ANOTHER ESCAPE, IN 3... 2... 1...
WHAT THE HEE-HAW?!
THERE AIN'T NO SHAKIN', LOU! MAYBE WE SHOULD HOTFOOT IT OUTTA HERE!
SORRY ABOUT THAT, FELLAS. BUT A FRIEND DEVELOPED THE ANTIDOTE TO YOUR LAUGHING GAS!
THERE'LL BE NO MORE EARTHQUAKES!
A FRIEND WITH AN ANTIDOTE? WHAT FRIEND?
THAT WOULD BE ME.
AFTER YOU GASSED ME... I COULDN'T MOVE. LUCKILY, STREAKY FETCHED THE ANTIDOTE FROM MY UTILITY BELT AND CURED ME...OF THAT INCESSANT LAUGHTER.
AND THANKS TO THEIR SUPER-SPEED... SUPERDOG AND STREAKY QUICKLY CURED ALL THE RATS, TOO.
OUTSIDE ...
THANKS FOR THE HELP, CHUMS... I'LL TAKE IT FROM HERE!
THERE'S ONE LAST THING I WANT TO DO WITH THESE GUYS.
WHOOOSH!
AW! I WANTED TO HAVE THE LAST LAUGH, LOU!

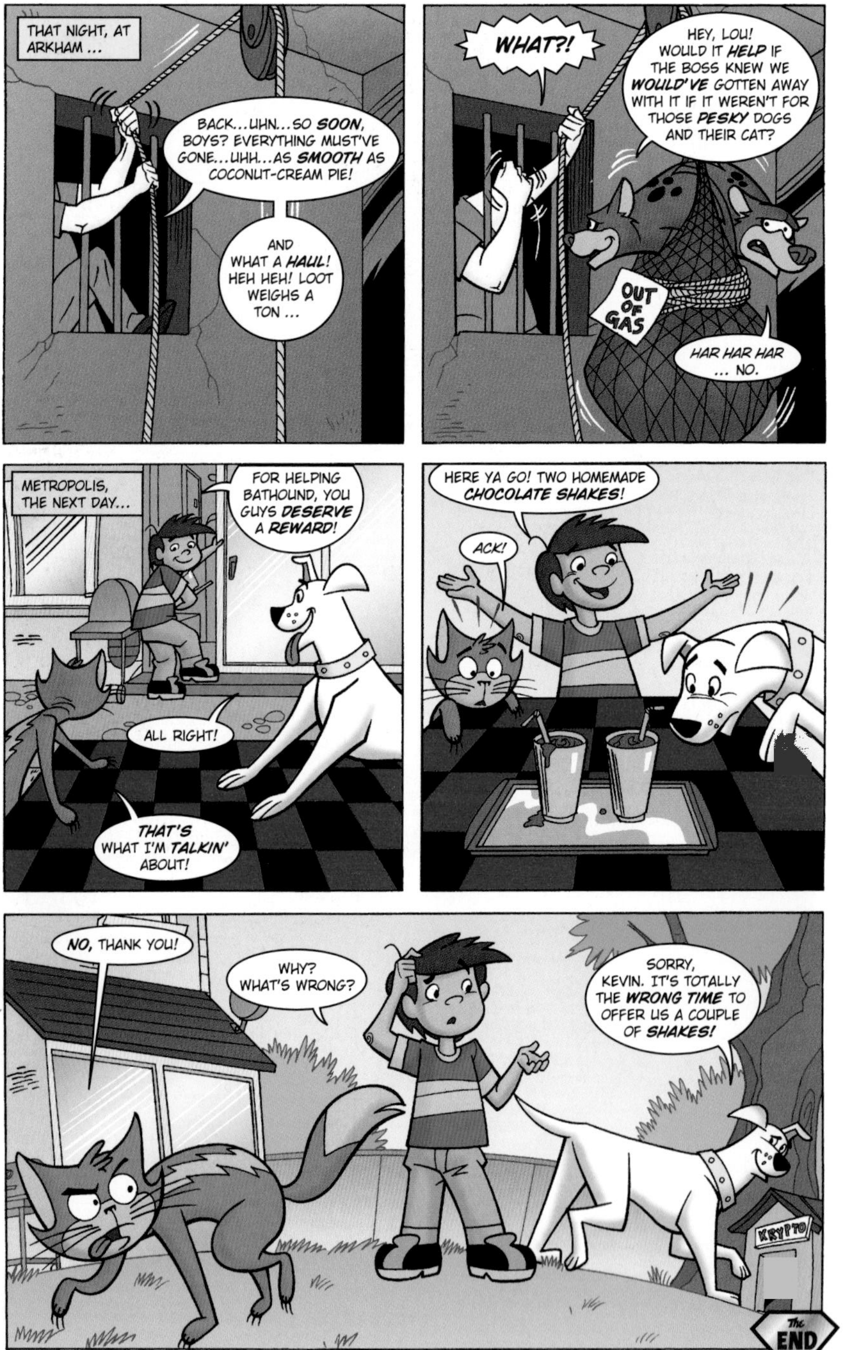
THAT NIGHT, AT ARKHAM ...
BACK...UHN...SO SOON, BOYS? EVERYTHING MUST'VE GONE...UHH...AS SMOOTH AS COCONUT-CREAM PIE!
AND WHAT A HAUL! HEH HEH! LOOT WEIGHS A TON ...
WHAT?!
HEY, LOU! WOULD IT HELP IF THE BOSS KNEW WE WOULD'VE GOTTEN AWAY WITH IT IF IT WEREN'T FOR THOSE PESKY DOGS AND THEIR CAT?
OUT OF GAS
HAR HAR HAR ... NO.
METROPOLIS, THE NEXT DAY...
FOR HELPING BATHOUND, YOU GUYS DESERVE A REWARD!
ALL RIGHT!
THAT'S WHAT I'M TALKIN' ABOUT!
HERE YA GO! TWO HOMEMADE CHOCOLATE SHAKES!
ACK!
NO, THANK YOU!
WHY? WHAT'S WRONG?
SORRY, KEVIN. IT'S TOTALLY THE WRONG TIME TO OFFER US A COUPLE OF SHAKES!
KRYPTO
The END

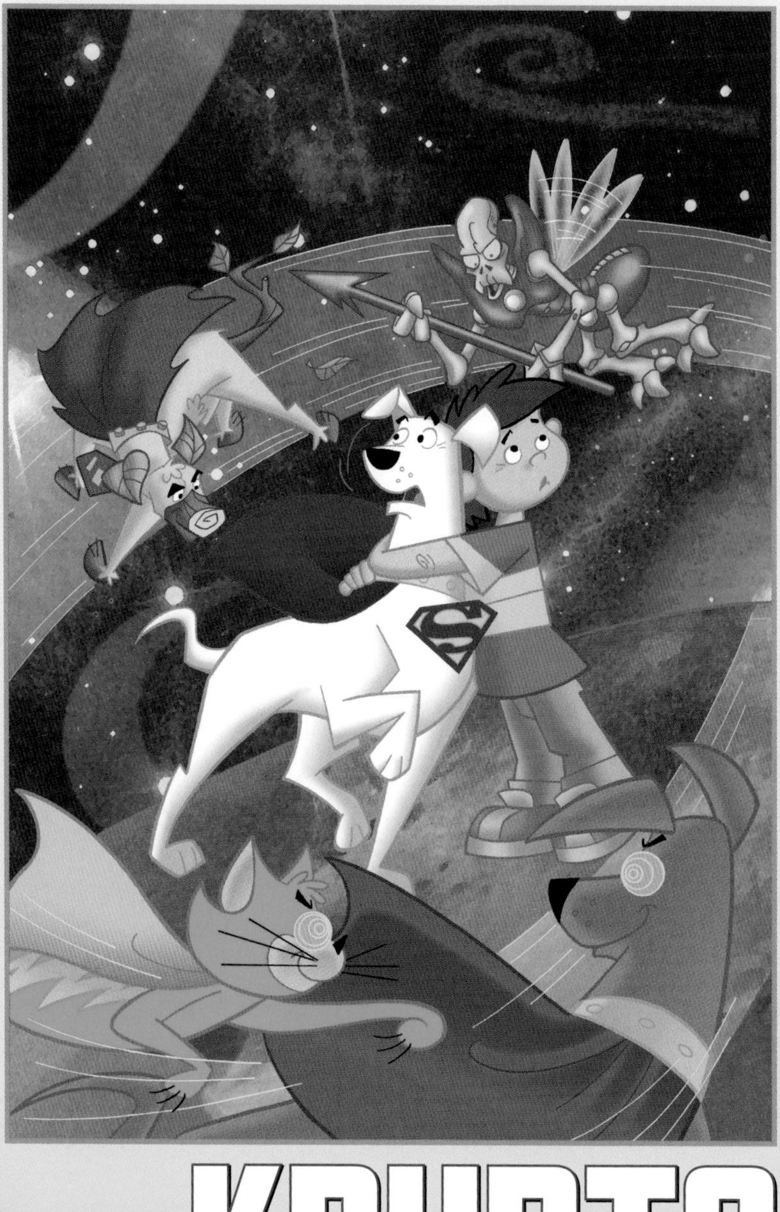

KRYPTO THE SUPERDOG

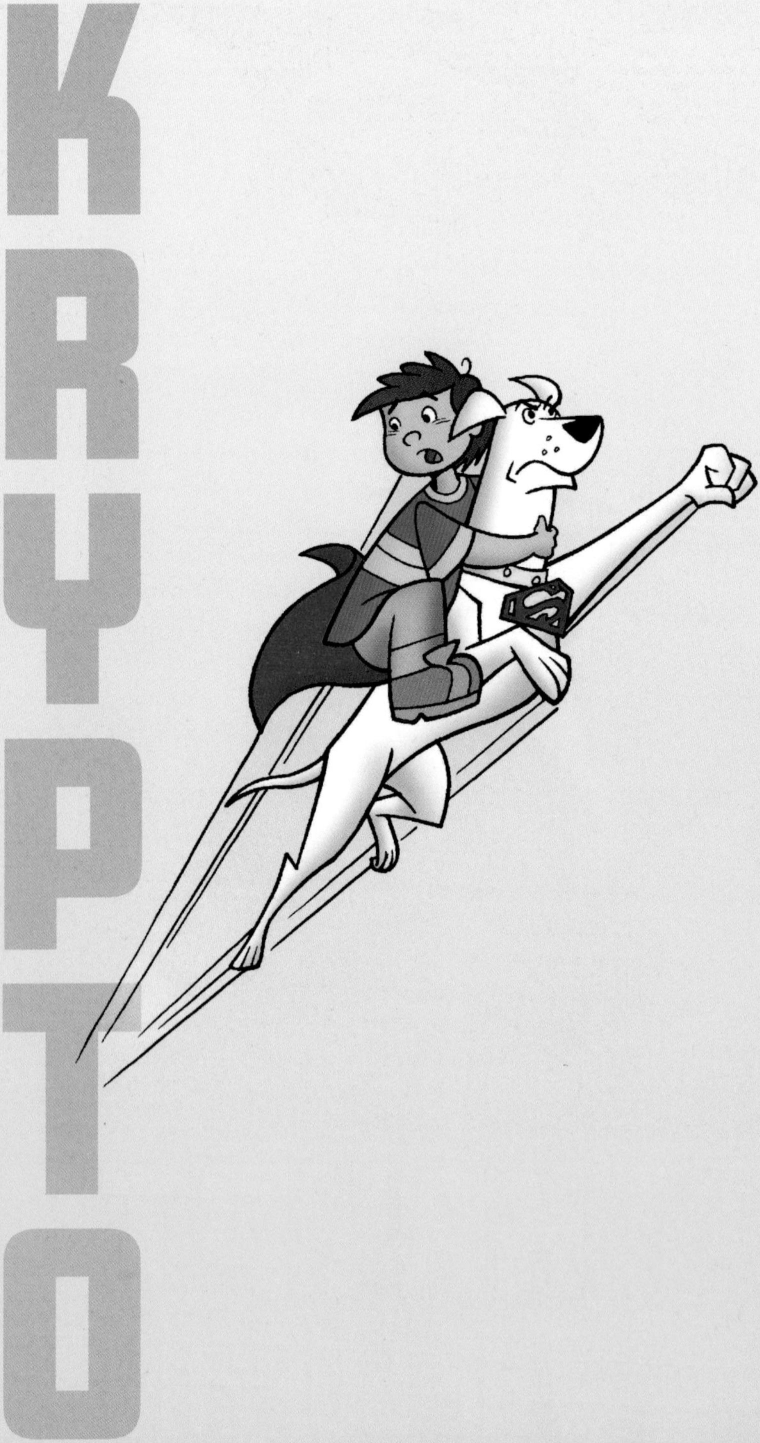
KRYPTO

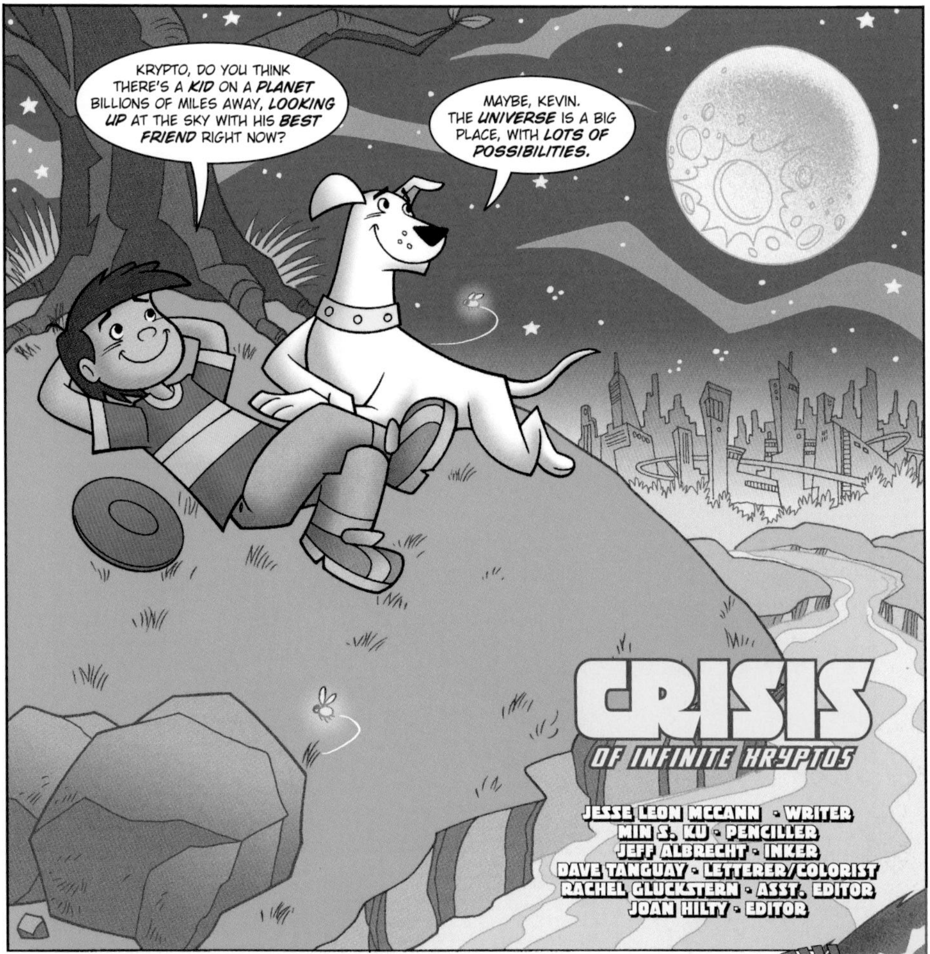
KRYPTO, DO YOU THINK THERE'S A KID ON A PLANET BILLIONS OF MILES AWAY, LOOKING UP AT THE SKY WITH HIS BEST FRIEND RIGHT NOW?
MAYBE, KEVIN. THE UNIVERSE IS A BIG PLACE, WITH LOTS OF POSSIBILITIES.
CRISIS
OF INFINITE KRYPTOS
JESSE LEON MCCANN - WRITER
MIN S. KU - PENCILLER
JEFF ALBRECHT - INKER
DAVE TANGUAY - LETTERER/COLORIST
RACHEL GLUCKSTERN - ASST. EDITOR
JOAN HILTY - EDITOR

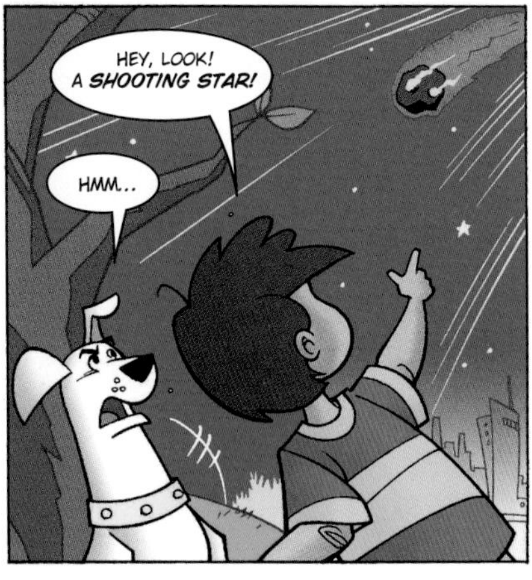
HEY, LOOK! A SHOOTING STAR!
HMM..

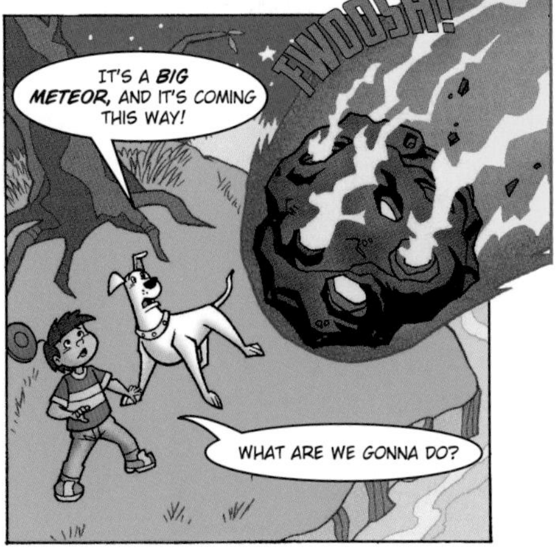
FWOOSH!
IT'S A BIG METEOR, AND IT'S COMING THIS WAY!
WHAT ARE WE GONNA DO?

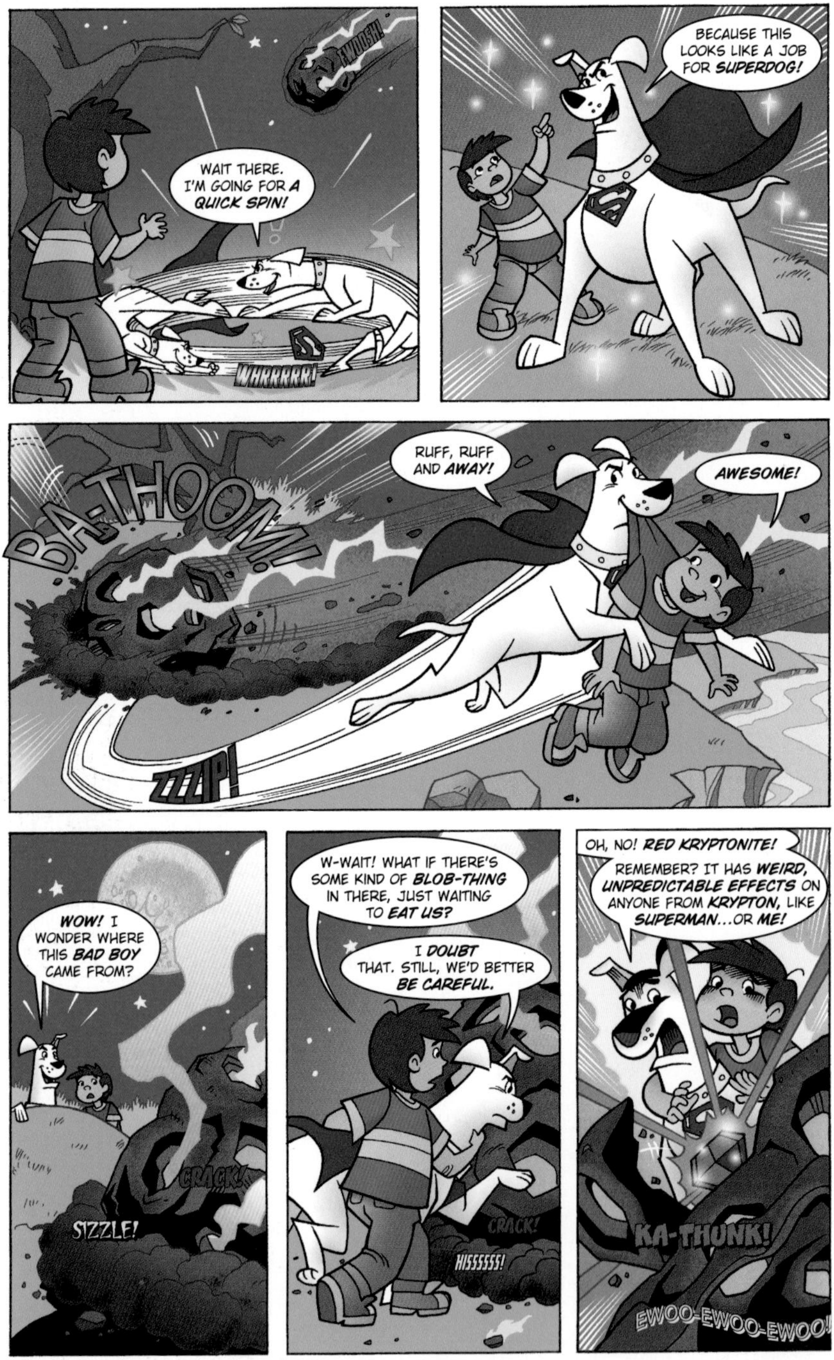
WHOOSH!
WAIT THERE. I'M GOING FOR A QUICK SPIN!
WHRRRRR!
BECAUSE THIS LOOKS LIKE A JOB FOR SUPERDOG!
BA-THOOM!
RUFF, RUFF AND AWAY!
AWESOME!
ZZZIP!
WOW! I WONDER WHERE THIS BAD BOY CAME FROM?
CRACK!
SIZZLE!
W-WAIT! WHAT IF THERE'S SOME KIND OF BLOB-THING IN THERE, JUST WAITING TO EAT US?
I DOUBT THAT. STILL, WE'D BETTER BE CAREFUL.
CRACK!
HISSSSSS!
OH, NO! RED KRYPTONITE!
REMEMBER? IT HAS WEIRD, UNPREDICTABLE EFFECTS ON ANYONE FROM KRYPTON, LIKE SUPERMAN...OR ME!
KA-THUNK!
EWOO-EWOO-EWOO!

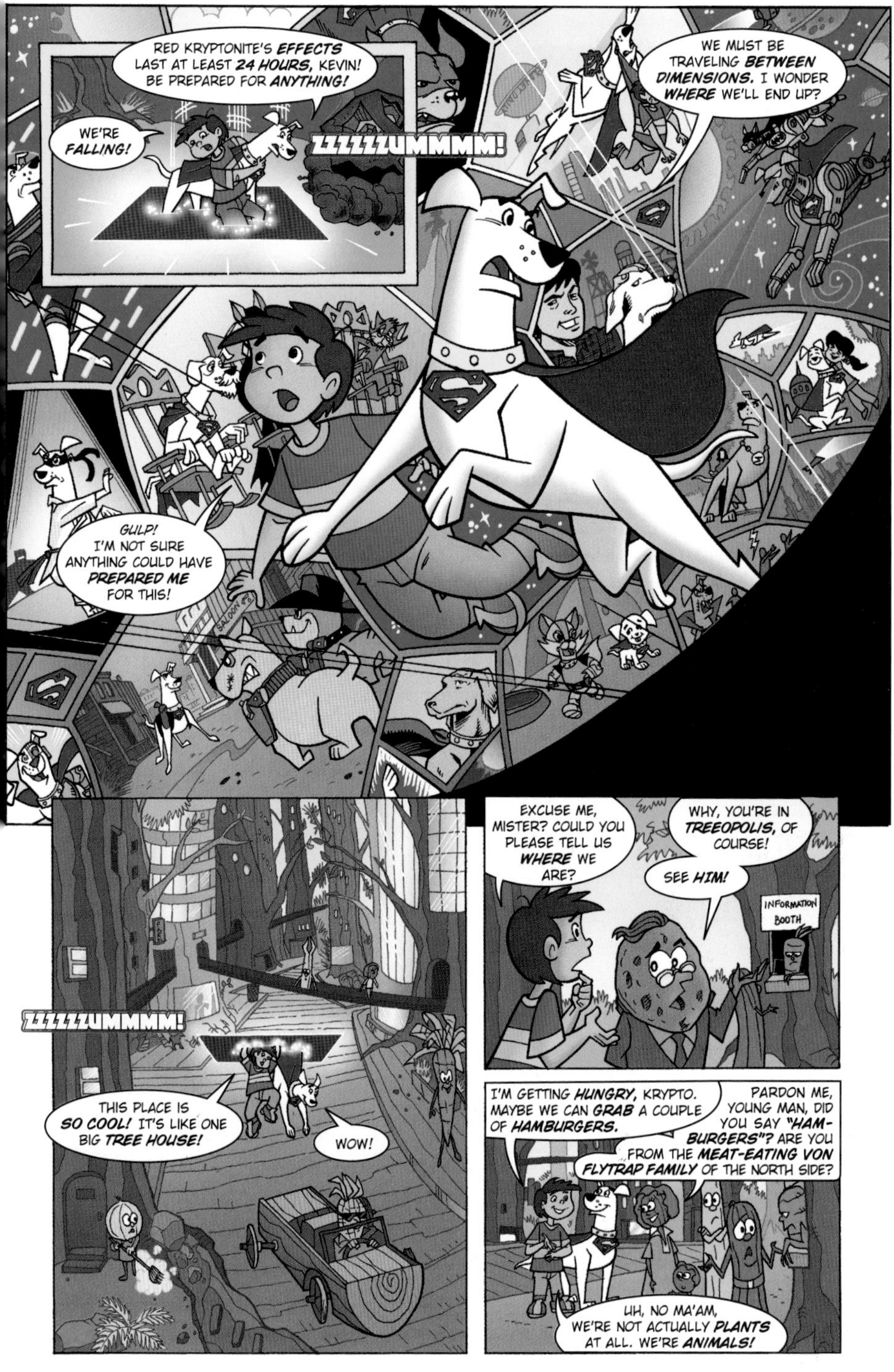
RED KRYPTONITE'S EFFECTS LAST AT LEAST 24 HOURS, KEVIN! BE PREPARED FOR ANYTHING!
WE'RE FALLING!
ZZZZZZUMMMMM!
WE MUST BE TRAVELING BETWEEN DIMENSIONS. I WONDER WHERE WE'LL END UP?
GULP! I'M NOT SURE ANYTHING COULD HAVE PREPARED ME FOR THIS!
SALOON
ZZZZZZUMMMMM!
THIS PLACE IS SO COOL! IT'S LIKE ONE BIG TREE HOUSE!
WOW!
EXCUSE ME, MISTER? COULD YOU PLEASE TELL US WHERE WE ARE?
WHY, YOU'RE IN TREEOPOLIS, OF COURSE!
SEE HIM!
INFORMATION BOOTH
I'M GETTING HUNGRY, KRYPTO. MAYBE WE CAN GRAB A COUPLE OF HAMBURGERS.
PARDON ME, YOUNG MAN, DID YOU SAY "HAMBURGERS"? ARE YOU FROM THE MEAT-EATING VON FLYTRAP FAMILY OF THE NORTH SIDE?
UH, NO MA'AM, WE'RE NOT ACTUALLY PLANTS AT ALL. WE'RE ANIMALS!

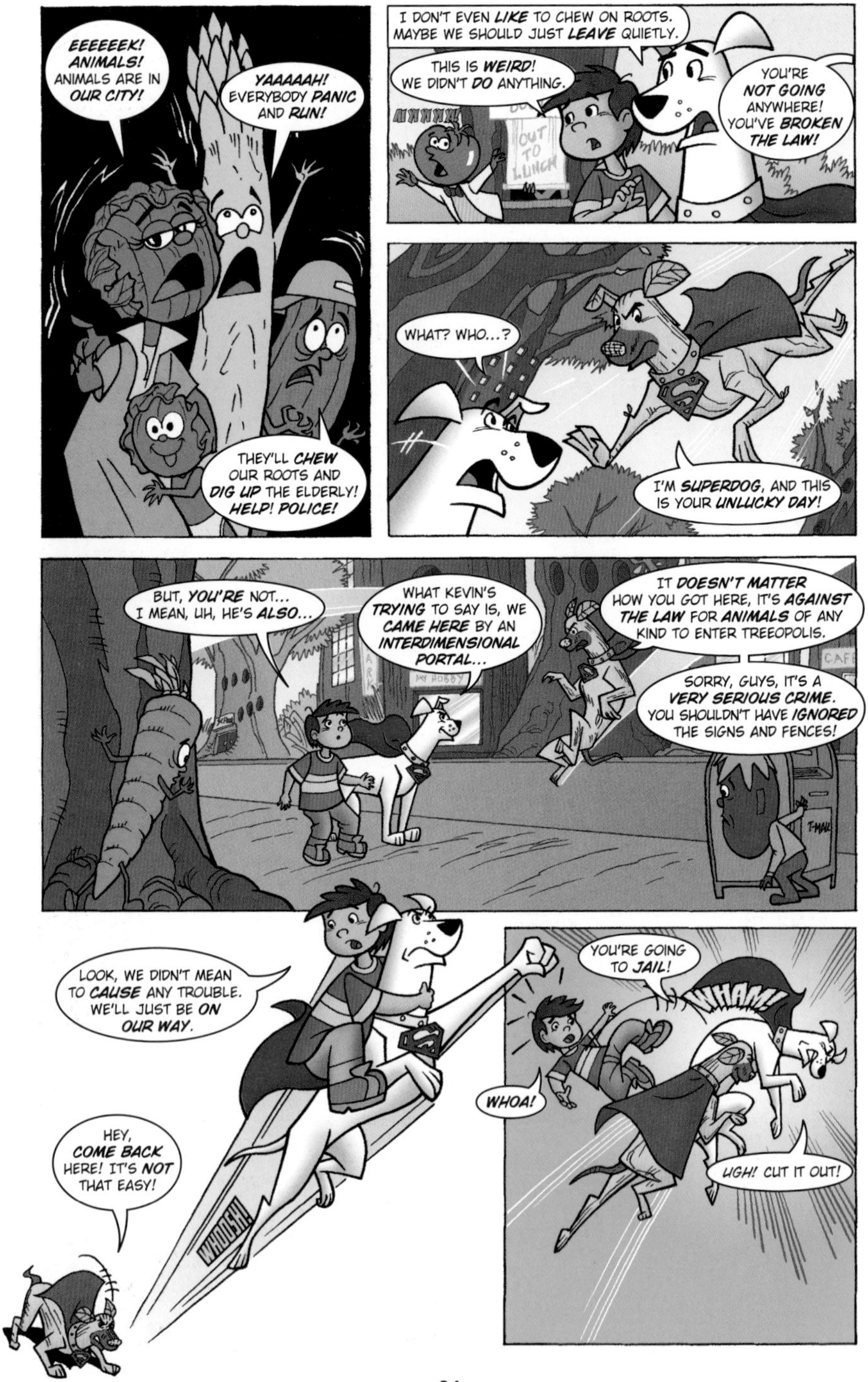

EEEEEEK! ANIMALS! ANIMALS ARE IN OUR CITY!
YAAAAAAH! EVERYBODY PANIC AND RUN!
THEY'LL CHEW OUR ROOTS AND DIG UP THE ELDERLY! HELP! POLICE!
I DON'T EVEN LIKE TO CHEW ON ROOTS. MAYBE WE SHOULD JUST LEAVE QUIETLY.
THIS IS WEIRD! WE DIDN'T DO ANYTHING.
YOU'RE NOT GOING ANYWHERE! YOU'VE BROKEN THE LAW!
OUT TO LUNCH
WHAT? WHO...?
I'M SUPERDOG, AND THIS IS YOUR UNLUCKY DAY!
BUT, YOU'RE NOT... I MEAN, UH, HE'S ALSO...
WHAT KEVIN'S TRYING TO SAY IS, WE CAME HERE BY AN INTERDIMENSIONAL PORTAL...
IT DOESN'T MATTER HOW YOU GOT HERE, IT'S AGAINST THE LAW FOR ANIMALS OF ANY KIND TO ENTER TREEOPOLIS.
SORRY, GUYS, IT'S A VERY SERIOUS CRIME. YOU SHOULDN'T HAVE IGNORED THE SIGNS AND FENCES!
T-MAIL
LOOK, WE DIDN'T MEAN TO CAUSE ANY TROUBLE. WE'LL JUST BE ON OUR WAY.
HEY, COME BACK HERE! IT'S NOT THAT EASY!
WHOOSH!
YOU'RE GOING TO JAIL!
WHAM!
WHOA!
UGH! CUT IT OUT!

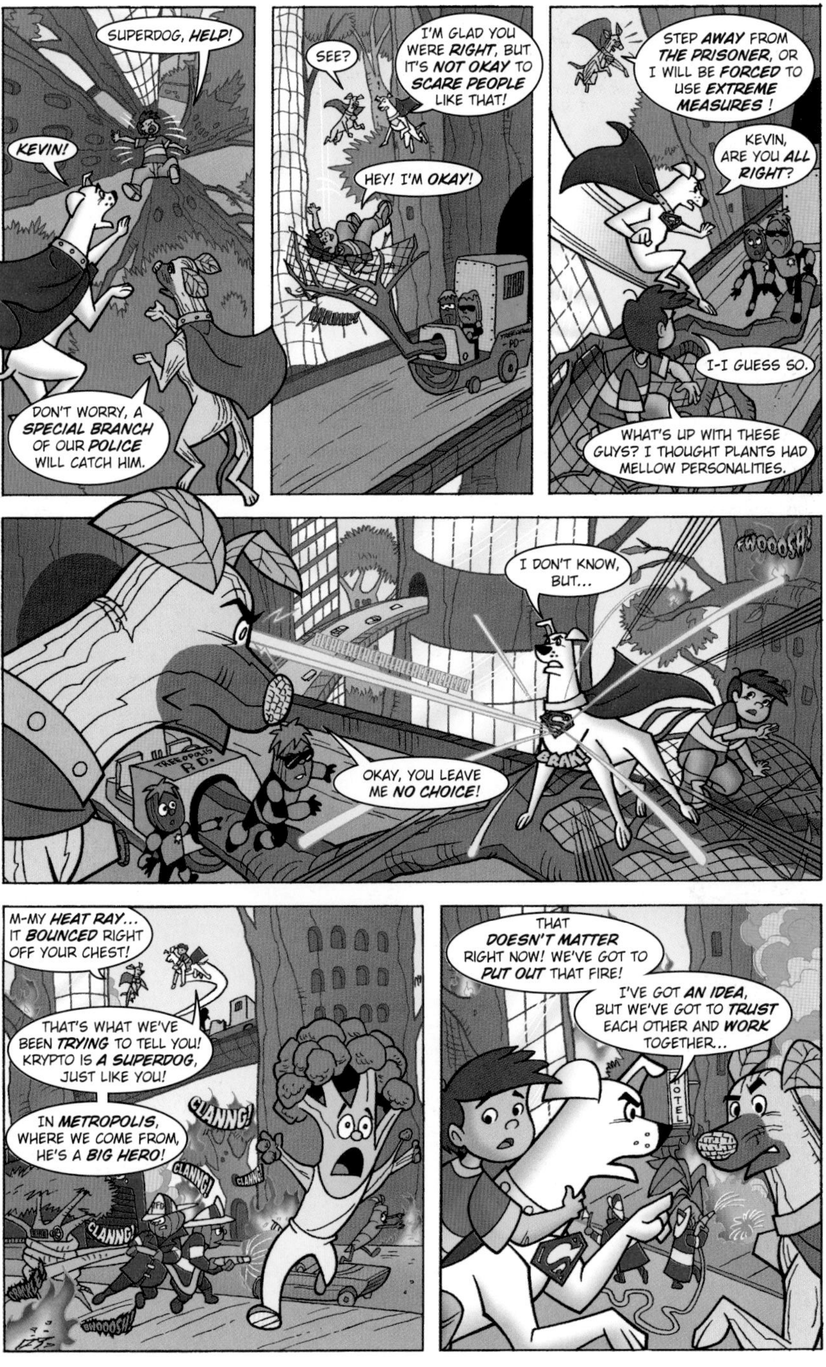
SUPERDOG, HELP!
KEVIN!
DON'T WORRY, A SPECIAL BRANCH OF OUR POLICE WILL CATCH HIM.
SEE?
I'M GLAD YOU WERE RIGHT, BUT IT'S NOT OKAY TO SCARE PEOPLE LIKE THAT!
HEY! I'M OKAY!
STEP AWAY FROM THE PRISONER, OR I WILL BE FORCED TO USE EXTREME MEASURES !
KEVIN, ARE YOU ALL RIGHT?
I-I GUESS SO.
WHAT'S UP WITH THESE GUYS? I THOUGHT PLANTS HAD MELLOW PERSONALITIES.
FWOOOSH!
I DON'T KNOW, BUT...
TREEOPOLIS P.D.
OKAY, YOU LEAVE ME NO CHOICE!
BRAK!
M-MY HEAT RAY... IT BOUNCED RIGHT OFF YOUR CHEST!
THAT'S WHAT WE'VE BEEN TRYING TO TELL YOU! KRYPTO IS A SUPERDOG, JUST LIKE YOU!
IN METROPOLIS, WHERE WE COME FROM, HE'S A BIG HERO!
CLANNG!
CLANNG!
CLANNG!
THAT DOESN'T MATTER RIGHT NOW! WE'VE GOT TO PUT OUT THAT FIRE!
I'VE GOT AN IDEA, BUT WE'VE GOT TO TRUST EACH OTHER AND WORK TOGETHER...
MOTEL

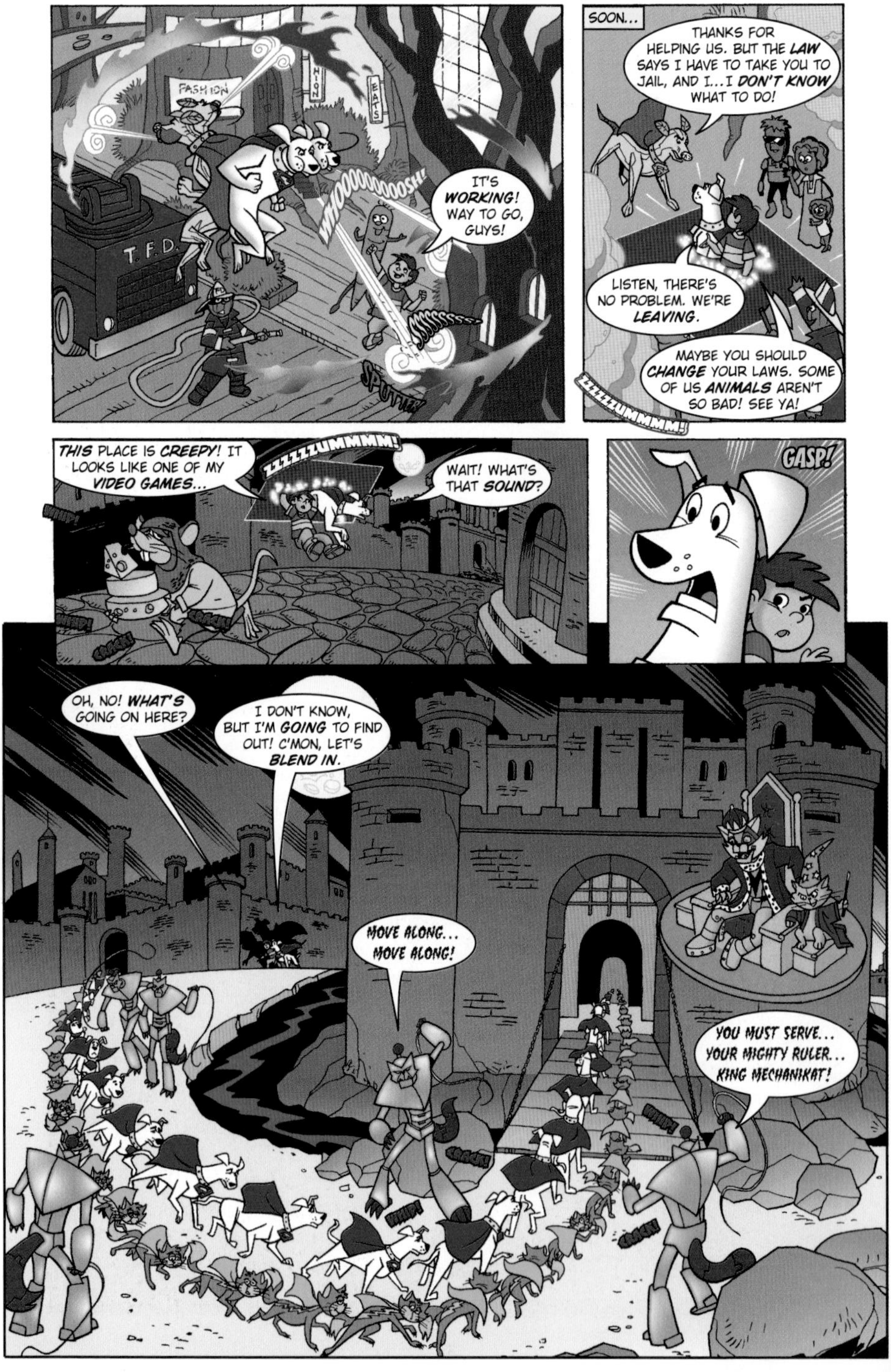

FASHION
EATS
T. F. D.
WHOOOOOOOOOOSH!
IT'S WORKING! WAY TO GO, GUYS!
SSSSSSSS
SPUTTT
SOON...
THANKS FOR HELPING US. BUT THE LAW SAYS I HAVE TO TAKE YOU TO JAIL, AND I...I DON'T KNOW WHAT TO DO!
LISTEN, THERE'S NO PROBLEM. WE'RE LEAVING.
MAYBE YOU SHOULD CHANGE YOUR LAWS. SOME OF US ANIMALS AREN'T SO BAD! SEE YA!
ZZZZZZZUMMMMM!
ZZZZZZZUMMMMM!
THIS PLACE IS CREEPY! IT LOOKS LIKE ONE OF MY VIDEO GAMES...
WAIT! WHAT'S THAT SOUND?
CRACK!
GASP!
OH, NO! WHAT'S GOING ON HERE?
I DON'T KNOW, BUT I'M GOING TO FIND OUT! C'MON, LET'S BLEND IN.
MOVE ALONG... MOVE ALONG!
YOU MUST SERVE... YOUR MIGHTY RULER... KING MECHANIKAT!
CRACK!
WHIP!
CRACK!

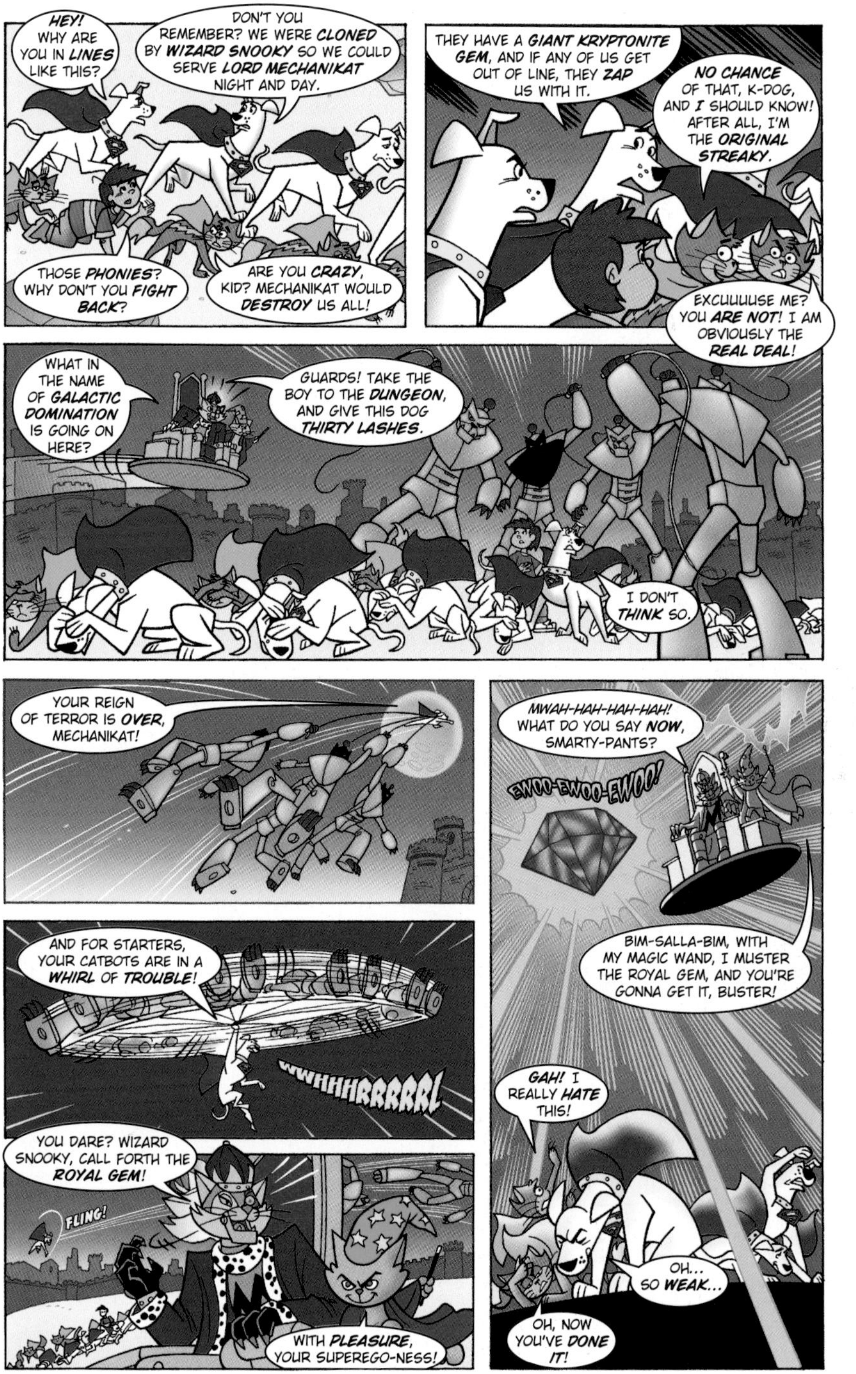
HEY! WHY ARE YOU IN LINES LIKE THIS?
DON'T YOU REMEMBER? WE WERE CLONED BY WIZARD SNOOKY SO WE COULD SERVE LORD MECHANIKAT NIGHT AND DAY.
THOSE PHONIES? WHY DON'T YOU FIGHT BACK?
ARE YOU CRAZY, KID? MECHANIKAT WOULD DESTROY US ALL!
THEY HAVE A GIANT KRYPTONITE GEM, AND IF ANY OF US GET OUT OF LINE, THEY ZAP US WITH IT.
NO CHANCE OF THAT, K-DOG, AND I SHOULD KNOW! AFTER ALL, I'M THE ORIGINAL STREAKY.
EXCUUUUSE ME? YOU ARE NOT! I AM OBVIOUSLY THE REAL DEAL!
WHAT IN THE NAME OF GALACTIC DOMINATION IS GOING ON HERE?
GUARDS! TAKE THE BOY TO THE DUNGEON, AND GIVE THIS DOG THIRTY LASHES.
I DON'T THINK SO.
YOUR REIGN OF TERROR IS OVER, MECHANIKAT!
AND FOR STARTERS, YOUR CATBOTS ARE IN A WHIRL OF TROUBLE!
WWHHHRRRRRL
YOU DARE? WIZARD SNOOKY, CALL FORTH THE ROYAL GEM!
FLING!
WITH PLEASURE, YOUR SUPEREGO-NESS!
MWAH-HAH-HAH-HAH! WHAT DO YOU SAY NOW, SMARTY-PANTS?
EWOO-EWOO-EWOO!
BIM-SALLA-BIM, WITH MY MAGIC WAND, I MUSTER THE ROYAL GEM, AND YOU'RE GONNA GET IT, BUSTER!
GAH! I REALLY HATE THIS!
OH... SO WEAK...
OH, NOW YOU'VE DONE IT!

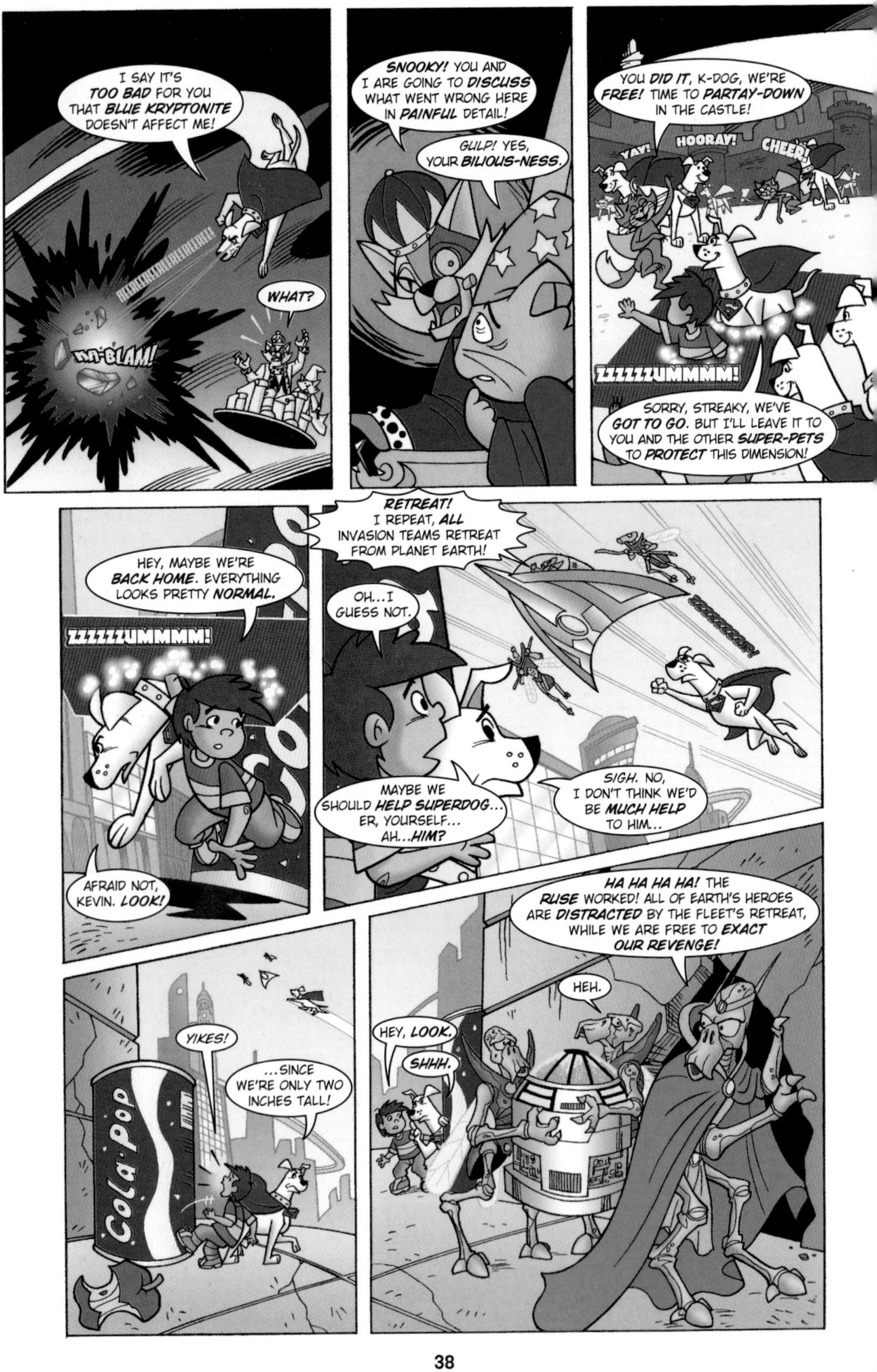
I SAY IT'S TOO BAD FOR YOU THAT BLUE KRYPTONITE DOESN'T AFFECT ME!
WHAT?
KA-BLAM!
SNOOKY! YOU AND I ARE GOING TO DISCUSS WHAT WENT WRONG HERE IN PAINFUL DETAIL!
GULP! YES, YOUR BILIOUS-NESS.
YOU DID IT, K-DOG, WE'RE FREE! TIME TO PARTAY-DOWN IN THE CASTLE!
YAY!
HOORAY!
CHEER!
ZZZZZZUMMMMM!
SORRY, STREAKY, WE'VE GOT TO GO. BUT I'LL LEAVE IT TO YOU AND THE OTHER SUPER-PETS TO PROTECT THIS DIMENSION!
HEY, MAYBE WE'RE BACK HOME. EVERYTHING LOOKS PRETTY NORMAL.
ZZZZZZUMMMMM!
AFRAID NOT, KEVIN. LOOK!
RETREAT! I REPEAT, ALL INVASION TEAMS RETREAT FROM PLANET EARTH!
OH...I GUESS NOT.
MAYBE WE SHOULD HELP SUPERDOG... ER, YOURSELF... AH...HIM?
SIGH. NO, I DON'T THINK WE'D BE MUCH HELP TO HIM...
YIKES!
...SINCE WE'RE ONLY TWO INCHES TALL!
Cola-Pop
HA HA HA HA! THE RUSE WORKED! ALL OF EARTH'S HEROES ARE DISTRACTED BY THE FLEET'S RETREAT, WHILE WE ARE FREE TO EXACT OUR REVENGE!
HEH.
HEY, LOOK.
SHHH.

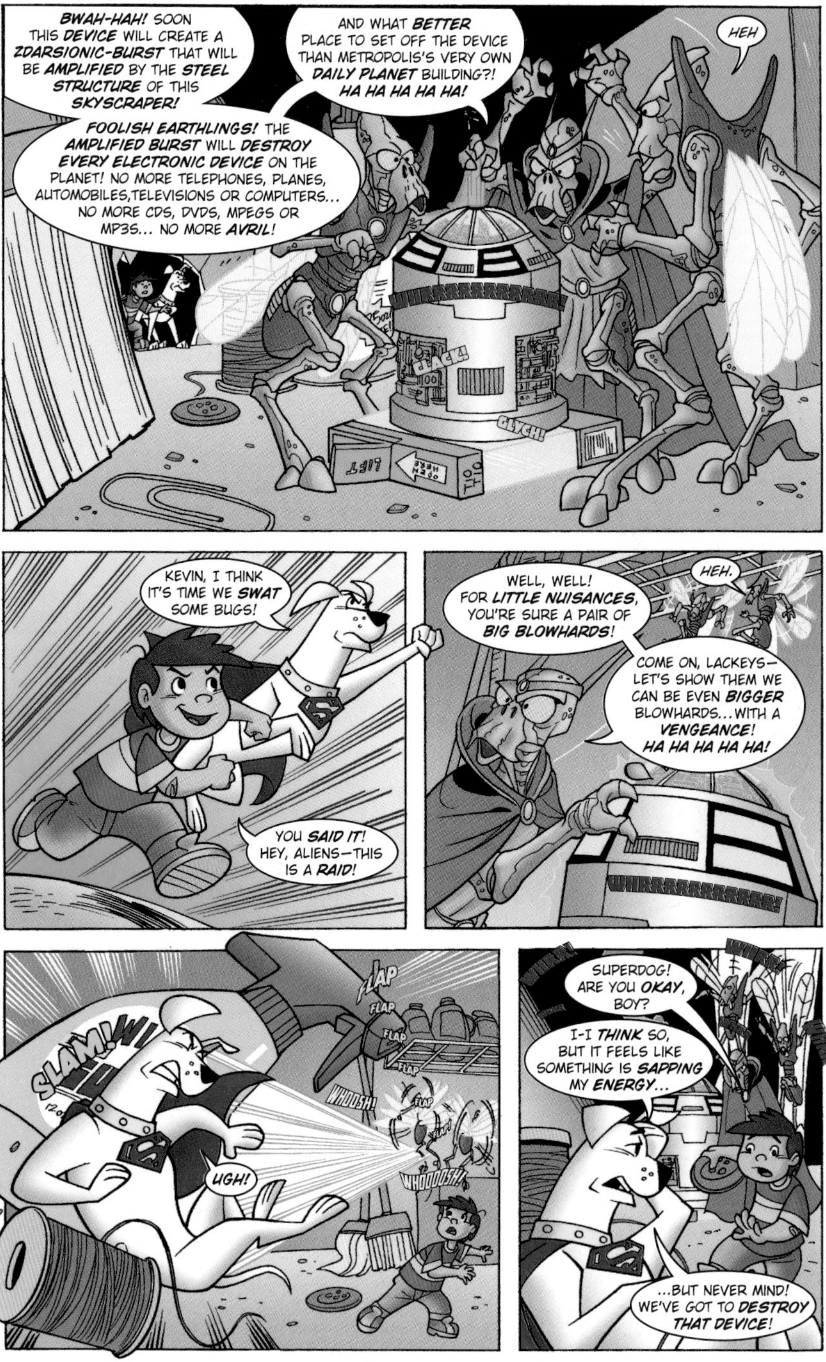
BWAH-HAH! SOON THIS DEVICE WILL CREATE A ZDARSIONIC-BURST THAT WILL BE AMPLIFIED BY THE STEEL STRUCTURE OF THIS SKYSCRAPER!
AND WHAT BETTER PLACE TO SET OFF THE DEVICE THAN METROPOLIS'S VERY OWN DAILY PLANET BUILDING?! HA HA HA HA HA!
HEH
FOOLISH EARTHLINGS! THE AMPLIFIED BURST WILL DESTROY EVERY ELECTRONIC DEVICE ON THE PLANET! NO MORE TELEPHONES, PLANES, AUTOMOBILES,TELEVISIONS OR COMPUTERS... NO MORE CDS, DVDS, MPEGS OR MP3S... NO MORE AVRIL!
WHIRRRRRRRRRRR!
CLACK!
GLYCH!
OPEN HERE
LIFT
KEVIN, I THINK IT'S TIME WE SWAT SOME BUGS!
YOU SAID IT! HEY, ALIENS—THIS IS A RAID!
WELL, WELL! FOR LITTLE NUISANCES, YOU'RE SURE A PAIR OF BIG BLOWHARDS!
HEH.
COME ON, LACKEYS— LET'S SHOW THEM WE CAN BE EVEN BIGGER BLOWHARDS...WITH A VENGEANCE! HA HA HA HA HA!
WHIRRRRRRRRRRR!
FLAP
FLAP
FLAP
FLAP
SLAM!
WHOOSH!
UGH!
WHOOOOSH!
SUPERDOG! ARE YOU OKAY, BOY?
I-I THINK SO, BUT IT FEELS LIKE SOMETHING IS SAPPING MY ENERGY...
...BUT NEVER MIND! WE'VE GOT TO DESTROY THAT DEVICE!

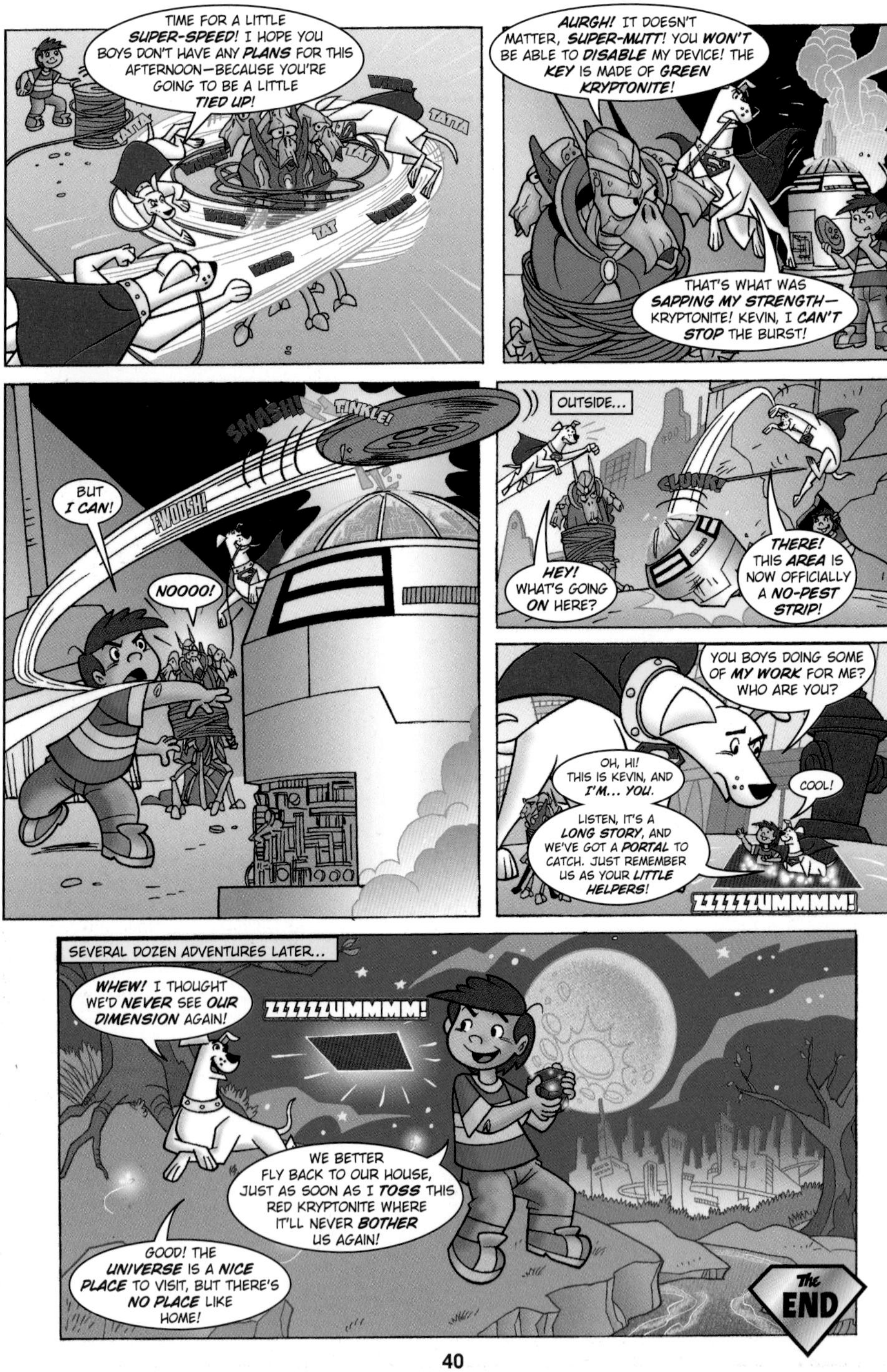

TIME FOR A LITTLE SUPER-SPEED! I HOPE YOU BOYS DON'T HAVE ANY PLANS FOR THIS AFTERNOON—BECAUSE YOU'RE GOING TO BE A LITTLE TIED UP!
WHIRR
TATTA
TAT
AURGH! IT DOESN'T MATTER, SUPER-MUTT! YOU WON'T BE ABLE TO DISABLE MY DEVICE! THE KEY IS MADE OF GREEN KRYPTONITE!
THAT'S WHAT WAS SAPPING MY STRENGTH—KRYPTONITE! KEVIN, I CAN'T STOP THE BURST!
SMASH!
TINKLE!
FWOOSH!
BUT I CAN!
NOOOO!
OUTSIDE...
CLUNK!
HEY! WHAT'S GOING ON HERE?
THERE! THIS AREA IS NOW OFFICIALLY A NO-PEST STRIP!
YOU BOYS DOING SOME OF MY WORK FOR ME? WHO ARE YOU?
OH, HI! THIS IS KEVIN, AND I'M... YOU.
COOL!
LISTEN, IT'S A LONG STORY, AND WE'VE GOT A PORTAL TO CATCH. JUST REMEMBER US AS YOUR LITTLE HELPERS!
ZZZZZZUMMMM!
SEVERAL DOZEN ADVENTURES LATER..
WHEW! I THOUGHT WE'D NEVER SEE OUR DIMENSION AGAIN!
ZZZZZZUMMMM!
WE BETTER FLY BACK TO OUR HOUSE, JUST AS SOON AS I TOSS THIS RED KRYPTONITE WHERE IT'LL NEVER BOTHER US AGAIN!
GOOD! THE UNIVERSE IS A NICE PLACE TO VISIT, BUT THERE'S NO PLACE LIKE HOME!
The END

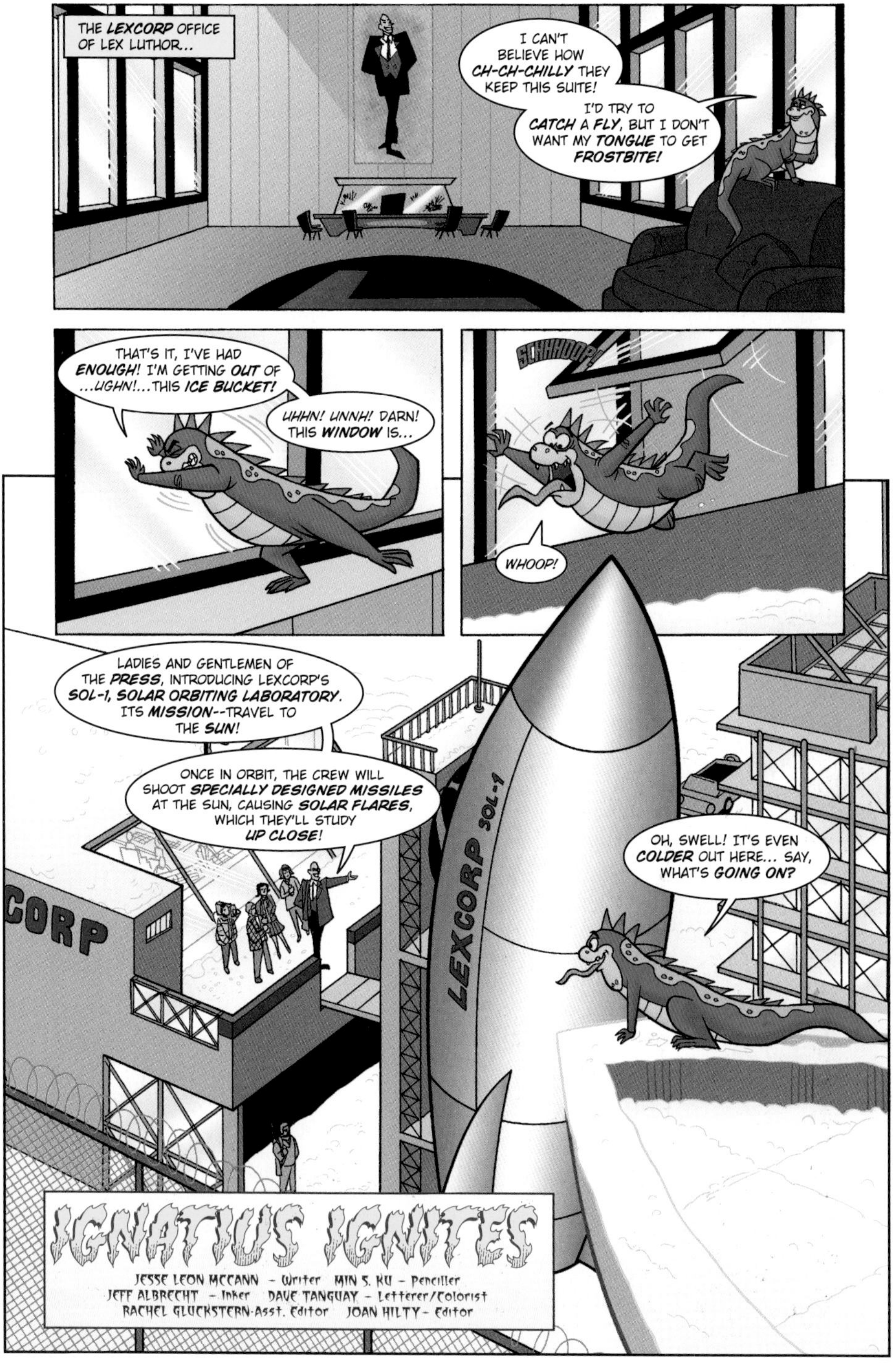
THE LEXCORP OFFICE OF LEX LUTHOR...
I CAN'T BELIEVE HOW CH-CH-CHILLY THEY KEEP THIS SUITE!
I'D TRY TO CATCH A FLY, BUT I DON'T WANT MY TONGUE TO GET FROSTBITE!
THAT'S IT, I'VE HAD ENOUGH! I'M GETTING OUT OF ...UGHN!...THIS ICE BUCKET!
UHHN! UNNH! DARN! THIS WINDOW IS...
SCHHHOOP!
WHOOP!
LADIES AND GENTLEMEN OF THE PRESS, INTRODUCING LEXCORP'S SOL-1, SOLAR ORBITING LABORATORY. ITS MISSION--TRAVEL TO THE SUN!
ONCE IN ORBIT, THE CREW WILL SHOOT SPECIALLY DESIGNED MISSILES AT THE SUN, CAUSING SOLAR FLARES, WHICH THEY'LL STUDY UP CLOSE!
OH, SWELL! IT'S EVEN COLDER OUT HERE... SAY, WHAT'S GOING ON?
CORP
LEXCORP SOL-1
IGNATIUS IGNITES
JESSE LEON MCCANN - Writer MIN S. KU - Penciller
JEFF ALBRECHT - Inker DAVE TANGUAY - Letterer/Colorist
RACHEL GLUCKSTERN-Asst. Editor JOAN HILTY- Editor

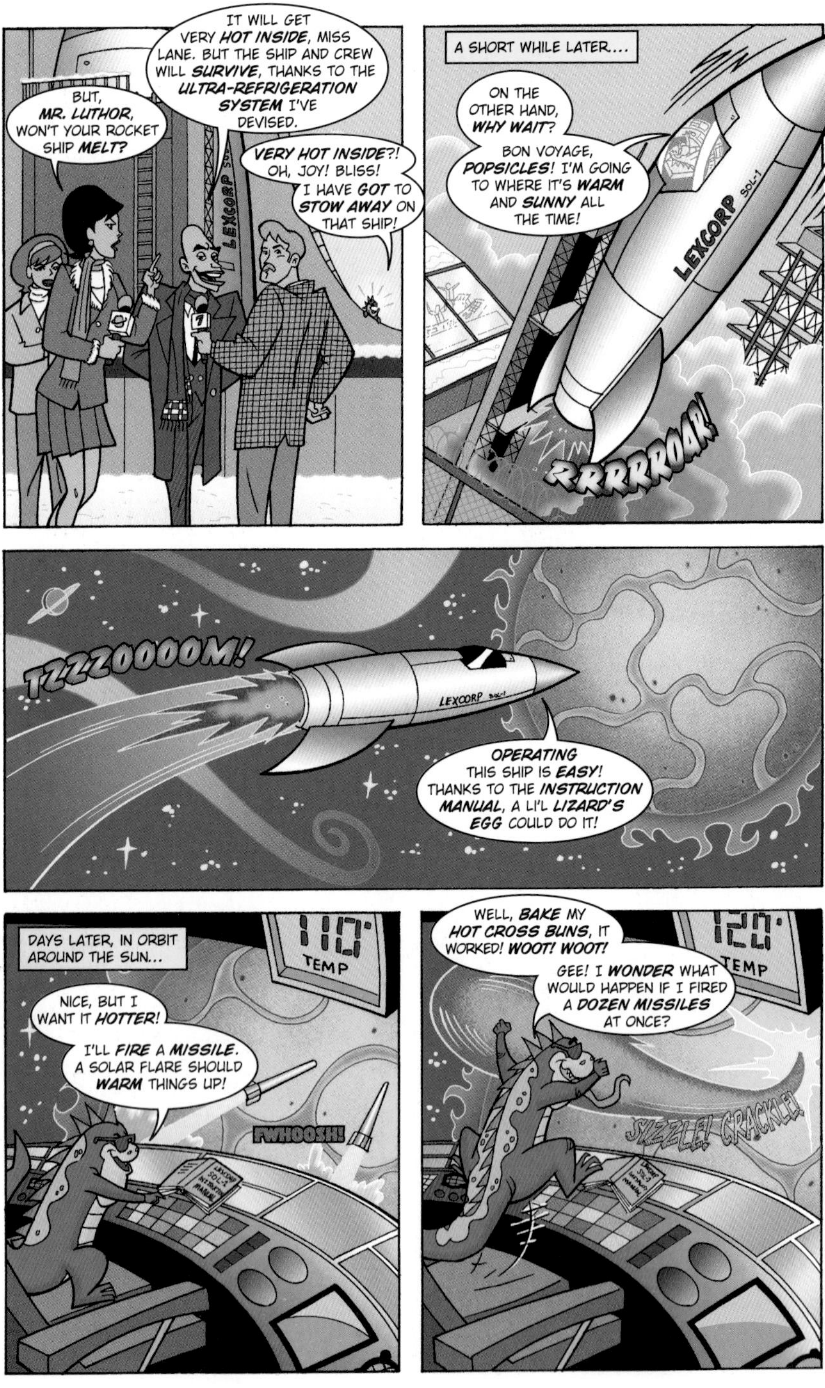
BUT, MR. LUTHOR, WON'T YOUR ROCKET SHIP MELT?
IT WILL GET VERY HOT INSIDE, MISS LANE. BUT THE SHIP AND CREW WILL SURVIVE, THANKS TO THE ULTRA-REFRIGERATION SYSTEM I'VE DEVISED.
VERY HOT INSIDE?! OH, JOY! BLISS!
I HAVE GOT TO STOW AWAY ON THAT SHIP!
LEXCORP
A SHORT WHILE LATER...
ON THE OTHER HAND, WHY WAIT?
BON VOYAGE, POPSICLES! I'M GOING TO WHERE IT'S WARM AND SUNNY ALL THE TIME!
LEXCORP SOL-1
RRRRROAR!
TZZZOOOOM!
LEXCORP SOL-1
OPERATING THIS SHIP IS EASY! THANKS TO THE INSTRUCTION MANUAL, A LI'L LIZARD'S EGG COULD DO IT!
DAYS LATER, IN ORBIT AROUND THE SUN...
110°
TEMP
NICE, BUT I WANT IT HOTTER!
I'LL FIRE A MISSILE. A SOLAR FLARE SHOULD WARM THINGS UP!
FWHOOSH!
WELL, BAKE MY HOT CROSS BUNS, IT WORKED! WOOT! WOOT!
GEE! I WONDER WHAT WOULD HAPPEN IF I FIRED A DOZEN MISSILES AT ONCE?
120°
TEMP
SIZZLE! CRACKLE!

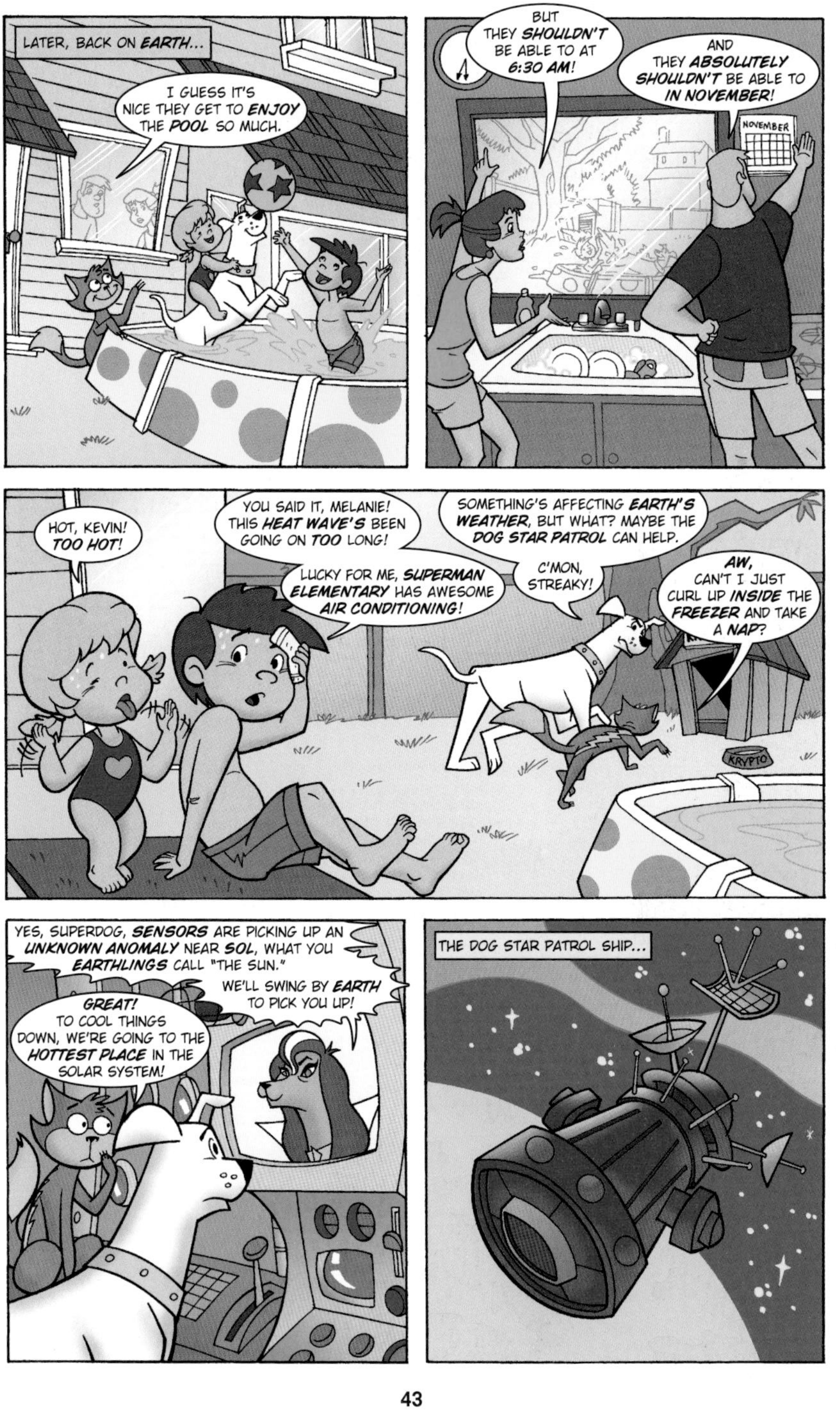
LATER, BACK ON EARTH...
I GUESS IT'S NICE THEY GET TO ENJOY THE POOL SO MUCH.
BUT THEY SHOULDN'T BE ABLE TO AT 6:30 AM!
AND THEY ABSOLUTELY SHOULDN'T BE ABLE TO IN NOVEMBER!
NOVEMBER
HOT, KEVIN! TOO HOT!
YOU SAID IT, MELANIE! THIS HEAT WAVE'S BEEN GOING ON TOO LONG!
LUCKY FOR ME, SUPERMAN ELEMENTARY HAS AWESOME AIR CONDITIONING!
SOMETHING'S AFFECTING EARTH'S WEATHER, BUT WHAT? MAYBE THE DOG STAR PATROL CAN HELP.
C'MON, STREAKY!
AW, CAN'T I JUST CURL UP INSIDE THE FREEZER AND TAKE A NAP?
KRYPTO
YES, SUPERDOG, SENSORS ARE PICKING UP AN UNKNOWN ANOMALY NEAR SOL, WHAT YOU EARTHLINGS CALL "THE SUN."
WE'LL SWING BY EARTH TO PICK YOU UP!
GREAT! TO COOL THINGS DOWN, WE'RE GOING TO THE HOTTEST PLACE IN THE SOLAR SYSTEM!
THE DOG STAR PATROL SHIP...

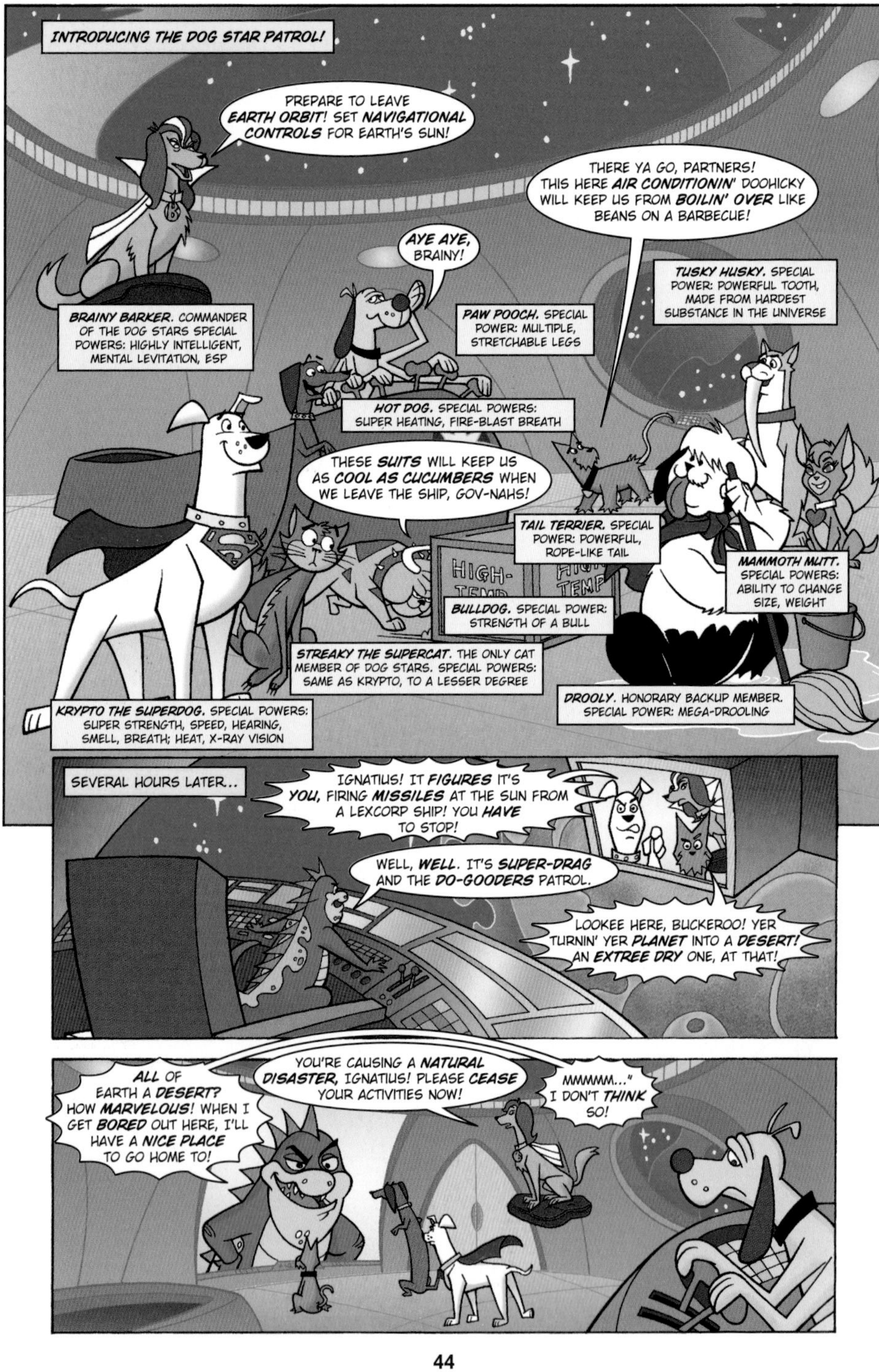

INTRODUCING THE DOG STAR PATROL!
PREPARE TO LEAVE EARTH ORBIT! SET NAVIGATIONAL CONTROLS FOR EARTH'S SUN!
THERE YA GO, PARTNERS! THIS HERE AIR CONDITIONIN' DOOHICKY WILL KEEP US FROM BOILIN' OVER LIKE BEANS ON A BARBECUE!
AYE AYE, BRAINY!
TUSKY HUSKY. SPECIAL POWER: POWERFUL TOOTH, MADE FROM HARDEST SUBSTANCE IN THE UNIVERSE
BRAINY BARKER. COMMANDER OF THE DOG STARS SPECIAL POWERS: HIGHLY INTELLIGENT, MENTAL LEVITATION, ESP
PAW POOCH. SPECIAL POWER: MULTIPLE, STRETCHABLE LEGS
HOT DOG. SPECIAL POWERS: SUPER HEATING, FIRE-BLAST BREATH
THESE SUITS WILL KEEP US AS COOL AS CUCUMBERS WHEN WE LEAVE THE SHIP, GOV-NAHS!
TAIL TERRIER. SPECIAL POWER: POWERFUL, ROPE-LIKE TAIL
MAMMOTH MUTT. SPECIAL POWERS: ABILITY TO CHANGE SIZE, WEIGHT
HIGH-TEMP
BULLDOG. SPECIAL POWER: STRENGTH OF A BULL
STREAKY THE SUPERCAT. THE ONLY CAT MEMBER OF DOG STARS. SPECIAL POWERS: SAME AS KRYPTO, TO A LESSER DEGREE
DROOLY. HONORARY BACKUP MEMBER. SPECIAL POWER: MEGA-DROOLING
KRYPTO THE SUPERDOG. SPECIAL POWERS: SUPER STRENGTH, SPEED, HEARING, SMELL, BREATH; HEAT, X-RAY VISION
SEVERAL HOURS LATER...
IGNATIUS! IT FIGURES IT'S YOU, FIRING MISSILES AT THE SUN FROM A LEXCORP SHIP! YOU HAVE TO STOP!
WELL, WELL. IT'S SUPER-DRAG AND THE DO-GOODERS PATROL.
LOOKEE HERE, BUCKEROO! YER TURNIN' YER PLANET INTO A DESERT! AN EXTREE DRY ONE, AT THAT!
ALL OF EARTH A DESERT? HOW MARVELOUS! WHEN I GET BORED OUT HERE, I'LL HAVE A NICE PLACE TO GO HOME TO!
YOU'RE CAUSING A NATURAL DISASTER, IGNATIUS! PLEASE CEASE YOUR ACTIVITIES NOW!
MMMMM..." I DON'T THINK SO!

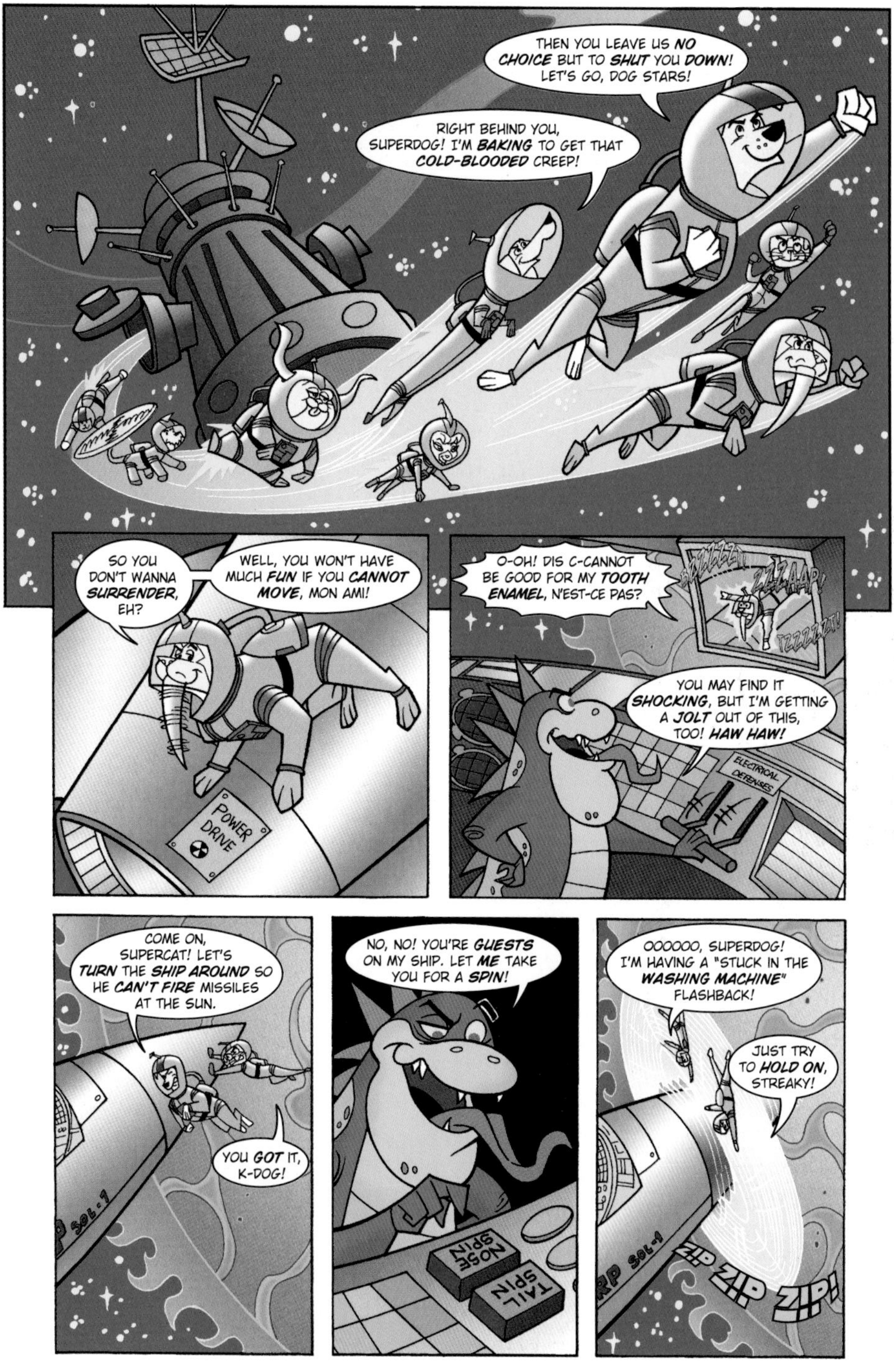
THEN YOU LEAVE US NO CHOICE BUT TO SHUT YOU DOWN! LET'S GO, DOG STARS!
RIGHT BEHIND YOU, SUPERDOG! I'M BAKING TO GET THAT COLD-BLOODED CREEP!
SO YOU DON'T WANNA SURRENDER, EH?
WELL, YOU WON'T HAVE MUCH FUN IF YOU CANNOT MOVE, MON AMI!
POWER DRIVE
O-OH! DIS C-CANNOT BE GOOD FOR MY TOOTH ENAMEL, N'EST-CE PAS?
ZZZAAP!
TZZZZZT!
YOU MAY FIND IT SHOCKING, BUT I'M GETTING A JOLT OUT OF THIS, TOO! HAW HAW!
ELECTRICAL DEFENSES
COME ON, SUPERCAT! LET'S TURN THE SHIP AROUND SO HE CAN'T FIRE MISSILES AT THE SUN.
YOU GOT IT, K-DOG!
SOL-1
NO, NO! YOU'RE GUESTS ON MY SHIP. LET ME TAKE YOU FOR A SPIN!
NOSE SPIN
TAIL SPIN
OOOOOO, SUPERDOG! I'M HAVING A "STUCK IN THE WASHING MACHINE" FLASHBACK!
JUST TRY TO HOLD ON, STREAKY!
SOL-1
ZIP ZIP ZIP!

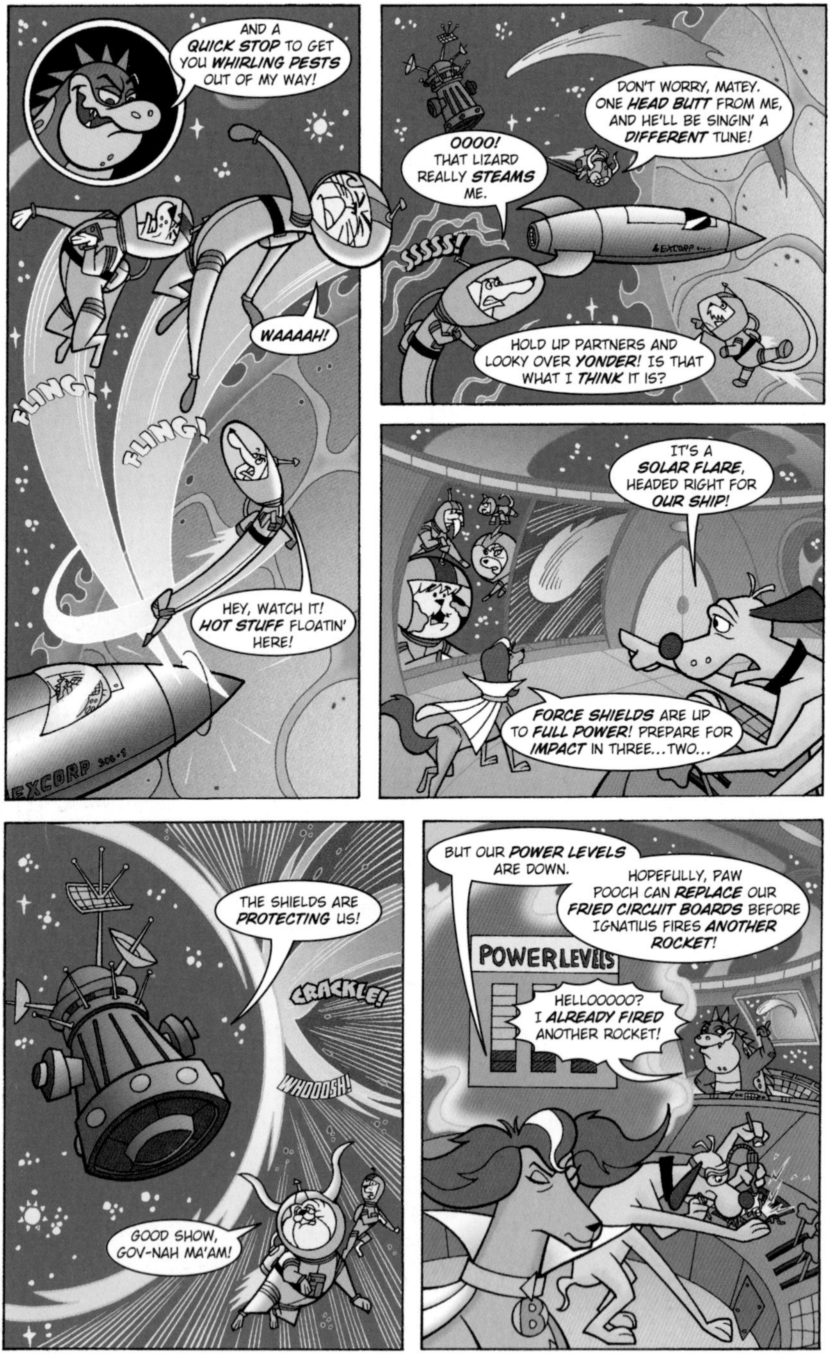

AND A QUICK STOP TO GET YOU WHIRLING PESTS OUT OF MY WAY!
WAAAAH!
FLING!
FLING!
HEY, WATCH IT! HOT STUFF FLOATIN' HERE!
EXCORP
DON'T WORRY, MATEY. ONE HEAD BUTT FROM ME, AND HE'LL BE SINGIN' A DIFFERENT TUNE!
OOOO! THAT LIZARD REALLY STEAMS ME.
SSSSS!
HOLD UP PARTNERS AND LOOKY OVER YONDER! IS THAT WHAT I THINK IT IS?
IT'S A SOLAR FLARE, HEADED RIGHT FOR OUR SHIP!
FORCE SHIELDS ARE UP TO FULL POWER! PREPARE FOR IMPACT IN THREE...TWO...
THE SHIELDS ARE PROTECTING US!
CRACKLE!
WHOOOSH!
GOOD SHOW, GOV-NAH MA'AM!
BUT OUR POWER LEVELS ARE DOWN.
HOPEFULLY, PAW POOCH CAN REPLACE OUR FRIED CIRCUIT BOARDS BEFORE IGNATIUS FIRES ANOTHER ROCKET!
POWER LEVELS
HELLOOOOO? I ALREADY FIRED ANOTHER ROCKET!

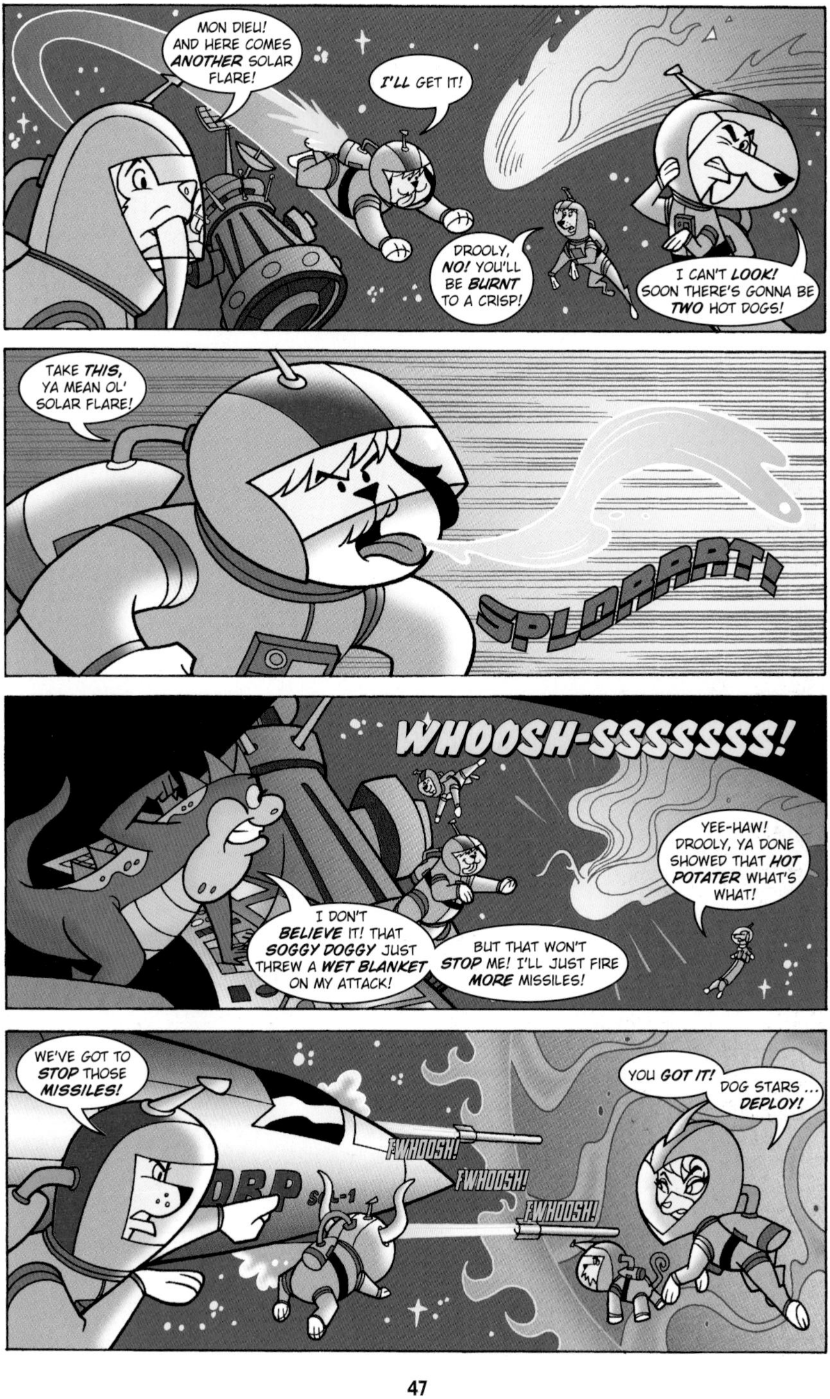
MON DIEU! AND HERE COMES ANOTHER SOLAR FLARE!
I'LL GET IT!
DROOLY, NO! YOU'LL BE BURNT TO A CRISP!
I CAN'T LOOK! SOON THERE'S GONNA BE TWO HOT DOGS!
TAKE THIS, YA MEAN OL' SOLAR FLARE!
SPLORRRT!
WHOOSH-SSSSSSS!
YEE-HAW! DROOLY, YA DONE SHOWED THAT HOT POTATER WHAT'S WHAT!
I DON'T BELIEVE IT! THAT SOGGY DOGGY JUST THREW A WET BLANKET ON MY ATTACK!
BUT THAT WON'T STOP ME! I'LL JUST FIRE MORE MISSILES!
WE'VE GOT TO STOP THOSE MISSILES!
FWHOOSH!
FWHOOSH!
FWHOOSH!
YOU GOT IT!
DOG STARS ... DEPLOY!

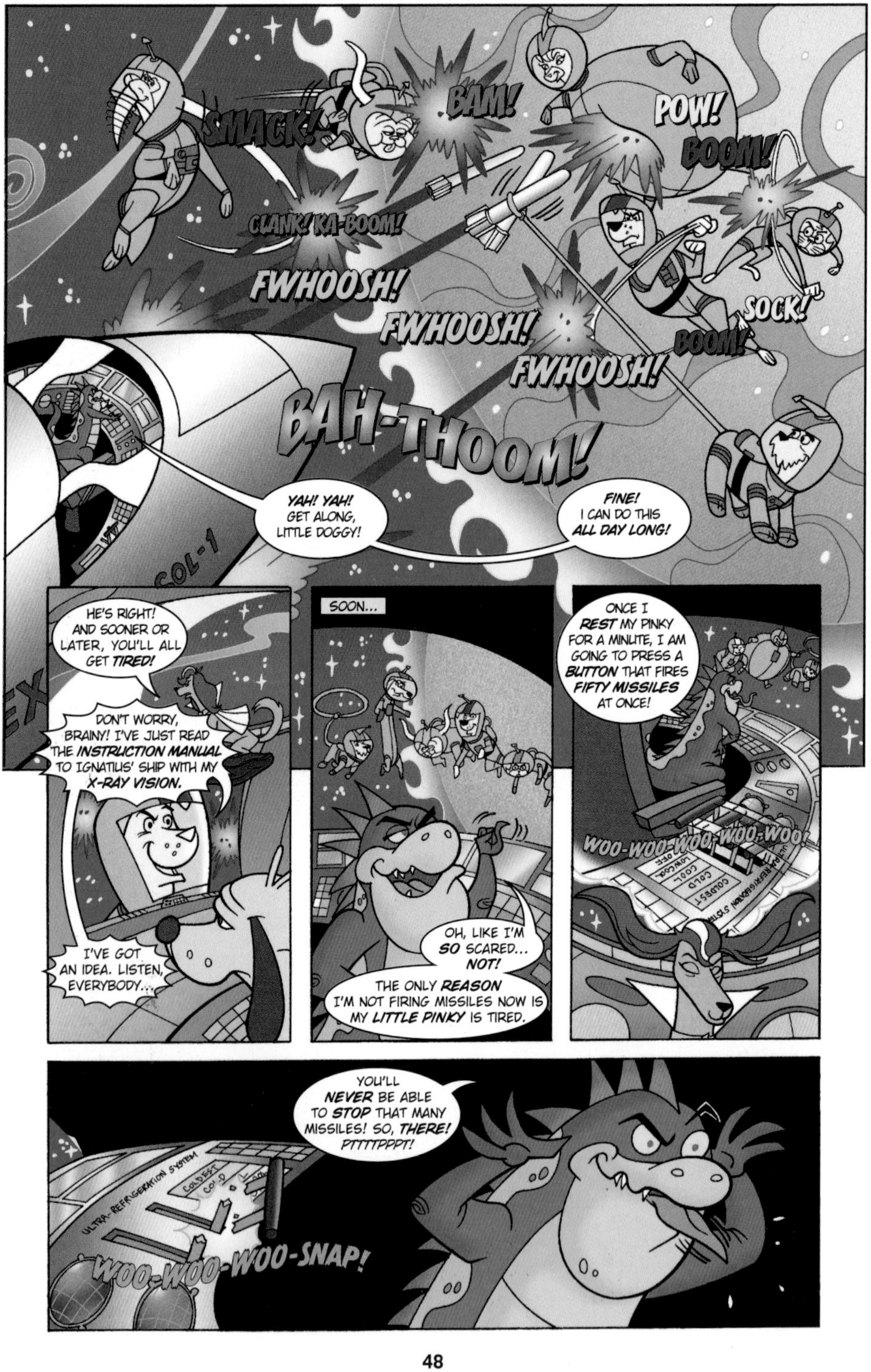
SMACK!
BAM!
POW!
BOOM!
CLANK! KA-BOOM!
FWHOOSH!
FWHOOSH!
FWHOOSH!
SOCK!
BOOM!
BAH-THOOM!
COL-1
YAH! YAH! GET ALONG, LITTLE DOGGY!
FINE! I CAN DO THIS ALL DAY LONG!
HE'S RIGHT! AND SOONER OR LATER, YOU'LL ALL GET TIRED!
DON'T WORRY, BRAINY! I'VE JUST READ THE INSTRUCTION MANUAL TO IGNATIUS' SHIP WITH MY X-RAY VISION.
I'VE GOT AN IDEA. LISTEN, EVERYBODY...
SOON...
OH, LIKE I'M SO SCARED... NOT!
THE ONLY REASON I'M NOT FIRING MISSILES NOW IS MY LITTLE PINKY IS TIRED.
ONCE I REST MY PINKY FOR A MINUTE, I AM GOING TO PRESS A BUTTON THAT FIRES FIFTY MISSILES AT ONCE!
WOO-WOO-WOO-WOO-WOO
YOU'LL NEVER BE ABLE TO STOP THAT MANY MISSILES! SO, THERE! PTTTTPPPT!
ULTRA-REFRIGERATION SYSTEM
COLDEST
COLD
WOO-WOO-WOO-SNAP!

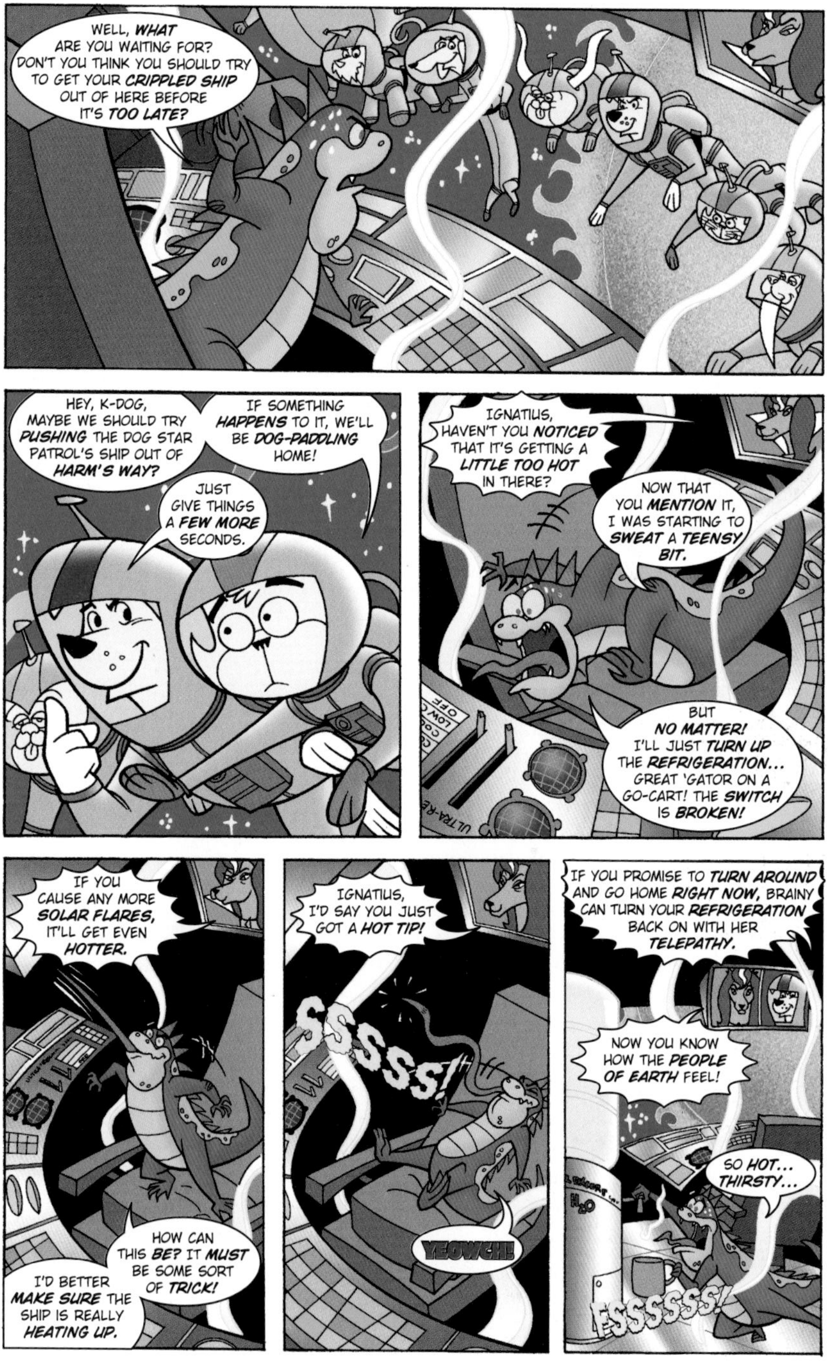
WELL, WHAT ARE YOU WAITING FOR? DON'T YOU THINK YOU SHOULD TRY TO GET YOUR CRIPPLED SHIP OUT OF HERE BEFORE IT'S TOO LATE?
HEY, K-DOG, MAYBE WE SHOULD TRY PUSHING THE DOG STAR PATROL'S SHIP OUT OF HARM'S WAY?
IF SOMETHING HAPPENS TO IT, WE'LL BE DOG-PADDLING HOME!
JUST GIVE THINGS A FEW MORE SECONDS.
IGNATIUS, HAVEN'T YOU NOTICED THAT IT'S GETTING A LITTLE TOO HOT IN THERE?
NOW THAT YOU MENTION IT, I WAS STARTING TO SWEAT A TEENSY BIT.
BUT NO MATTER! I'LL JUST TURN UP THE REFRIGERATION... GREAT 'GATOR ON A GO-CART! THE SWITCH IS BROKEN!
IF YOU CAUSE ANY MORE SOLAR FLARES, IT'LL GET EVEN HOTTER.
HOW CAN THIS BE? IT MUST BE SOME SORT OF TRICK!
I'D BETTER MAKE SURE THE SHIP IS REALLY HEATING UP.
IGNATIUS, I'D SAY YOU JUST GOT A HOT TIP!
SSSSS!
YEOWCH!
IF YOU PROMISE TO TURN AROUND AND GO HOME RIGHT NOW, BRAINY CAN TURN YOUR REFRIGERATION BACK ON WITH HER TELEPATHY.
NOW YOU KNOW HOW THE PEOPLE OF EARTH FEEL!
SO HOT... THIRSTY...
ESSSSSSS!

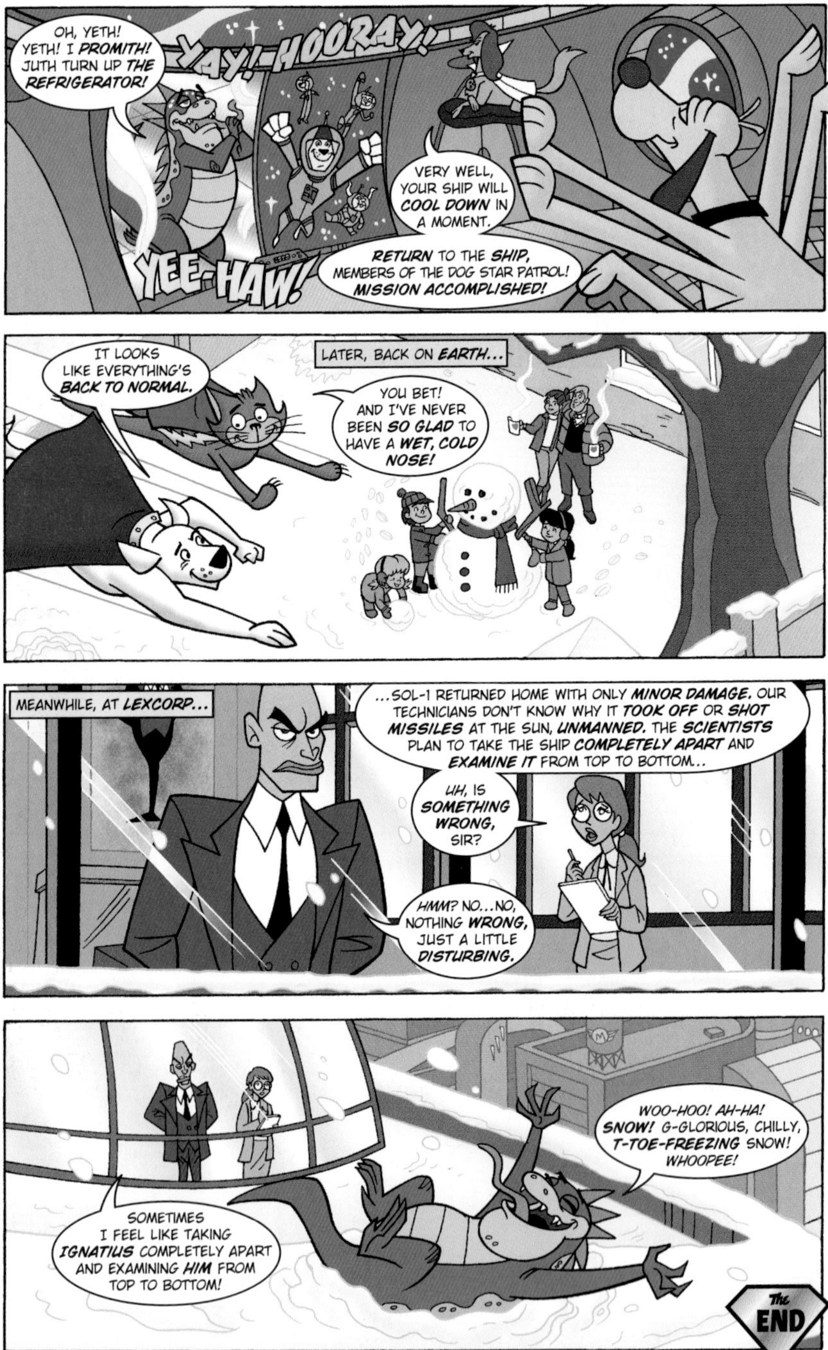
OH, YETH! YETH! I PROMITH! JUTH TURN UP THE REFRIGERATOR!
YAY! HOORAY!
VERY WELL, YOUR SHIP WILL COOL DOWN IN A MOMENT.
YEE-HAW!
RETURN TO THE SHIP, MEMBERS OF THE DOG STAR PATROL! MISSION ACCOMPLISHED!
LATER, BACK ON EARTH...
IT LOOKS LIKE EVERYTHING'S BACK TO NORMAL.
YOU BET! AND I'VE NEVER BEEN SO GLAD TO HAVE A WET, COLD NOSE!
MEANWHILE, AT LEXCORP...
...SOL-1 RETURNED HOME WITH ONLY MINOR DAMAGE. OUR TECHNICIANS DON'T KNOW WHY IT TOOK OFF OR SHOT MISSILES AT THE SUN, UNMANNED. THE SCIENTISTS PLAN TO TAKE THE SHIP COMPLETELY APART AND EXAMINE IT FROM TOP TO BOTTOM...
UH, IS SOMETHING WRONG, SIR?
HMM? NO...NO, NOTHING WRONG, JUST A LITTLE DISTURBING.
WOO-HOO! AH-HA! SNOW! G-GLORIOUS, CHILLY, T-TOE-FREEZING SNOW! WHOOPEE!
SOMETIMES I FEEL LIKE TAKING IGNATIUS COMPLETELY APART AND EXAMINING HIM FROM TOP TO BOTTOM!
The END

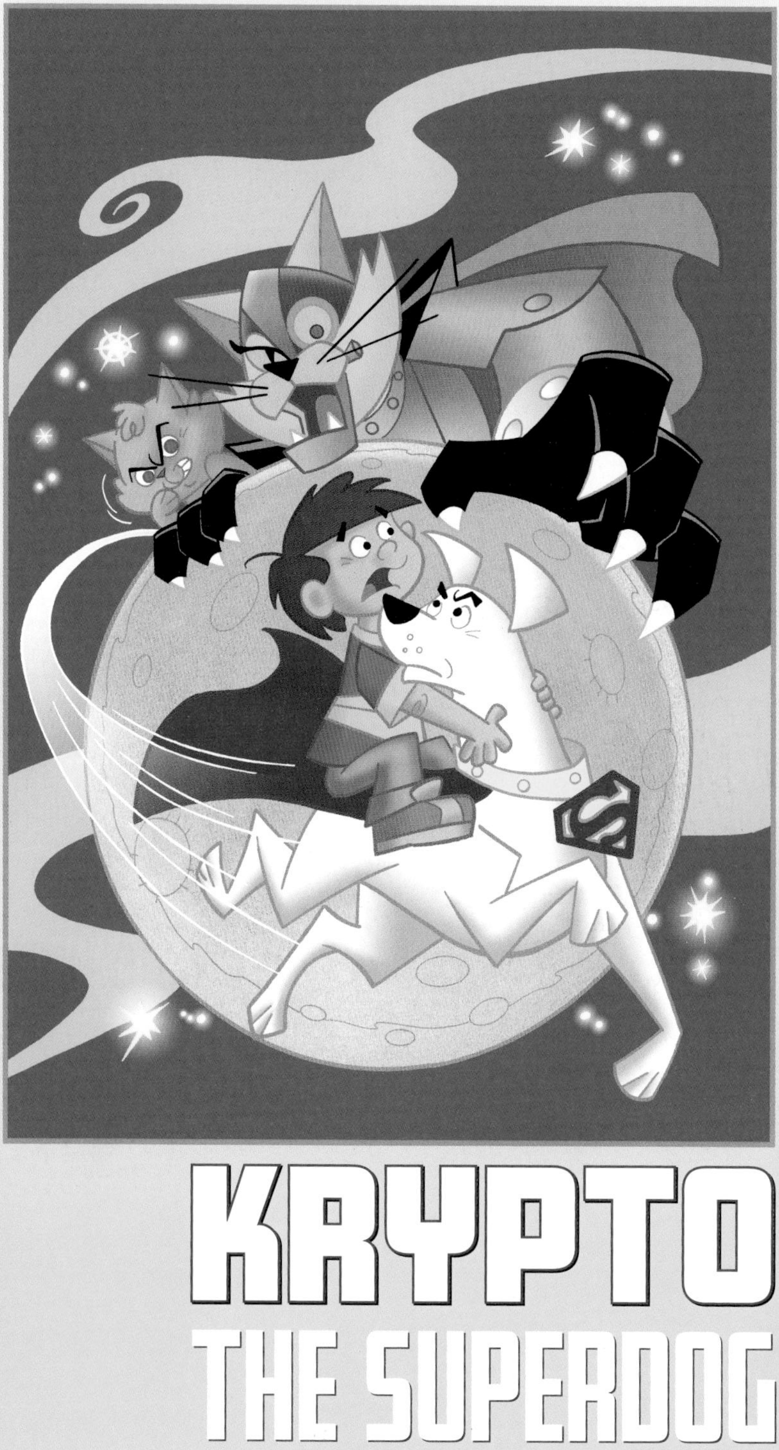

KRYPTO THE SUPERDOG

KRYPTO

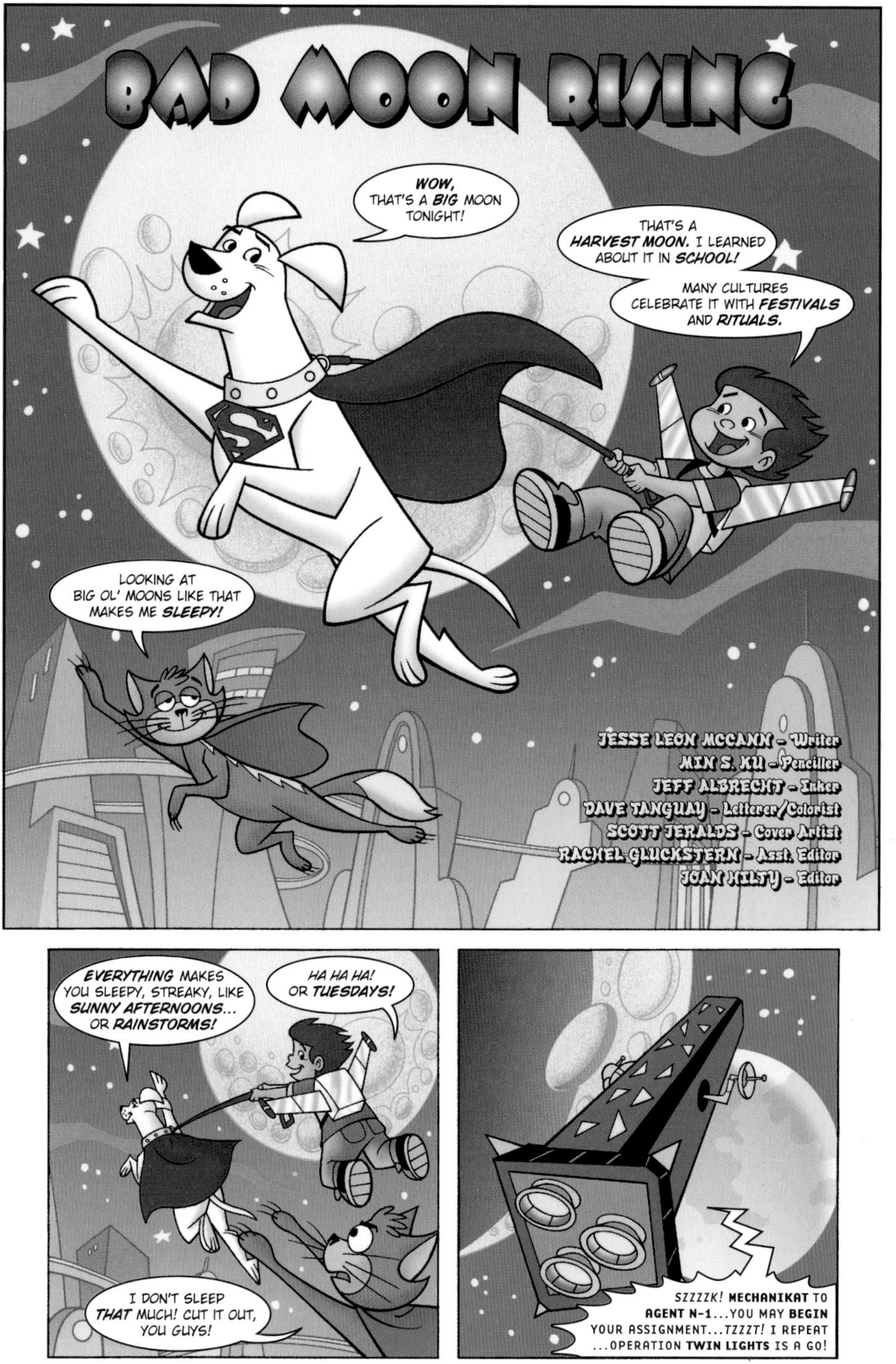
BAD MOON RISING
WOW, THAT'S A BIG MOON TONIGHT!
THAT'S A HARVEST MOON. I LEARNED ABOUT IT IN SCHOOL!
MANY CULTURES CELEBRATE IT WITH FESTIVALS AND RITUALS.
LOOKING AT BIG OL' MOONS LIKE THAT MAKES ME SLEEPY!
JESSE LEON MCCANN - Writer
MIN S. KU - Penciller
JEFF ALBRECHT - Inker
DAVE TANGUAY - Letterer/Colorist
SCOTT JERALDS - Cover Artist
RACHEL GLUCKSTERN - Asst. Editor
JOAN HILTY - Editor
EVERYTHING MAKES YOU SLEEPY, STREAKY, LIKE SUNNY AFTERNOONS... OR RAINSTORMS!
HA HA HA! OR TUESDAYS!
I DON'T SLEEP THAT MUCH! CUT IT OUT, YOU GUYS!
SZZZZK! MECHANIKAT TO AGENT N-1...YOU MAY BEGIN YOUR ASSIGNMENT...TZZZT! I REPEAT ...OPERATION TWIN LIGHTS IS A GO!

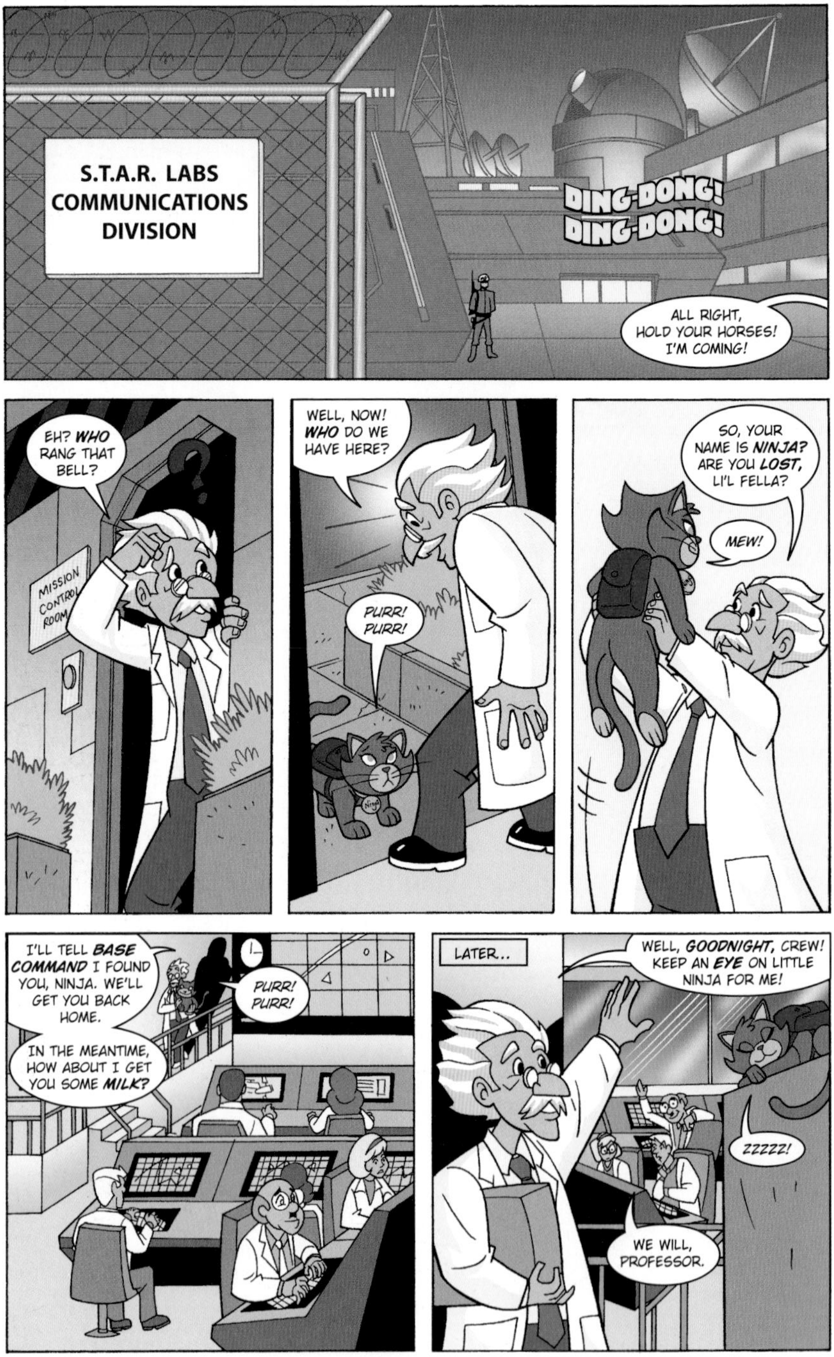
S.T.A.R. LABS COMMUNICATIONS DIVISION
DING-DONG! DING-DONG!
ALL RIGHT, HOLD YOUR HORSES! I'M COMING!
EH? WHO RANG THAT BELL?
MISSION CONTROL ROOM
WELL, NOW! WHO DO WE HAVE HERE?
PURR! PURR!
SO, YOUR NAME IS NINJA? ARE YOU LOST, LI'L FELLA?
MEW!
I'LL TELL BASE COMMAND I FOUND YOU, NINJA. WE'LL GET YOU BACK HOME.
IN THE MEANTIME, HOW ABOUT I GET YOU SOME MILK?
PURR! PURR!
LATER...
WELL, GOODNIGHT, CREW! KEEP AN EYE ON LITTLE NINJA FOR ME!
ZZZZZ!
WE WILL, PROFESSOR.

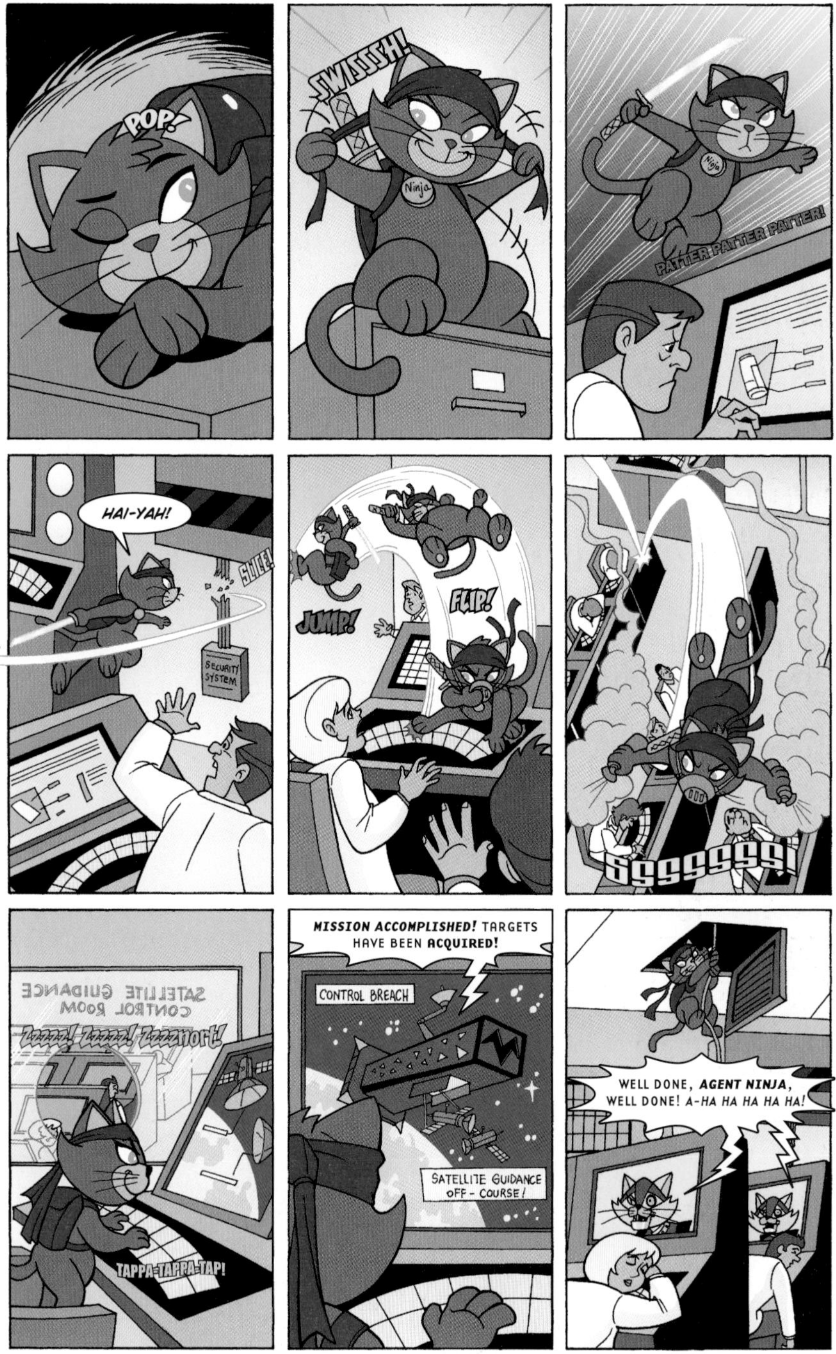
POP!
SWISSSH!
Ninja
Ninja
PATTER PATTER PATTER!
HAI-YAH!
SLICE!
SECURITY SYSTEM
JUMP!
FLIP!
SSSSSSS!
SATELLITE GUIDANCE CONTROL ROOM
Zzzzzz! Zzzzzz! Zzzznort!
TAPPA-TAPPA-TAP!
MISSION ACCOMPLISHED! TARGETS HAVE BEEN **ACQUIRED!**
CONTROL BREACH
SATELLITE GUIDANCE OFF-COURSE!
WELL DONE, **AGENT NINJA**, WELL DONE! A-HA HA HA HA HA!

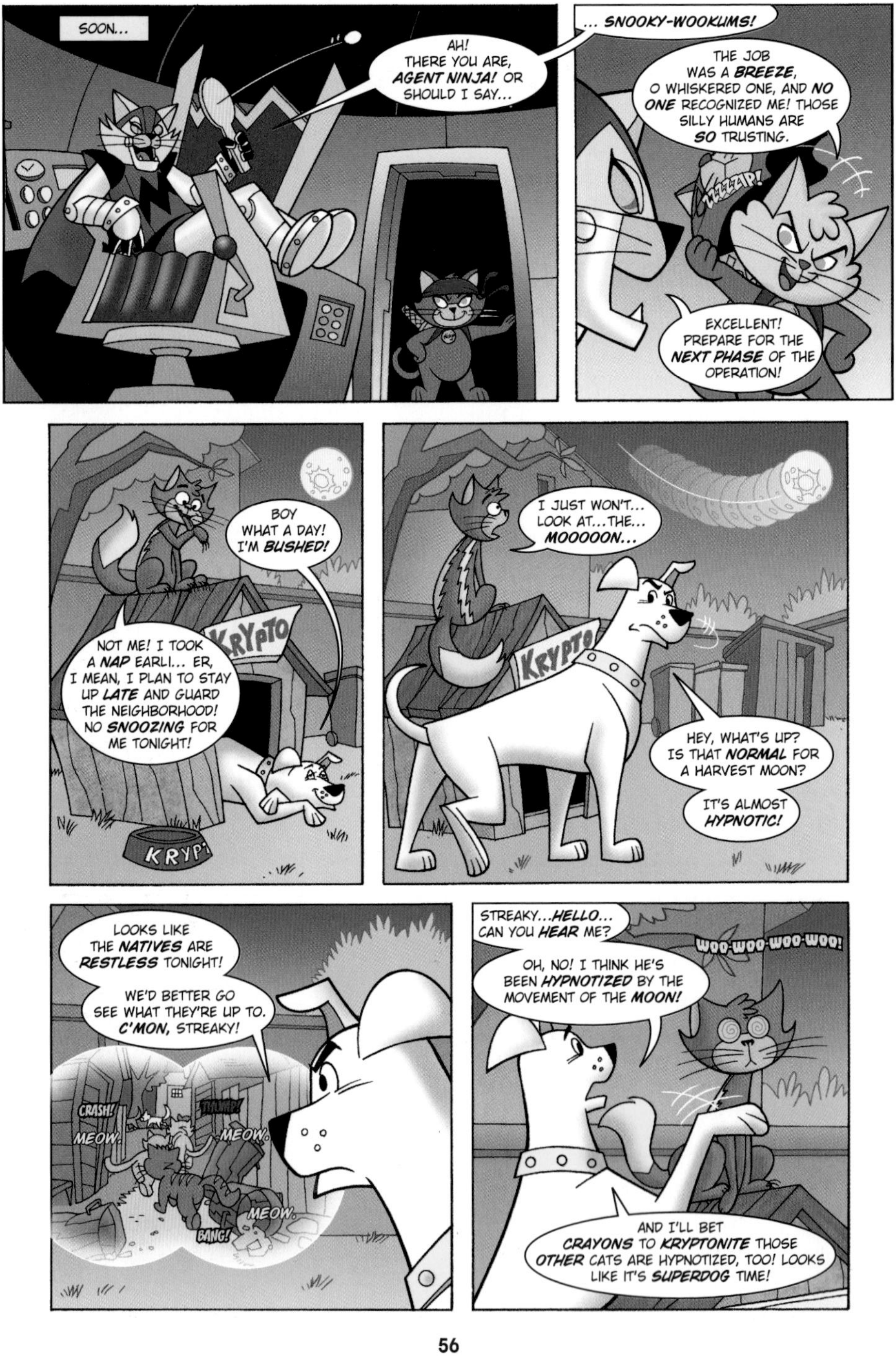
SOON...
AH! THERE YOU ARE, AGENT NINJA! OR SHOULD I SAY...
... SNOOKY-WOOKUMS!
THE JOB WAS A BREEZE, O WHISKERED ONE, AND NO ONE RECOGNIZED ME! THOSE SILLY HUMANS ARE SO TRUSTING.
ZZZZZAP!
EXCELLENT! PREPARE FOR THE NEXT PHASE OF THE OPERATION!
BOY WHAT A DAY! I'M BUSHED!
KRYPTO
NOT ME! I TOOK A NAP EARLI... ER, I MEAN, I PLAN TO STAY UP LATE AND GUARD THE NEIGHBORHOOD! NO SNOOZING FOR ME TONIGHT!
KRYP
I JUST WON'T... LOOK AT...THE... MOOOOON...
KRYPTO
HEY, WHAT'S UP? IS THAT NORMAL FOR A HARVEST MOON?
IT'S ALMOST HYPNOTIC!
LOOKS LIKE THE NATIVES ARE RESTLESS TONIGHT!
WE'D BETTER GO SEE WHAT THEY'RE UP TO. C'MON, STREAKY!
CRASH!
THUMP!
MEOW.
MEOW.
MEOW.
BANG!
STREAKY...HELLO... CAN YOU HEAR ME?
WOO-WOO-WOO-WOO!
OH, NO! I THINK HE'S BEEN HYPNOTIZED BY THE MOVEMENT OF THE MOON!
AND I'LL BET CRAYONS TO KRYPTONITE THOSE OTHER CATS ARE HYPNOTIZED, TOO! LOOKS LIKE IT'S SUPERDOG TIME!

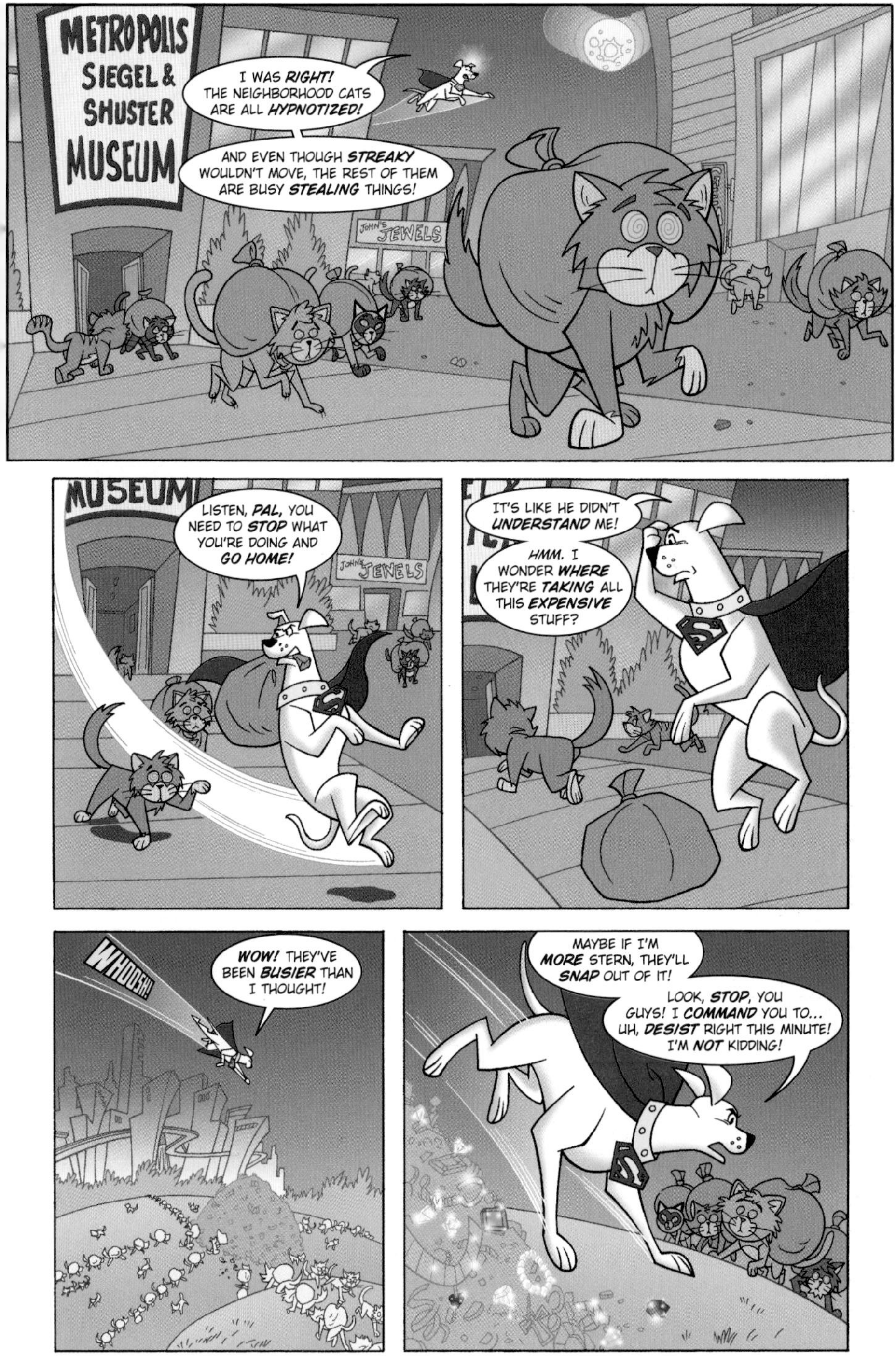
METROPOLIS SIEGEL & SHUSTER MUSEUM
I WAS RIGHT! THE NEIGHBORHOOD CATS ARE ALL HYPNOTIZED!
AND EVEN THOUGH STREAKY WOULDN'T MOVE, THE REST OF THEM ARE BUSY STEALING THINGS!
JOHN'S JEWELS
LISTEN, PAL, YOU NEED TO STOP WHAT YOU'RE DOING AND GO HOME!
IT'S LIKE HE DIDN'T UNDERSTAND ME!
HMM. I WONDER WHERE THEY'RE TAKING ALL THIS EXPENSIVE STUFF?
WHOOSH!
WOW! THEY'VE BEEN BUSIER THAN I THOUGHT!
MAYBE IF I'M MORE STERN, THEY'LL SNAP OUT OF IT!
LOOK, STOP, YOU GUYS! I COMMAND YOU TO... UH, DESIST RIGHT THIS MINUTE! I'M NOT KIDDING!

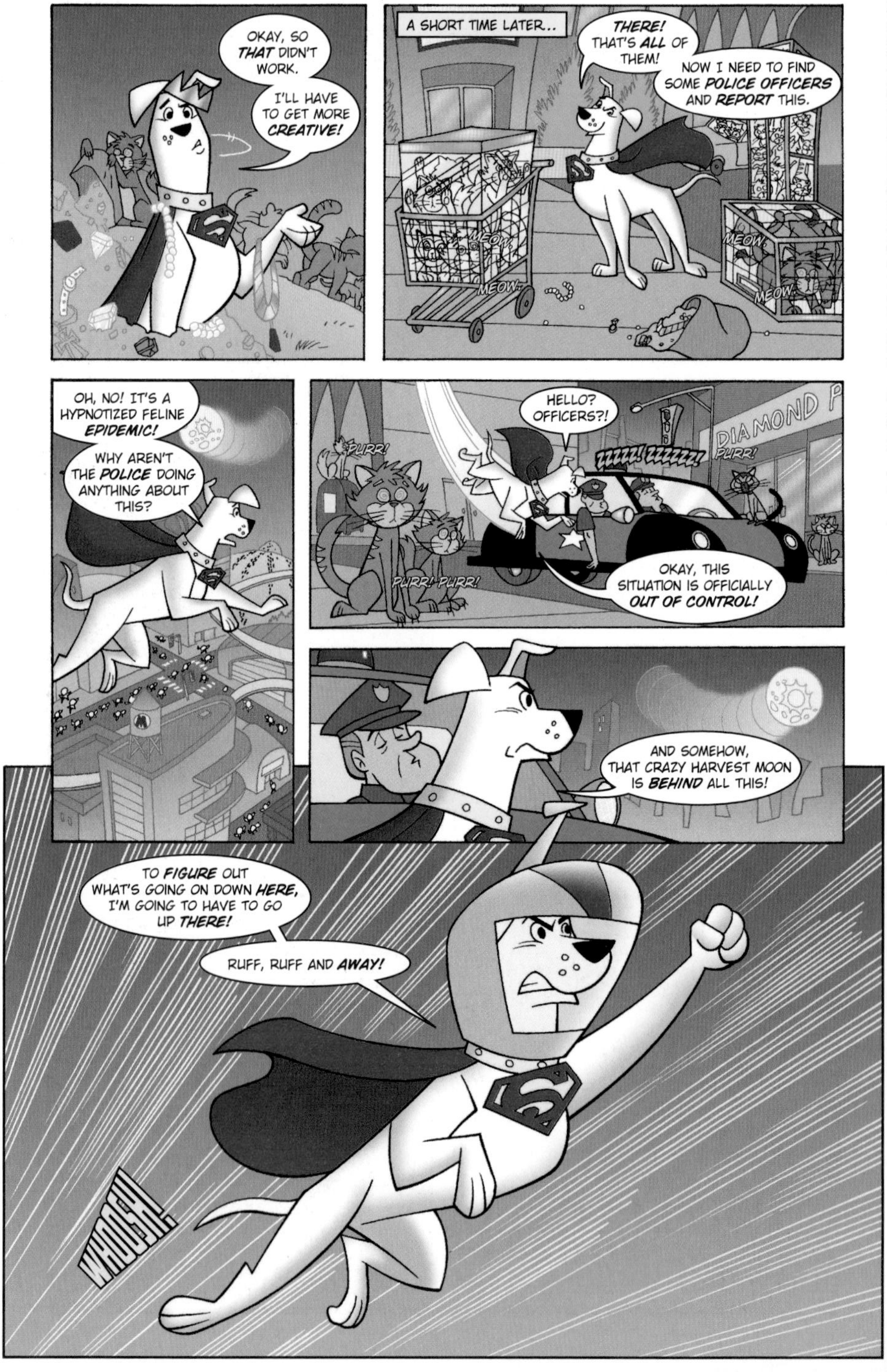

OKAY, SO ***THAT*** DIDN'T WORK.
I'LL HAVE TO GET MORE ***CREATIVE!***
A SHORT TIME LATER...
THERE! THAT'S ***ALL*** OF THEM!
NOW I NEED TO FIND SOME ***POLICE OFFICERS*** AND ***REPORT*** THIS.
MEOW.
MEOW.
MEOW.
MEOW.
OH, NO! IT'S A HYPNOTIZED FELINE ***EPIDEMIC!***
WHY AREN'T THE ***POLICE*** DOING ANYTHING ABOUT THIS?
HELLO? OFFICERS?!
PURR!
DIAMOND
ZZZZZZ! ZZZZZZZ!
PURR!
PURR! PURR!
OKAY, THIS SITUATION IS OFFICIALLY ***OUT OF CONTROL!***
AND SOMEHOW, THAT CRAZY HARVEST MOON IS ***BEHIND*** ALL THIS!
TO ***FIGURE*** OUT WHAT'S GOING ON DOWN ***HERE,*** I'M GOING TO HAVE TO GO UP ***THERE!***
RUFF, RUFF AND ***AWAY!***
WHOOSH!

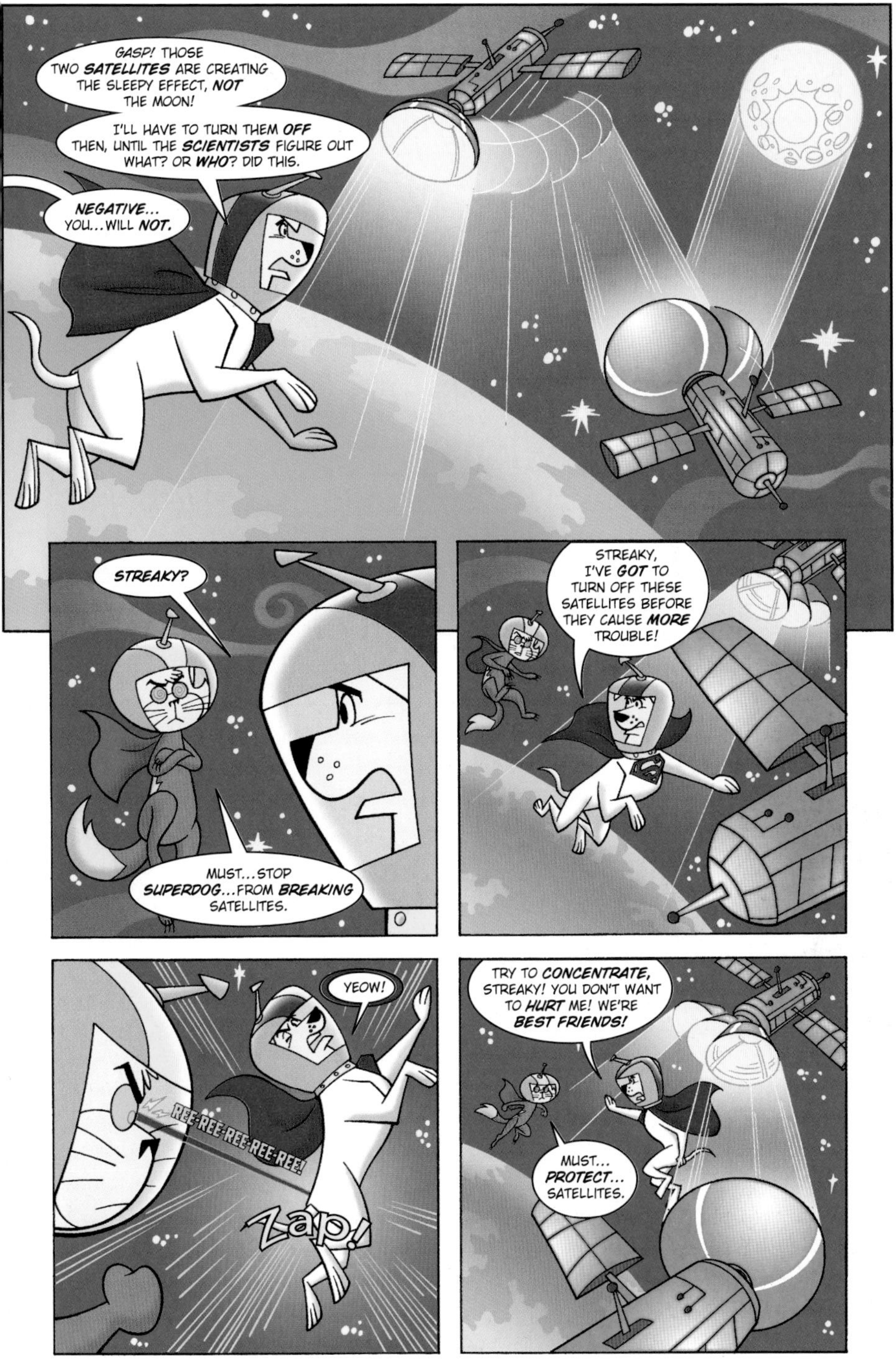

GASP! THOSE TWO SATELLITES ARE CREATING THE SLEEPY EFFECT, NOT THE MOON!
I'LL HAVE TO TURN THEM OFF THEN, UNTIL THE SCIENTISTS FIGURE OUT WHAT? OR WHO? DID THIS.
NEGATIVE... YOU...WILL NOT.
STREAKY?
MUST...STOP SUPERDOG...FROM BREAKING SATELLITES.
STREAKY, I'VE GOT TO TURN OFF THESE SATELLITES BEFORE THEY CAUSE MORE TROUBLE!
YEOW!
REE-REE-REE-REE-REE!
ZAP!
TRY TO CONCENTRATE, STREAKY! YOU DON'T WANT TO HURT ME! WE'RE BEST FRIENDS!
MUST... PROTECT... SATELLITES.

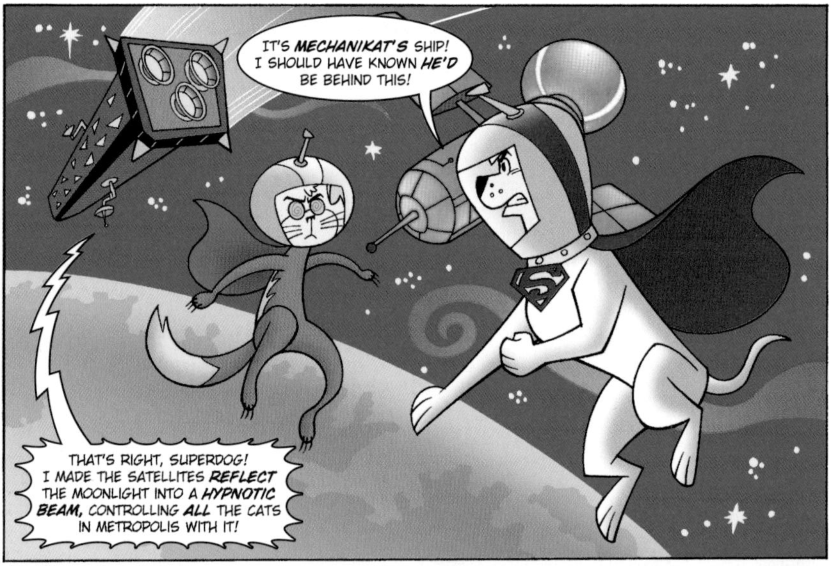
IT'S MECHANIKAT'S SHIP! I SHOULD HAVE KNOWN HE'D BE BEHIND THIS!
THAT'S RIGHT, SUPERDOG! I MADE THE SATELLITES REFLECT THE MOONLIGHT INTO A HYPNOTIC BEAM, CONTROLLING ALL THE CATS IN METROPOLIS WITH IT!

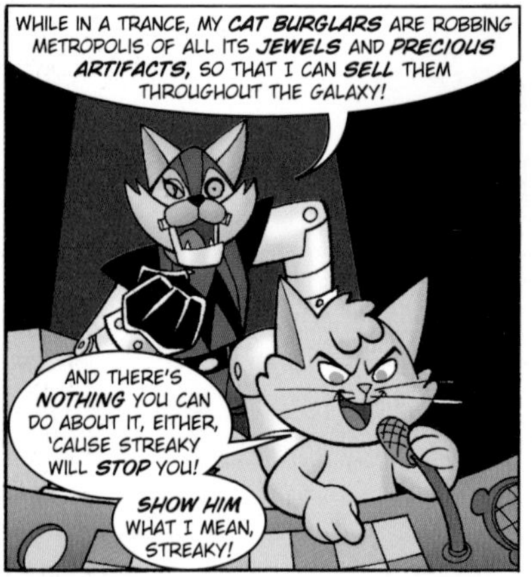
WHILE IN A TRANCE, MY CAT BURGLARS ARE ROBBING METROPOLIS OF ALL ITS JEWELS AND PRECIOUS ARTIFACTS, SO THAT I CAN SELL THEM THROUGHOUT THE GALAXY!
AND THERE'S NOTHING YOU CAN DO ABOUT IT, EITHER, 'CAUSE STREAKY WILL STOP YOU!
SHOW HIM WHAT I MEAN, STREAKY!

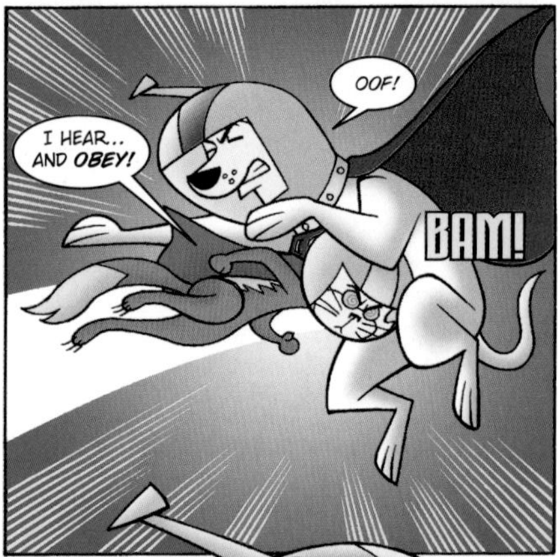
OOF!
I HEAR... AND OBEY!
BAM!

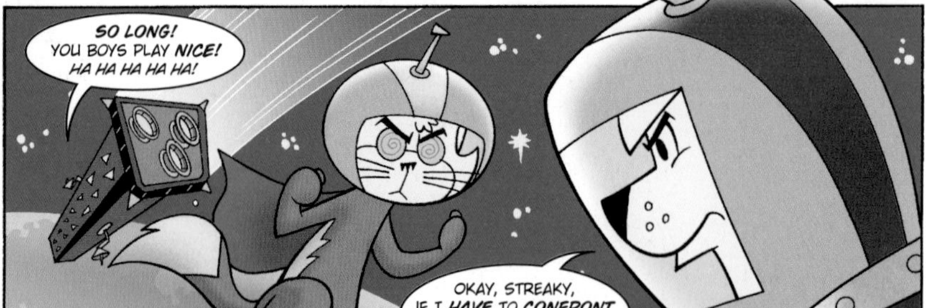
SO LONG! YOU BOYS PLAY NICE! HA HA HA HA HA!
OKAY, STREAKY, IF I HAVE TO CONFRONT YOU, IT'S GOING TO BE ON MY OWN TERMS.

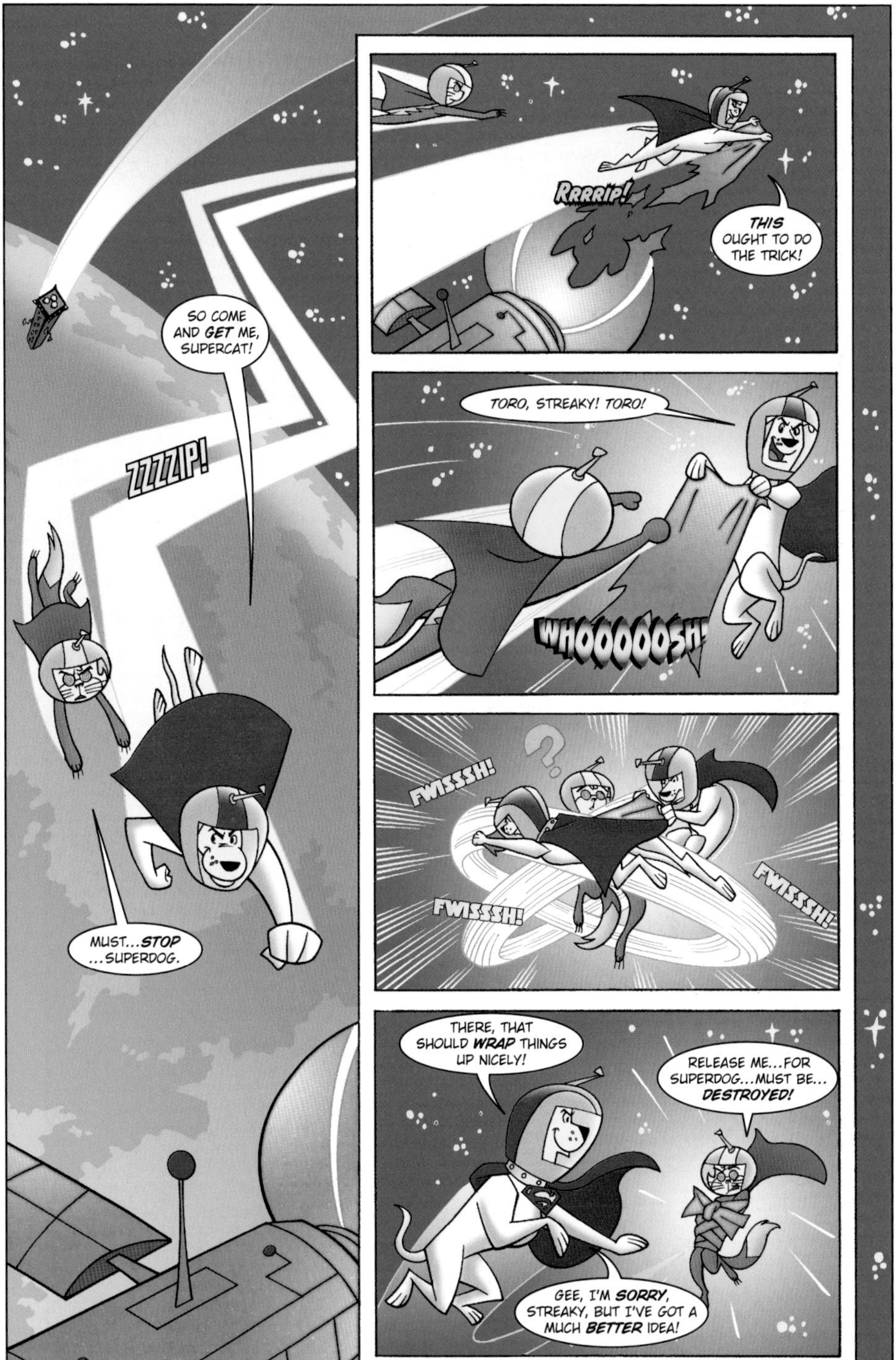
SO COME AND GET ME, SUPERCAT!
ZZZZIP!
MUST...STOP ...SUPERDOG.
RRRRIP!
THIS OUGHT TO DO THE TRICK!
TORO, STREAKY! TORO!
WHOOOOOOSH!
FWISSSH!
FWISSSH!
FWISSSH!
THERE, THAT SHOULD WRAP THINGS UP NICELY!
RELEASE ME...FOR SUPERDOG...MUST BE... DESTROYED!
GEE, I'M SORRY, STREAKY, BUT I'VE GOT A MUCH BETTER IDEA!

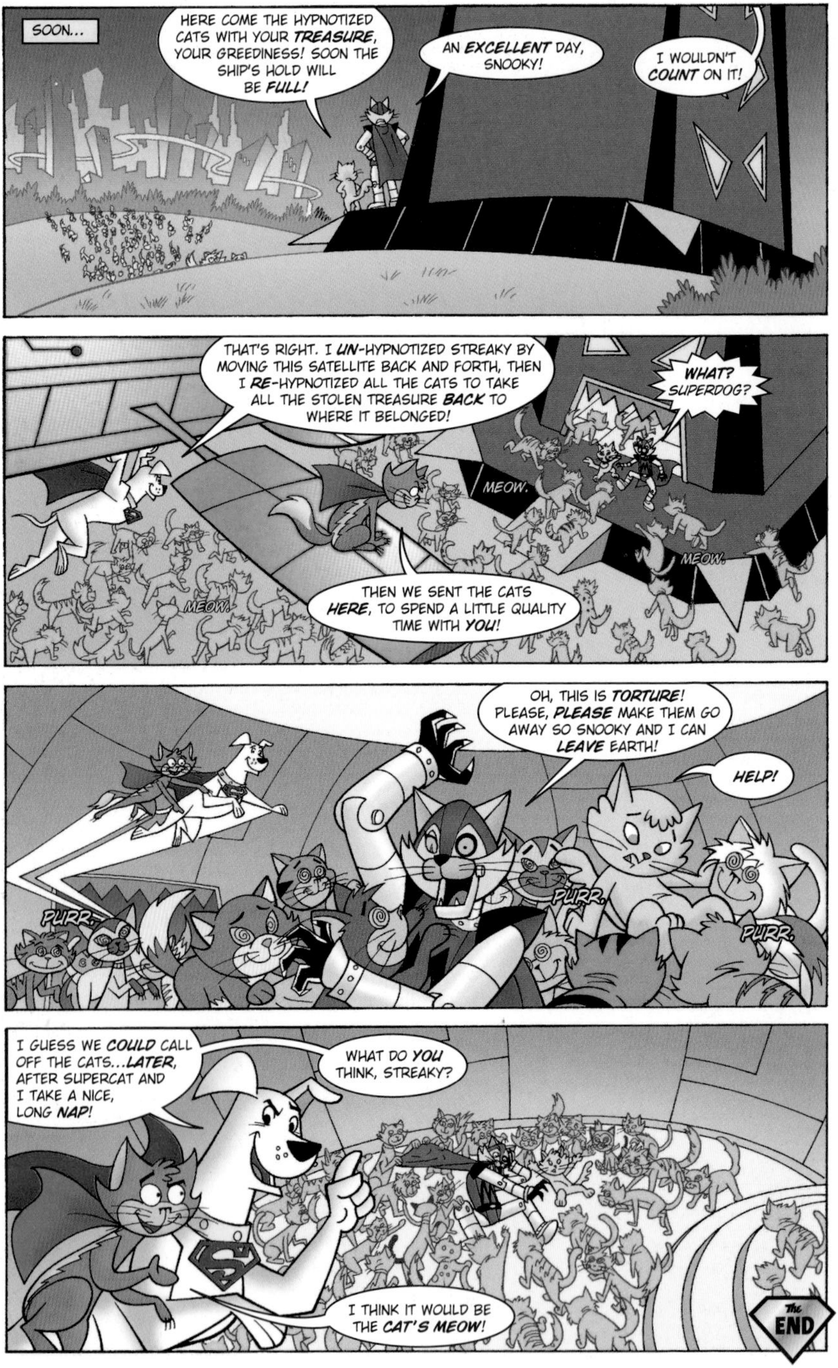
SOON...
HERE COME THE HYPNOTIZED CATS WITH YOUR TREASURE, YOUR GREEDINESS! SOON THE SHIP'S HOLD WILL BE FULL!
AN EXCELLENT DAY, SNOOKY!
I WOULDN'T COUNT ON IT!
THAT'S RIGHT. I UN-HYPNOTIZED STREAKY BY MOVING THIS SATELLITE BACK AND FORTH, THEN I RE-HYPNOTIZED ALL THE CATS TO TAKE ALL THE STOLEN TREASURE BACK TO WHERE IT BELONGED!
WHAT? SUPERDOG?
MEOW.
MEOW.
MEOW.
THEN WE SENT THE CATS HERE, TO SPEND A LITTLE QUALITY TIME WITH YOU!
OH, THIS IS TORTURE! PLEASE, PLEASE MAKE THEM GO AWAY SO SNOOKY AND I CAN LEAVE EARTH!
HELP!
PURR.
PURR.
PURR.
I GUESS WE COULD CALL OFF THE CATS...LATER, AFTER SUPERCAT AND I TAKE A NICE, LONG NAP!
WHAT DO YOU THINK, STREAKY?
I THINK IT WOULD BE THE CAT'S MEOW!
The END

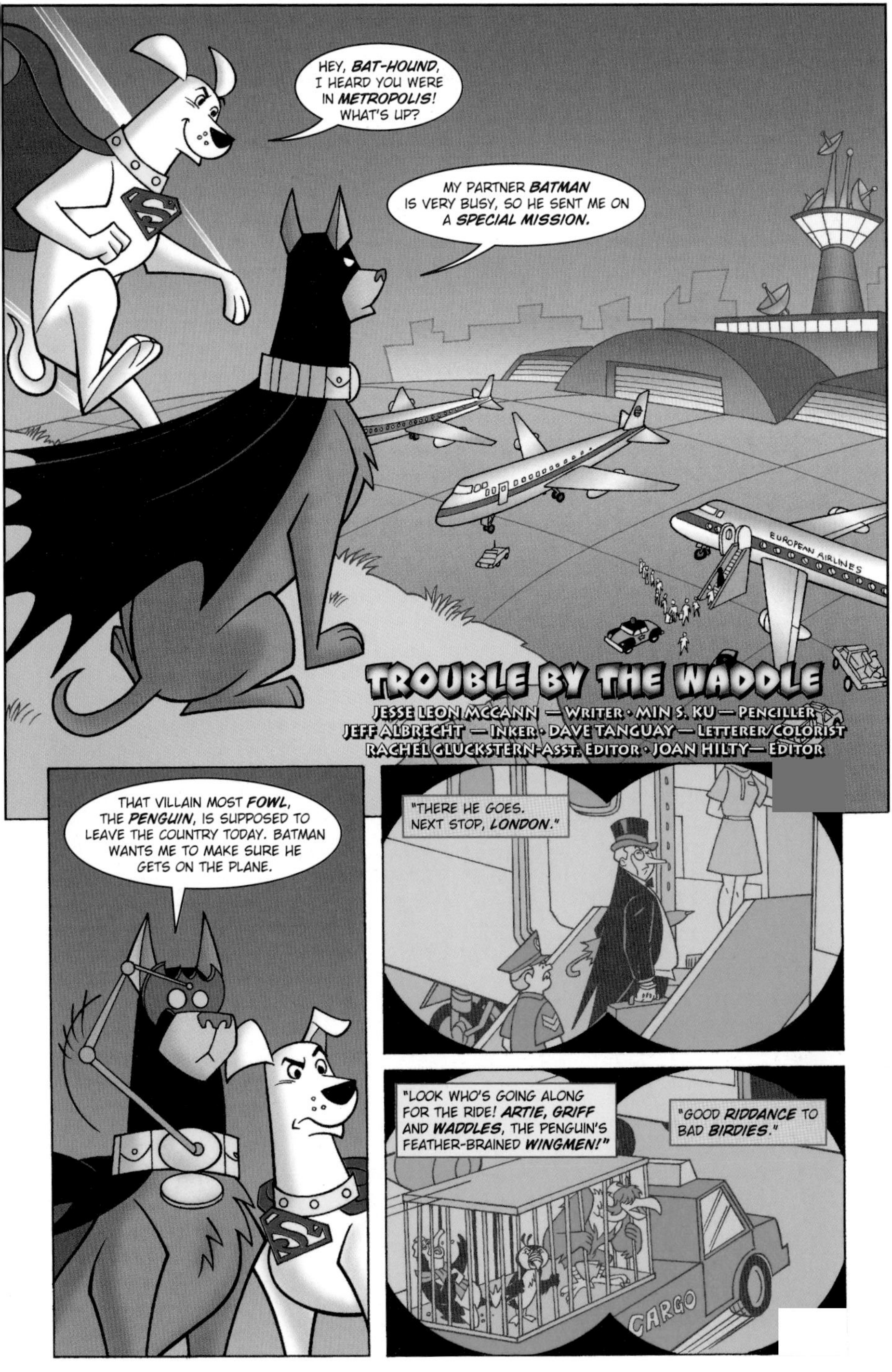
HEY, BAT-HOUND, I HEARD YOU WERE IN METROPOLIS! WHAT'S UP?
MY PARTNER BATMAN IS VERY BUSY, SO HE SENT ME ON A SPECIAL MISSION.
EUROPEAN AIRLINES
TROUBLE BY THE WADDLE
JESSE LEON MCCANN — WRITER · MIN S. KU — PENCILLER
JEFF ALBRECHT — INKER · DAVE TANGUAY — LETTERER/COLORIST
RACHEL GLUCKSTERN-ASST. EDITOR · JOAN HILTY— EDITOR
THAT VILLAIN MOST FOWL, THE PENGUIN, IS SUPPOSED TO LEAVE THE COUNTRY TODAY. BATMAN WANTS ME TO MAKE SURE HE GETS ON THE PLANE.
"THERE HE GOES. NEXT STOP, LONDON."
"LOOK WHO'S GOING ALONG FOR THE RIDE! ARTIE, GRIFF AND WADDLES, THE PENGUIN'S FEATHER-BRAINED WINGMEN!"
"GOOD RIDDANCE TO BAD BIRDIES."
CARGO

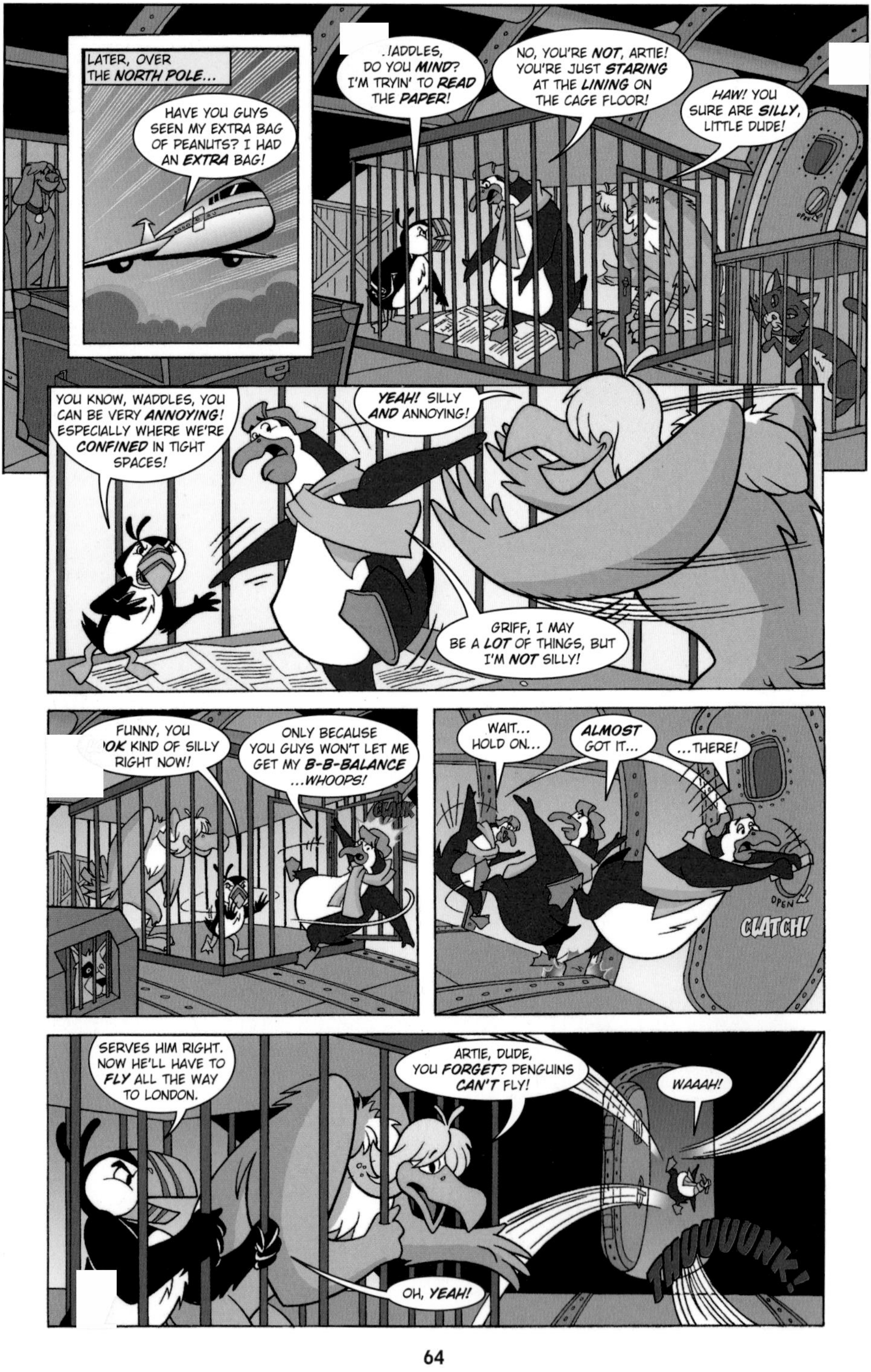
LATER, OVER THE NORTH POLE...
HAVE YOU GUYS SEEN MY EXTRA BAG OF PEANUTS? I HAD AN EXTRA BAG!
ADDLES, DO YOU MIND? I'M TRYIN' TO READ THE PAPER!
NO, YOU'RE NOT, ARTIE! YOU'RE JUST STARING AT THE LINING ON THE CAGE FLOOR!
HAW! YOU SURE ARE SILLY, LITTLE DUDE!
YOU KNOW, WADDLES, YOU CAN BE VERY ANNOYING! ESPECIALLY WHERE WE'RE CONFINED IN TIGHT SPACES!
YEAH! SILLY AND ANNOYING!
GRIFF, I MAY BE A LOT OF THINGS, BUT I'M NOT SILLY!
FUNNY, YOU OK KIND OF SILLY RIGHT NOW!
ONLY BECAUSE YOU GUYS WON'T LET ME GET MY B-B-BALANCE ...WHOOPS!
WAIT... HOLD ON...
ALMOST GOT IT...
...THERE!
OPEN
CLATCH!
SERVES HIM RIGHT. NOW HE'LL HAVE TO FLY ALL THE WAY TO LONDON.
ARTIE, DUDE, YOU FORGET? PENGUINS CAN'T FLY!
WAAAH!
THUUUUUNK!
OH, YEAH!

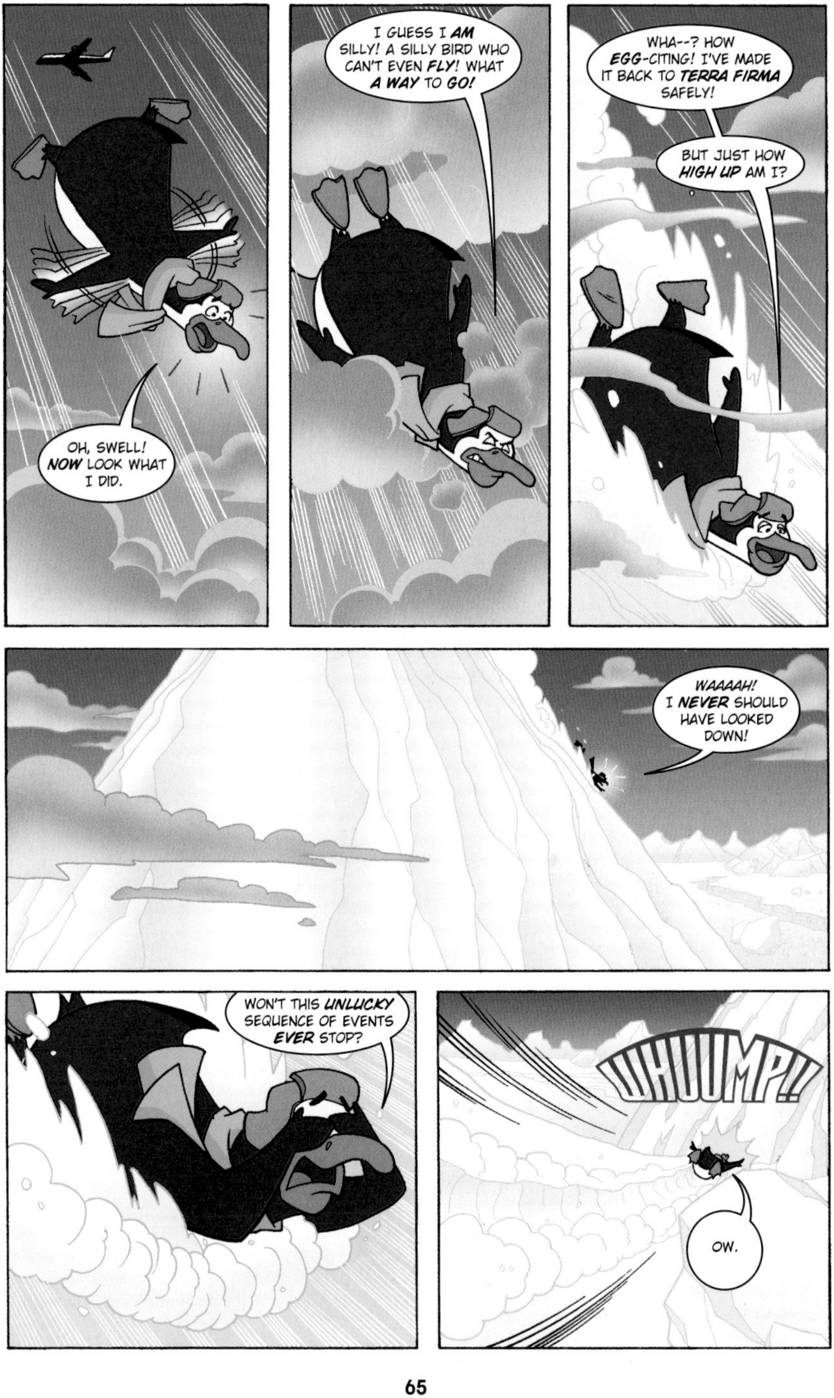
OH, SWELL! NOW LOOK WHAT I DID.
I GUESS I AM SILLY! A SILLY BIRD WHO CAN'T EVEN FLY! WHAT A WAY TO GO!
WHA--? HOW EGG-CITING! I'VE MADE IT BACK TO TERRA FIRMA SAFELY!
BUT JUST HOW HIGH UP AM I?
WAAAAH! I NEVER SHOULD HAVE LOOKED DOWN!
WON'T THIS UNLUCKY SEQUENCE OF EVENTS EVER STOP?
WHUUMP!!
OW.

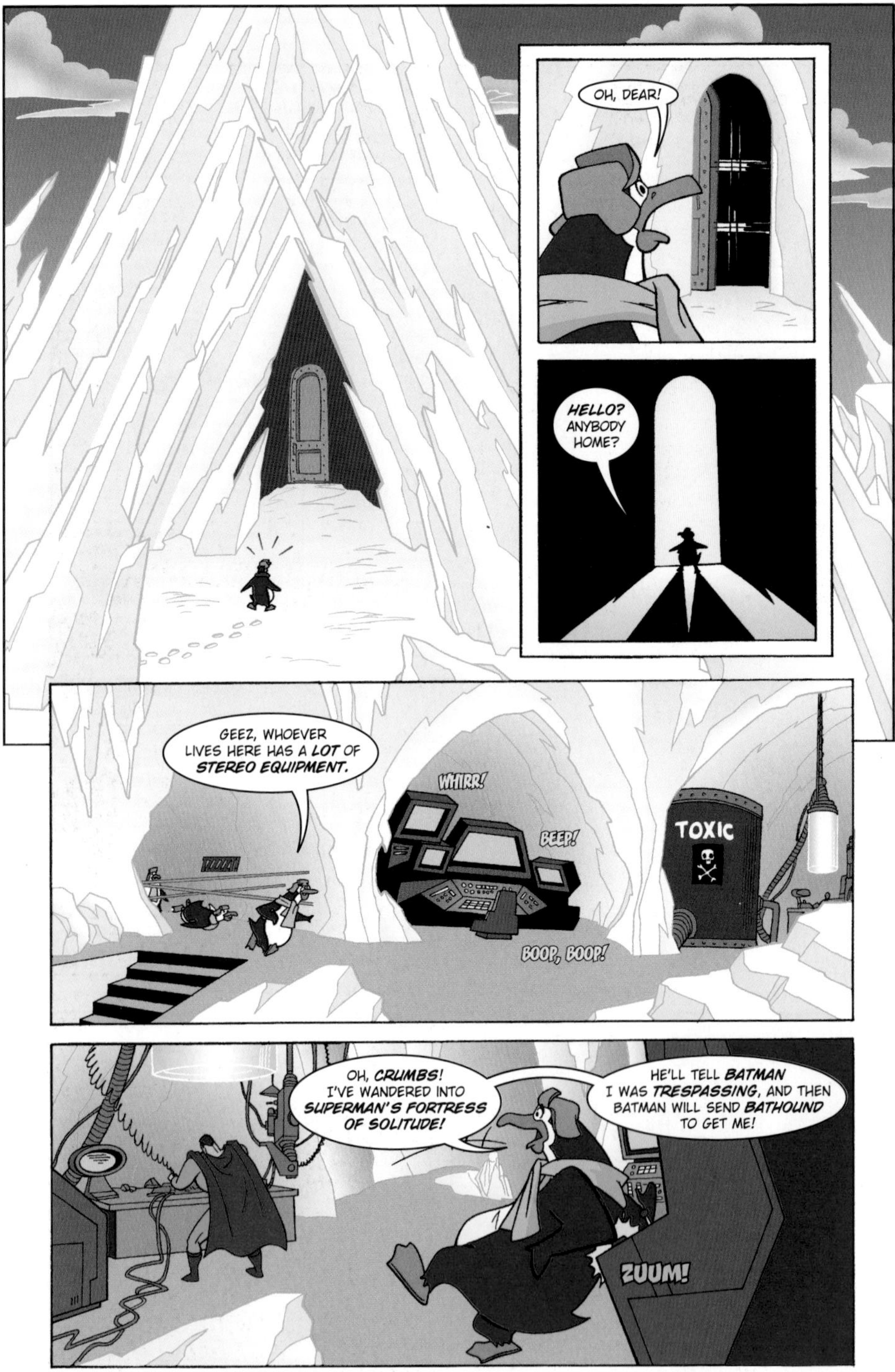
OH, DEAR!
HELLO? ANYBODY HOME?
GEEZ, WHOEVER LIVES HERE HAS A LOT OF STEREO EQUIPMENT.
WHIRR!
BEEP!
TOXIC
BOOP, BOOP!
OH, CRUMBS! I'VE WANDERED INTO SUPERMAN'S FORTRESS OF SOLITUDE!
HE'LL TELL BATMAN I WAS TRESPASSING, AND THEN BATMAN WILL SEND BATHOUND TO GET ME!
ZUUM!

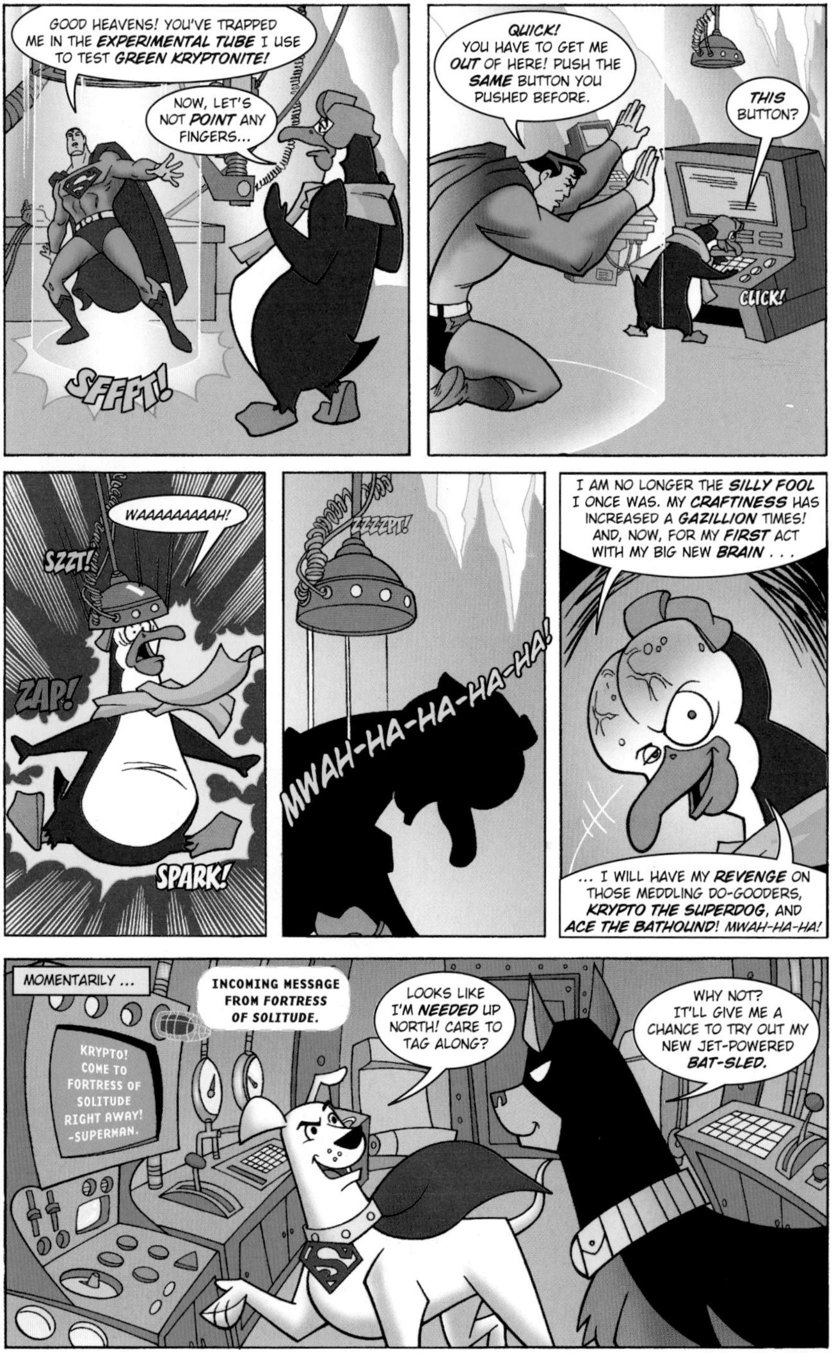
GOOD HEAVENS! YOU'VE TRAPPED ME IN THE EXPERIMENTAL TUBE I USE TO TEST GREEN KRYPTONITE!
NOW, LET'S NOT POINT ANY FINGERS...
SFFPT!
QUICK! YOU HAVE TO GET ME OUT OF HERE! PUSH THE SAME BUTTON YOU PUSHED BEFORE.
THIS BUTTON?
CLICK!
WAAAAAAAAAH!
SZZT!
ZAP!
SPARK!
ZZZZAPT!
MWAH-HA-HA-HA-HA!
I AM NO LONGER THE SILLY FOOL I ONCE WAS. MY CRAFTINESS HAS INCREASED A GAZILLION TIMES! AND, NOW, FOR MY FIRST ACT WITH MY BIG NEW BRAIN . . .
... I WILL HAVE MY REVENGE ON THOSE MEDDLING DO-GOODERS, KRYPTO THE SUPERDOG, AND ACE THE BATHOUND! MWAH-HA-HA!
MOMENTARILY ...
INCOMING MESSAGE FROM FORTRESS OF SOLITUDE.
KRYPTO! COME TO FORTRESS OF SOLITUDE RIGHT AWAY! -SUPERMAN.
LOOKS LIKE I'M NEEDED UP NORTH! CARE TO TAG ALONG?
WHY NOT? IT'LL GIVE ME A CHANCE TO TRY OUT MY NEW JET-POWERED BAT-SLED.

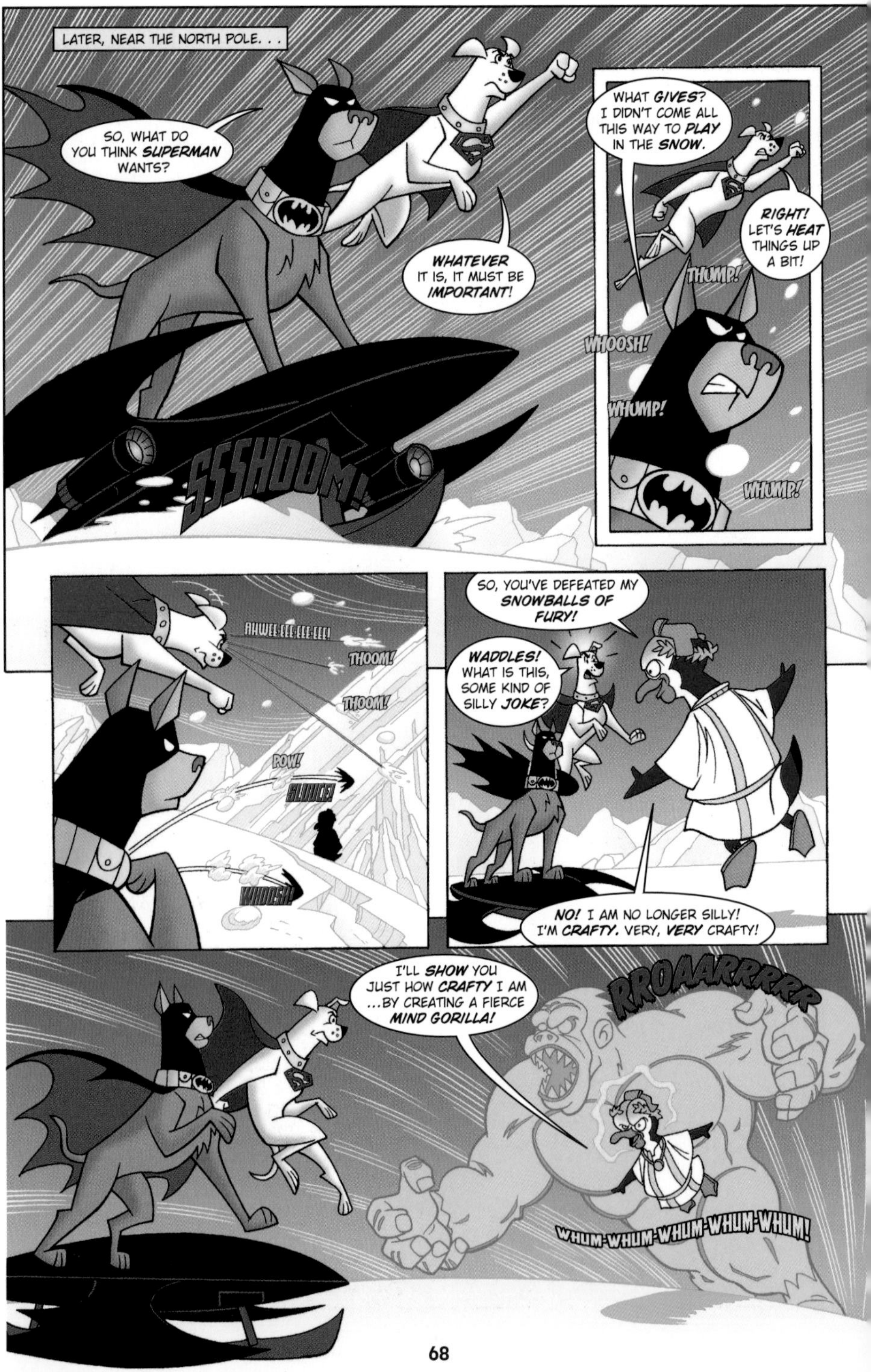
LATER, NEAR THE NORTH POLE. . .
SO, WHAT DO YOU THINK SUPERMAN WANTS?
WHATEVER IT IS, IT MUST BE IMPORTANT!
SSSHOOM!
WHAT GIVES? I DIDN'T COME ALL THIS WAY TO PLAY IN THE SNOW.
RIGHT! LET'S HEAT THINGS UP A BIT!
THUMP!
WHOOSH!
WHUMP!
WHUMP!
AHWEE-EEE-EEE-EEE!
THOOM!
THOOM!
POW!
SLUUCE!
WHOOSH!
SO, YOU'VE DEFEATED MY SNOWBALLS OF FURY!
WADDLES! WHAT IS THIS, SOME KIND OF SILLY JOKE?
NO! I AM NO LONGER SILLY! I'M CRAFTY. VERY, VERY CRAFTY!
I'LL SHOW YOU JUST HOW CRAFTY I AM ...BY CREATING A FIERCE MIND GORILLA!
RROAARRRRR
WHUM-WHUM-WHUM-WHUM-WHUM!

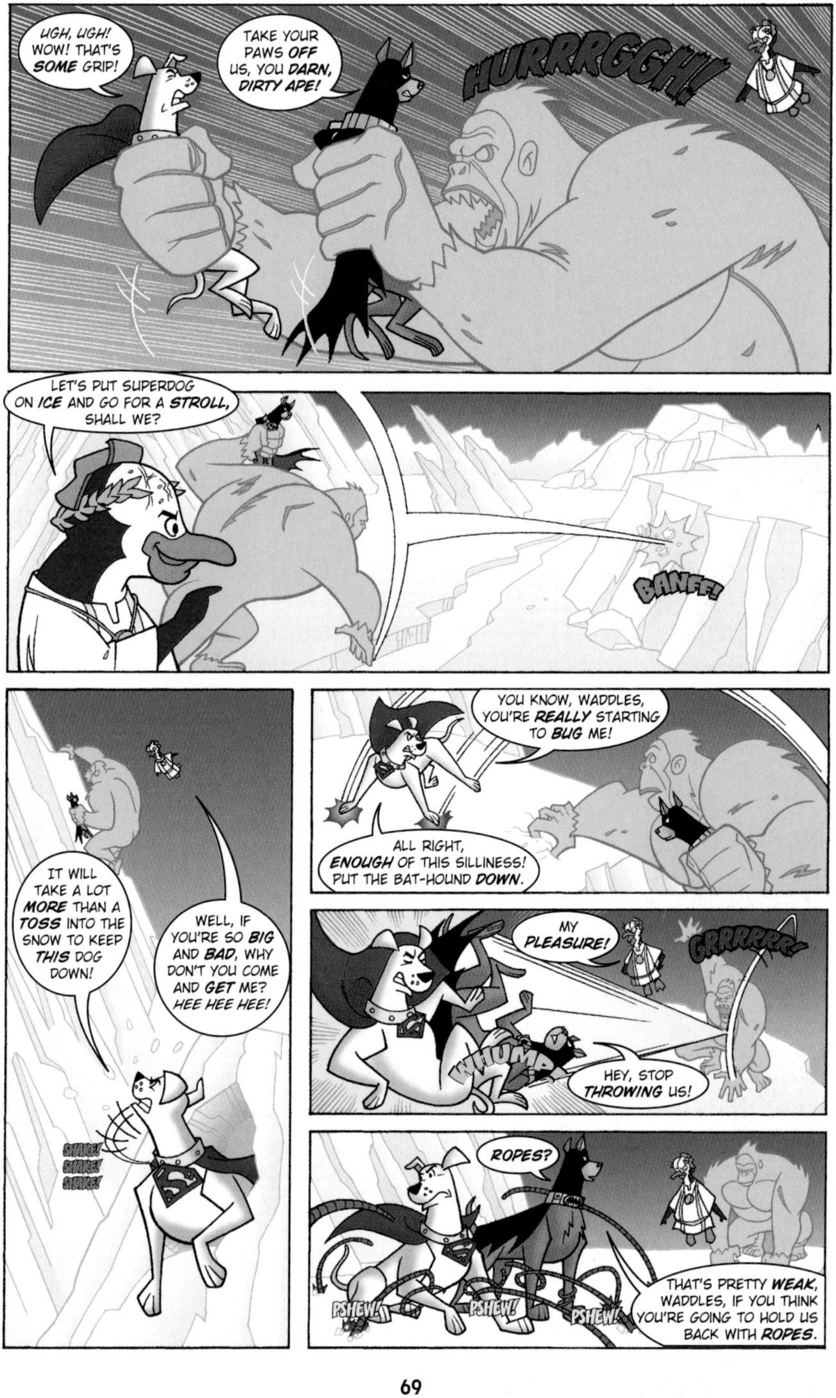
UGH, UGH! WOW! THAT'S **SOME** GRIP!
TAKE YOUR PAWS **OFF** US, YOU **DARN, DIRTY APE!**
HURRRRGGH!
LET'S PUT SUPERDOG ON **ICE** AND GO FOR A **STROLL,** SHALL WE?
BANFF!
IT WILL TAKE A LOT **MORE** THAN A **TOSS** INTO THE SNOW TO KEEP **THIS** DOG DOWN!
WELL, IF YOU'RE SO **BIG** AND **BAD**, WHY DON'T YOU COME AND **GET** ME? **HEE HEE HEE!**
SHAKE! SHAKE! SHAKE!
YOU KNOW, WADDLES, YOU'RE **REALLY** STARTING TO **BUG** ME!
ALL RIGHT, **ENOUGH** OF THIS SILLINESS! PUT THE BAT-HOUND **DOWN**.
MY **PLEASURE!**
GRRRRRR!
WHUMP
HEY, STOP **THROWING** US!
ROPES?
PSHEW! PSHEW! PSHEW!
THAT'S PRETTY **WEAK**, WADDLES, IF YOU THINK YOU'RE GOING TO HOLD US BACK WITH **ROPES**.

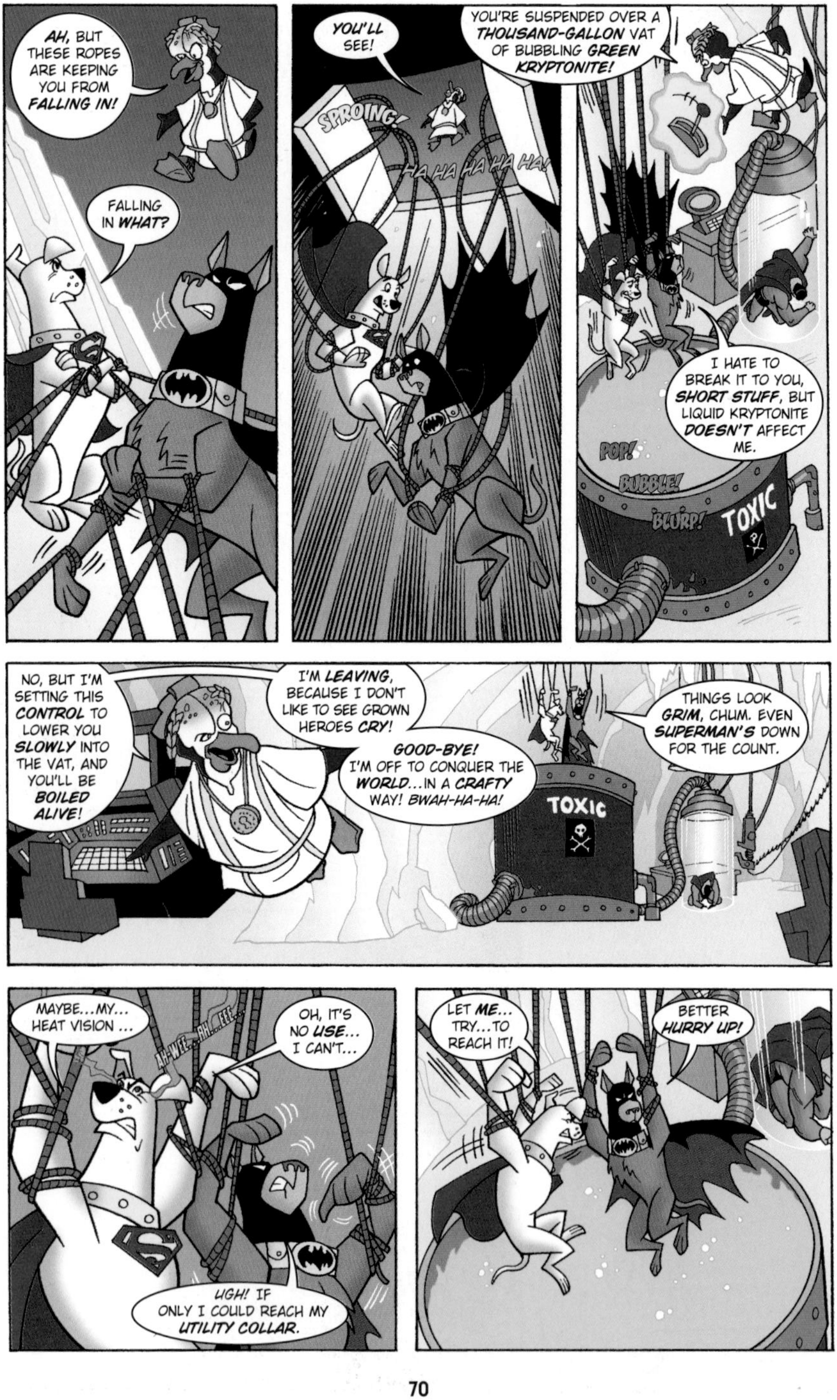
AH, BUT THESE ROPES ARE KEEPING YOU FROM FALLING IN!
FALLING IN WHAT?
YOU'LL SEE!
SPROING!
HA HA HA HA HA!
YOU'RE SUSPENDED OVER A THOUSAND-GALLON VAT OF BUBBLING GREEN KRYPTONITE!
I HATE TO BREAK IT TO YOU, SHORT STUFF, BUT LIQUID KRYPTONITE DOESN'T AFFECT ME.
POP!
BUBBLE!
BLURP!
TOXIC
NO, BUT I'M SETTING THIS CONTROL TO LOWER YOU SLOWLY INTO THE VAT, AND YOU'LL BE BOILED ALIVE!
I'M LEAVING, BECAUSE I DON'T LIKE TO SEE GROWN HEROES CRY!
GOOD-BYE! I'M OFF TO CONQUER THE WORLD...IN A CRAFTY WAY! BWAH-HA-HA!
THINGS LOOK GRIM, CHUM. EVEN SUPERMAN'S DOWN FOR THE COUNT.
TOXIC
MAYBE...MY... HEAT VISION ...
OH, IT'S NO USE... I CAN'T...
UGH! IF ONLY I COULD REACH MY UTILITY COLLAR.
LET ME... TRY...TO REACH IT!
BETTER HURRY UP!

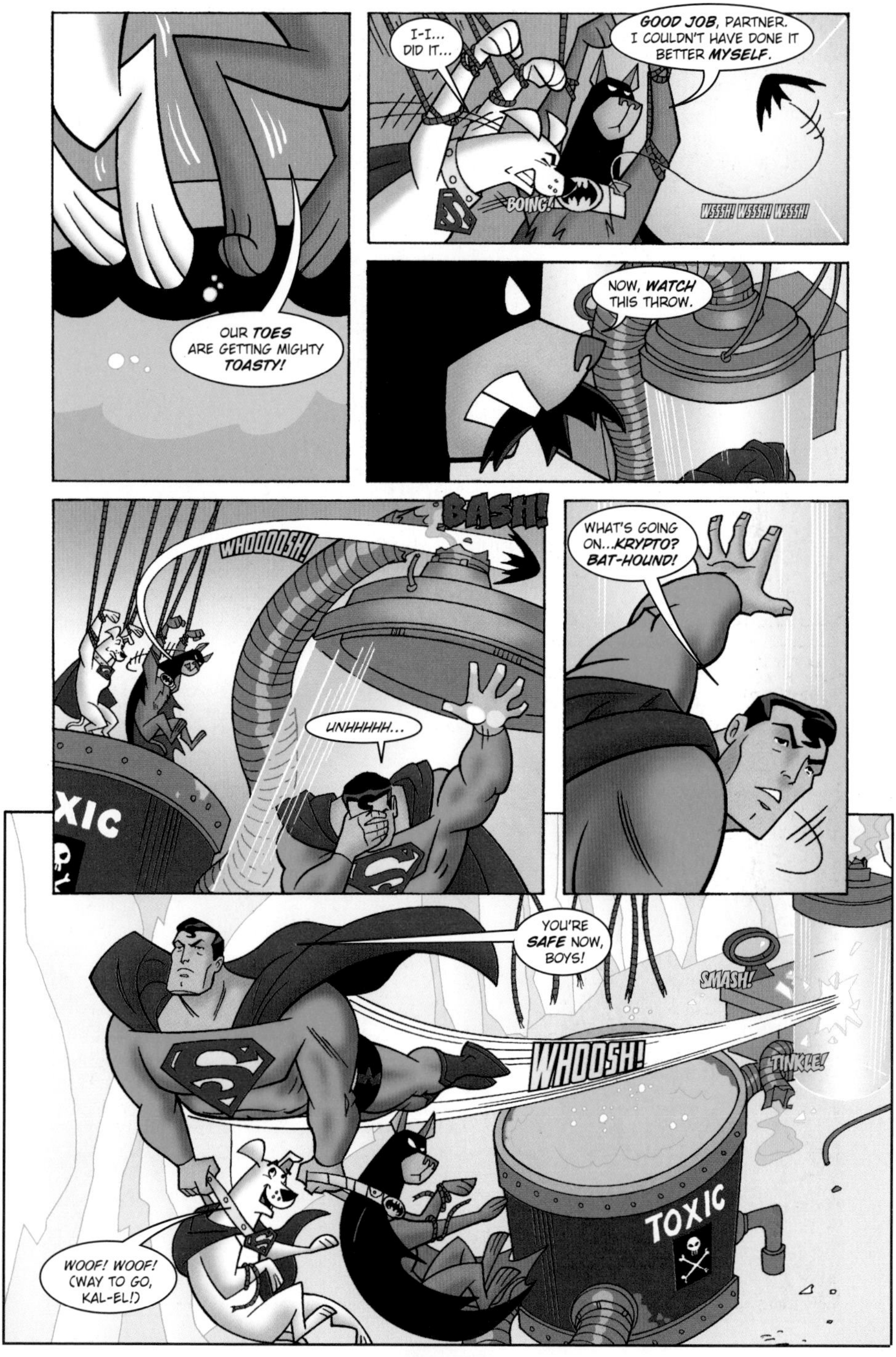
OUR TOES ARE GETTING MIGHTY TOASTY!
I-I... DID IT...
GOOD JOB, PARTNER. I COULDN'T HAVE DONE IT BETTER MYSELF.
BOING!
WSSSH! WSSSH! WSSSH!
NOW, WATCH THIS THROW.
BASH!
WHOOOOSH!
UNHHHHH...
TOXIC
WHAT'S GOING ON...KRYPTO? BAT-HOUND!
YOU'RE SAFE NOW, BOYS!
SMASH!
WHOOSH!
TINKLE!
TOXIC
WOOF! WOOF! (WAY TO GO, KAL-EL!)

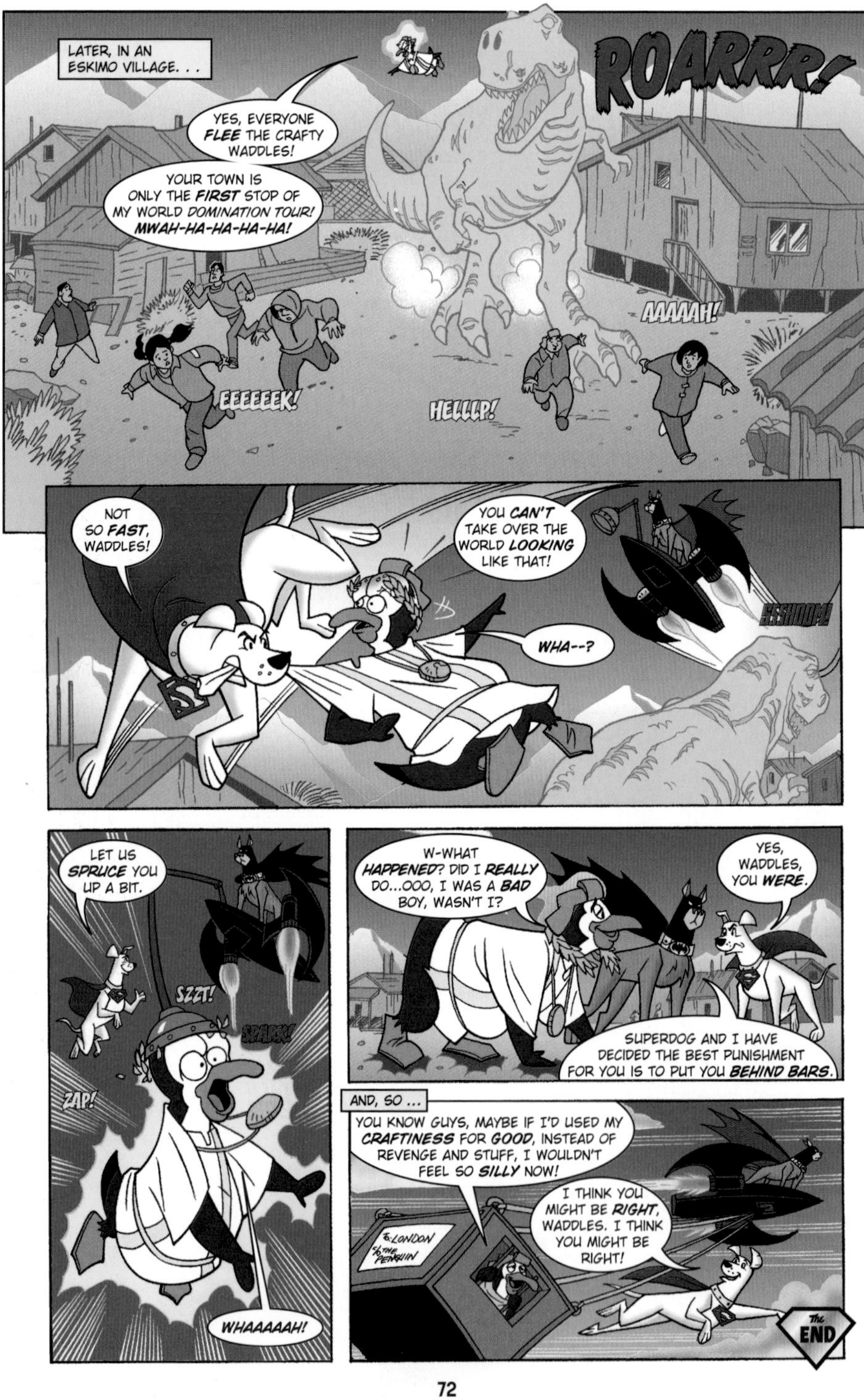

LATER, IN AN ESKIMO VILLAGE. . .
ROARRR!
YES, EVERYONE FLEE THE CRAFTY WADDLES!
YOUR TOWN IS ONLY THE FIRST STOP OF MY WORLD DOMINATION TOUR! MWAH-HA-HA-HA-HA!
AAAAAH!
EEEEEEK!
HELLLP!
NOT SO FAST, WADDLES!
YOU CAN'T TAKE OVER THE WORLD LOOKING LIKE THAT!
SSSHOOM!
WHA--?
LET US SPRUCE YOU UP A BIT.
SZZT!
SPARK!
ZAP!
WHAAAAAH!
W-WHAT HAPPENED? DID I REALLY DO...OOO, I WAS A BAD BOY, WASN'T I?
YES, WADDLES, YOU WERE.
SUPERDOG AND I HAVE DECIDED THE BEST PUNISHMENT FOR YOU IS TO PUT YOU BEHIND BARS.
AND, SO ...
YOU KNOW GUYS, MAYBE IF I'D USED MY CRAFTINESS FOR GOOD, INSTEAD OF REVENGE AND STUFF, I WOULDN'T FEEL SO SILLY NOW!
I THINK YOU MIGHT BE RIGHT, WADDLES. I THINK YOU MIGHT BE RIGHT!
To: LONDON c/o THE PENGUIN
The END

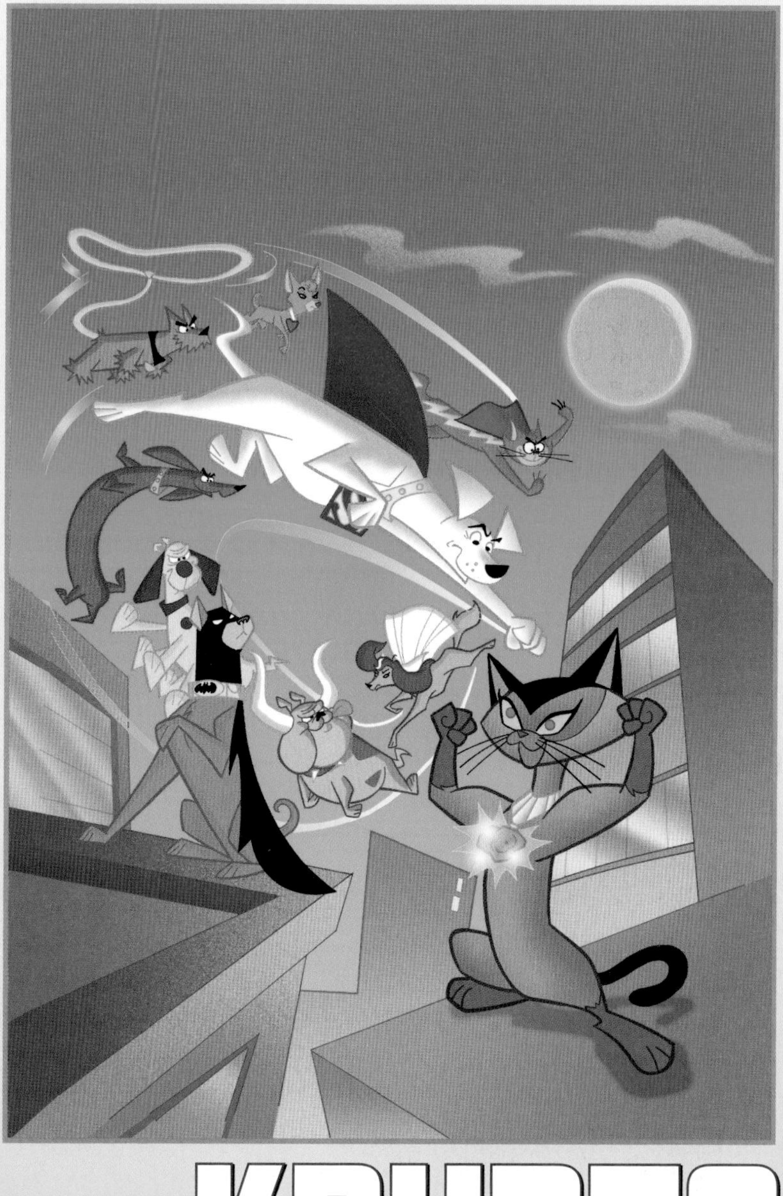

KRYPTO THE SUPERDOG

KRYPTO

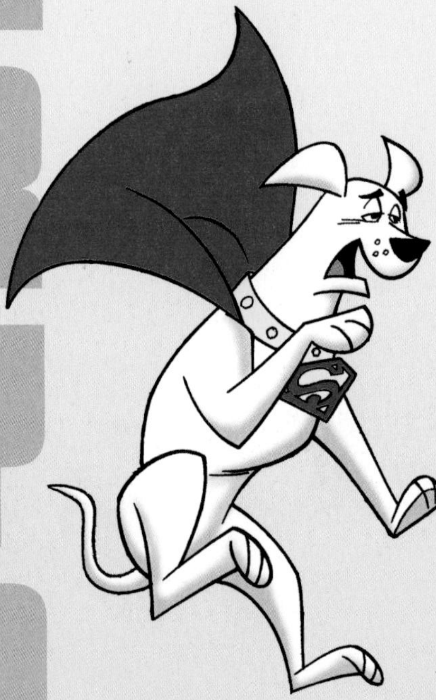

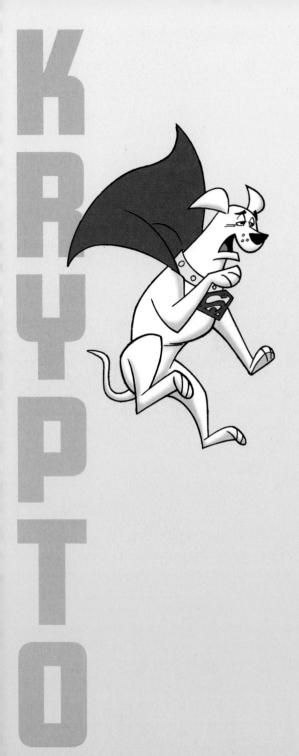

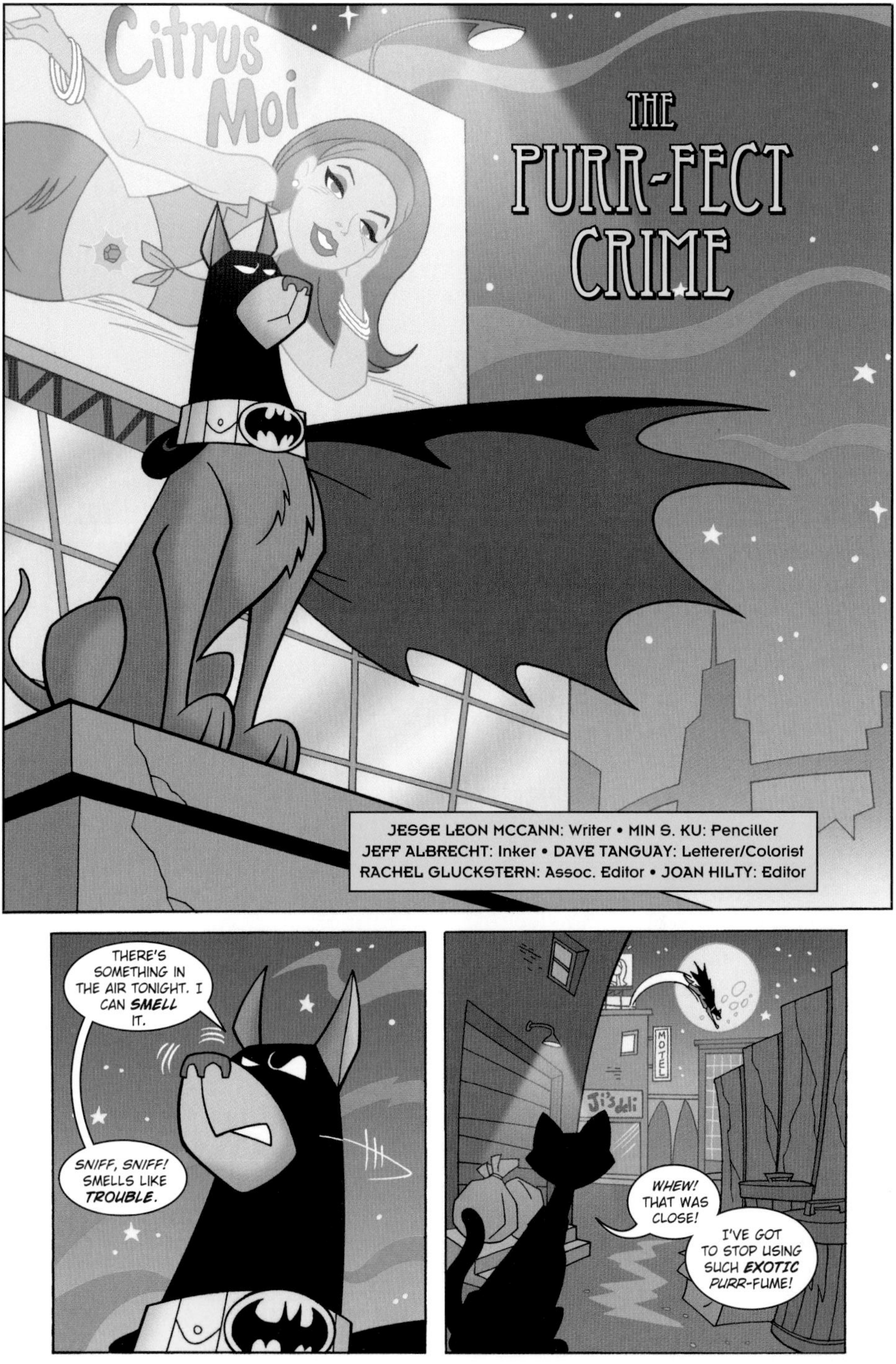
Citrus Moi
THE PURR-FECT CRIME
JESSE LEON MCCANN: Writer • MIN S. KU: Penciller
JEFF ALBRECHT: Inker • DAVE TANGUAY: Letterer/Colorist
RACHEL GLUCKSTERN: Assoc. Editor • JOAN HILTY: Editor
THERE'S SOMETHING IN THE AIR TONIGHT. I CAN SMELL IT.
SNIFF, SNIFF! SMELLS LIKE TROUBLE.
MOTEL
Ji's deli
WHEW! THAT WAS CLOSE!
I'VE GOT TO STOP USING SUCH EXOTIC PURR-FUME!

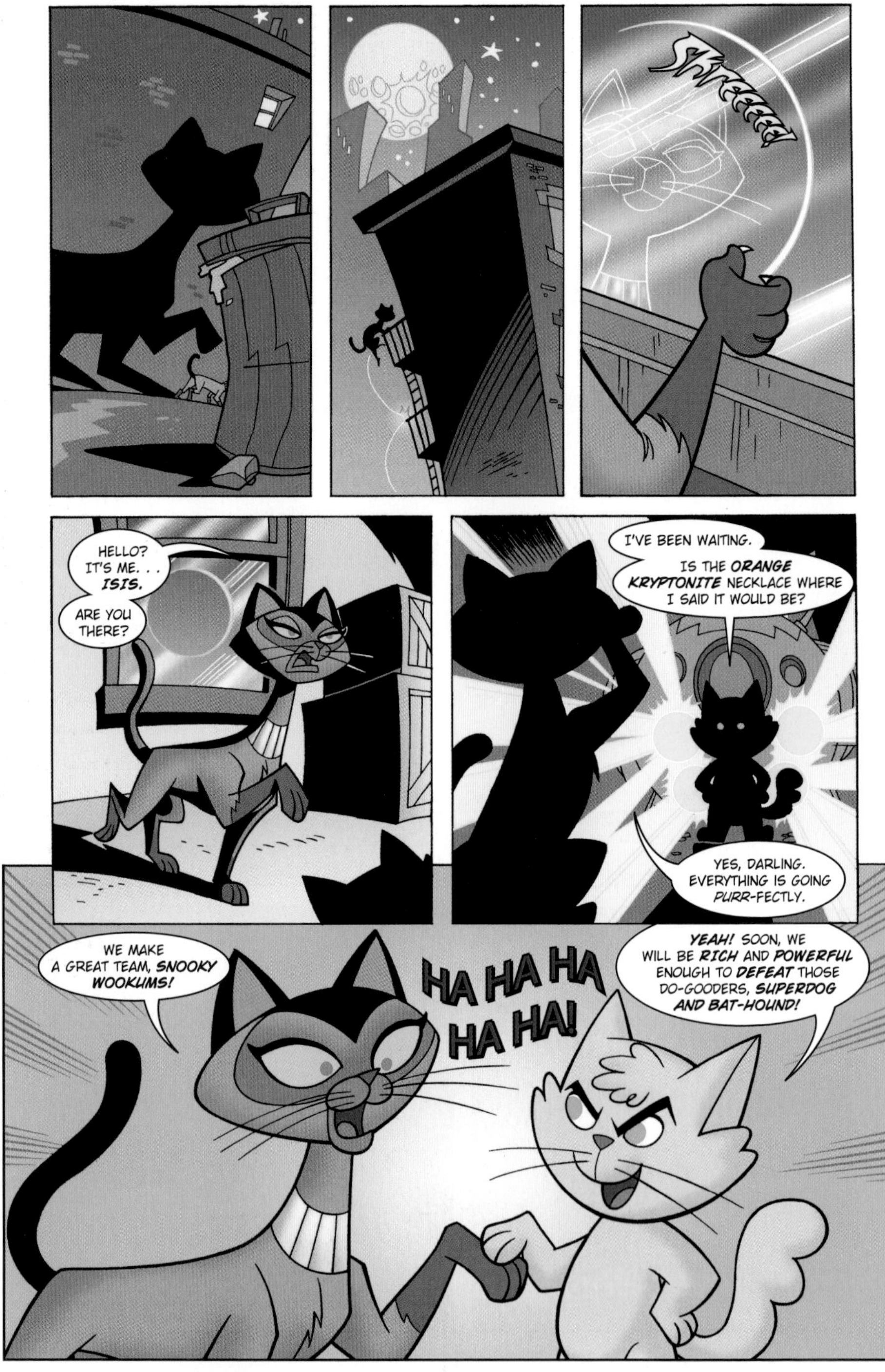
SKREEEEE
HELLO? IT'S ME. . . ISIS.
ARE YOU THERE?
I'VE BEEN WAITING.
IS THE ORANGE KRYPTONITE NECKLACE WHERE I SAID IT WOULD BE?
YES, DARLING. EVERYTHING IS GOING PURR-FECTLY.
WE MAKE A GREAT TEAM, SNOOKY WOOKUMS!
HA HA HA HA HA!
YEAH! SOON, WE WILL BE RICH AND POWERFUL ENOUGH TO DEFEAT THOSE DO-GOODERS, SUPERDOG AND BAT-HOUND!

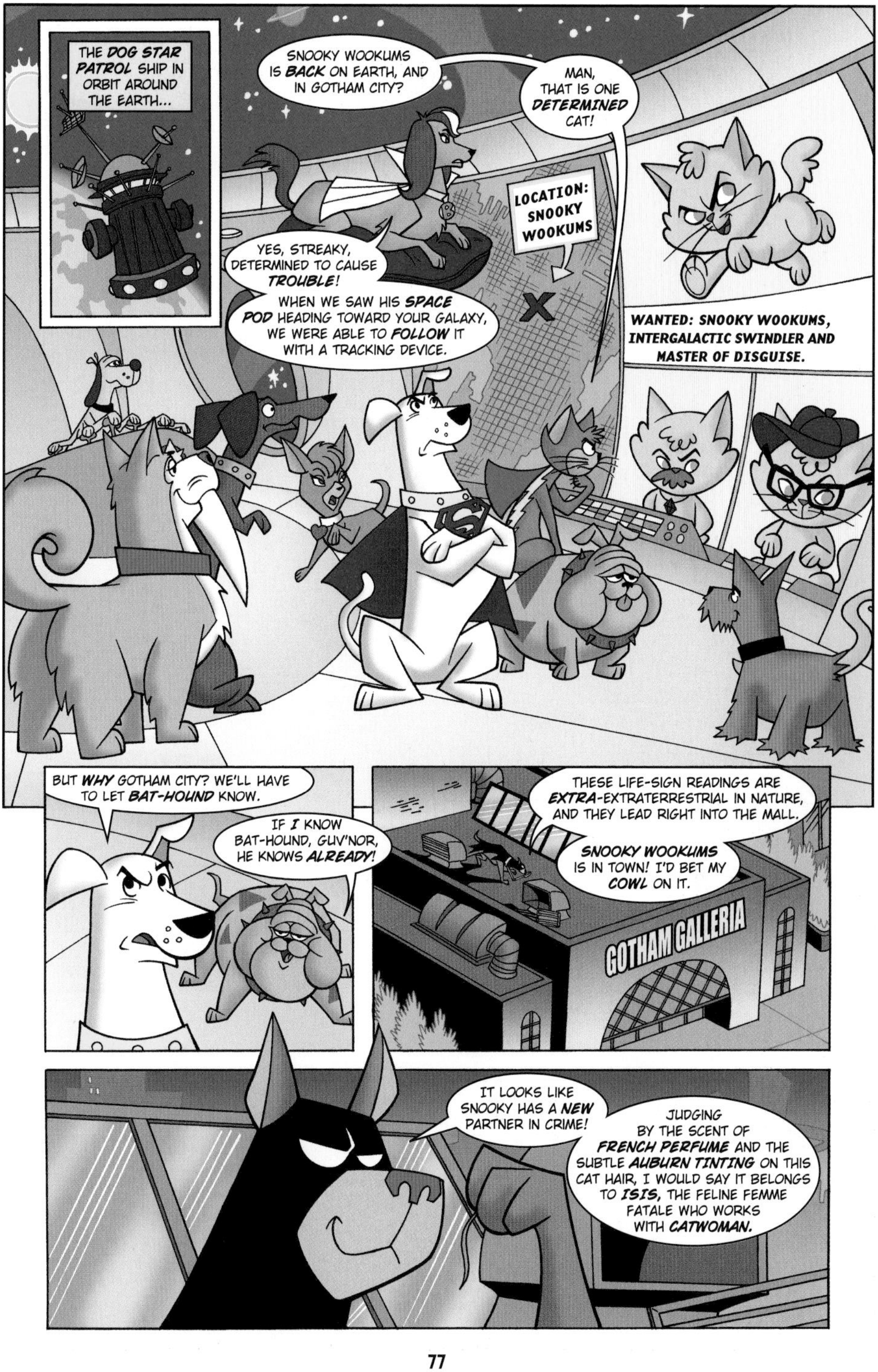
THE DOG STAR PATROL SHIP IN ORBIT AROUND THE EARTH...
SNOOKY WOOKUMS IS BACK ON EARTH, AND IN GOTHAM CITY?
MAN, THAT IS ONE DETERMINED CAT!
LOCATION: SNOOKY WOOKUMS
YES, STREAKY, DETERMINED TO CAUSE TROUBLE!
WHEN WE SAW HIS SPACE POD HEADING TOWARD YOUR GALAXY, WE WERE ABLE TO FOLLOW IT WITH A TRACKING DEVICE.
WANTED: SNOOKY WOOKUMS, INTERGALACTIC SWINDLER AND MASTER OF DISGUISE.
BUT WHY GOTHAM CITY? WE'LL HAVE TO LET BAT-HOUND KNOW.
IF I KNOW BAT-HOUND, GUV'NOR, HE KNOWS ALREADY!
THESE LIFE-SIGN READINGS ARE EXTRA-EXTRATERRESTRIAL IN NATURE, AND THEY LEAD RIGHT INTO THE MALL.
SNOOKY WOOKUMS IS IN TOWN! I'D BET MY COWL ON IT.
GOTHAM GALLERIA
IT LOOKS LIKE SNOOKY HAS A NEW PARTNER IN CRIME!
JUDGING BY THE SCENT OF FRENCH PERFUME AND THE SUBTLE AUBURN TINTING ON THIS CAT HAIR, I WOULD SAY IT BELONGS TO ISIS, THE FELINE FEMME FATALE WHO WORKS WITH CATWOMAN.

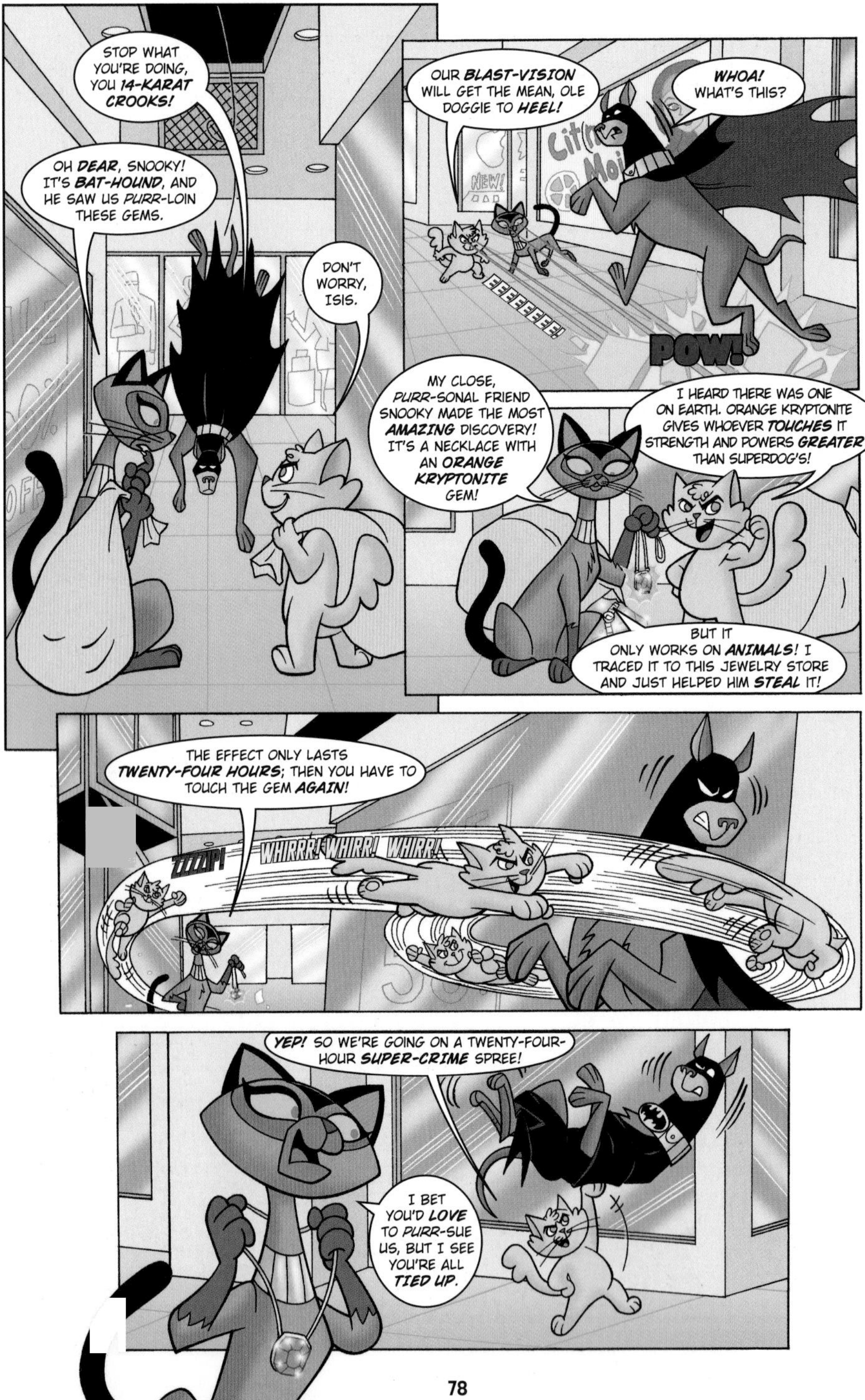

STOP WHAT YOU'RE DOING, YOU 14-KARAT CROOKS!
OH DEAR, SNOOKY! IT'S BAT-HOUND, AND HE SAW US PURR-LOIN THESE GEMS.
DON'T WORRY, ISIS.
OUR BLAST-VISION WILL GET THE MEAN, OLE DOGGIE TO HEEL!
WHOA! WHAT'S THIS?
EEEEEEEE!
POW!
MY CLOSE, PURR-SONAL FRIEND SNOOKY MADE THE MOST AMAZING DISCOVERY! IT'S A NECKLACE WITH AN ORANGE KRYPTONITE GEM!
I HEARD THERE WAS ONE ON EARTH. ORANGE KRYPTONITE GIVES WHOEVER TOUCHES IT STRENGTH AND POWERS GREATER THAN SUPERDOG'S!
BUT IT ONLY WORKS ON ANIMALS! I TRACED IT TO THIS JEWELRY STORE AND JUST HELPED HIM STEAL IT!
THE EFFECT ONLY LASTS TWENTY-FOUR HOURS; THEN YOU HAVE TO TOUCH THE GEM AGAIN!
ZZZZIP!
WHIRRR! WHIRR! WHIRR!
YEP! SO WE'RE GOING ON A TWENTY-FOUR-HOUR SUPER-CRIME SPREE!
I BET YOU'D LOVE TO PURR-SUE US, BUT I SEE YOU'RE ALL TIED UP.

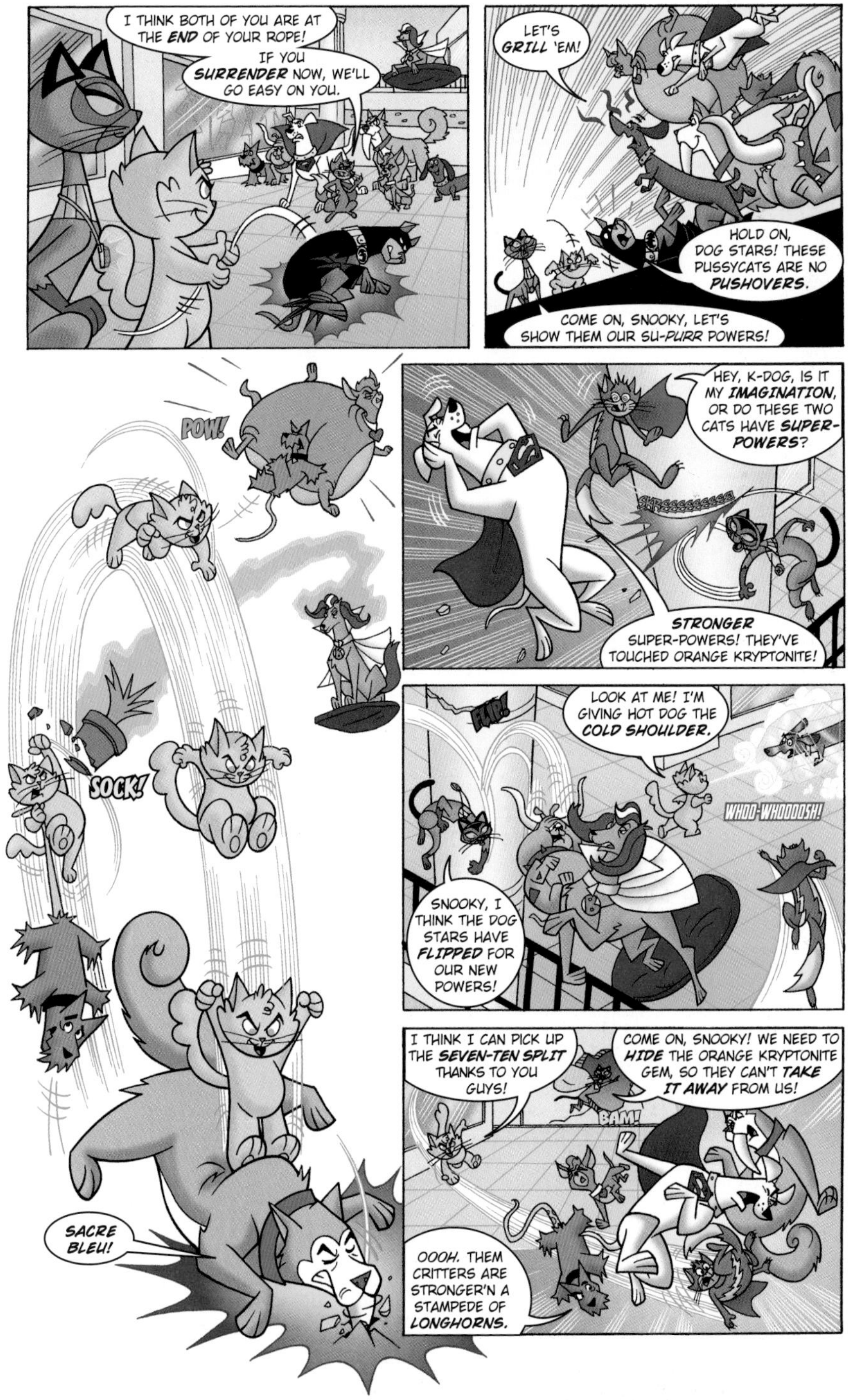
I THINK BOTH OF YOU ARE AT THE END OF YOUR ROPE!
IF YOU SURRENDER NOW, WE'LL GO EASY ON YOU.
LET'S GRILL 'EM!
HOLD ON, DOG STARS! THESE PUSSYCATS ARE NO PUSHOVERS.
COME ON, SNOOKY, LET'S SHOW THEM OUR SU-PURR POWERS!
POW!
SOCK!
SACRE BLEU!
HEY, K-DOG, IS IT MY IMAGINATION, OR DO THESE TWO CATS HAVE SUPER-POWERS?
STRONGER SUPER-POWERS! THEY'VE TOUCHED ORANGE KRYPTONITE!
FLIP!
LOOK AT ME! I'M GIVING HOT DOG THE COLD SHOULDER.
WHOO-WHOOOOSH!
SNOOKY, I THINK THE DOG STARS HAVE FLIPPED FOR OUR NEW POWERS!
I THINK I CAN PICK UP THE SEVEN-TEN SPLIT THANKS TO YOU GUYS!
COME ON, SNOOKY! WE NEED TO HIDE THE ORANGE KRYPTONITE GEM, SO THEY CAN'T TAKE IT AWAY FROM US!
BAM!
OOOH. THEM CRITTERS ARE STRONGER'N A STAMPEDE OF LONGHORNS.

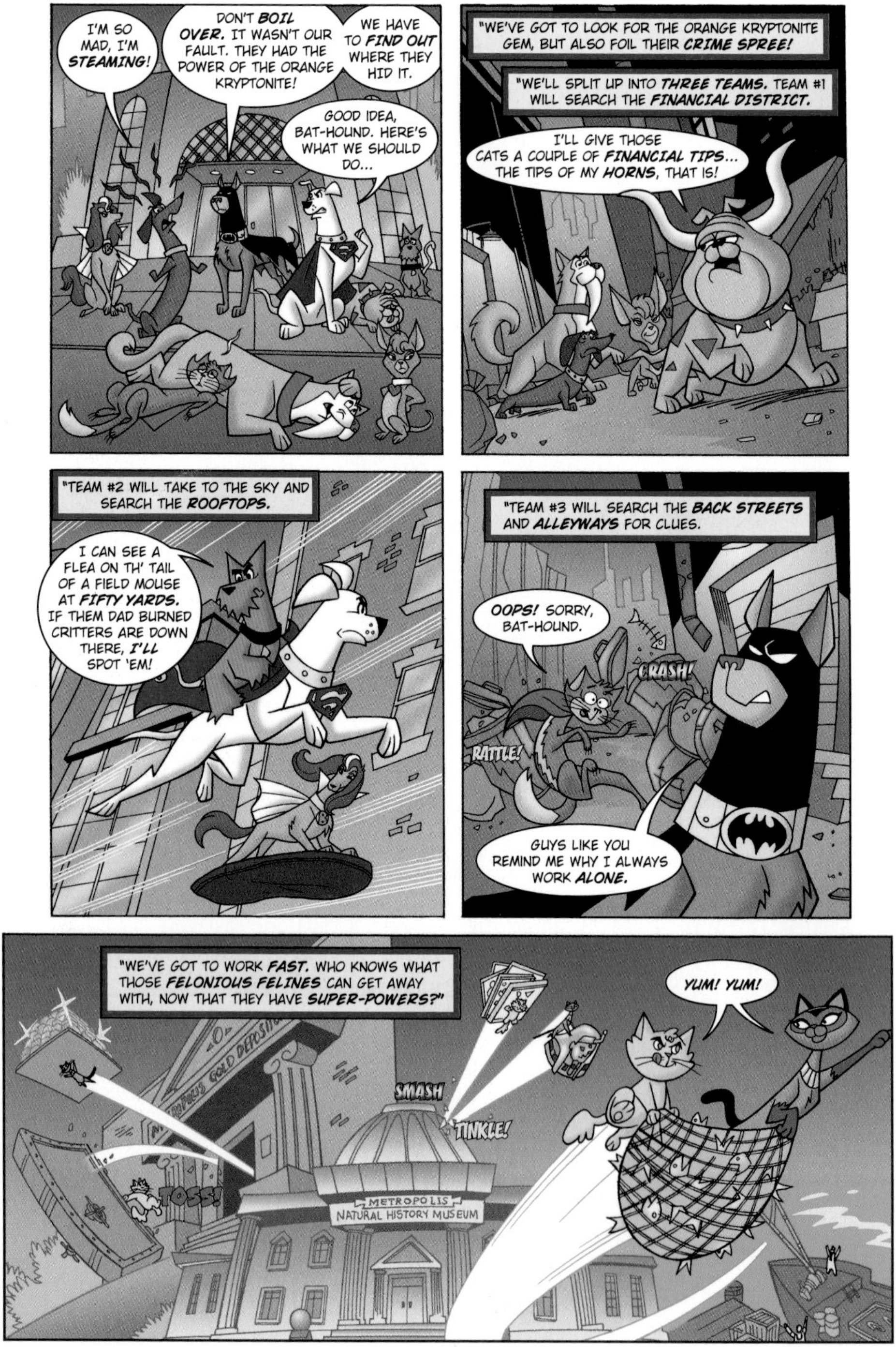

I'M SO MAD, I'M STEAMING!
DON'T BOIL OVER. IT WASN'T OUR FAULT. THEY HAD THE POWER OF THE ORANGE KRYPTONITE!
WE HAVE TO FIND OUT WHERE THEY HID IT.
GOOD IDEA, BAT-HOUND. HERE'S WHAT WE SHOULD DO...
"WE'VE GOT TO LOOK FOR THE ORANGE KRYPTONITE GEM, BUT ALSO FOIL THEIR CRIME SPREE!
"WE'LL SPLIT UP INTO THREE TEAMS. TEAM #1 WILL SEARCH THE FINANCIAL DISTRICT.
I'LL GIVE THOSE CATS A COUPLE OF FINANCIAL TIPS... THE TIPS OF MY HORNS, THAT IS!
"TEAM #2 WILL TAKE TO THE SKY AND SEARCH THE ROOFTOPS.
I CAN SEE A FLEA ON TH' TAIL OF A FIELD MOUSE AT FIFTY YARDS. IF THEM DAD BURNED CRITTERS ARE DOWN THERE, I'LL SPOT 'EM!
"TEAM #3 WILL SEARCH THE BACK STREETS AND ALLEYWAYS FOR CLUES.
OOPS! SORRY, BAT-HOUND.
CRASH!
RATTLE!
GUYS LIKE YOU REMIND ME WHY I ALWAYS WORK ALONE.
"WE'VE GOT TO WORK FAST. WHO KNOWS WHAT THOSE FELONIOUS FELINES CAN GET AWAY WITH, NOW THAT THEY HAVE SUPER-POWERS?"
YUM! YUM!
SMASH
TINKLE!
TOSS!
METROPOLIS NATURAL HISTORY MUSEUM

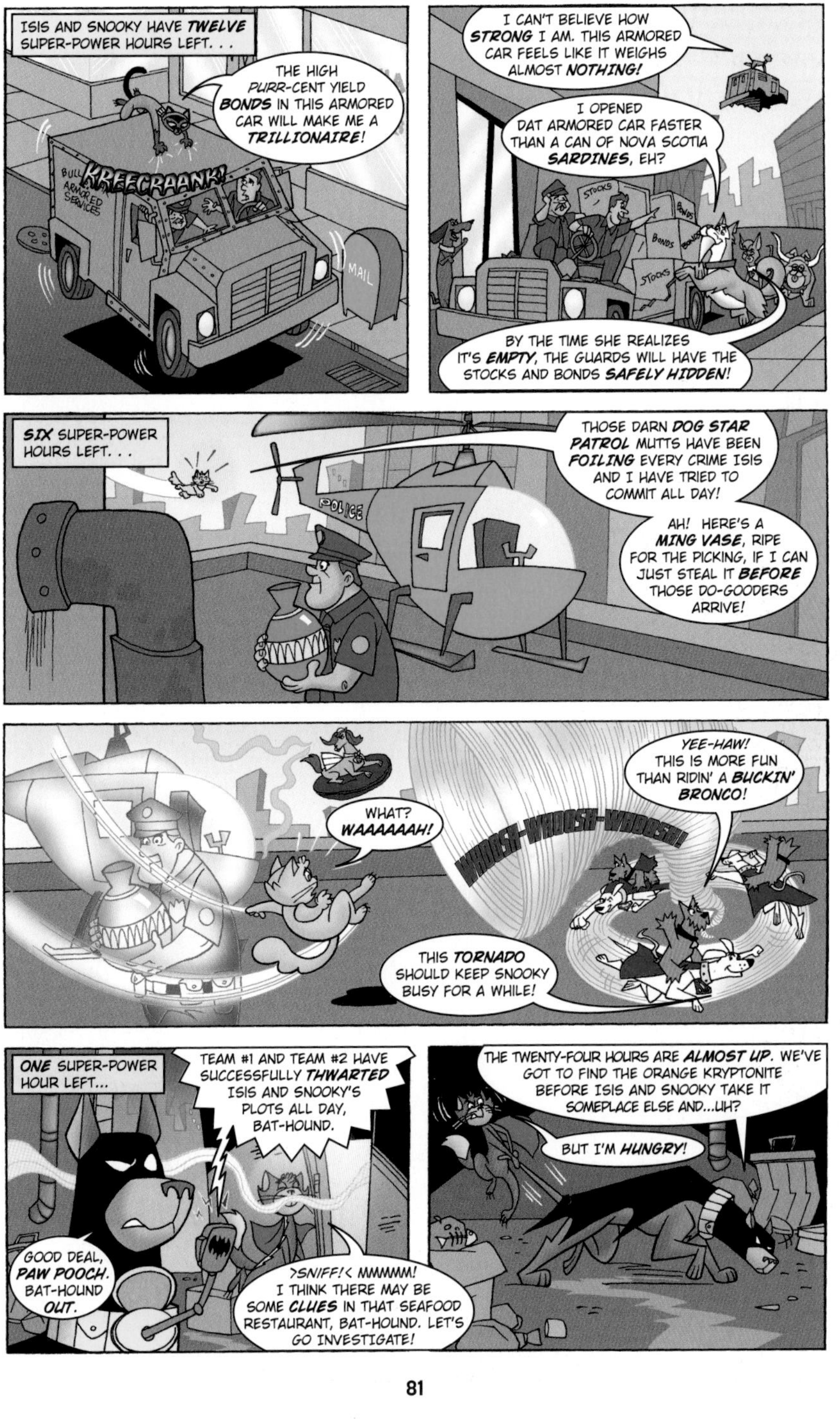
ISIS AND SNOOKY HAVE TWELVE SUPER-POWER HOURS LEFT. . .
THE HIGH PURR-CENT YIELD BONDS IN THIS ARMORED CAR WILL MAKE ME A TRILLIONAIRE!
KREEGRAANK!
BULL ARMORED SERVICES
MAIL
I CAN'T BELIEVE HOW STRONG I AM. THIS ARMORED CAR FEELS LIKE IT WEIGHS ALMOST NOTHING!
I OPENED DAT ARMORED CAR FASTER THAN A CAN OF NOVA SCOTIA SARDINES, EH?
STOCKS
BONDS
STOCKS
BY THE TIME SHE REALIZES IT'S EMPTY, THE GUARDS WILL HAVE THE STOCKS AND BONDS SAFELY HIDDEN!
SIX SUPER-POWER HOURS LEFT. . .
THOSE DARN DOG STAR PATROL MUTTS HAVE BEEN FOILING EVERY CRIME ISIS AND I HAVE TRIED TO COMMIT ALL DAY!
AH! HERE'S A MING VASE, RIPE FOR THE PICKING, IF I CAN JUST STEAL IT BEFORE THOSE DO-GOODERS ARRIVE!
POLICE
YEE-HAW! THIS IS MORE FUN THAN RIDIN' A BUCKIN' BRONCO!
WHAT? WAAAAAAH!
WHOOSH-WHOOSH-WHOOSH!
THIS TORNADO SHOULD KEEP SNOOKY BUSY FOR A WHILE!
ONE SUPER-POWER HOUR LEFT...
TEAM #1 AND TEAM #2 HAVE SUCCESSFULLY THWARTED ISIS AND SNOOKY'S PLOTS ALL DAY, BAT-HOUND.
GOOD DEAL, PAW POOCH. BAT-HOUND OUT.
>SNIFF!< MMMMM! I THINK THERE MAY BE SOME CLUES IN THAT SEAFOOD RESTAURANT, BAT-HOUND. LET'S GO INVESTIGATE!
THE TWENTY-FOUR HOURS ARE ALMOST UP. WE'VE GOT TO FIND THE ORANGE KRYPTONITE BEFORE ISIS AND SNOOKY TAKE IT SOMEPLACE ELSE AND...UH?
BUT I'M HUNGRY!

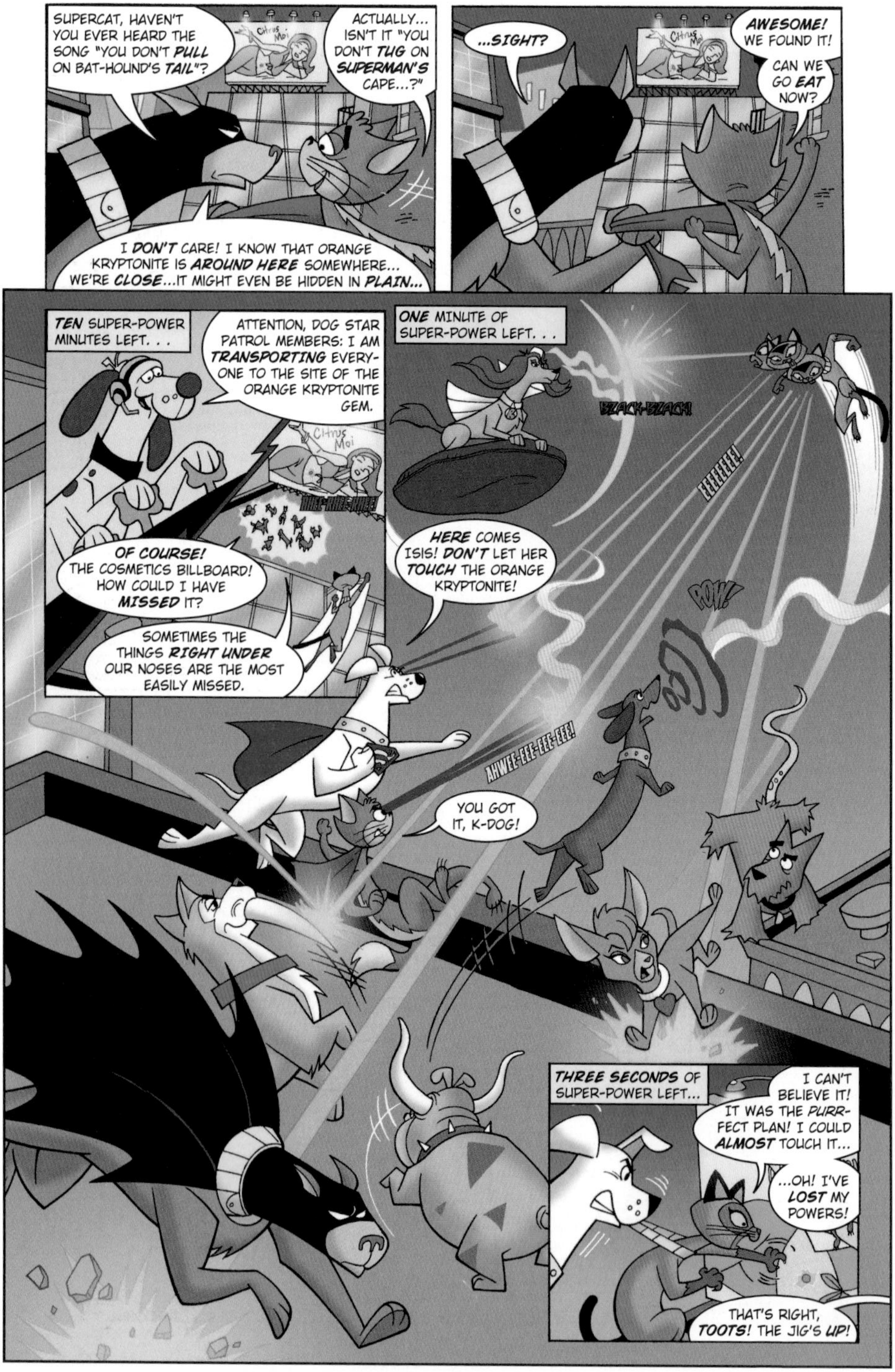

SUPERCAT, HAVEN'T YOU EVER HEARD THE SONG "YOU DON'T PULL ON BAT-HOUND'S TAIL"?
ACTUALLY... ISN'T IT "YOU DON'T TUG ON SUPERMAN'S CAPE...?"
Citrus Moi
I DON'T CARE! I KNOW THAT ORANGE KRYPTONITE IS AROUND HERE SOMEWHERE... WE'RE CLOSE...IT MIGHT EVEN BE HIDDEN IN PLAIN...
...SIGHT?
AWESOME! WE FOUND IT!
CAN WE GO EAT NOW?
TEN SUPER-POWER MINUTES LEFT. . .
ATTENTION, DOG STAR PATROL MEMBERS: I AM TRANSPORTING EVERYONE TO THE SITE OF THE ORANGE KRYPTONITE GEM.
OF COURSE! THE COSMETICS BILLBOARD! HOW COULD I HAVE MISSED IT?
SOMETIMES THE THINGS RIGHT UNDER OUR NOSES ARE THE MOST EASILY MISSED.
ONE MINUTE OF SUPER-POWER LEFT. . .
BZACK-BZACK!
EEEEEEE!
HERE COMES ISIS! DON'T LET HER TOUCH THE ORANGE KRYPTONITE!
POW!
AHWEE-EEE-EEE-EEE!
YOU GOT IT, K-DOG!
THREE SECONDS OF SUPER-POWER LEFT...
I CAN'T BELIEVE IT! IT WAS THE PURR-FECT PLAN! I COULD ALMOST TOUCH IT...
...OH! I'VE LOST MY POWERS!
THAT'S RIGHT, TOOTS! THE JIG'S UP!

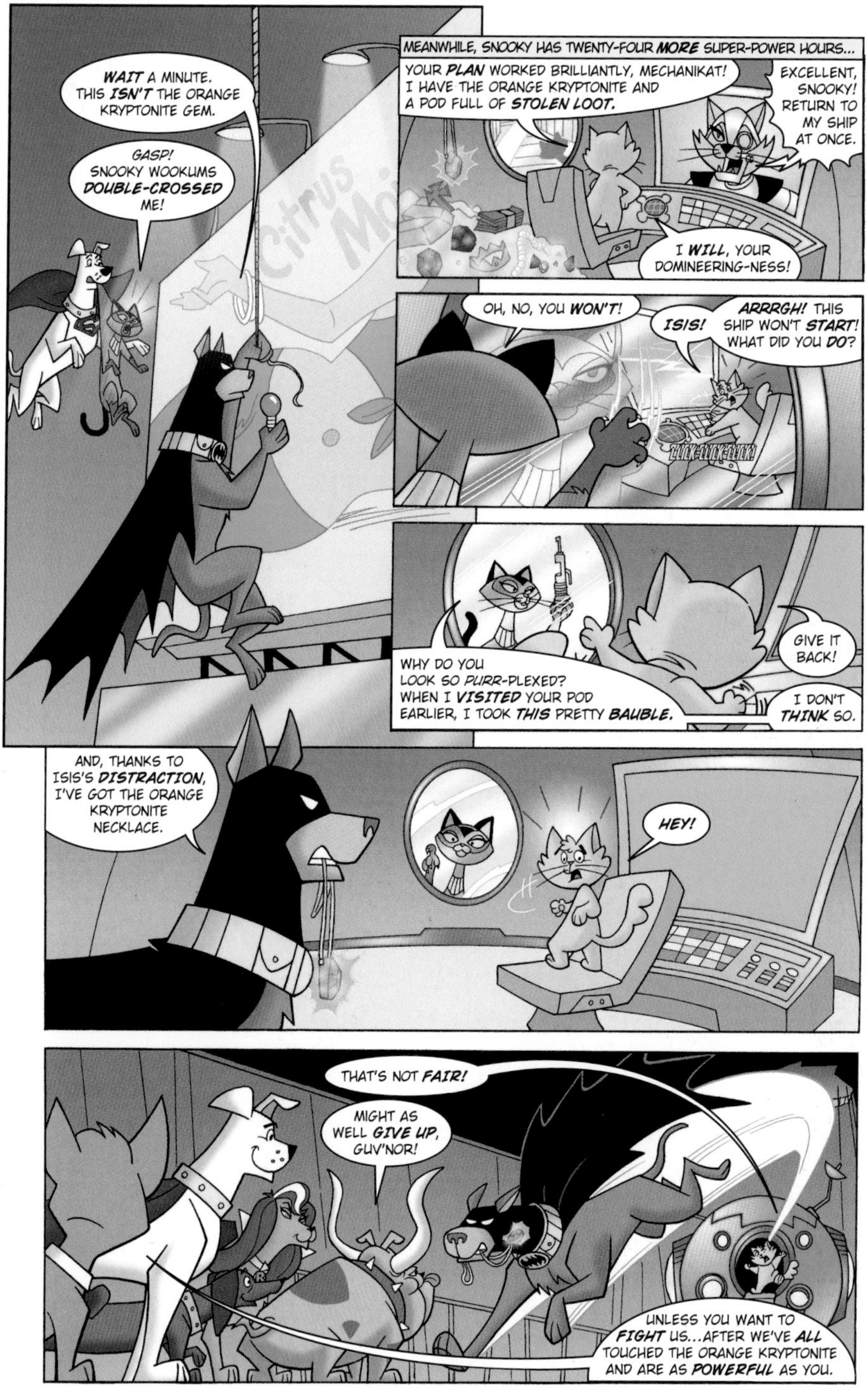
WAIT A MINUTE. THIS ISN'T THE ORANGE KRYPTONITE GEM.
GASP! SNOOKY WOOKUMS DOUBLE-CROSSED ME!
MEANWHILE, SNOOKY HAS TWENTY-FOUR MORE SUPER-POWER HOURS...
YOUR PLAN WORKED BRILLIANTLY, MECHANIKAT! I HAVE THE ORANGE KRYPTONITE AND A POD FULL OF STOLEN LOOT.
EXCELLENT, SNOOKY! RETURN TO MY SHIP AT ONCE.
I WILL, YOUR DOMINEERING-NESS!
OH, NO, YOU WON'T!
ISIS!
ARRRGH! THIS SHIP WON'T START! WHAT DID YOU DO?
CLICK-CLICK-CLICK!
WHY DO YOU LOOK SO PURR-PLEXED? WHEN I VISITED YOUR POD EARLIER, I TOOK THIS PRETTY BAUBLE.
GIVE IT BACK!
I DON'T THINK SO.
AND, THANKS TO ISIS'S DISTRACTION, I'VE GOT THE ORANGE KRYPTONITE NECKLACE.
HEY!
THAT'S NOT FAIR!
MIGHT AS WELL GIVE UP, GUV'NOR!
UNLESS YOU WANT TO FIGHT US...AFTER WE'VE ALL TOUCHED THE ORANGE KRYPTONITE AND ARE AS POWERFUL AS YOU.

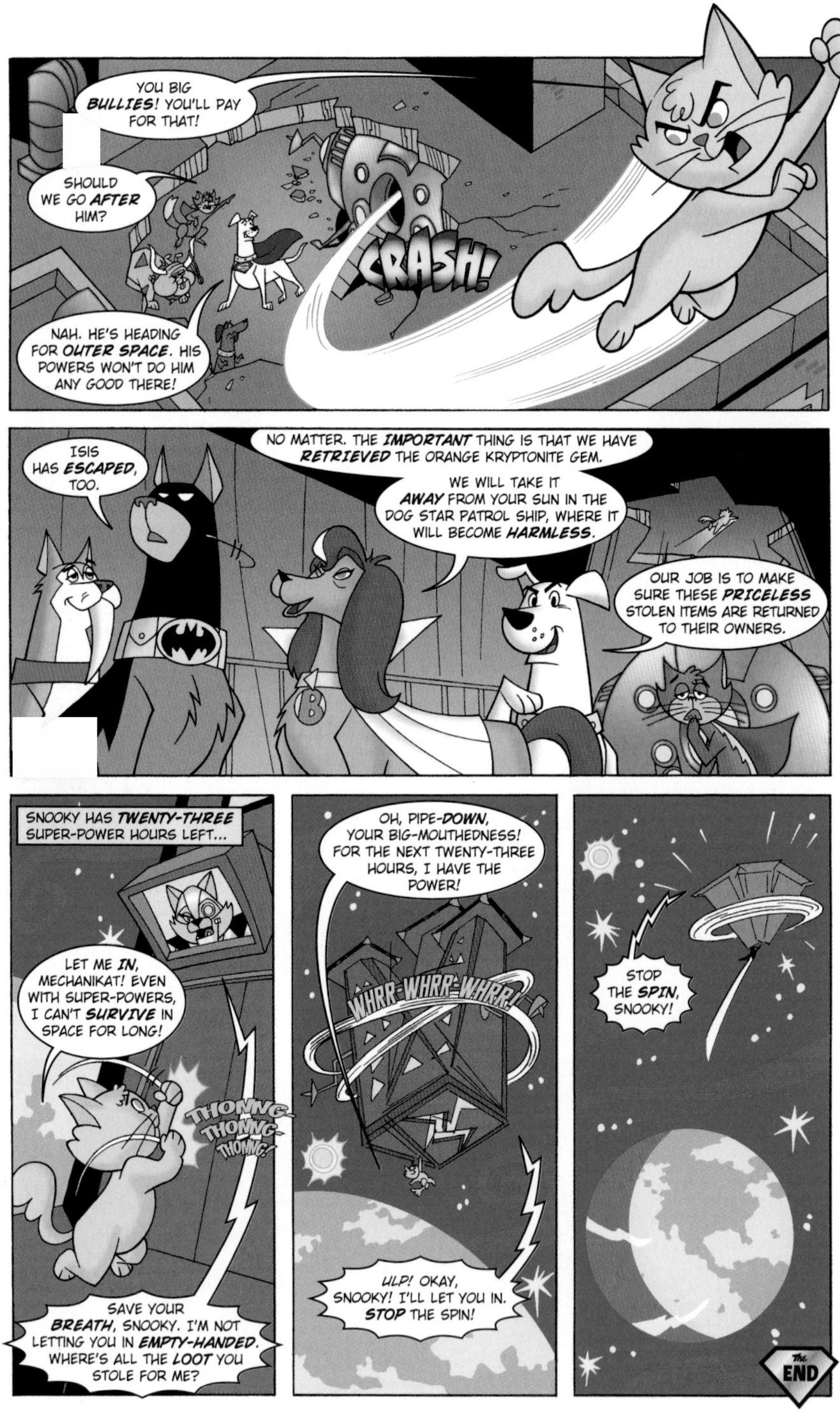

YOU BIG BULLIES! YOU'LL PAY FOR THAT!
SHOULD WE GO AFTER HIM?
CRASH!
NAH. HE'S HEADING FOR OUTER SPACE. HIS POWERS WON'T DO HIM ANY GOOD THERE!
ISIS HAS ESCAPED, TOO.
NO MATTER. THE IMPORTANT THING IS THAT WE HAVE RETRIEVED THE ORANGE KRYPTONITE GEM.
WE WILL TAKE IT AWAY FROM YOUR SUN IN THE DOG STAR PATROL SHIP, WHERE IT WILL BECOME HARMLESS.
OUR JOB IS TO MAKE SURE THESE PRICELESS STOLEN ITEMS ARE RETURNED TO THEIR OWNERS.
SNOOKY HAS TWENTY-THREE SUPER-POWER HOURS LEFT...
LET ME IN, MECHANIKAT! EVEN WITH SUPER-POWERS, I CAN'T SURVIVE IN SPACE FOR LONG!
THONNG-THONNG-THONNG!
SAVE YOUR BREATH, SNOOKY. I'M NOT LETTING YOU IN EMPTY-HANDED. WHERE'S ALL THE LOOT YOU STOLE FOR ME?
OH, PIPE-DOWN, YOUR BIG-MOUTHEDNESS! FOR THE NEXT TWENTY-THREE HOURS, I HAVE THE POWER!
WHRR-WHRR-WHRR!
ULP! OKAY, SNOOKY! I'LL LET YOU IN. STOP THE SPIN!
STOP THE SPIN, SNOOKY!
The END

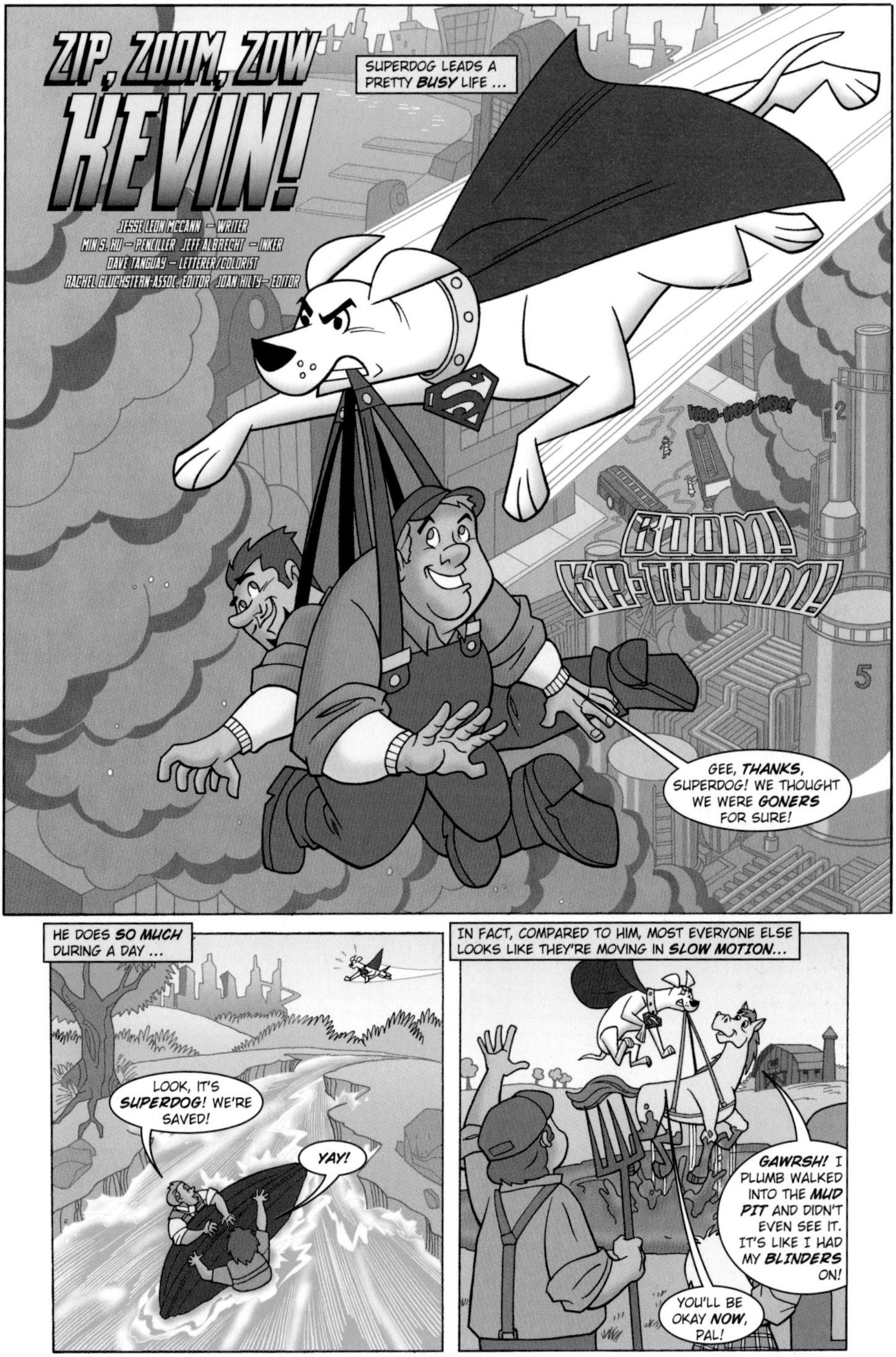
ZIP, ZOOM, ZOW KEVIN!
JESSE LEON MCCANN — WRITER
MIN S. KU — PENCILLER JEFF ALBRECHT — INKER
DAVE TANGUAY — LETTERER/COLORIST
RACHEL GLUCKSTERN-ASSOC. EDITOR JOAN HILTY— EDITOR
SUPERDOG LEADS A PRETTY BUSY LIFE ...
WOO-WOO-WOO!
BOOM! KA-THOOM!
GEE, THANKS, SUPERDOG! WE THOUGHT WE WERE GONERS FOR SURE!
HE DOES SO MUCH DURING A DAY ...
LOOK, IT'S SUPERDOG! WE'RE SAVED!
YAY!
IN FACT, COMPARED TO HIM, MOST EVERYONE ELSE LOOKS LIKE THEY'RE MOVING IN SLOW MOTION...
GAWRSH! I PLUMB WALKED INTO THE MUD PIT AND DIDN'T EVEN SEE IT. IT'S LIKE I HAD MY BLINDERS ON!
YOU'LL BE OKAY NOW, PAL!

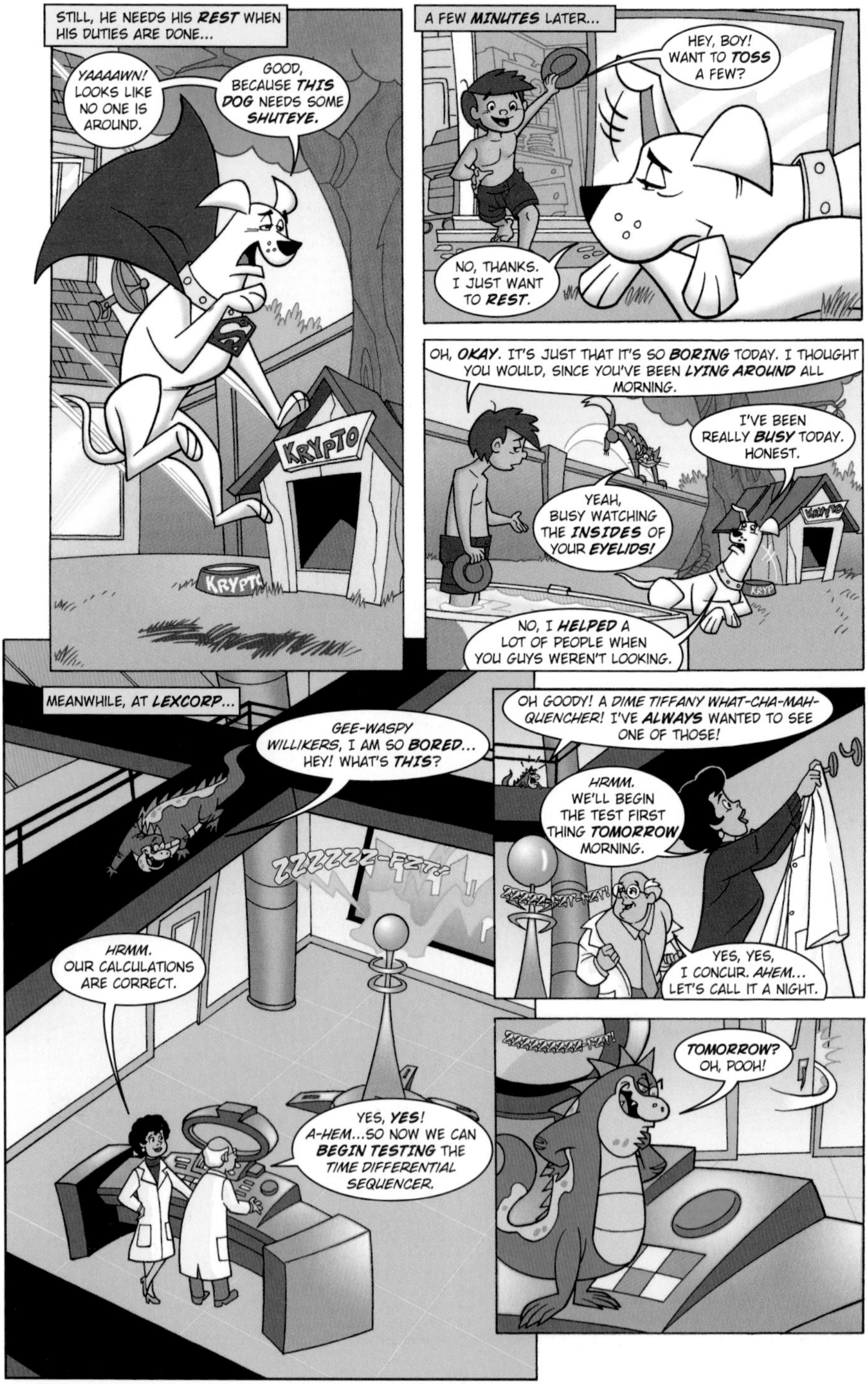
STILL, HE NEEDS HIS REST WHEN HIS DUTIES ARE DONE...
YAAAAWN! LOOKS LIKE NO ONE IS AROUND.
GOOD, BECAUSE THIS DOG NEEDS SOME SHUTEYE.
KRYPTO
KRYPTO
A FEW MINUTES LATER...
HEY, BOY! WANT TO TOSS A FEW?
NO, THANKS. I JUST WANT TO REST.
OH, OKAY. IT'S JUST THAT IT'S SO BORING TODAY. I THOUGHT YOU WOULD, SINCE YOU'VE BEEN LYING AROUND ALL MORNING.
I'VE BEEN REALLY BUSY TODAY. HONEST.
YEAH, BUSY WATCHING THE INSIDES OF YOUR EYELIDS!
NO, I HELPED A LOT OF PEOPLE WHEN YOU GUYS WEREN'T LOOKING.
MEANWHILE, AT LEXCORP...
GEE-WASPY WILLIKERS, I AM SO BORED... HEY! WHAT'S THIS?
HRMM. OUR CALCULATIONS ARE CORRECT.
YES, YES! A-HEM...SO NOW WE CAN BEGIN TESTING THE TIME DIFFERENTIAL SEQUENCER.
OH GOODY! A DIME TIFFANY WHAT-CHA-MAH-QUENCHER! I'VE ALWAYS WANTED TO SEE ONE OF THOSE!
HRMM. WE'LL BEGIN THE TEST FIRST THING TOMORROW MORNING.
YES, YES, I CONCUR. AHEM... LET'S CALL IT A NIGHT.
TOMORROW? OH, POOH!

WHY *WAIT?* I WANT TO WATCH IT WORK *NOW!*

CLICK-CHICK!

ZZZZZ-FZT-FZZT-ZZZT!

...AND THAT WAS THE STORY OF MY *GREATEST* ADVENTURE EVER! NOW, TWO DAYS AFTER THAT...

OH, MAN! COULD THIS *SLOW, BORING* DAY GET ANY *WORSE?*

HEY KEVIN, I'M ALL *RESTED!* LET'S PLAY!

ZZZOT ZZZ!

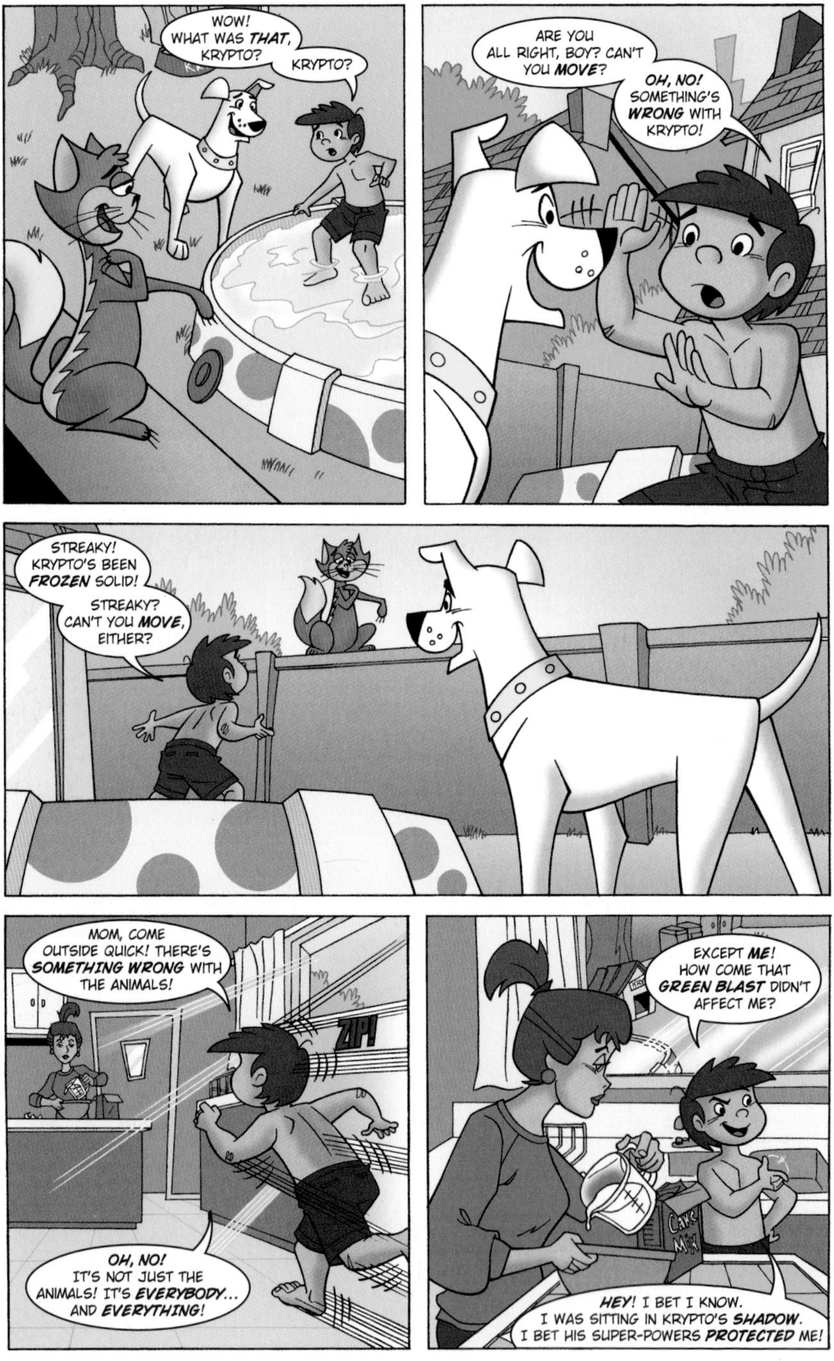
WOW! WHAT WAS THAT, KRYPTO?
KRYPTO?
ARE YOU ALL RIGHT, BOY? CAN'T YOU MOVE?
OH, NO! SOMETHING'S WRONG WITH KRYPTO!
STREAKY! KRYPTO'S BEEN FROZEN SOLID!
STREAKY? CAN'T YOU MOVE, EITHER?
MOM, COME OUTSIDE QUICK! THERE'S SOMETHING WRONG WITH THE ANIMALS!
ZIP!
OH, NO! IT'S NOT JUST THE ANIMALS! IT'S EVERYBODY... AND EVERYTHING!
EXCEPT ME! HOW COME THAT GREEN BLAST DIDN'T AFFECT ME?
HEY! I BET I KNOW. I WAS SITTING IN KRYPTO'S SHADOW. I BET HIS SUPER-POWERS PROTECTED ME!

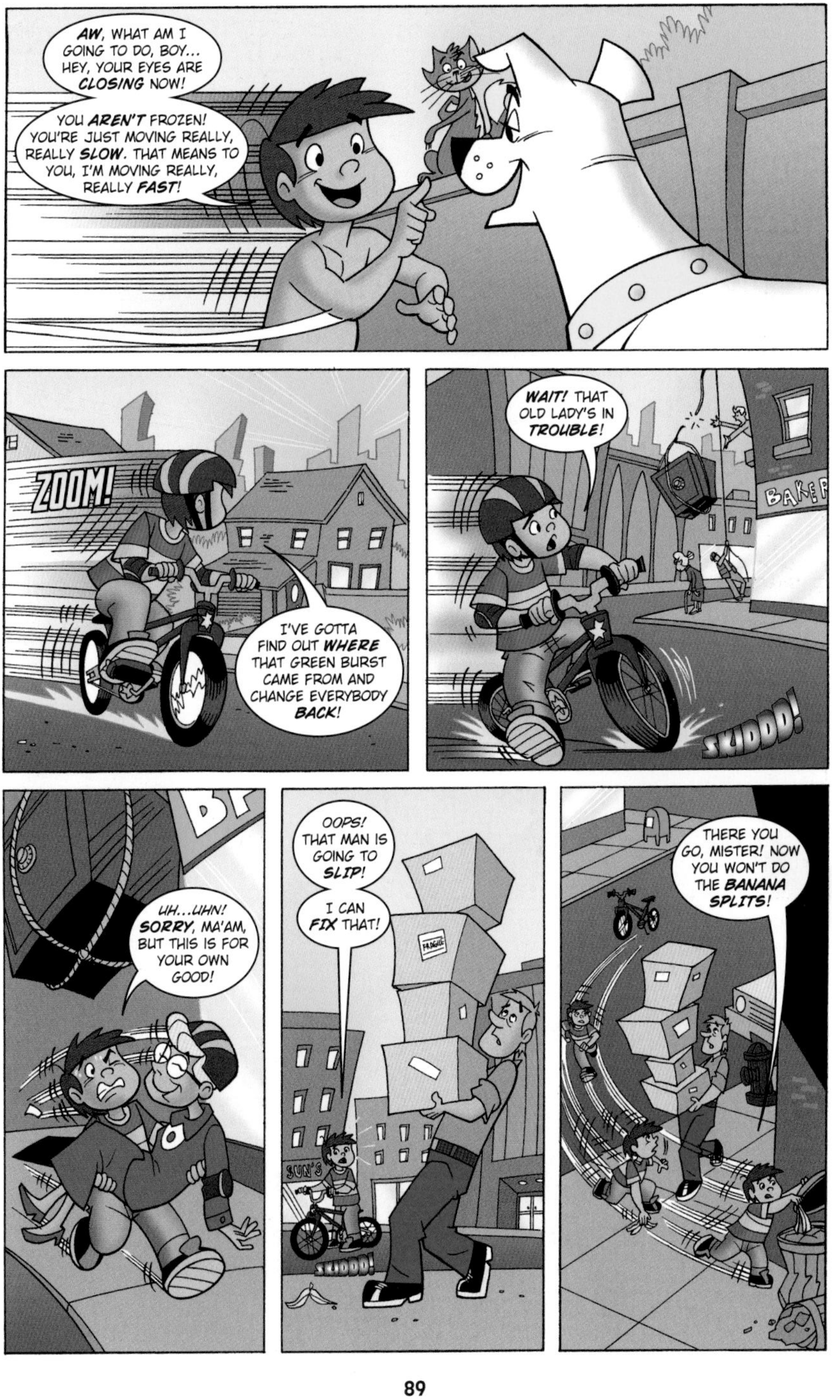
AW, WHAT AM I GOING TO DO, BOY... HEY, YOUR EYES ARE CLOSING NOW!
YOU AREN'T FROZEN! YOU'RE JUST MOVING REALLY, REALLY SLOW. THAT MEANS TO YOU, I'M MOVING REALLY, REALLY FAST!
ZOOM!
I'VE GOTTA FIND OUT WHERE THAT GREEN BURST CAME FROM AND CHANGE EVERYBODY BACK!
WAIT! THAT OLD LADY'S IN TROUBLE!
SKIDDD!
UH...UHN! SORRY, MA'AM, BUT THIS IS FOR YOUR OWN GOOD!
OOPS! THAT MAN IS GOING TO SLIP!
I CAN FIX THAT!
FRAGILE
SUN'S
SKIDDD!
THERE YOU GO, MISTER! NOW YOU WON'T DO THE BANANA SPLITS!

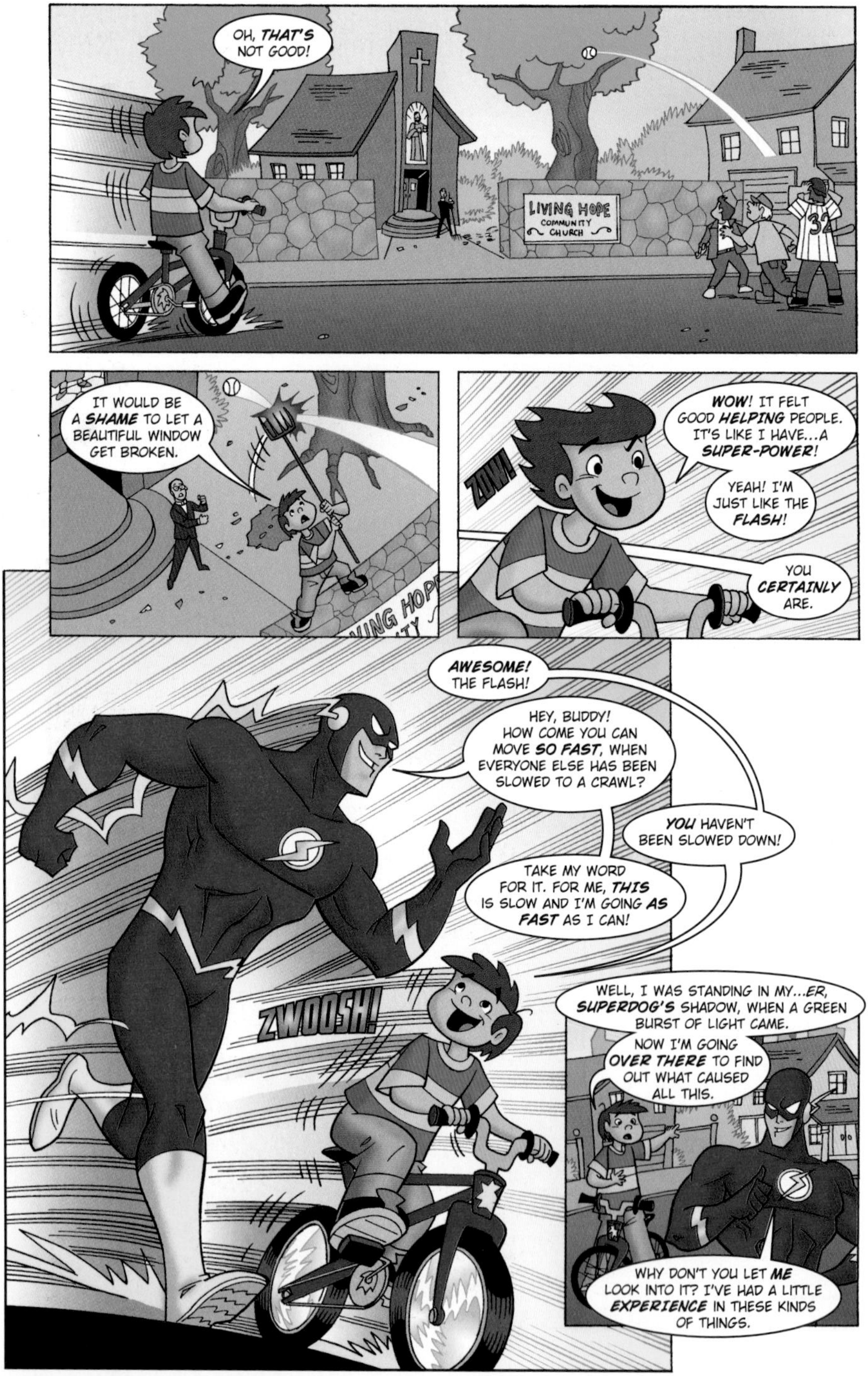
OH, THAT'S NOT GOOD!
LIVING HOPE COMMUNITY CHURCH
IT WOULD BE A SHAME TO LET A BEAUTIFUL WINDOW GET BROKEN.
ZOW!
WOW! IT FELT GOOD HELPING PEOPLE. IT'S LIKE I HAVE...A SUPER-POWER!
YEAH! I'M JUST LIKE THE FLASH!
YOU CERTAINLY ARE.
AWESOME! THE FLASH!
HEY, BUDDY! HOW COME YOU CAN MOVE SO FAST, WHEN EVERYONE ELSE HAS BEEN SLOWED TO A CRAWL?
YOU HAVEN'T BEEN SLOWED DOWN!
TAKE MY WORD FOR IT. FOR ME, THIS IS SLOW AND I'M GOING AS FAST AS I CAN!
ZWOOSH!
WELL, I WAS STANDING IN MY...ER, SUPERDOG'S SHADOW, WHEN A GREEN BURST OF LIGHT CAME.
NOW I'M GOING OVER THERE TO FIND OUT WHAT CAUSED ALL THIS.
WHY DON'T YOU LET ME LOOK INTO IT? I'VE HAD A LITTLE EXPERIENCE IN THESE KINDS OF THINGS.

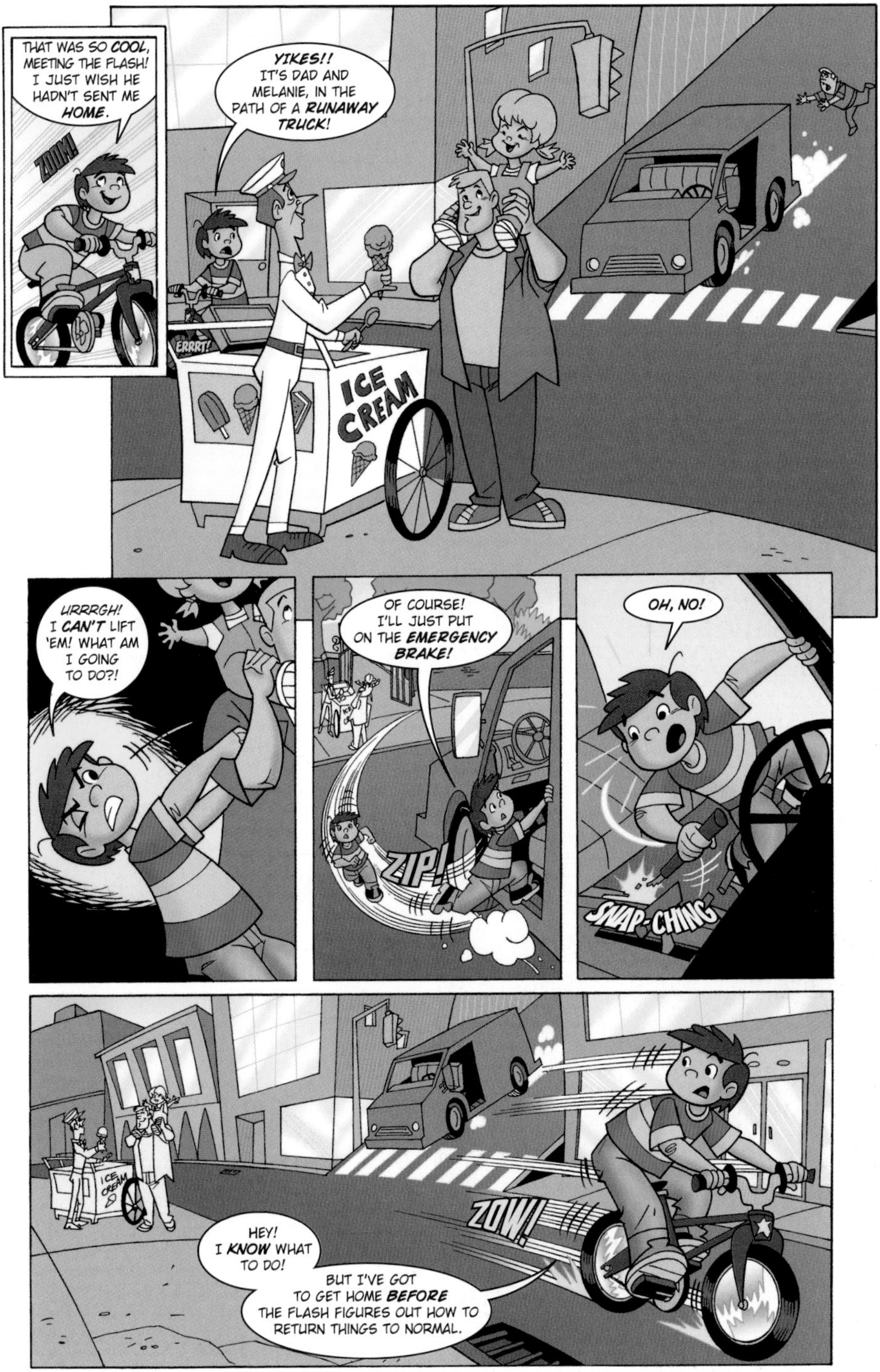
THAT WAS SO COOL, MEETING THE FLASH! I JUST WISH HE HADN'T SENT ME HOME.
ZOOM!
YIKES!! IT'S DAD AND MELANIE, IN THE PATH OF A RUNAWAY TRUCK!
ERRRT!
ICE CREAM
URRRGH! I CAN'T LIFT 'EM! WHAT AM I GOING TO DO?!
OF COURSE! I'LL JUST PUT ON THE EMERGENCY BRAKE!
ZIP!
OH, NO!
SNAP-CHING
HEY! I KNOW WHAT TO DO!
BUT I'VE GOT TO GET HOME BEFORE THE FLASH FIGURES OUT HOW TO RETURN THINGS TO NORMAL.
ZOW!

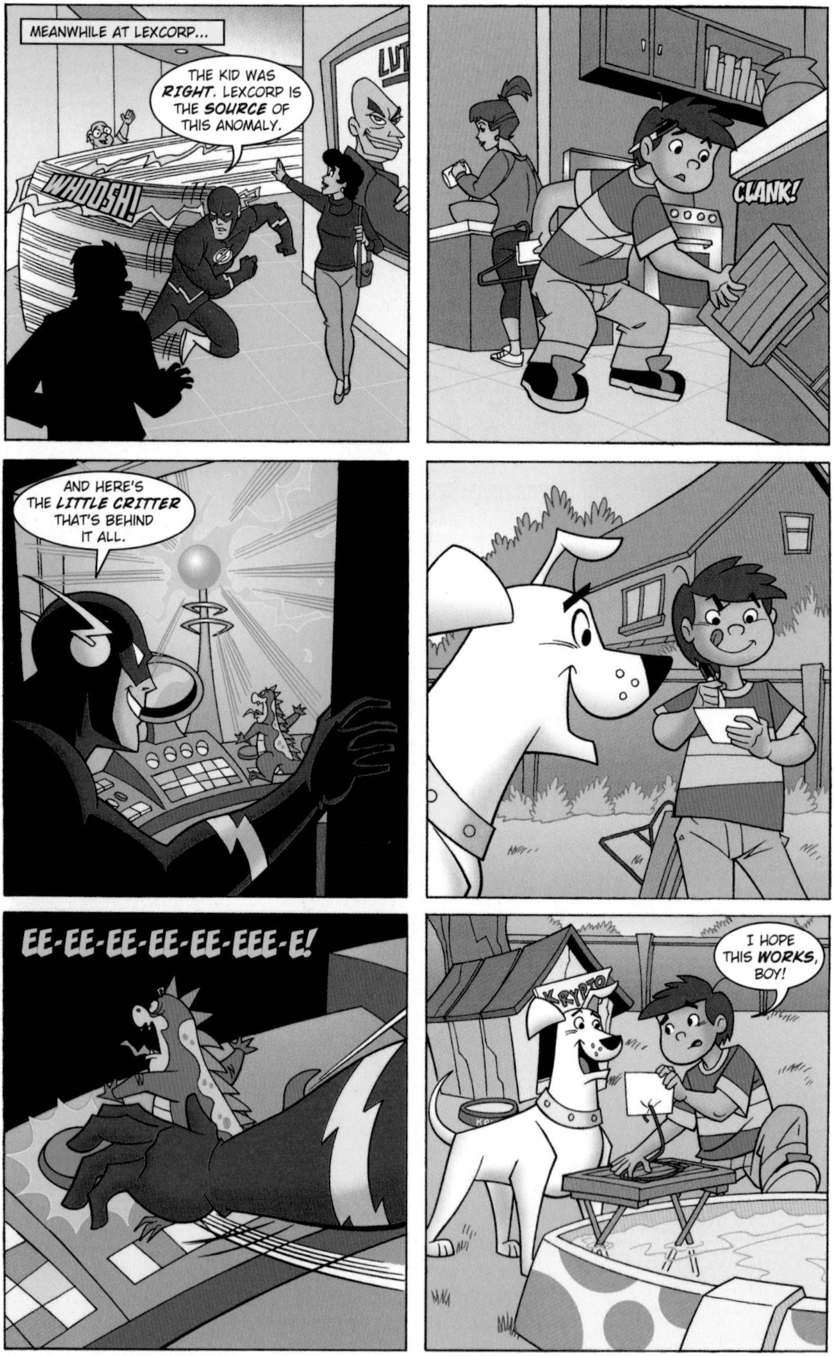
MEANWHILE AT LEXCORP...
THE KID WAS RIGHT. LEXCORP IS THE SOURCE OF THIS ANOMALY.
WHOOSH!
CLANK!
AND HERE'S THE LITTLE CRITTER THAT'S BEHIND IT ALL.
EE-EE-EE-EE-EE-EEE-E!
KRYPTO
I HOPE THIS WORKS, BOY!

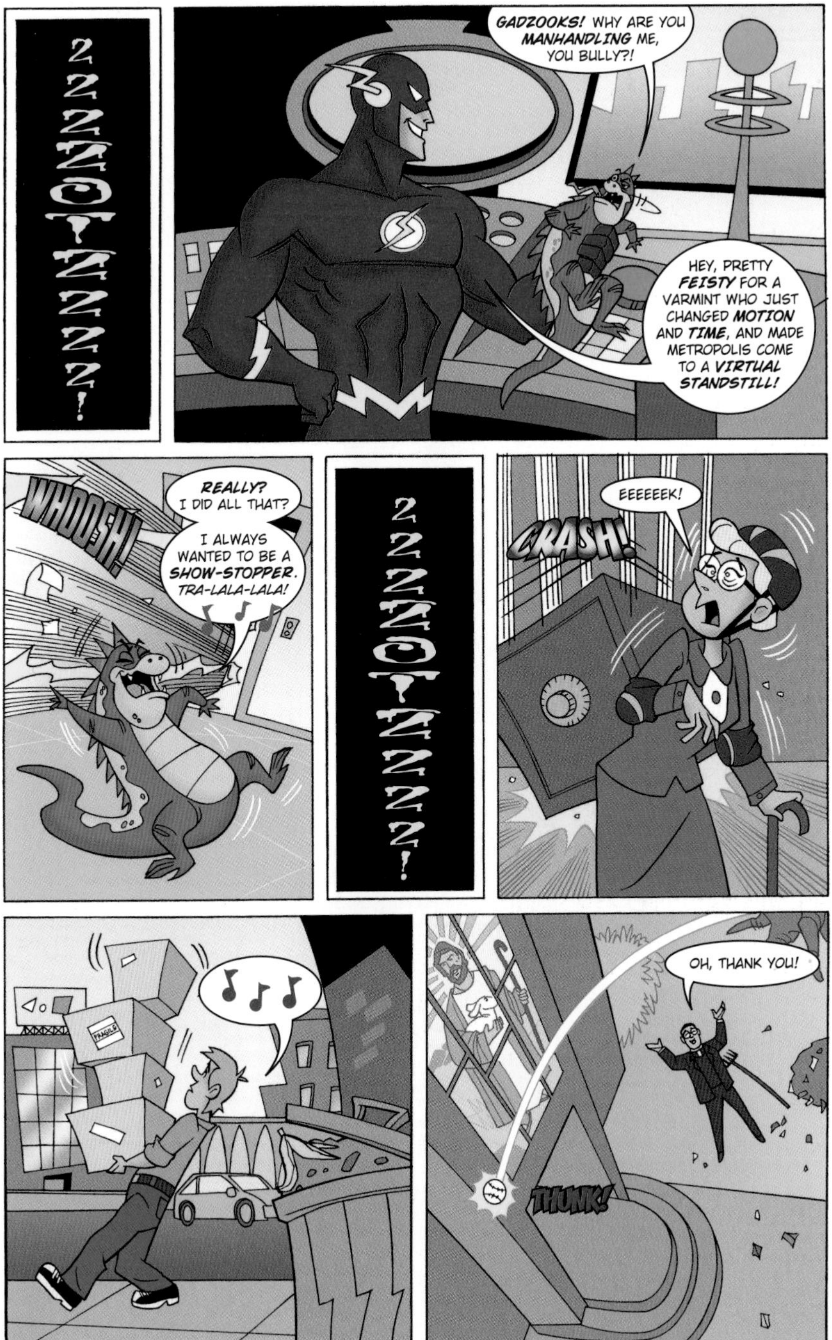
ZZZZOTZZZZ!
GADZOOKS! WHY ARE YOU MANHANDLING ME, YOU BULLY?!
HEY, PRETTY FEISTY FOR A VARMINT WHO JUST CHANGED MOTION AND TIME, AND MADE METROPOLIS COME TO A VIRTUAL STANDSTILL!
WHOOSH!
REALLY? I DID ALL THAT?
I ALWAYS WANTED TO BE A SHOW-STOPPER. TRA-LALA-LALA!
ZZZZOTZZZZ!
EEEEEEK!
CRASH!
FRAGILE
OH, THANK YOU!
THUNK!

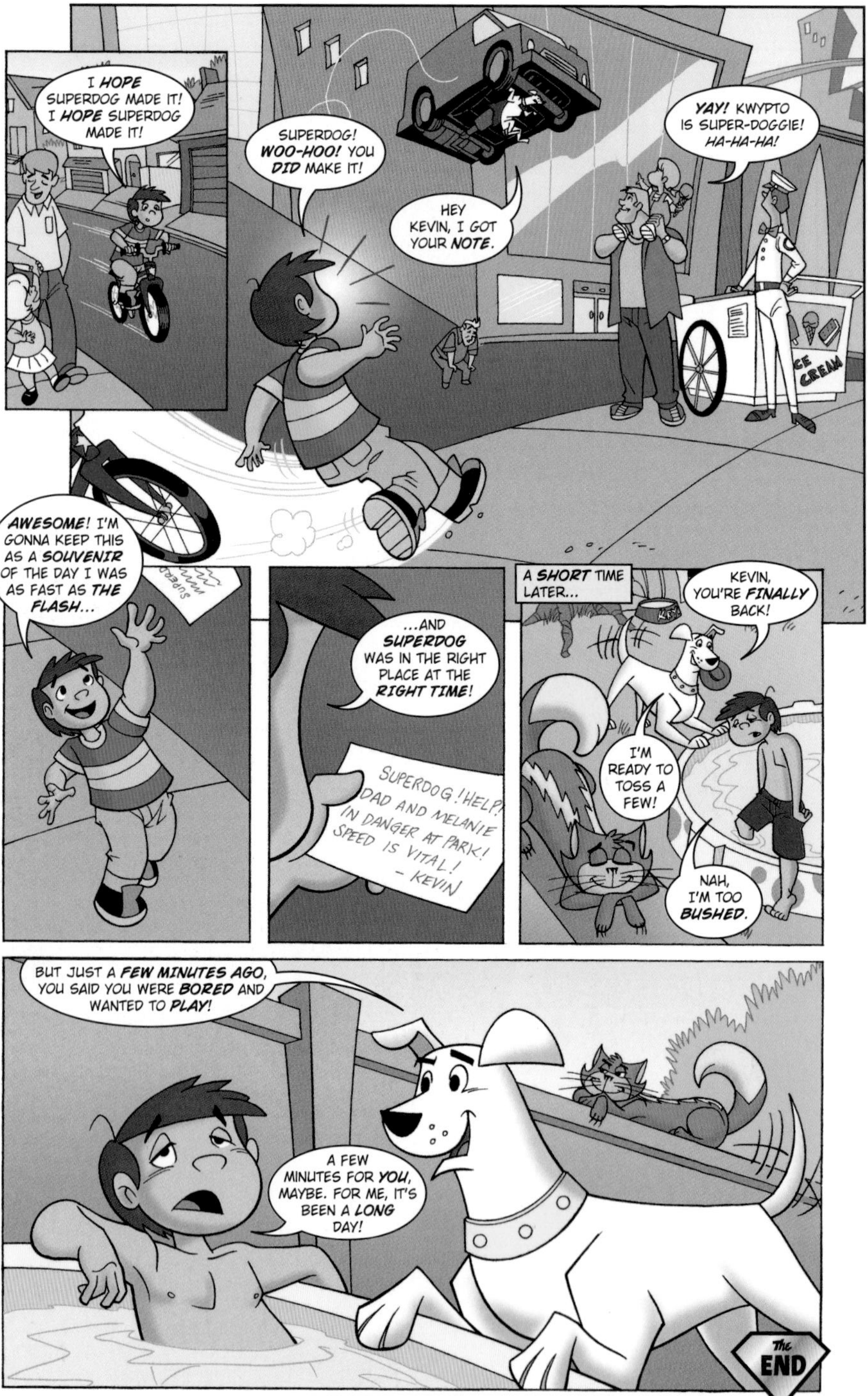

I HOPE SUPERDOG MADE IT! I HOPE SUPERDOG MADE IT!
SUPERDOG! WOO-HOO! YOU DID MAKE IT!
HEY KEVIN, I GOT YOUR NOTE.
YAY! KWYPTO IS SUPER-DOGGIE! HA-HA-HA!
ICE CREAM
AWESOME! I'M GONNA KEEP THIS AS A SOUVENIR OF THE DAY I WAS AS FAST AS THE FLASH...
...AND SUPERDOG WAS IN THE RIGHT PLACE AT THE RIGHT TIME!
SUPERDOG! HELP! DAD AND MELANIE IN DANGER AT PARK! SPEED IS VITAL! - KEVIN
A SHORT TIME LATER...
KEVIN, YOU'RE FINALLY BACK!
I'M READY TO TOSS A FEW!
NAH, I'M TOO BUSHED.
BUT JUST A FEW MINUTES AGO, YOU SAID YOU WERE BORED AND WANTED TO PLAY!
A FEW MINUTES FOR YOU, MAYBE. FOR ME, IT'S BEEN A LONG DAY!
The END

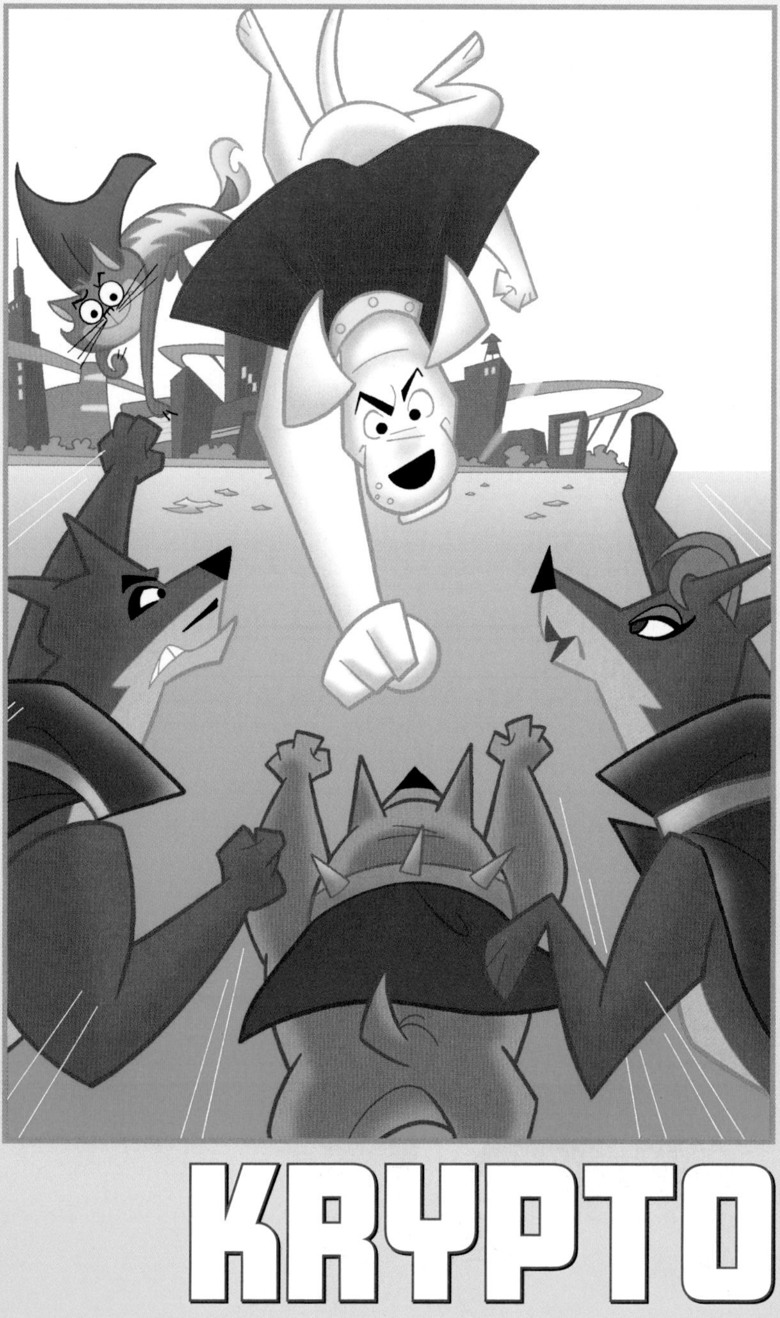

KRYPTO THE SUPERDOG

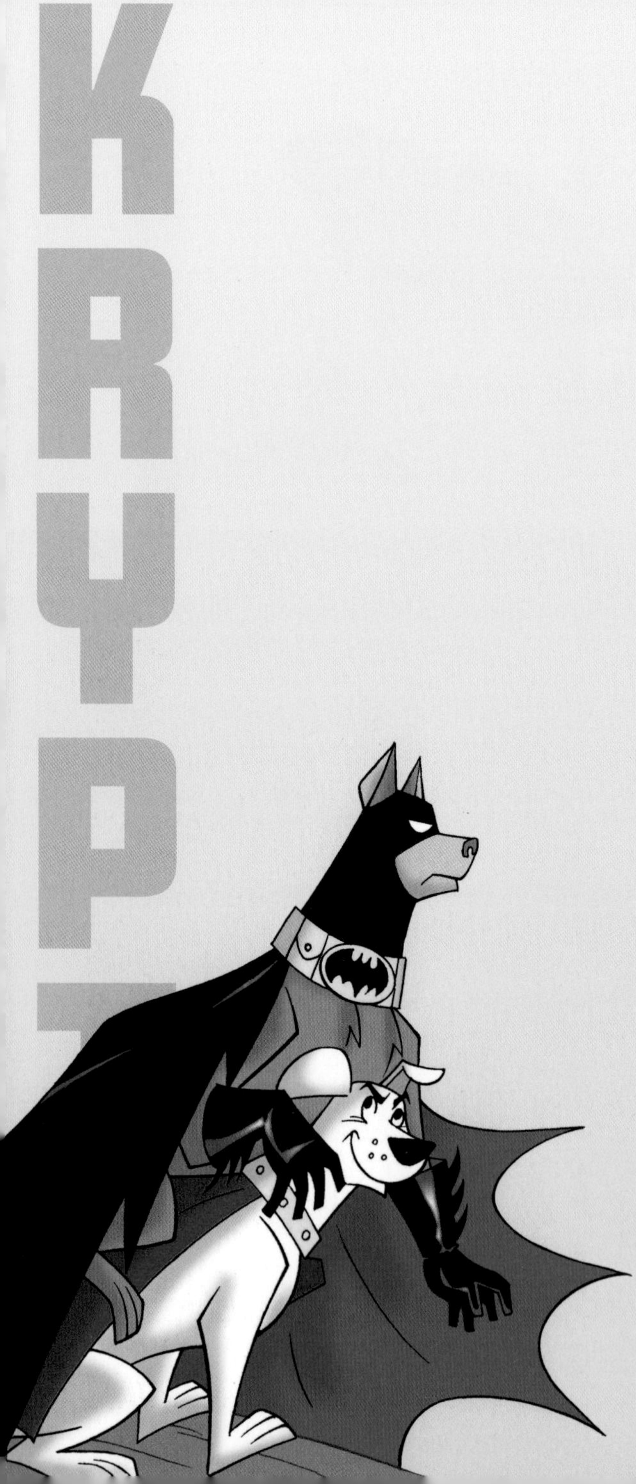
KRYP

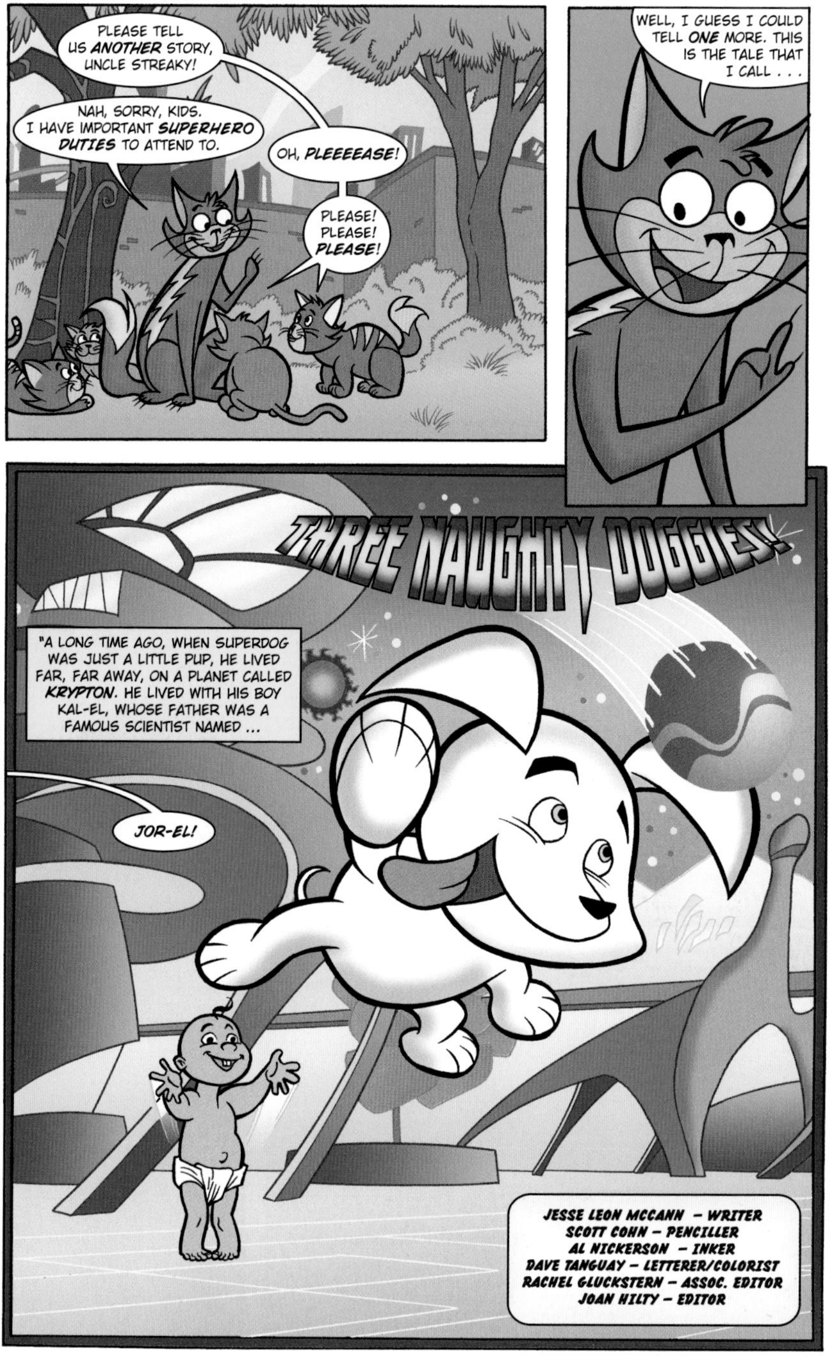
PLEASE TELL US ANOTHER STORY, UNCLE STREAKY!
NAH, SORRY, KIDS. I HAVE IMPORTANT SUPERHERO DUTIES TO ATTEND TO.
OH, PLEEEEASE!
PLEASE! PLEASE! PLEASE!
WELL, I GUESS I COULD TELL ONE MORE. THIS IS THE TALE THAT I CALL . . .
THREE NAUGHTY DOGGIES!
"A LONG TIME AGO, WHEN SUPERDOG WAS JUST A LITTLE PUP, HE LIVED FAR, FAR AWAY, ON A PLANET CALLED KRYPTON. HE LIVED WITH HIS BOY KAL-EL, WHOSE FATHER WAS A FAMOUS SCIENTIST NAMED ...
JOR-EL!
JESSE LEON MCCANN – WRITER
SCOTT COHN – PENCILLER
AL NICKERSON – INKER
DAVE TANGUAY – LETTERER/COLORIST
RACHEL GLUCKSTERN – ASSOC. EDITOR
JOAN HILTY – EDITOR

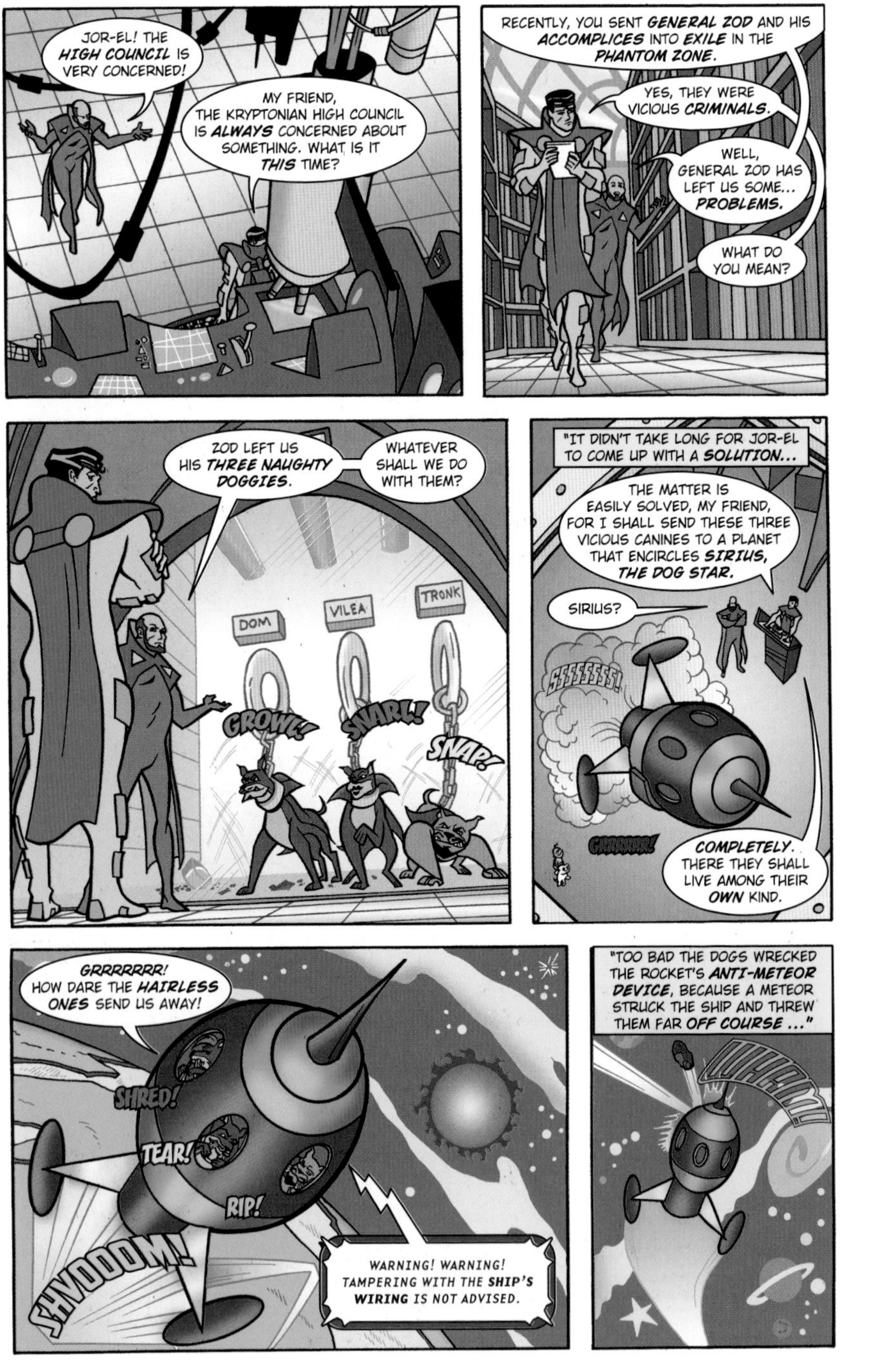

JOR-EL! THE HIGH COUNCIL IS VERY CONCERNED!
MY FRIEND, THE KRYPTONIAN HIGH COUNCIL IS ALWAYS CONCERNED ABOUT SOMETHING. WHAT IS IT THIS TIME?
RECENTLY, YOU SENT GENERAL ZOD AND HIS ACCOMPLICES INTO EXILE IN THE PHANTOM ZONE.
YES, THEY WERE VICIOUS CRIMINALS.
WELL, GENERAL ZOD HAS LEFT US SOME... PROBLEMS.
WHAT DO YOU MEAN?
ZOD LEFT US HIS THREE NAUGHTY DOGGIES.
WHATEVER SHALL WE DO WITH THEM?
DOM
VILEA
TRONK
GROWL!
SNARL!
SNAP!
"IT DIDN'T TAKE LONG FOR JOR-EL TO COME UP WITH A SOLUTION...
THE MATTER IS EASILY SOLVED, MY FRIEND, FOR I SHALL SEND THESE THREE VICIOUS CANINES TO A PLANET THAT ENCIRCLES SIRIUS, THE DOG STAR.
SIRIUS?
SSSSSSSS!
GRRRRRRR!
COMPLETELY. THERE THEY SHALL LIVE AMONG THEIR OWN KIND.
GRRRRRRR! HOW DARE THE HAIRLESS ONES SEND US AWAY!
SHRED!
TEAR!
RIP!
SHVOOOM!
WARNING! WARNING! TAMPERING WITH THE SHIP'S WIRING IS NOT ADVISED.
"TOO BAD THE DOGS WRECKED THE ROCKET'S ANTI-METEOR DEVICE, BECAUSE A METEOR STRUCK THE SHIP AND THREW THEM FAR OFF COURSE ..."
WHAM!

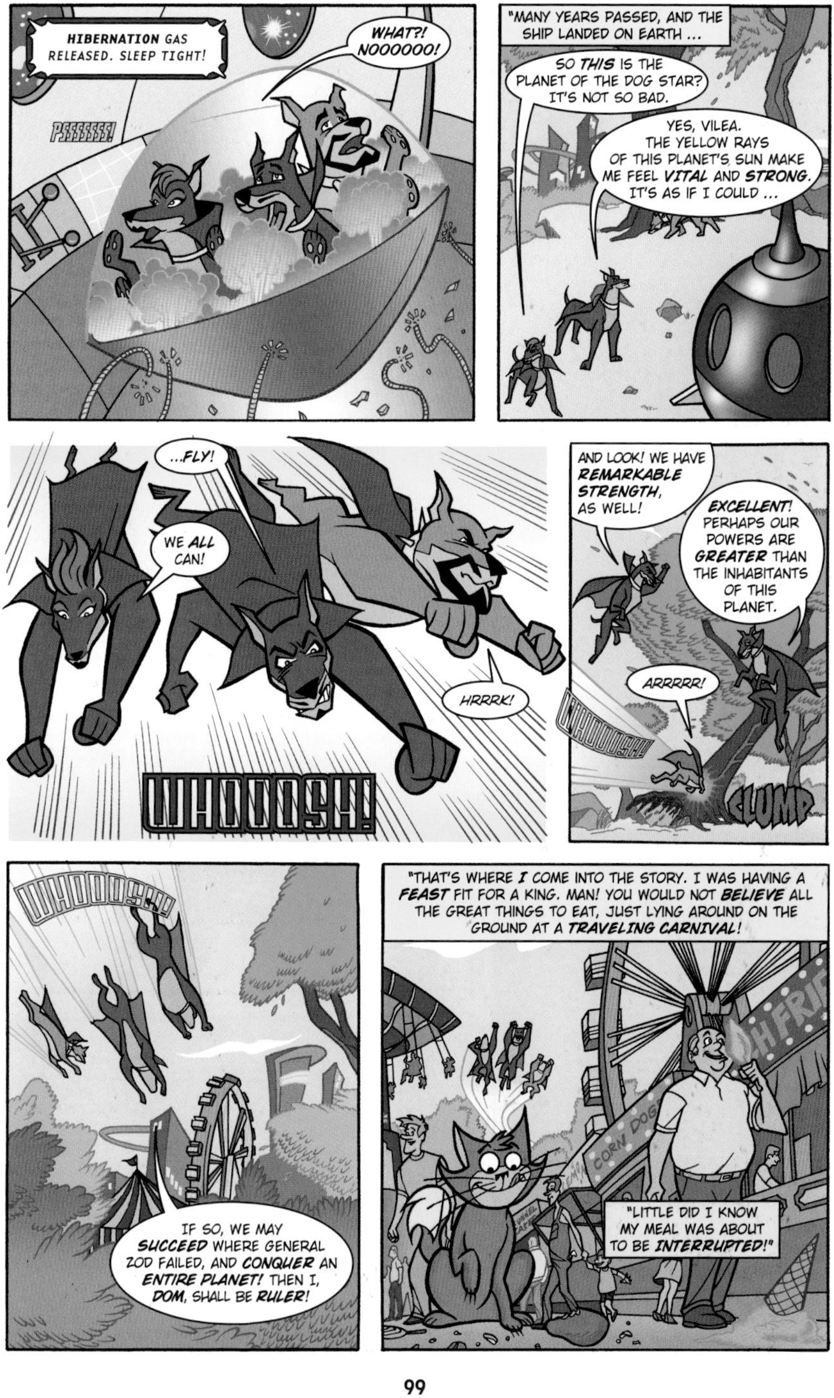
HIBERNATION GAS RELEASED. SLEEP TIGHT!
WHAT?! NOOOOOO!
PSSSSSSS!
"MANY YEARS PASSED, AND THE SHIP LANDED ON EARTH ...
SO THIS IS THE PLANET OF THE DOG STAR? IT'S NOT SO BAD.
YES, VILEA. THE YELLOW RAYS OF THIS PLANET'S SUN MAKE ME FEEL VITAL AND STRONG. IT'S AS IF I COULD ...
...FLY!
WE ALL CAN!
HRRRK!
WHOOOSH!
AND LOOK! WE HAVE REMARKABLE STRENGTH, AS WELL!
EXCELLENT! PERHAPS OUR POWERS ARE GREATER THAN THE INHABITANTS OF THIS PLANET.
ARRRRR!
WHOOOSH!
CLUMP
WHOOOSH!
IF SO, WE MAY SUCCEED WHERE GENERAL ZOD FAILED, AND CONQUER AN ENTIRE PLANET! THEN I, DOM, SHALL BE RULER!
"THAT'S WHERE I COME INTO THE STORY. I WAS HAVING A FEAST FIT FOR A KING. MAN! YOU WOULD NOT BELIEVE ALL THE GREAT THINGS TO EAT, JUST LYING AROUND ON THE GROUND AT A TRAVELING CARNIVAL!
CORN DOGS
"LITTLE DID I KNOW MY MEAL WAS ABOUT TO BE INTERRUPTED!"

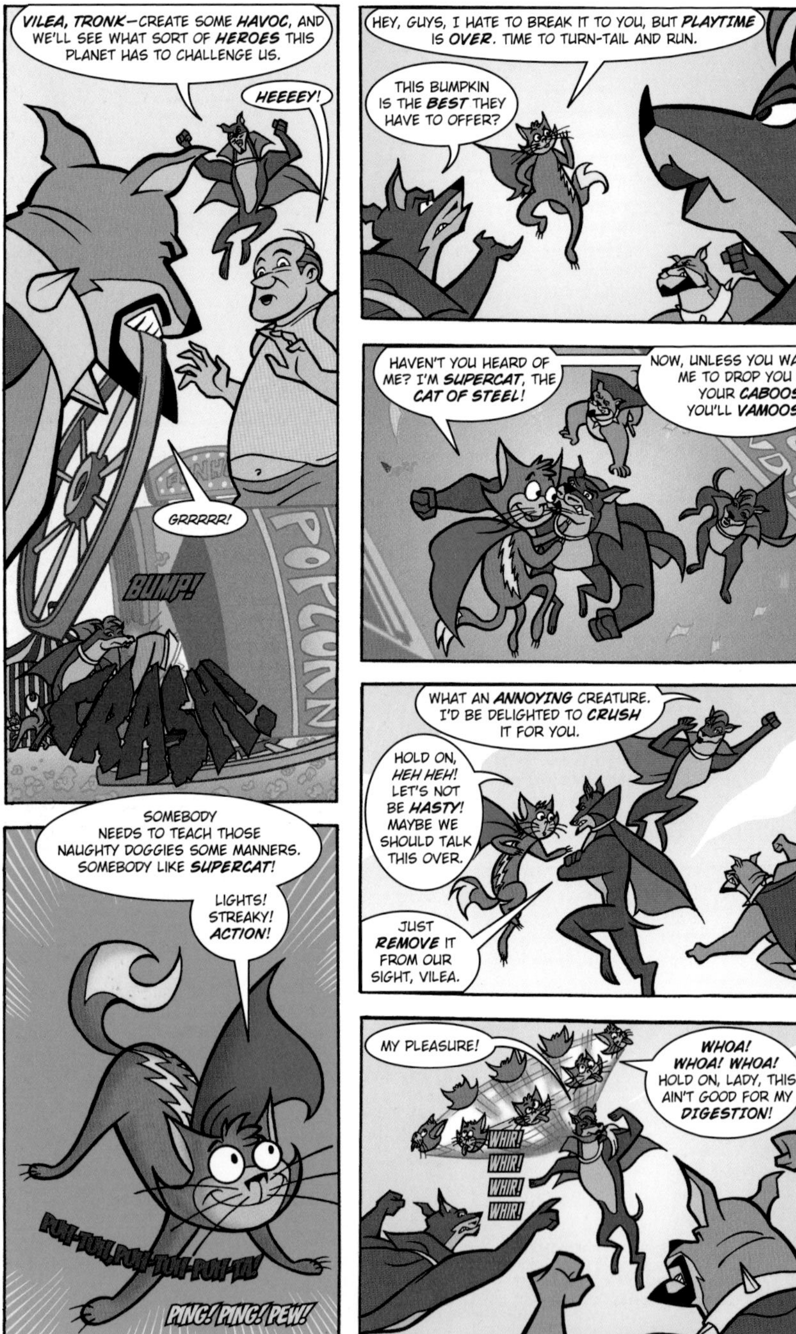
VILEA, TRONK—CREATE SOME HAVOC, AND WE'LL SEE WHAT SORT OF HEROES THIS PLANET HAS TO CHALLENGE US.
HEEEEY!
GRRRRR!
POPCORN
BUMP!
CRASH!
SOMEBODY NEEDS TO TEACH THOSE NAUGHTY DOGGIES SOME MANNERS. SOMEBODY LIKE SUPERCAT!
LIGHTS! STREAKY! ACTION!
PUH-TUH, PUH-TUH-PUH-TA!
PING! PING! PEW!
HEY, GUYS, I HATE TO BREAK IT TO YOU, BUT PLAYTIME IS OVER. TIME TO TURN-TAIL AND RUN.
THIS BUMPKIN IS THE BEST THEY HAVE TO OFFER?
HAVEN'T YOU HEARD OF ME? I'M SUPERCAT, THE CAT OF STEEL!
NOW, UNLESS YOU WANT ME TO DROP YOU ON YOUR CABOOSE, YOU'LL VAMOOSE.
WHAT AN ANNOYING CREATURE. I'D BE DELIGHTED TO CRUSH IT FOR YOU.
HOLD ON, HEH HEH! LET'S NOT BE HASTY! MAYBE WE SHOULD TALK THIS OVER.
JUST REMOVE IT FROM OUR SIGHT, VILEA.
MY PLEASURE!
WHOA! WHOA! WHOA! HOLD ON, LADY, THIS AIN'T GOOD FOR MY DIGESTION!
WHIR!
WHIR!
WHIR!
WHIR!

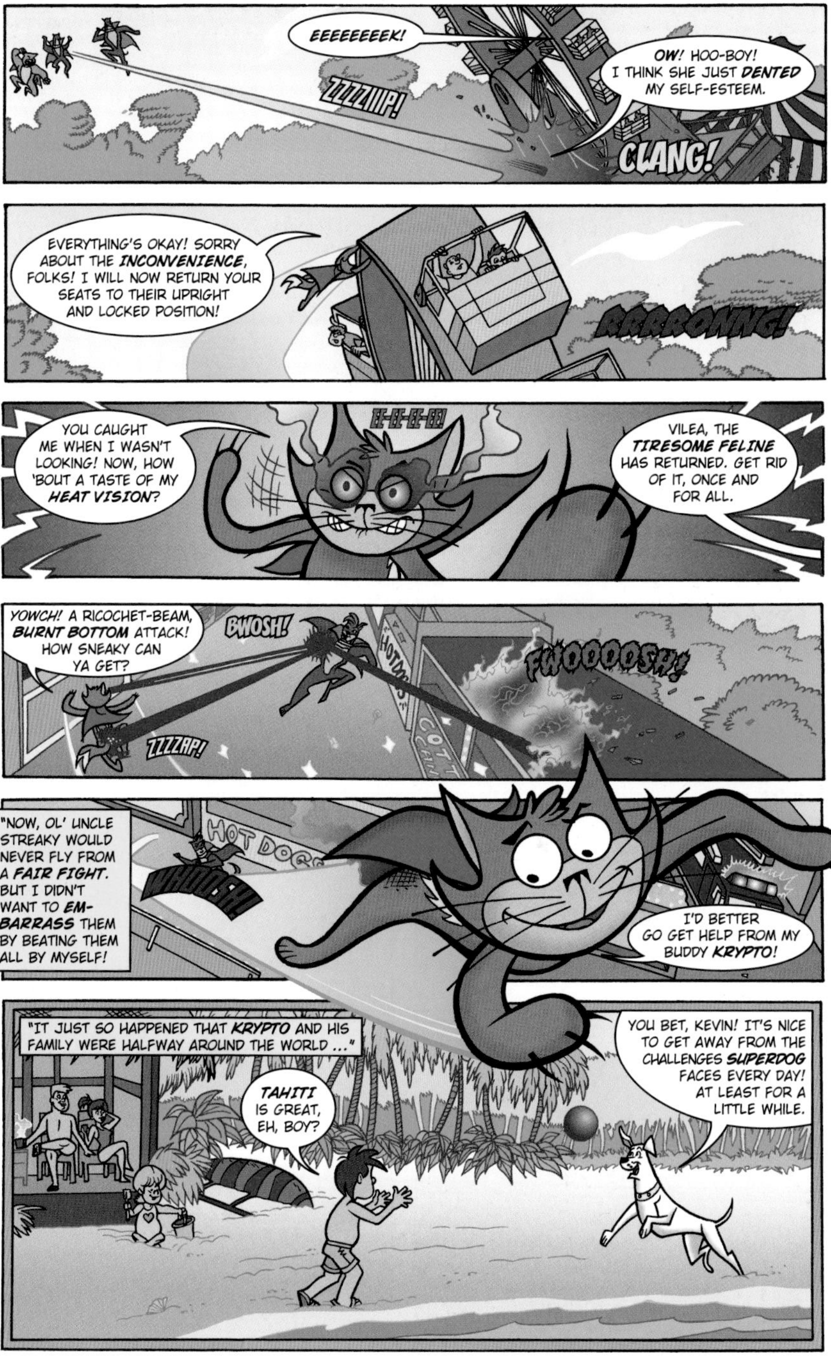
EEEEEEEEK!
ZZZZIIP!
OW! HOO-BOY! I THINK SHE JUST DENTED MY SELF-ESTEEM.
CLANG!
EVERYTHING'S OKAY! SORRY ABOUT THE INCONVENIENCE, FOLKS! I WILL NOW RETURN YOUR SEATS TO THEIR UPRIGHT AND LOCKED POSITION!
RRRRONNNG!
YOU CAUGHT ME WHEN I WASN'T LOOKING! NOW, HOW 'BOUT A TASTE OF MY HEAT VISION?
EE-EE-EE-EE!
VILEA, THE TIRESOME FELINE HAS RETURNED. GET RID OF IT, ONCE AND FOR ALL.
YOWCH! A RICOCHET-BEAM, BURNT BOTTOM ATTACK! HOW SNEAKY CAN YA GET?
BWOSH!
FWOOOOOSH!
ZZZZAP!
"NOW, OL' UNCLE STREAKY WOULD NEVER FLY FROM A FAIR FIGHT. BUT I DIDN'T WANT TO EMBARRASS THEM BY BEATING THEM ALL BY MYSELF!
HOT DOGS
WHOOSH!
I'D BETTER GO GET HELP FROM MY BUDDY KRYPTO!
"IT JUST SO HAPPENED THAT KRYPTO AND HIS FAMILY WERE HALFWAY AROUND THE WORLD ..."
TAHITI IS GREAT, EH, BOY?
YOU BET, KEVIN! IT'S NICE TO GET AWAY FROM THE CHALLENGES SUPERDOG FACES EVERY DAY! AT LEAST FOR A LITTLE WHILE.

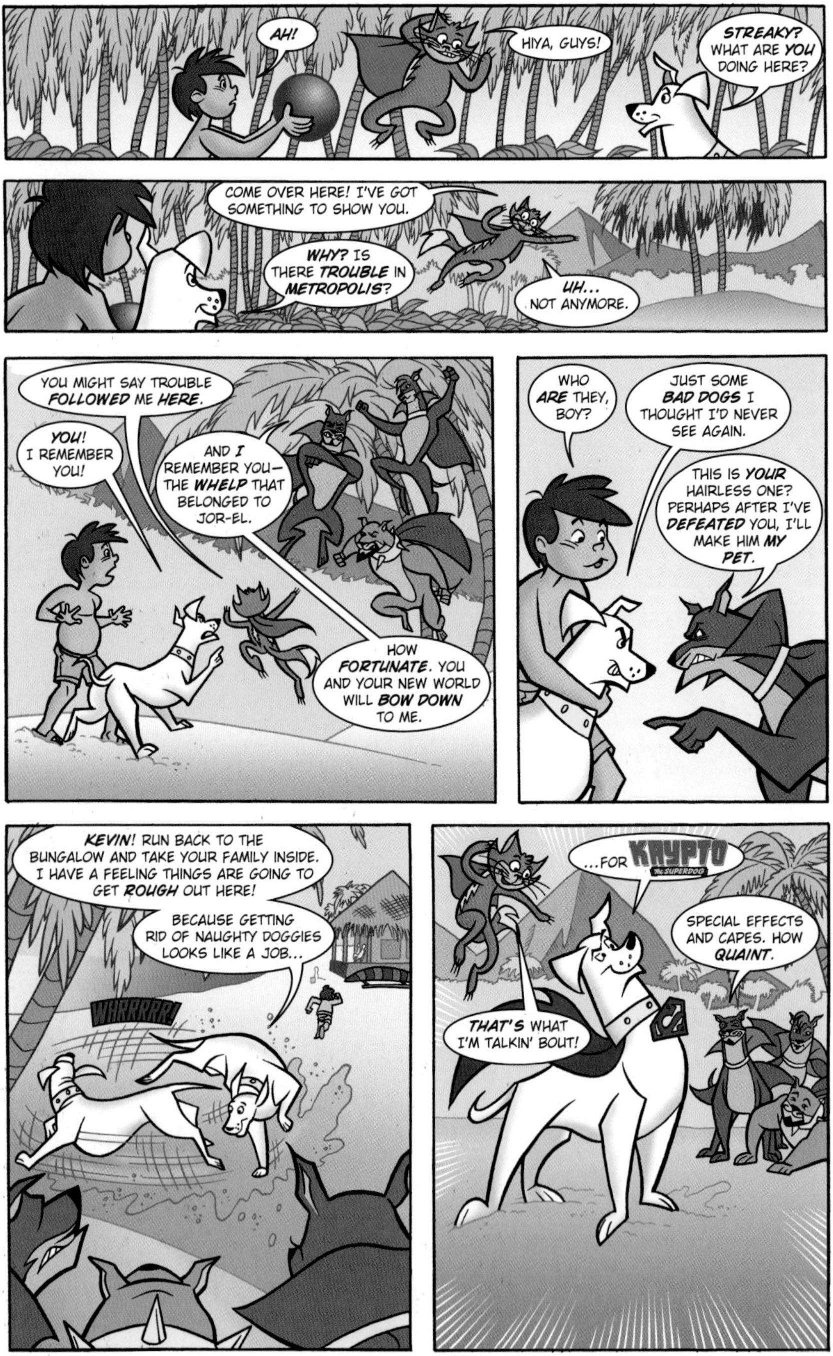
AH!
HIYA, GUYS!
STREAKY? WHAT ARE YOU DOING HERE?
COME OVER HERE! I'VE GOT SOMETHING TO SHOW YOU.
WHY? IS THERE TROUBLE IN METROPOLIS?
UH... NOT ANYMORE.
YOU MIGHT SAY TROUBLE FOLLOWED ME HERE.
YOU! I REMEMBER YOU!
AND I REMEMBER YOU— THE WHELP THAT BELONGED TO JOR-EL.
HOW FORTUNATE. YOU AND YOUR NEW WORLD WILL BOW DOWN TO ME.
WHO ARE THEY, BOY?
JUST SOME BAD DOGS I THOUGHT I'D NEVER SEE AGAIN.
THIS IS YOUR HAIRLESS ONE? PERHAPS AFTER I'VE DEFEATED YOU, I'LL MAKE HIM MY PET.
KEVIN! RUN BACK TO THE BUNGALOW AND TAKE YOUR FAMILY INSIDE. I HAVE A FEELING THINGS ARE GOING TO GET ROUGH OUT HERE!
BECAUSE GETTING RID OF NAUGHTY DOGGIES LOOKS LIKE A JOB...
WHRRRR!
...FOR KRYPTO THE SUPERDOG
SPECIAL EFFECTS AND CAPES. HOW QUAINT.
THAT'S WHAT I'M TALKIN' BOUT!

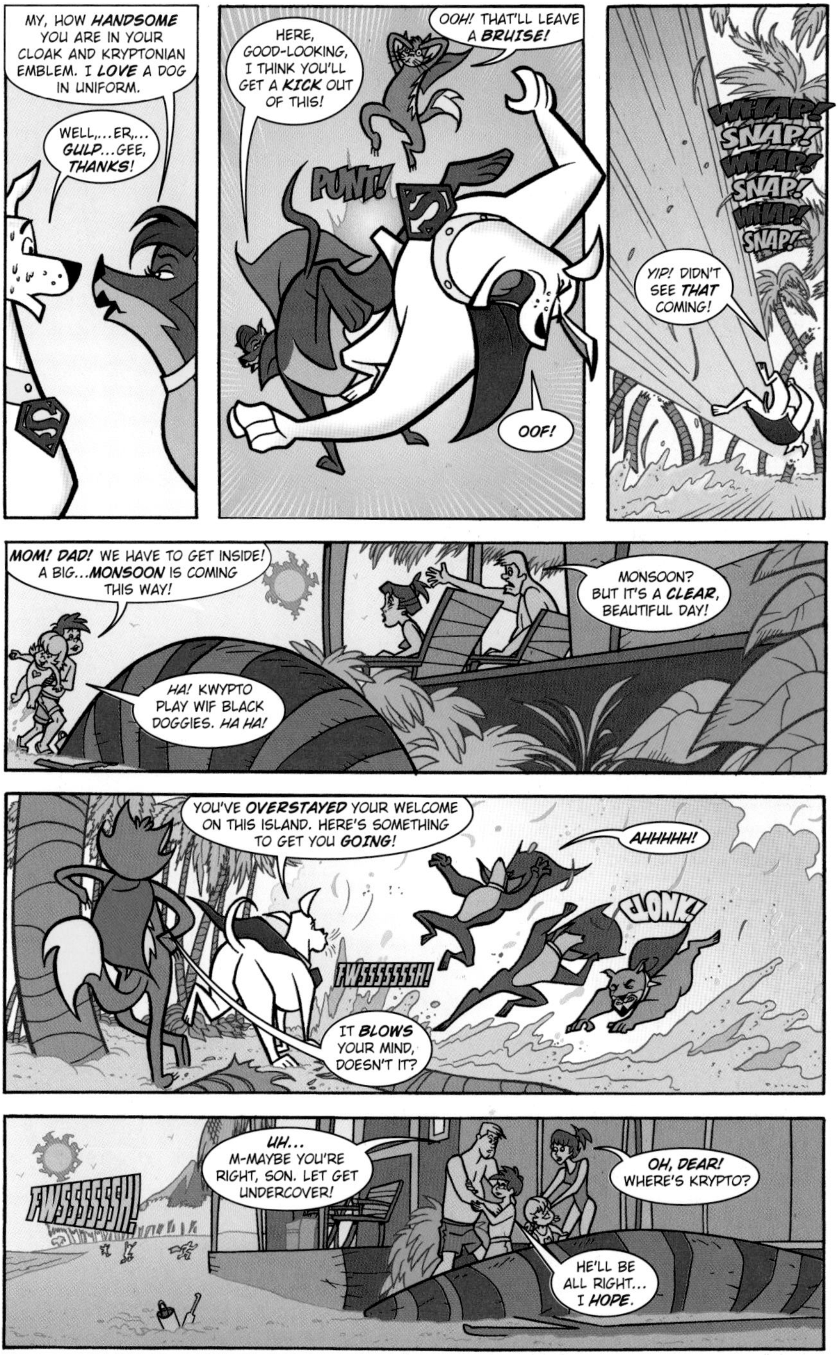
MY, HOW HANDSOME YOU ARE IN YOUR CLOAK AND KRYPTONIAN EMBLEM. I LOVE A DOG IN UNIFORM.
WELL,...ER,... GULP...GEE, THANKS!
HERE, GOOD-LOOKING, I THINK YOU'LL GET A KICK OUT OF THIS!
PUNT!
OOH! THAT'LL LEAVE A BRUISE!
OOF!
WHAP! SNAP! WHAP! SNAP! WHAP! SNAP!
YIP! DIDN'T SEE THAT COMING!
MOM! DAD! WE HAVE TO GET INSIDE! A BIG...MONSOON IS COMING THIS WAY!
MONSOON? BUT IT'S A CLEAR, BEAUTIFUL DAY!
HA! KWYPTO PLAY WIF BLACK DOGGIES. HA HA!
YOU'VE OVERSTAYED YOUR WELCOME ON THIS ISLAND. HERE'S SOMETHING TO GET YOU GOING!
AHHHHH!
CLONK!
FWSSSSSSSH!
IT BLOWS YOUR MIND, DOESN'T IT?
FWSSSSSSH!
UH... M-MAYBE YOU'RE RIGHT, SON. LET GET UNDERCOVER!
OH, DEAR! WHERE'S KRYPTO?
HE'LL BE ALL RIGHT... I HOPE.

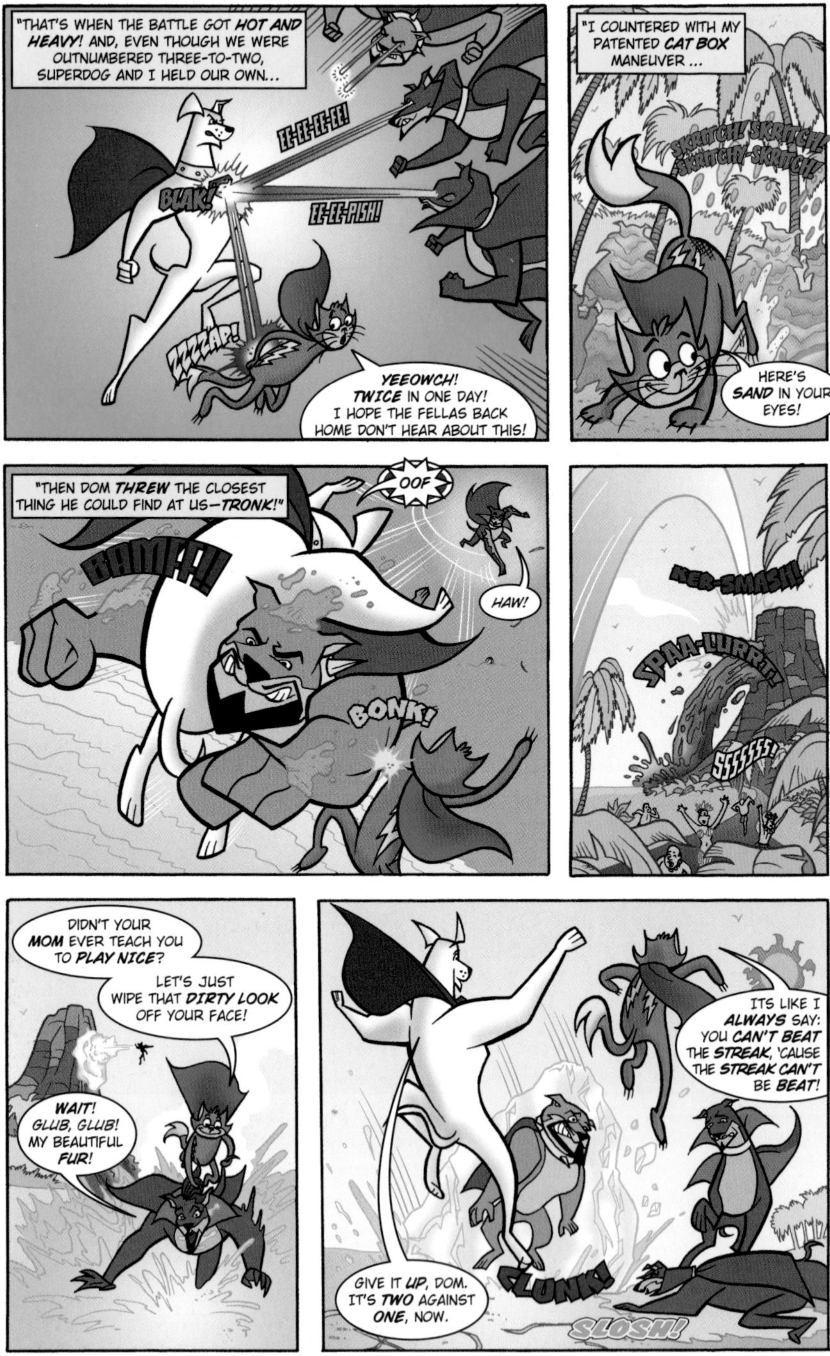
"THAT'S WHEN THE BATTLE GOT HOT AND HEAVY! AND, EVEN THOUGH WE WERE OUTNUMBERED THREE-TO-TWO, SUPERDOG AND I HELD OUR OWN...
EE-EE-EE-EE!
BLAK!
EE-EE-PISH!
ZZZZAP!
YEEOWCH! TWICE IN ONE DAY! I HOPE THE FELLAS BACK HOME DON'T HEAR ABOUT THIS!
"I COUNTERED WITH MY PATENTED CAT BOX MANEUVER ...
SKRITCH! SKRITCH! SKRITCH! SKRITCH!
HERE'S SAND IN YOUR EYES!
"THEN DOM THREW THE CLOSEST THING HE COULD FIND AT US—TRONK!"
OOF
BAMF!!
HAW!
BONK!
KER-SMASH!
SPAA-LURRT!
SSSSSSS!
DIDN'T YOUR MOM EVER TEACH YOU TO PLAY NICE?
LET'S JUST WIPE THAT DIRTY LOOK OFF YOUR FACE!
WAIT! GLUB, GLUB! MY BEAUTIFUL FUR!
ITS LIKE I ALWAYS SAY: YOU CAN'T BEAT THE STREAK, 'CAUSE THE STREAK CAN'T BE BEAT!
GIVE IT UP, DOM. IT'S TWO AGAINST ONE, NOW.
CLUNK!
SLOSH!

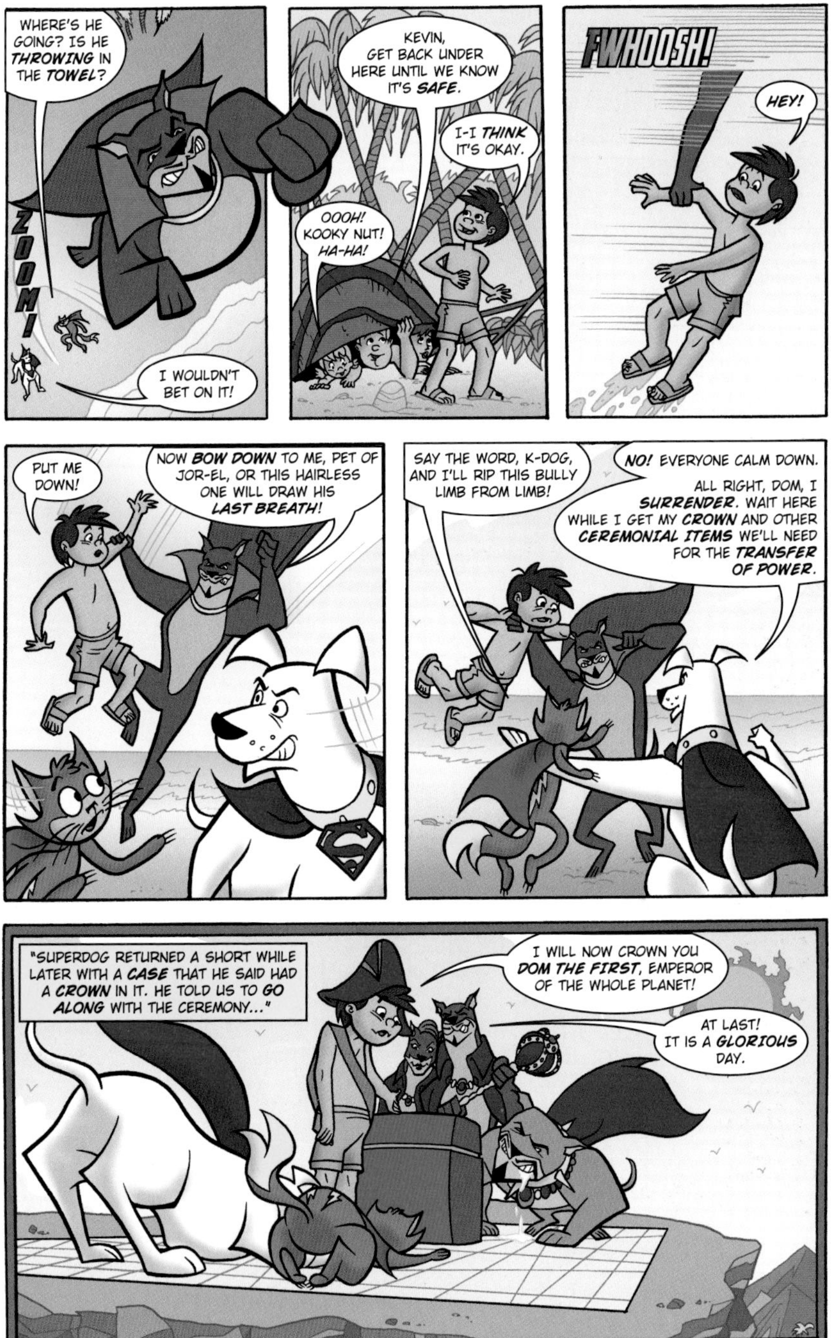
WHERE'S HE GOING? IS HE THROWING IN THE TOWEL?
ZOOM!
I WOULDN'T BET ON IT!
KEVIN, GET BACK UNDER HERE UNTIL WE KNOW IT'S SAFE.
I-I THINK IT'S OKAY.
OOOH! KOOKY NUT! HA-HA!
FWHOOSH!
HEY!
PUT ME DOWN!
NOW BOW DOWN TO ME, PET OF JOR-EL, OR THIS HAIRLESS ONE WILL DRAW HIS LAST BREATH!
SAY THE WORD, K-DOG, AND I'LL RIP THIS BULLY LIMB FROM LIMB!
NO! EVERYONE CALM DOWN.
ALL RIGHT, DOM, I SURRENDER. WAIT HERE WHILE I GET MY CROWN AND OTHER CEREMONIAL ITEMS WE'LL NEED FOR THE TRANSFER OF POWER.
"SUPERDOG RETURNED A SHORT WHILE LATER WITH A CASE THAT HE SAID HAD A CROWN IN IT. HE TOLD US TO GO ALONG WITH THE CEREMONY..."
I WILL NOW CROWN YOU DOM THE FIRST, EMPEROR OF THE WHOLE PLANET!
AT LAST! IT IS A GLORIOUS DAY.

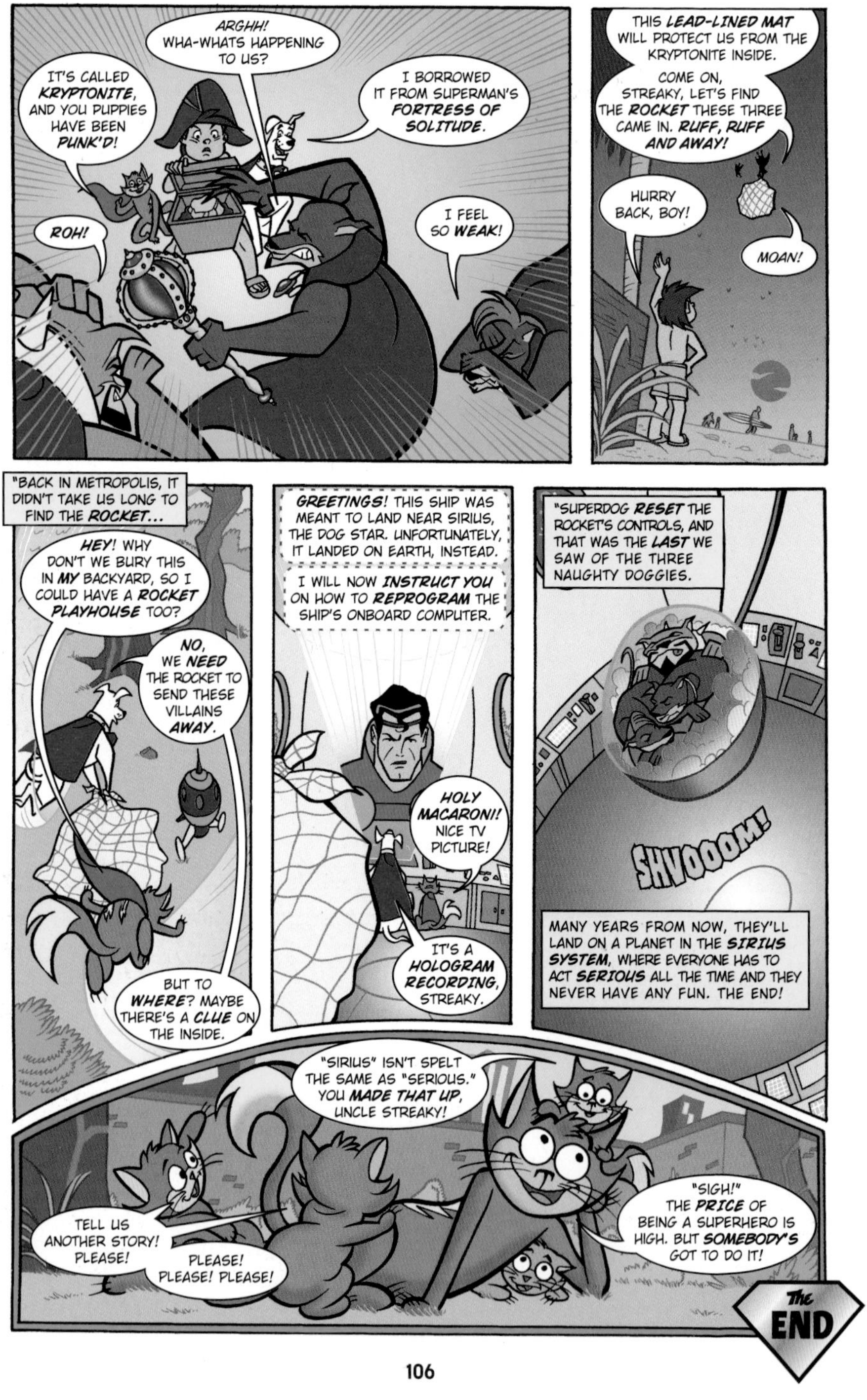
ARGHH! WHA-WHATS HAPPENING TO US?
IT'S CALLED KRYPTONITE, AND YOU PUPPIES HAVE BEEN PUNK'D!
I BORROWED IT FROM SUPERMAN'S FORTRESS OF SOLITUDE.
ROH!
I FEEL SO WEAK!
THIS LEAD-LINED MAT WILL PROTECT US FROM THE KRYPTONITE INSIDE.
COME ON, STREAKY, LET'S FIND THE ROCKET THESE THREE CAME IN. RUFF, RUFF AND AWAY!
HURRY BACK, BOY!
MOAN!
"BACK IN METROPOLIS, IT DIDN'T TAKE US LONG TO FIND THE ROCKET...
HEY! WHY DON'T WE BURY THIS IN MY BACKYARD, SO I COULD HAVE A ROCKET PLAYHOUSE TOO?
NO, WE NEED THE ROCKET TO SEND THESE VILLAINS AWAY.
BUT TO WHERE? MAYBE THERE'S A CLUE ON THE INSIDE.
GREETINGS! THIS SHIP WAS MEANT TO LAND NEAR SIRIUS, THE DOG STAR. UNFORTUNATELY, IT LANDED ON EARTH, INSTEAD.
I WILL NOW INSTRUCT YOU ON HOW TO REPROGRAM THE SHIP'S ONBOARD COMPUTER.
HOLY MACARONI! NICE TV PICTURE!
IT'S A HOLOGRAM RECORDING, STREAKY.
"SUPERDOG RESET THE ROCKET'S CONTROLS, AND THAT WAS THE LAST WE SAW OF THE THREE NAUGHTY DOGGIES.
SHVOOOM!
MANY YEARS FROM NOW, THEY'LL LAND ON A PLANET IN THE SIRIUS SYSTEM, WHERE EVERYONE HAS TO ACT SERIOUS ALL THE TIME AND THEY NEVER HAVE ANY FUN. THE END!
"SIRIUS" ISN'T SPELT THE SAME AS "SERIOUS." YOU MADE THAT UP, UNCLE STREAKY!
TELL US ANOTHER STORY! PLEASE!
PLEASE! PLEASE! PLEASE!
"SIGH!" THE PRICE OF BEING A SUPERHERO IS HIGH. BUT SOMEBODY'S GOT TO DO IT!
The END

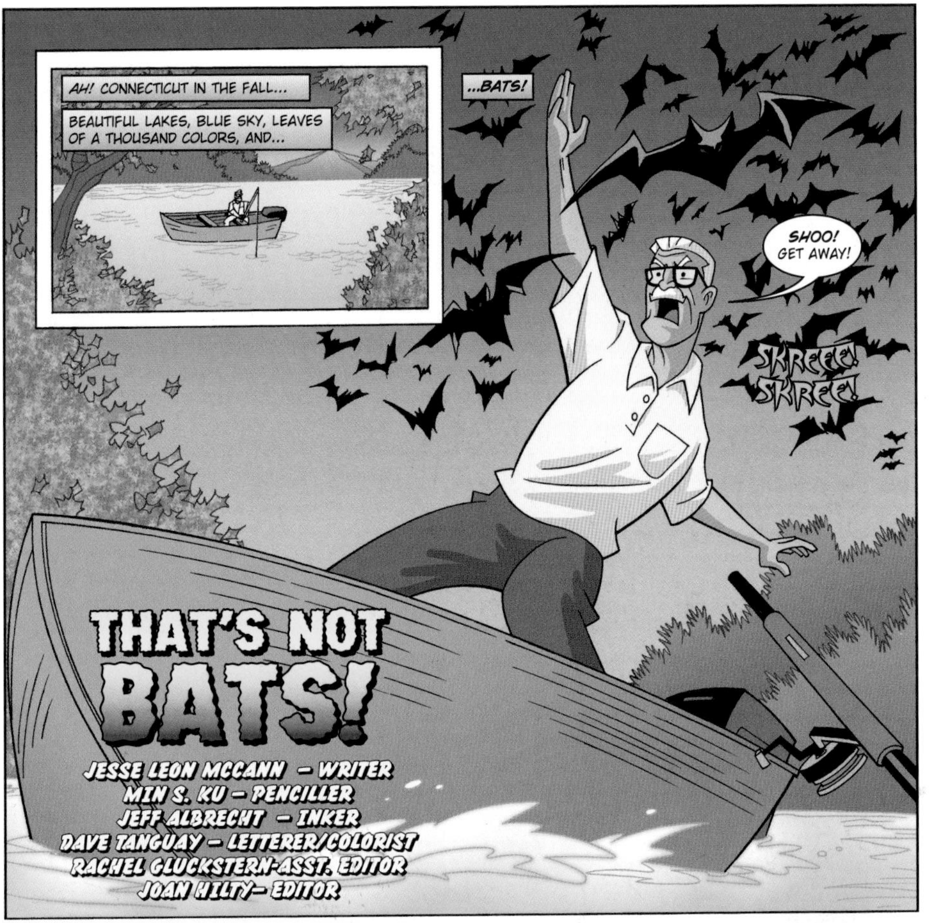
AH! CONNECTICUT IN THE FALL...
BEAUTIFUL LAKES, BLUE SKY, LEAVES OF A THOUSAND COLORS, AND...
...BATS!
SHOO! GET AWAY!
SKREEE! SKREEE!
THAT'S NOT BATS!
JESSE LEON MCCANN - WRITER
MIN S. KU - PENCILLER
JEFF ALBRECHT - INKER
DAVE TANGUAY - LETTERER/COLORIST
RACHEL GLUCKSTERN-ASST. EDITOR
JOAN HILTY- EDITOR

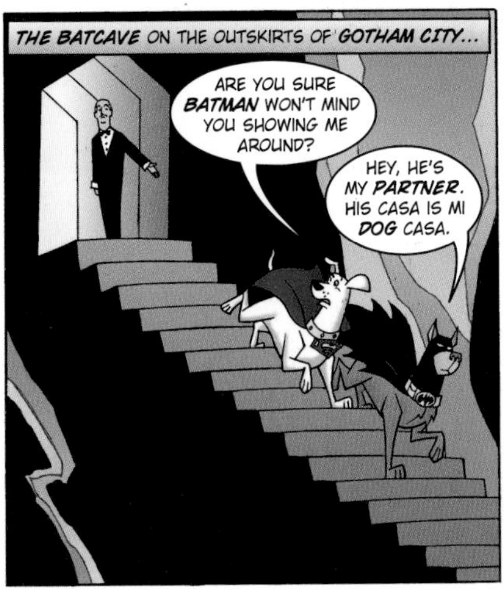
THE BATCAVE ON THE OUTSKIRTS OF GOTHAM CITY...
ARE YOU SURE BATMAN WON'T MIND YOU SHOWING ME AROUND?
HEY, HE'S MY PARTNER. HIS CASA IS MI DOG CASA.

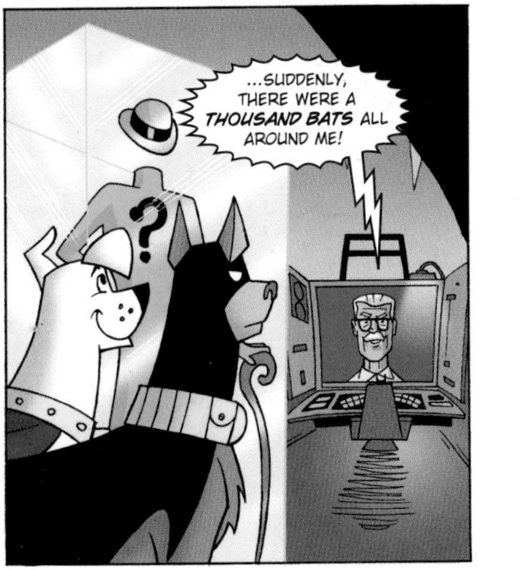
...SUDDENLY, THERE WERE A THOUSAND BATS ALL AROUND ME!

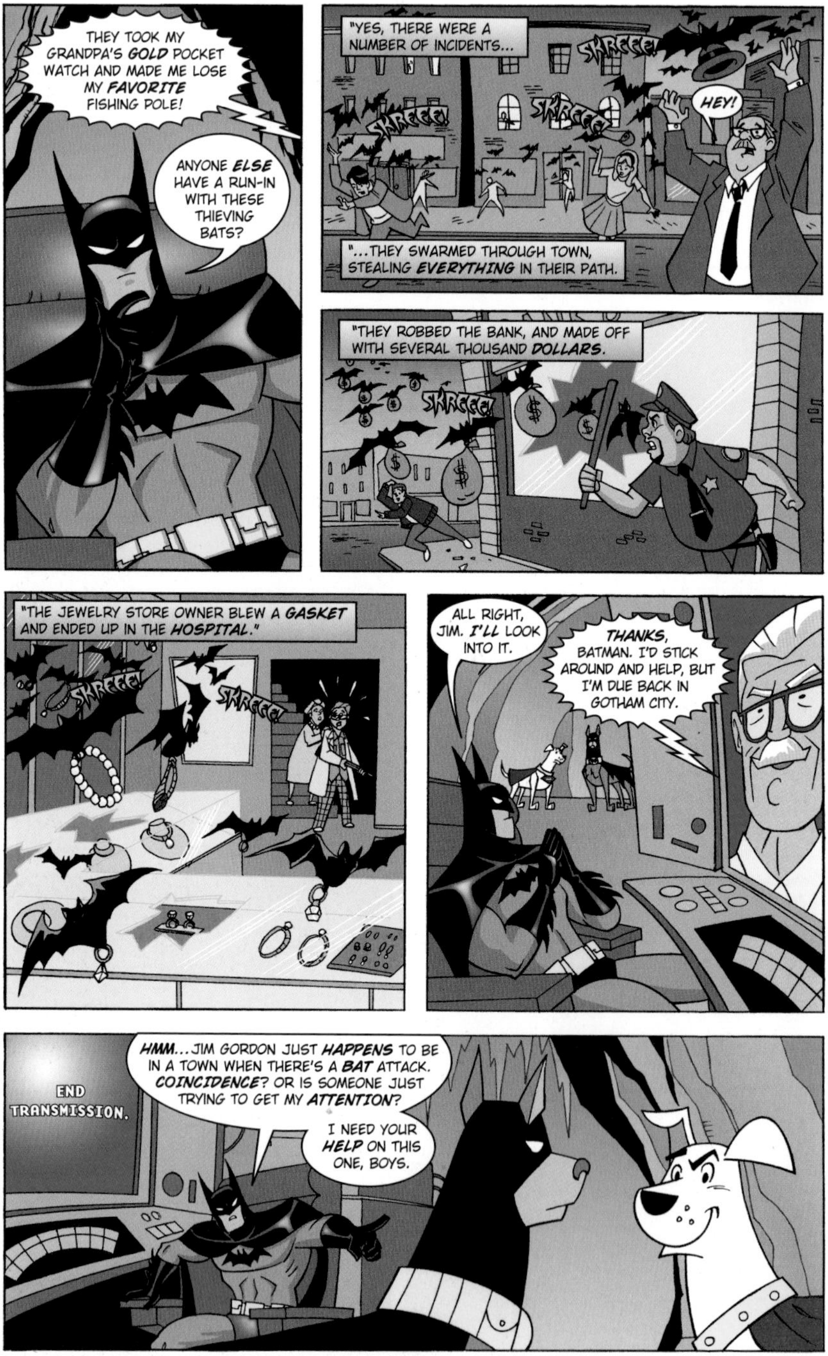
THEY TOOK MY GRANDPA'S **GOLD** POCKET WATCH AND MADE ME LOSE MY **FAVORITE** FISHING POLE!
ANYONE **ELSE** HAVE A RUN-IN WITH THESE THIEVING BATS?
"YES, THERE WERE A NUMBER OF INCIDENTS...
SKREEE!
SKREEE!
SKREEE!
HEY!
"...THEY SWARMED THROUGH TOWN, STEALING **EVERYTHING** IN THEIR PATH.
"THEY ROBBED THE BANK, AND MADE OFF WITH SEVERAL THOUSAND **DOLLARS**.
SKREEE!
"THE JEWELRY STORE OWNER BLEW A **GASKET** AND ENDED UP IN THE **HOSPITAL**."
SKREEE!
SKREEE!
ALL RIGHT, JIM. **I'LL** LOOK INTO IT.
THANKS, BATMAN. I'D STICK AROUND AND HELP, BUT I'M DUE BACK IN GOTHAM CITY.
END TRANSMISSION.
HMM... JIM GORDON JUST **HAPPENS** TO BE IN A TOWN WHEN THERE'S A **BAT** ATTACK. **COINCIDENCE**? OR IS SOMEONE JUST TRYING TO GET MY **ATTENTION**?
I NEED YOUR **HELP** ON THIS ONE, BOYS.

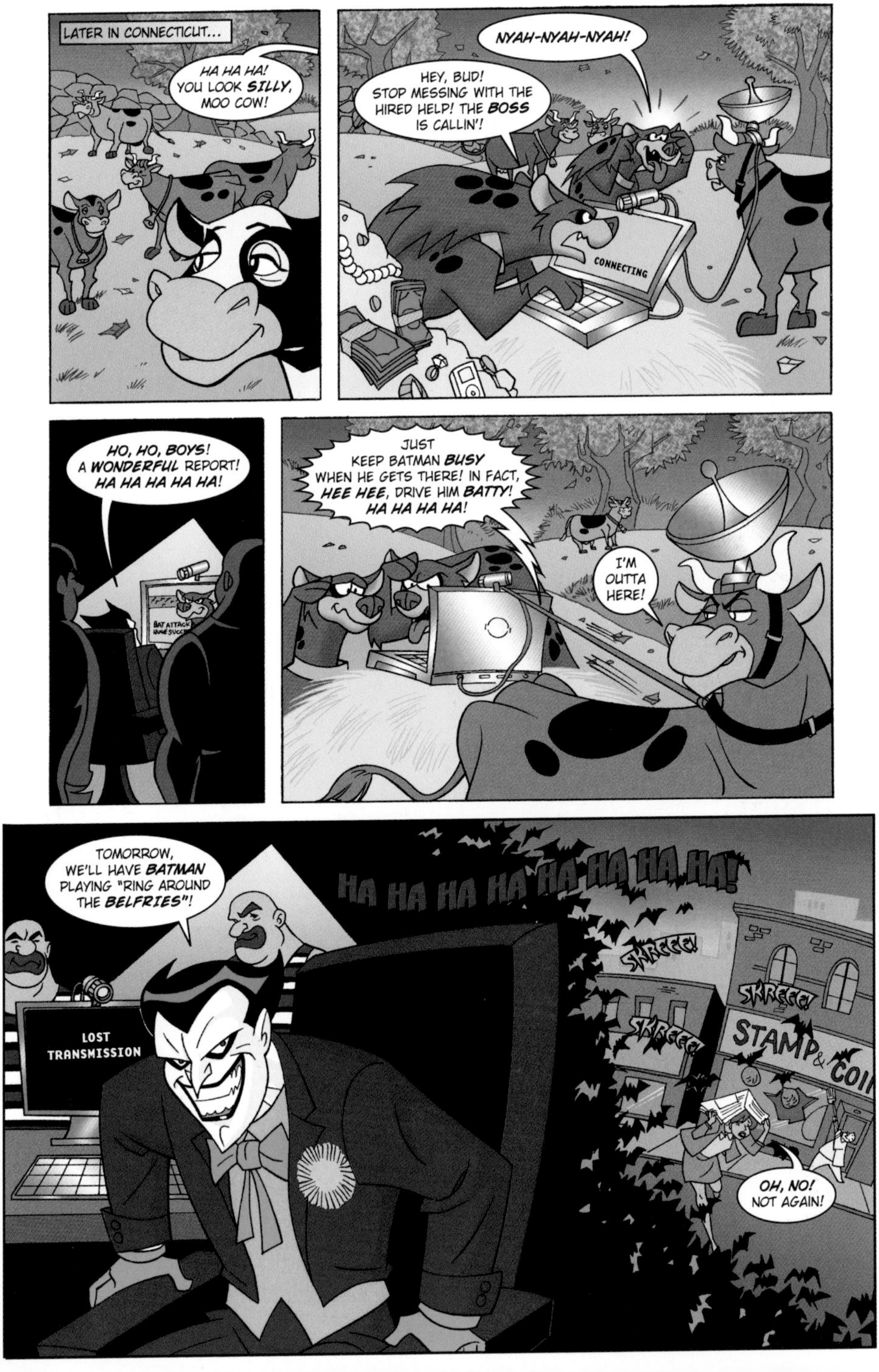
LATER IN CONNECTICUT...
HA HA HA! YOU LOOK SILLY, MOO COW!
NYAH-NYAH-NYAH!
HEY, BUD! STOP MESSING WITH THE HIRED HELP! THE BOSS IS CALLIN'!
CONNECTING
HO, HO, BOYS! A WONDERFUL REPORT! HA HA HA HA HA!
JUST KEEP BATMAN BUSY WHEN HE GETS THERE! IN FACT, HEE HEE, DRIVE HIM BATTY! HA HA HA HA!
I'M OUTTA HERE!
TOMORROW, WE'LL HAVE BATMAN PLAYING "RING AROUND THE BELFRIES"!
HA HA HA HA HA HA HA HA!
LOST TRANSMISSION
SKREEE!
SKREEE!
SKREEE!
STAMP & COIN
OH, NO! NOT AGAIN!

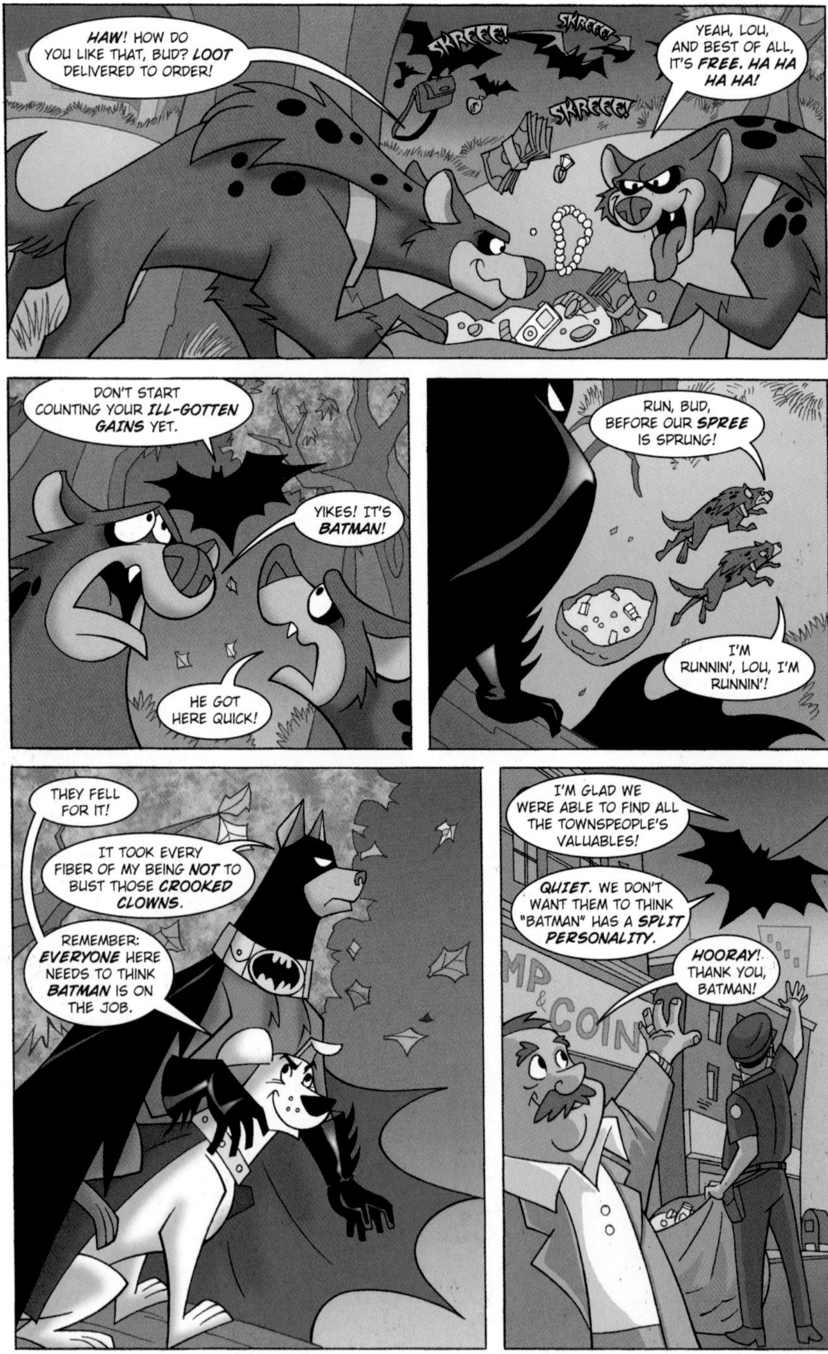
HAW! HOW DO YOU LIKE THAT, BUD? LOOT DELIVERED TO ORDER!
SKREEE!
SKREEE!
SKREEE!
YEAH, LOU, AND BEST OF ALL, IT'S FREE. HA HA HA HA!
DON'T START COUNTING YOUR ILL-GOTTEN GAINS YET.
YIKES! IT'S BATMAN!
HE GOT HERE QUICK!
RUN, BUD, BEFORE OUR SPREE IS SPRUNG!
I'M RUNNIN', LOU, I'M RUNNIN'!
THEY FELL FOR IT!
IT TOOK EVERY FIBER OF MY BEING NOT TO BUST THOSE CROOKED CLOWNS.
REMEMBER: EVERYONE HERE NEEDS TO THINK BATMAN IS ON THE JOB.
I'M GLAD WE WERE ABLE TO FIND ALL THE TOWNSPEOPLE'S VALUABLES!
QUIET. WE DON'T WANT THEM TO THINK "BATMAN" HAS A SPLIT PERSONALITY.
HOORAY! THANK YOU, BATMAN!
MP & COIN

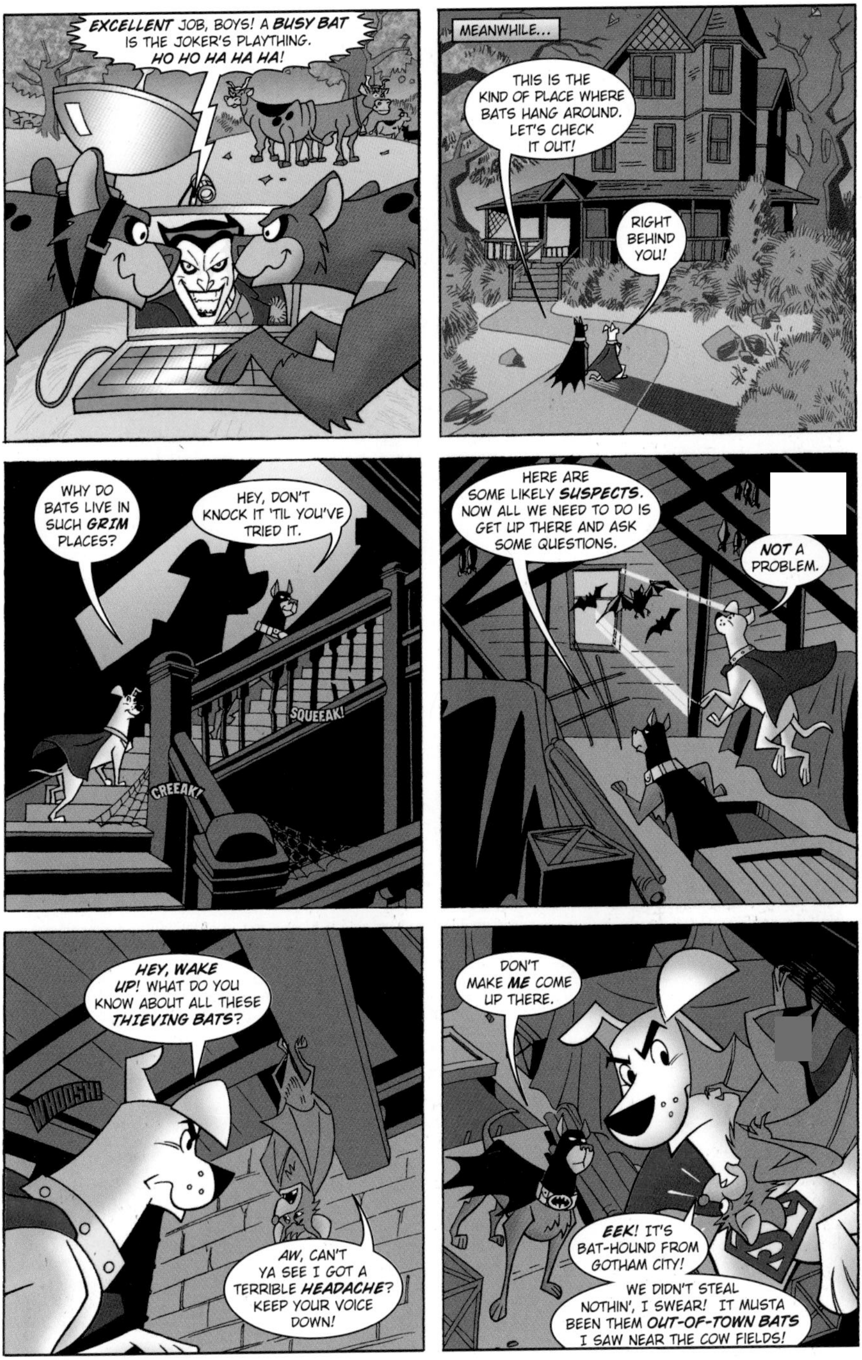

EXCELLENT JOB, BOYS! A BUSY BAT IS THE JOKER'S PLAYTHING. HO HO HA HA HA!
MEANWHILE...
THIS IS THE KIND OF PLACE WHERE BATS HANG AROUND. LET'S CHECK IT OUT!
RIGHT BEHIND YOU!
WHY DO BATS LIVE IN SUCH GRIM PLACES?
HEY, DON'T KNOCK IT 'TIL YOU'VE TRIED IT.
SQUEEAK!
CREEAK!
HERE ARE SOME LIKELY SUSPECTS. NOW ALL WE NEED TO DO IS GET UP THERE AND ASK SOME QUESTIONS.
NOT A PROBLEM.
HEY, WAKE UP! WHAT DO YOU KNOW ABOUT ALL THESE THIEVING BATS?
WHOOSH!
AW, CAN'T YA SEE I GOT A TERRIBLE HEADACHE? KEEP YOUR VOICE DOWN!
DON'T MAKE ME COME UP THERE.
EEK! IT'S BAT-HOUND FROM GOTHAM CITY!
WE DIDN'T STEAL NOTHIN', I SWEAR! IT MUSTA BEEN THEM OUT-OF-TOWN BATS I SAW NEAR THE COW FIELDS!

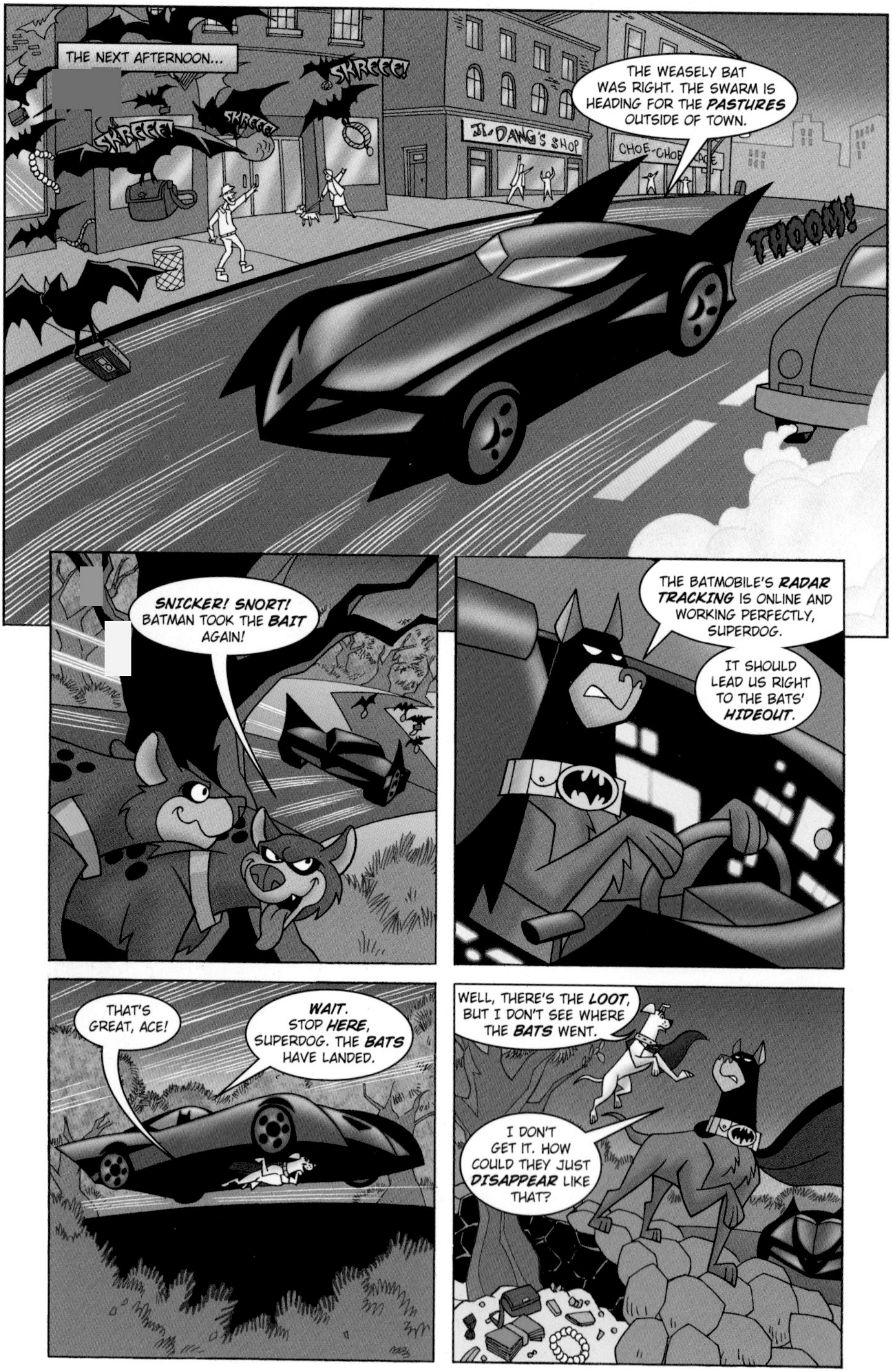
THE NEXT AFTERNOON...
SKREEE!
SKREEE!
THE WEASELY BAT WAS RIGHT. THE SWARM IS HEADING FOR THE PASTURES OUTSIDE OF TOWN.
THOOM!
SNICKER! SNORT! BATMAN TOOK THE BAIT AGAIN!
THE BATMOBILE'S RADAR TRACKING IS ONLINE AND WORKING PERFECTLY, SUPERDOG.
IT SHOULD LEAD US RIGHT TO THE BATS' HIDEOUT.
THAT'S GREAT, ACE!
WAIT. STOP HERE, SUPERDOG. THE BATS HAVE LANDED.
WELL, THERE'S THE LOOT, BUT I DON'T SEE WHERE THE BATS WENT.
I DON'T GET IT. HOW COULD THEY JUST DISAPPEAR LIKE THAT?

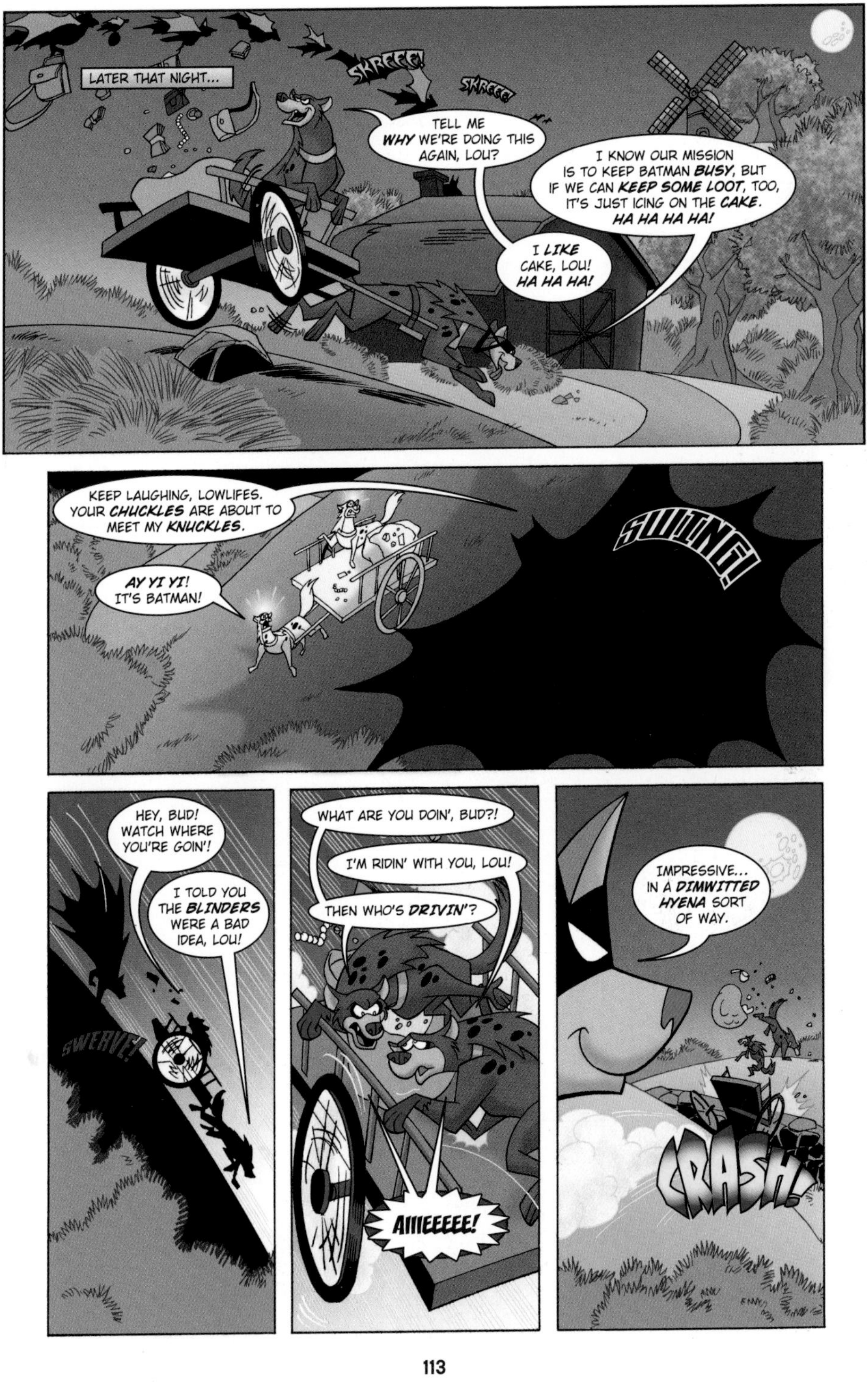
LATER THAT NIGHT...
SKREEE!
SKREEE!
TELL ME WHY WE'RE DOING THIS AGAIN, LOU?
I KNOW OUR MISSION IS TO KEEP BATMAN BUSY, BUT IF WE CAN KEEP SOME LOOT, TOO, IT'S JUST ICING ON THE CAKE. HA HA HA HA!
I LIKE CAKE, LOU! HA HA HA!
KEEP LAUGHING, LOWLIFES. YOUR CHUCKLES ARE ABOUT TO MEET MY KNUCKLES.
SWING!
AY YI YI! IT'S BATMAN!
HEY, BUD! WATCH WHERE YOU'RE GOIN'!
I TOLD YOU THE BLINDERS WERE A BAD IDEA, LOU!
SWERVE!
WHAT ARE YOU DOIN', BUD?!
I'M RIDIN' WITH YOU, LOU!
THEN WHO'S DRIVIN'?
AIIIEEEEE!
IMPRESSIVE... IN A DIMWITTED HYENA SORT OF WAY.
CRASH!

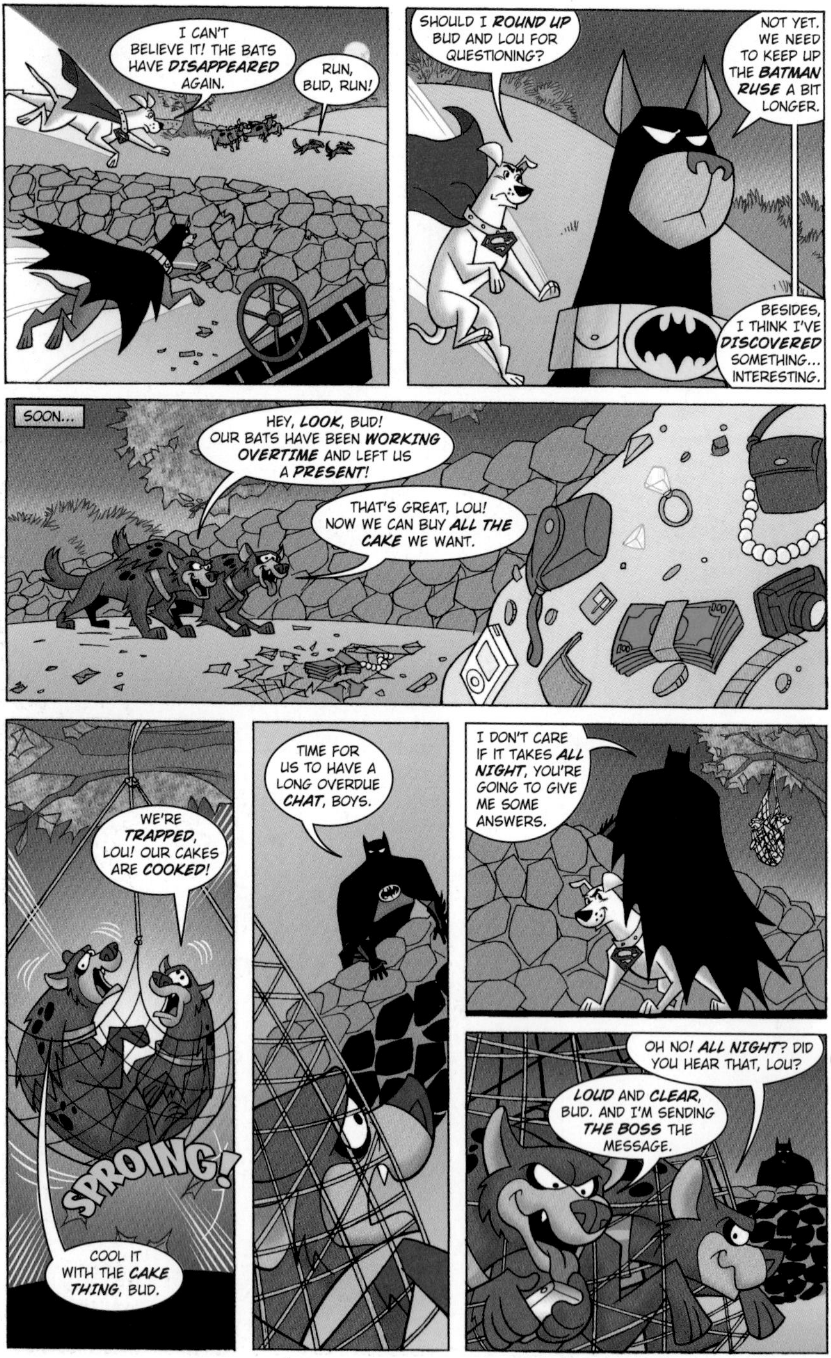
I CAN'T BELIEVE IT! THE BATS HAVE DISAPPEARED AGAIN.
RUN, BUD, RUN!
SHOULD I ROUND UP BUD AND LOU FOR QUESTIONING?
NOT YET. WE NEED TO KEEP UP THE BATMAN RUSE A BIT LONGER.
BESIDES, I THINK I'VE DISCOVERED SOMETHING... INTERESTING.
SOON...
HEY, LOOK, BUD! OUR BATS HAVE BEEN WORKING OVERTIME AND LEFT US A PRESENT!
THAT'S GREAT, LOU! NOW WE CAN BUY ALL THE CAKE WE WANT.
WE'RE TRAPPED, LOU! OUR CAKES ARE COOKED!
SPROING!
COOL IT WITH THE CAKE THING, BUD.
TIME FOR US TO HAVE A LONG OVERDUE CHAT, BOYS.
I DON'T CARE IF IT TAKES ALL NIGHT, YOU'RE GOING TO GIVE ME SOME ANSWERS.
OH NO! ALL NIGHT? DID YOU HEAR THAT, LOU?
LOUD AND CLEAR, BUD. AND I'M SENDING THE BOSS THE MESSAGE.

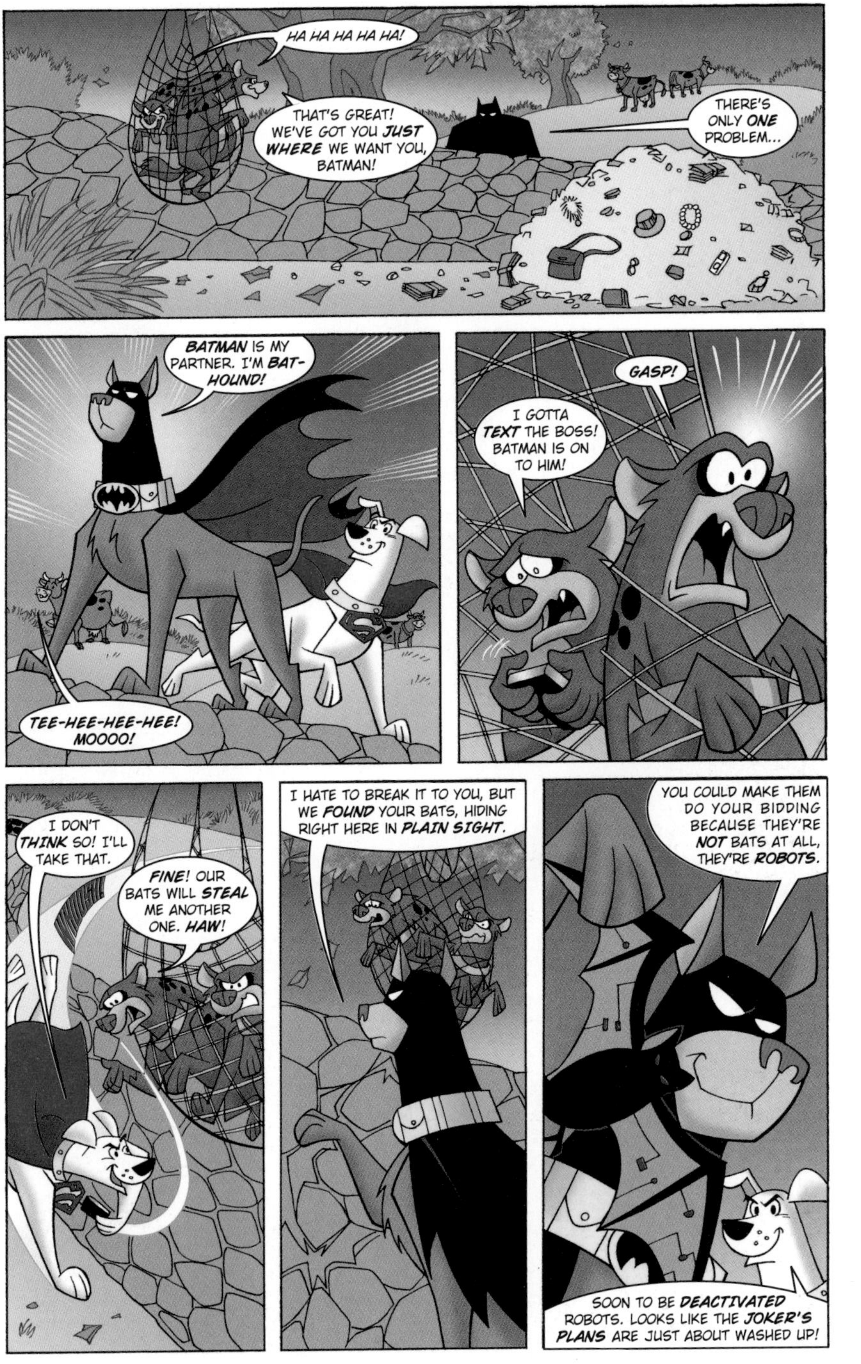
HA HA HA HA HA!
THAT'S GREAT! WE'VE GOT YOU JUST WHERE WE WANT YOU, BATMAN!
THERE'S ONLY ONE PROBLEM...
BATMAN IS MY PARTNER. I'M BAT-HOUND!
TEE-HEE-HEE-HEE! MOOOO!
GASP!
I GOTTA TEXT THE BOSS! BATMAN IS ON TO HIM!
I DON'T THINK SO! I'LL TAKE THAT.
FINE! OUR BATS WILL STEAL ME ANOTHER ONE. HAW!
I HATE TO BREAK IT TO YOU, BUT WE FOUND YOUR BATS, HIDING RIGHT HERE IN PLAIN SIGHT.
YOU COULD MAKE THEM DO YOUR BIDDING BECAUSE THEY'RE NOT BATS AT ALL, THEY'RE ROBOTS.
SOON TO BE DEACTIVATED ROBOTS. LOOKS LIKE THE JOKER'S PLANS ARE JUST ABOUT WASHED UP!

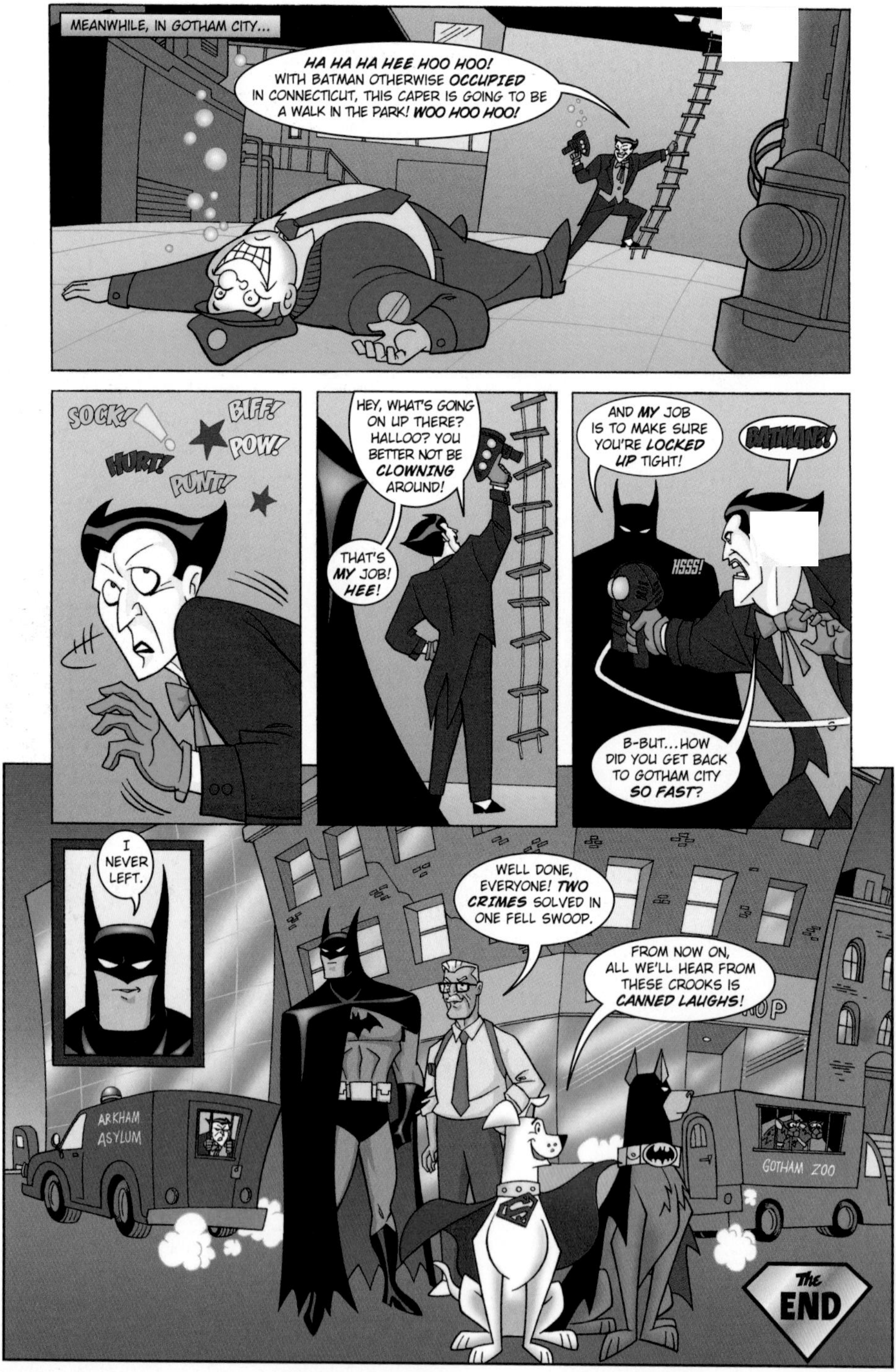
MEANWHILE, IN GOTHAM CITY...
HA HA HA HEE HOO HOO! WITH BATMAN OTHERWISE OCCUPIED IN CONNECTICUT, THIS CAPER IS GOING TO BE A WALK IN THE PARK! WOO HOO HOO!
SOCK!
BIFF!
POW!
HURT!
PUNT!
HEY, WHAT'S GOING ON UP THERE? HALLOO? YOU BETTER NOT BE CLOWNING AROUND!
THAT'S MY JOB! HEE!
AND MY JOB IS TO MAKE SURE YOU'RE LOCKED UP TIGHT!
BATMAN?!
HSSS!
B-BUT...HOW DID YOU GET BACK TO GOTHAM CITY SO FAST?
I NEVER LEFT.
WELL DONE, EVERYONE! TWO CRIMES SOLVED IN ONE FELL SWOOP.
FROM NOW ON, ALL WE'LL HEAR FROM THESE CROOKS IS CANNED LAUGHS!
ARKHAM ASYLUM
GOTHAM ZOO
The END

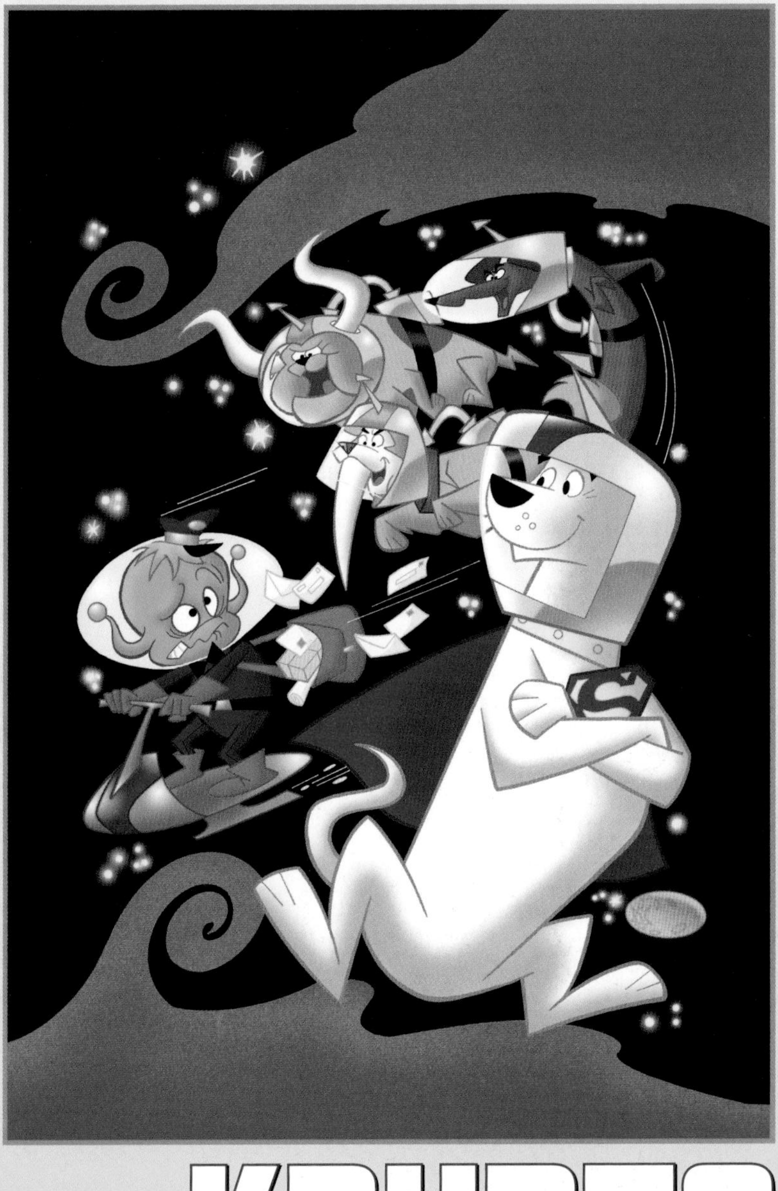

KRYPTO THE SUPERDOG

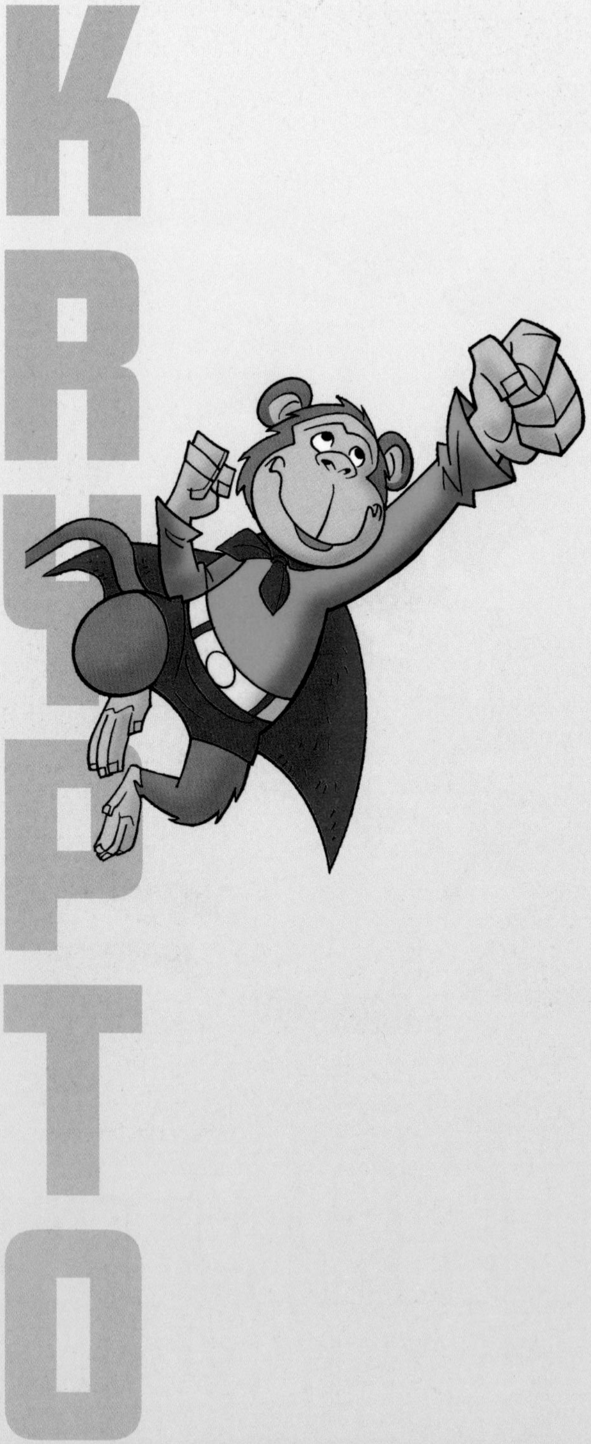

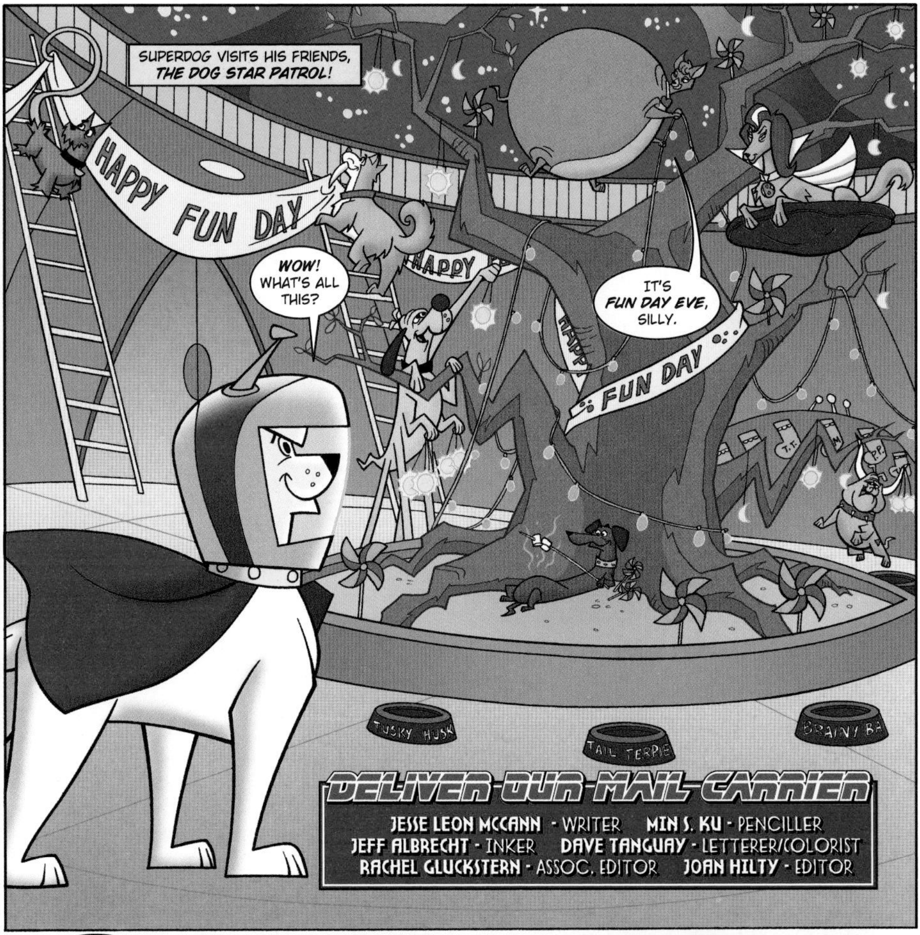
SUPERDOG VISITS HIS FRIENDS, THE DOG STAR PATROL!
HAPPY FUN DAY
WOW! WHAT'S ALL THIS?
IT'S FUN DAY EVE, SILLY.
TUSKY HUSK
TAIL TERRIE
BRAINY BA
DELIVER OUR MAIL CARRIER
JESSE LEON MCCANN - WRITER MIN S. KU - PENCILLER
JEFF ALBRECHT - INKER DAVE TANGUAY - LETTERER/COLORIST
RACHEL GLUCKSTERN - ASSOC. EDITOR JOAN HILTY - EDITOR

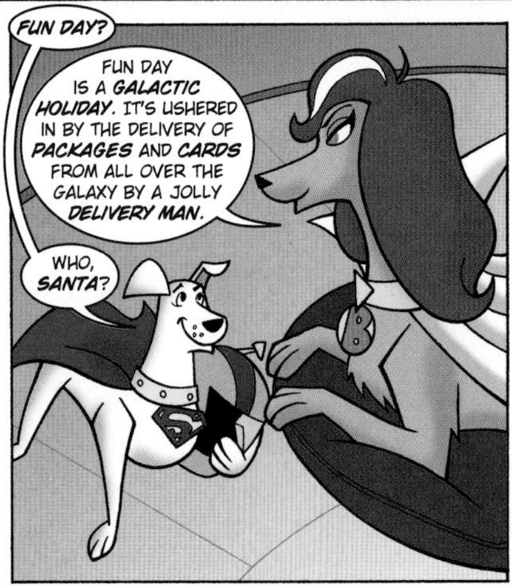
FUN DAY?
FUN DAY IS A GALACTIC HOLIDAY. IT'S USHERED IN BY THE DELIVERY OF PACKAGES AND CARDS FROM ALL OVER THE GALAXY BY A JOLLY DELIVERY MAN.
WHO, SANTA?

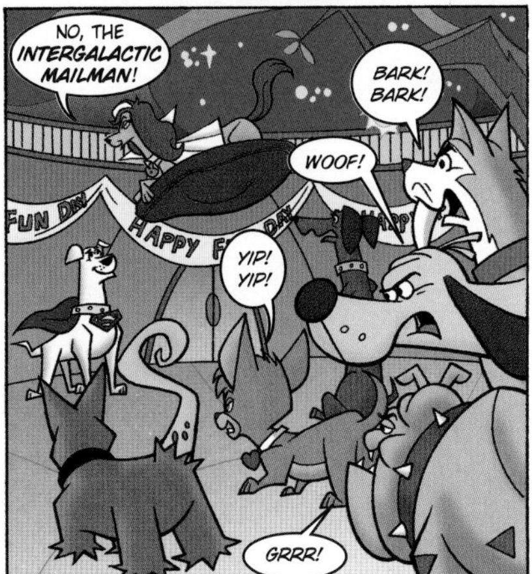
NO, THE INTERGALACTIC MAILMAN!
BARK! BARK!
WOOF!
YIP! YIP!
GRRR!

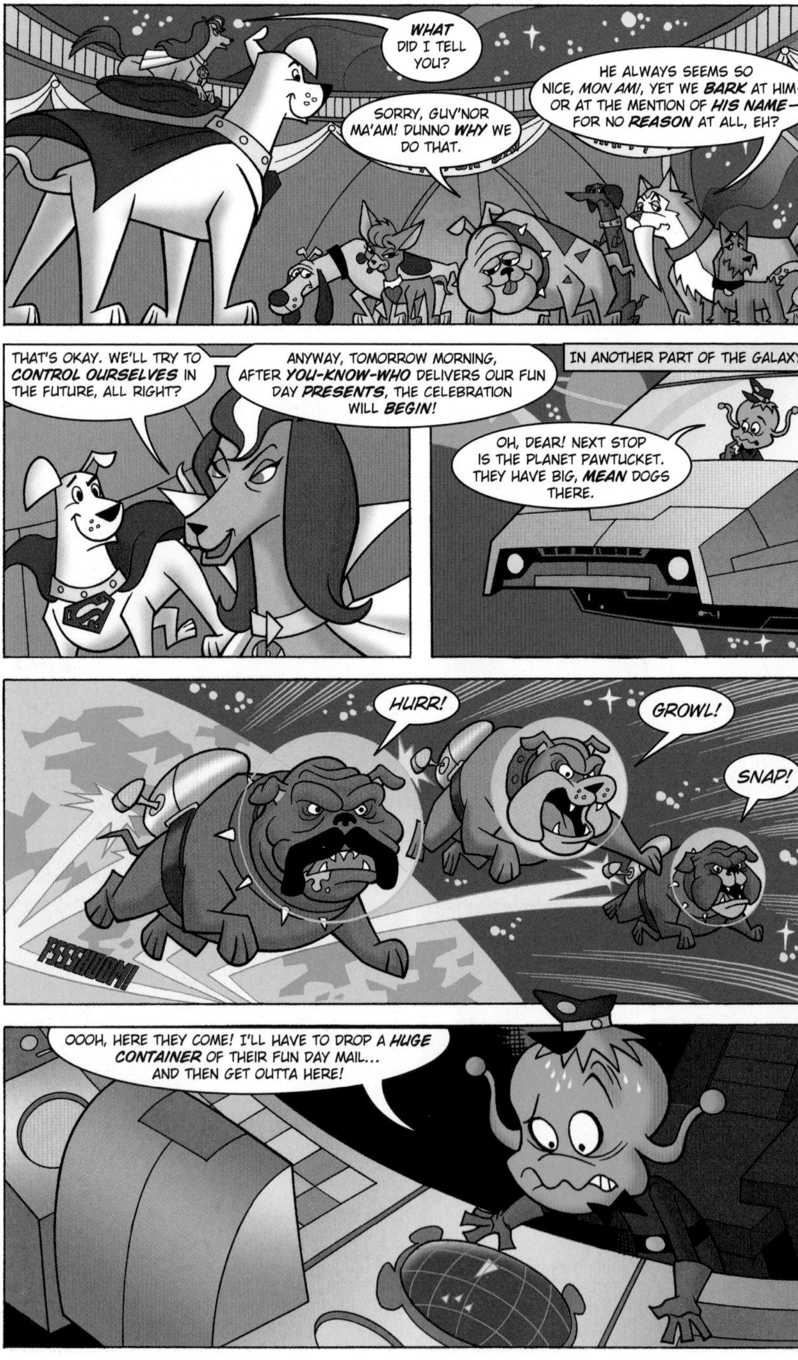
WHAT DID I TELL YOU?
SORRY, GUV'NOR MA'AM! DUNNO WHY WE DO THAT.
HE ALWAYS SEEMS SO NICE, MON AMI, YET WE BARK AT HIM— OR AT THE MENTION OF HIS NAME— FOR NO REASON AT ALL, EH?
THAT'S OKAY. WE'LL TRY TO CONTROL OURSELVES IN THE FUTURE, ALL RIGHT?
ANYWAY, TOMORROW MORNING, AFTER YOU-KNOW-WHO DELIVERS OUR FUN DAY PRESENTS, THE CELEBRATION WILL BEGIN!
IN ANOTHER PART OF THE GALAXY...
OH, DEAR! NEXT STOP IS THE PLANET PAWTUCKET. THEY HAVE BIG, MEAN DOGS THERE.
HURR!
GROWL!
SNAP!
FSSSHOOM!
OOOH, HERE THEY COME! I'LL HAVE TO DROP A HUGE CONTAINER OF THEIR FUN DAY MAIL... AND THEN GET OUTTA HERE!

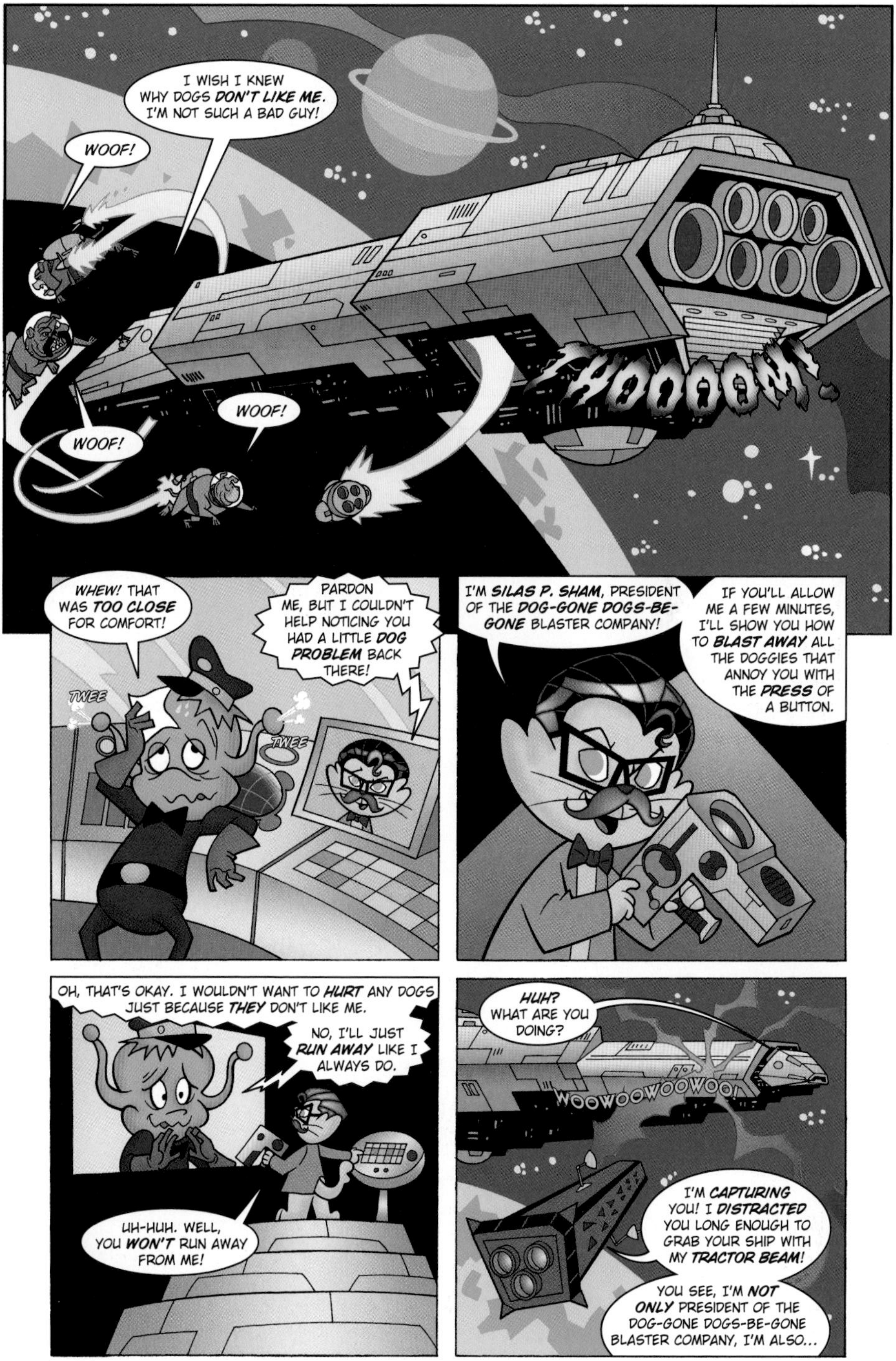
I WISH I KNEW WHY DOGS DON'T LIKE ME. I'M NOT SUCH A BAD GUY!
WOOF!
WOOF!
WOOF!
WHOOOOM!
WHEW! THAT WAS TOO CLOSE FOR COMFORT!
PARDON ME, BUT I COULDN'T HELP NOTICING YOU HAD A LITTLE DOG PROBLEM BACK THERE!
TWEE
TWEE
I'M SILAS P. SHAM, PRESIDENT OF THE DOG-GONE DOGS-BE-GONE BLASTER COMPANY!
IF YOU'LL ALLOW ME A FEW MINUTES, I'LL SHOW YOU HOW TO BLAST AWAY ALL THE DOGGIES THAT ANNOY YOU WITH THE PRESS OF A BUTTON.
OH, THAT'S OKAY. I WOULDN'T WANT TO HURT ANY DOGS JUST BECAUSE THEY DON'T LIKE ME.
NO, I'LL JUST RUN AWAY LIKE I ALWAYS DO.
UH-HUH. WELL, YOU WON'T RUN AWAY FROM ME!
HUH? WHAT ARE YOU DOING?
WOOWOOWOOWOO!
I'M CAPTURING YOU! I DISTRACTED YOU LONG ENOUGH TO GRAB YOUR SHIP WITH MY TRACTOR BEAM!
YOU SEE, I'M NOT ONLY PRESIDENT OF THE DOG-GONE DOGS-BE-GONE BLASTER COMPANY, I'M ALSO...

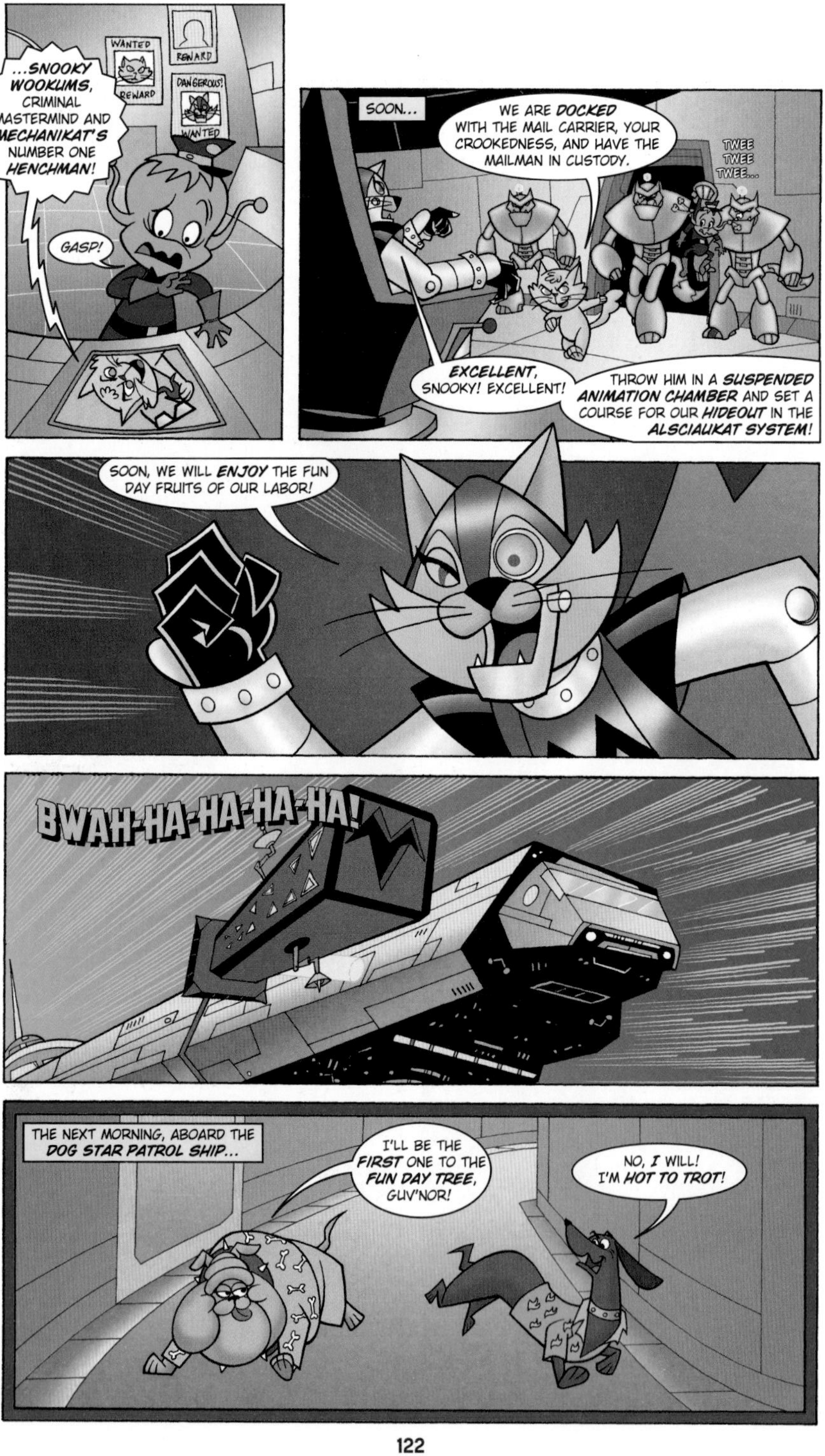
WANTED
REWARD
REWARD
DANGEROUS!
WANTED
...SNOOKY WOOKUMS, CRIMINAL MASTERMIND AND MECHANIKAT'S NUMBER ONE HENCHMAN!
GASP!
SOON...
WE ARE DOCKED WITH THE MAIL CARRIER, YOUR CROOKEDNESS, AND HAVE THE MAILMAN IN CUSTODY.
TWEE TWEE TWEE...
EXCELLENT, SNOOKY! EXCELLENT!
THROW HIM IN A SUSPENDED ANIMATION CHAMBER AND SET A COURSE FOR OUR HIDEOUT IN THE ALSCIAUKAT SYSTEM!
SOON, WE WILL ENJOY THE FUN DAY FRUITS OF OUR LABOR!
BWAH-HA-HA-HA-HA!
THE NEXT MORNING, ABOARD THE DOG STAR PATROL SHIP...
I'LL BE THE FIRST ONE TO THE FUN DAY TREE, GUV'NOR!
NO, I WILL! I'M HOT TO TROT!

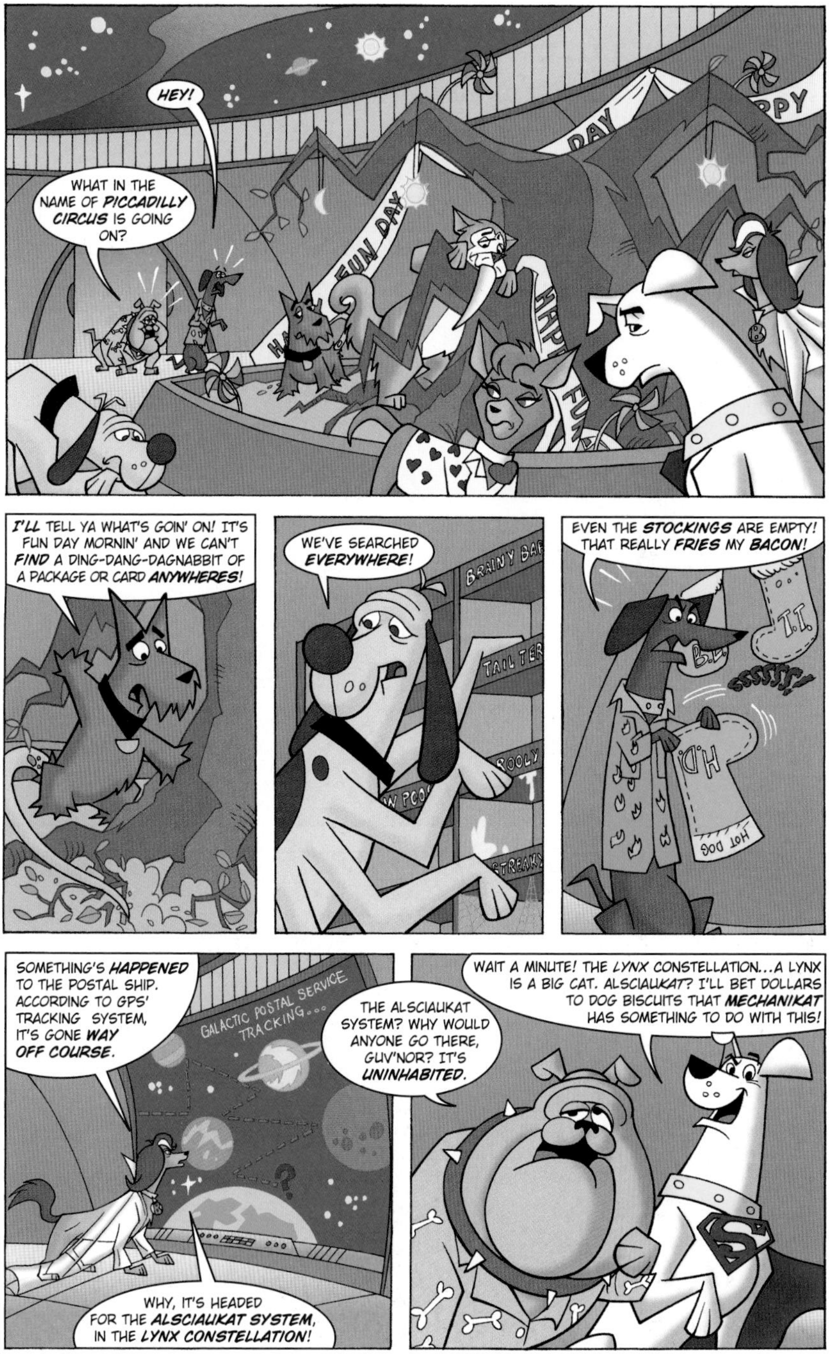
HEY!
WHAT IN THE NAME OF *PICCADILLY CIRCUS* IS GOING ON?
HAPPY FUN DAY
I'LL TELL YA WHAT'S GOIN' ON! IT'S FUN DAY MORNIN' AND WE CAN'T *FIND* A DING-DANG-DAGNABBIT OF A PACKAGE OR CARD *ANYWHERES*!
WE'VE SEARCHED *EVERYWHERE*!
EVEN THE *STOCKINGS* ARE EMPTY! THAT REALLY *FRIES* MY *BACON*!
SSSSSS!
SOMETHING'S *HAPPENED* TO THE POSTAL SHIP. ACCORDING TO GPS' TRACKING SYSTEM, IT'S GONE *WAY OFF COURSE*.
GALACTIC POSTAL SERVICE TRACKING...
WHY, IT'S HEADED FOR THE *ALSCIAUKAT SYSTEM*, IN THE *LYNX CONSTELLATION*!
THE ALSCIAUKAT SYSTEM? WHY WOULD ANYONE GO THERE, GUV'NOR? IT'S *UNINHABITED*.
WAIT A MINUTE! THE *LYNX* CONSTELLATION...A LYNX IS A BIG CAT. ALSCIAU*KAT*? I'LL BET DOLLARS TO DOG BISCUITS THAT *MECHANIKAT* HAS SOMETHING TO DO WITH THIS!

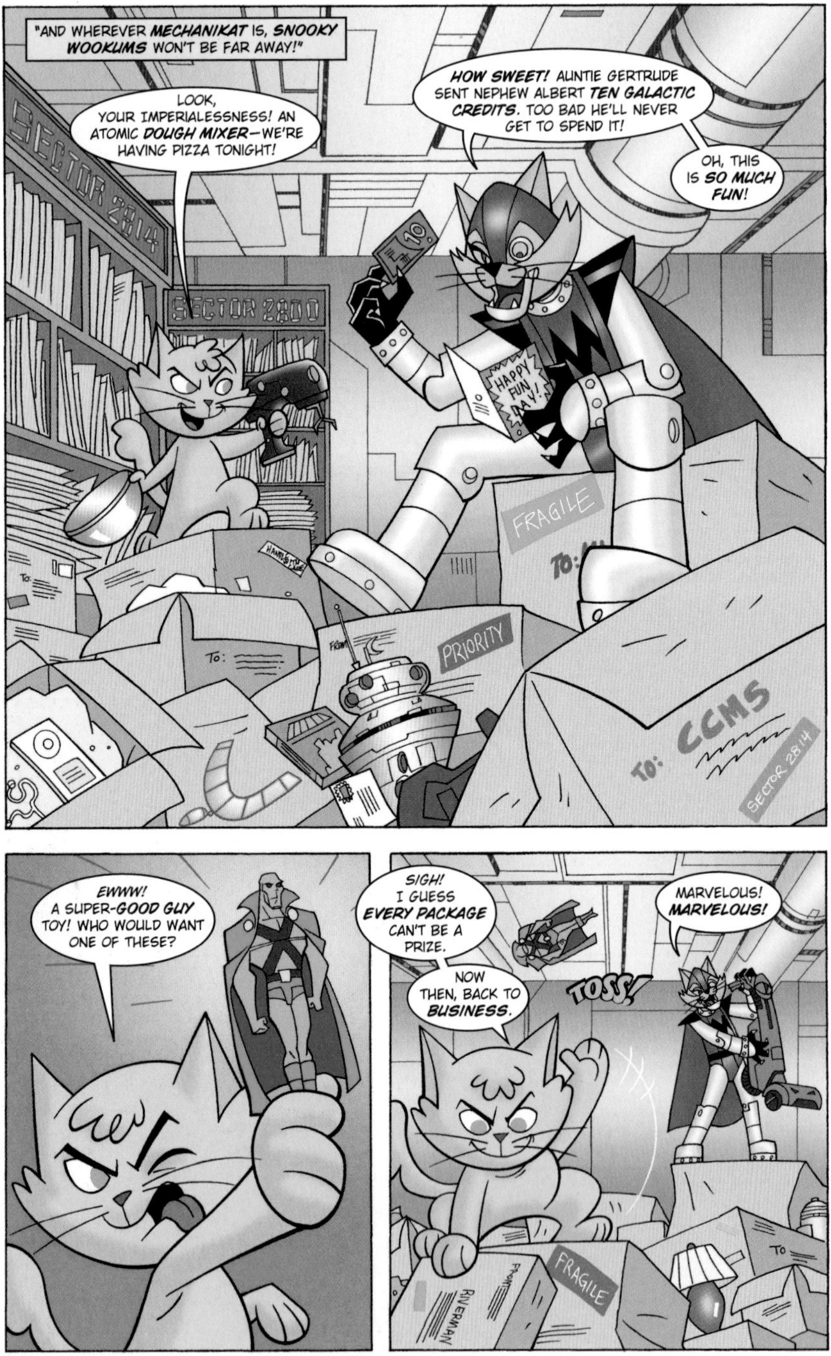
"AND WHEREVER MECHANIKAT IS, SNOOKY WOOKUMS WON'T BE FAR AWAY!"
LOOK, YOUR IMPERIALESSNESS! AN ATOMIC DOUGH MIXER—WE'RE HAVING PIZZA TONIGHT!
HOW SWEET! AUNTIE GERTRUDE SENT NEPHEW ALBERT TEN GALACTIC CREDITS. TOO BAD HE'LL NEVER GET TO SPEND IT!
OH, THIS IS SO MUCH FUN!
SECTOR 2814
SECTOR 2800
HAPPY FUN DAY!
FRAGILE
PRIORITY
TO: CCMS
SECTOR 2814
EWWW! A SUPER-GOOD GUY TOY! WHO WOULD WANT ONE OF THESE?
SIGH! I GUESS EVERY PACKAGE CAN'T BE A PRIZE.
NOW THEN, BACK TO BUSINESS.
MARVELOUS! MARVELOUS!
TOSS!
FRAGILE
RIVERMAN

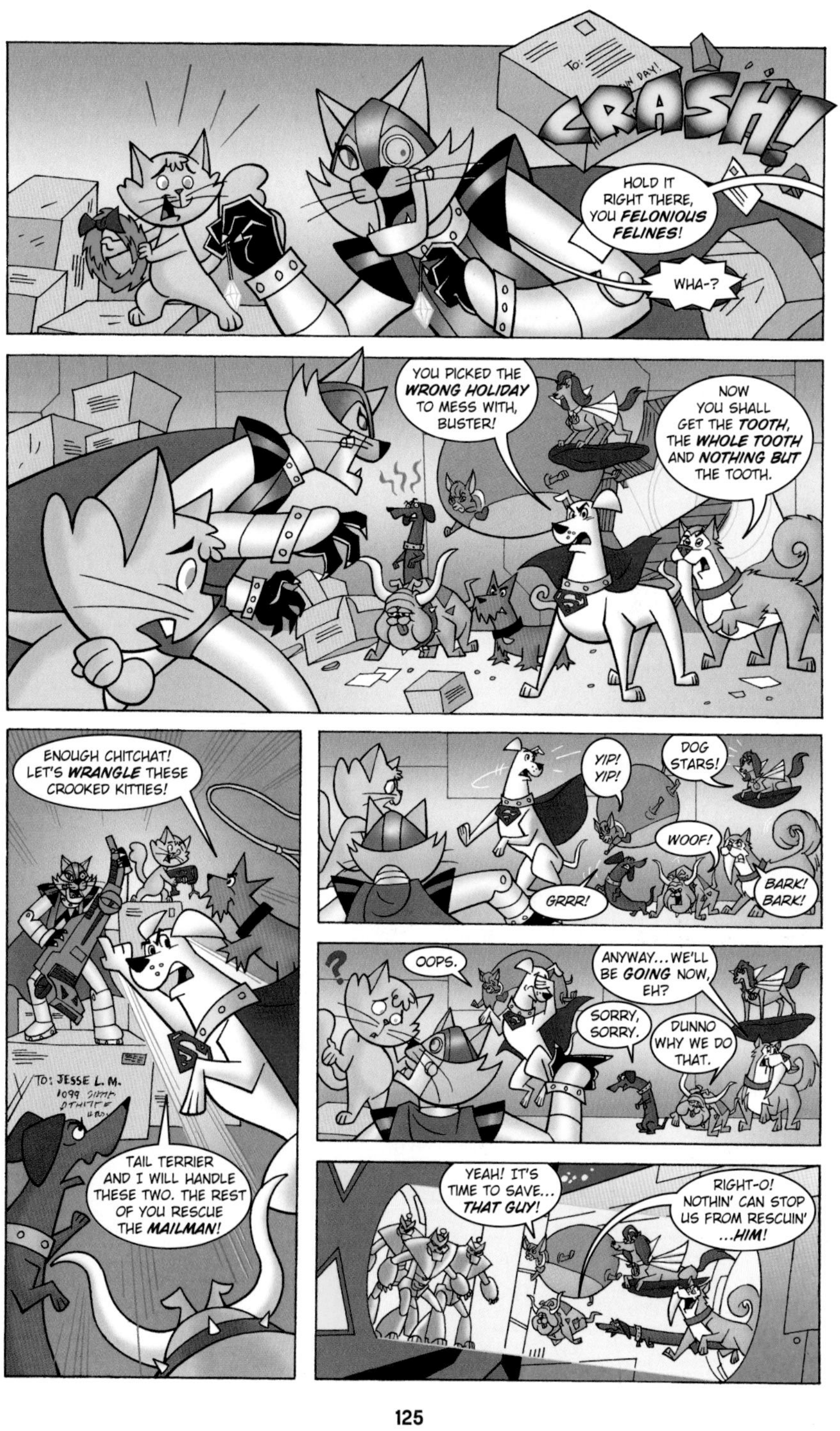
To:
CRASH!
HOLD IT RIGHT THERE, YOU FELONIOUS FELINES!
WHA-?
YOU PICKED THE WRONG HOLIDAY TO MESS WITH, BUSTER!
NOW YOU SHALL GET THE TOOTH, THE WHOLE TOOTH AND NOTHING BUT THE TOOTH.
ENOUGH CHITCHAT! LET'S WRANGLE THESE CROOKED KITTIES!
TO: JESSE L.M.
TAIL TERRIER AND I WILL HANDLE THESE TWO. THE REST OF YOU RESCUE THE MAILMAN!
YIP! YIP!
DOG STARS!
WOOF!
GRRR!
BARK! BARK!
OOPS.
ANYWAY... WE'LL BE GOING NOW, EH?
SORRY, SORRY.
DUNNO WHY WE DO THAT.
YEAH! IT'S TIME TO SAVE... THAT GUY!
RIGHT-O! NOTHIN' CAN STOP US FROM RESCUIN' ...HIM!

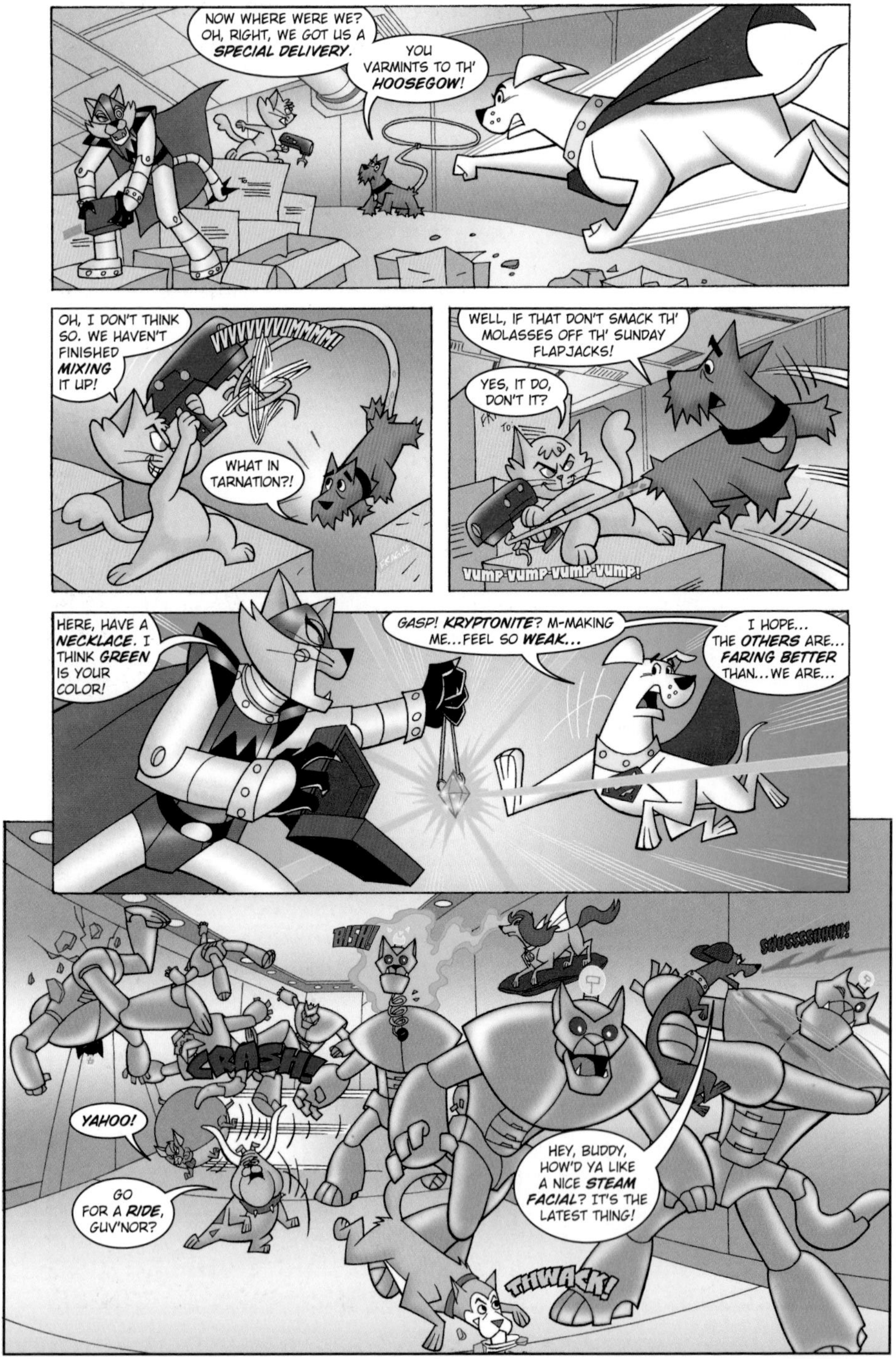
NOW WHERE WERE WE? OH, RIGHT, WE GOT US A SPECIAL DELIVERY.
YOU VARMINTS TO TH' HOOSEGOW!
OH, I DON'T THINK SO. WE HAVEN'T FINISHED MIXING IT UP!
VVVVVVVVUMMMM!
WHAT IN TARNATION?!
WELL, IF THAT DON'T SMACK TH' MOLASSES OFF TH' SUNDAY FLAPJACKS!
YES, IT DO, DON'T IT?
VUMP-VUMP-VUMP-VUMP!
HERE, HAVE A NECKLACE. I THINK GREEN IS YOUR COLOR!
GASP! KRYPTONITE? M-MAKING ME...FEEL SO WEAK...
I HOPE... THE OTHERS ARE... FARING BETTER THAN...WE ARE...
BISH!
SHUSSSSHHHH!
CRASH!
YAHOO!
GO FOR A RIDE, GUV'NOR?
HEY, BUDDY, HOW'D YA LIKE A NICE STEAM FACIAL? IT'S THE LATEST THING!
THWACK!

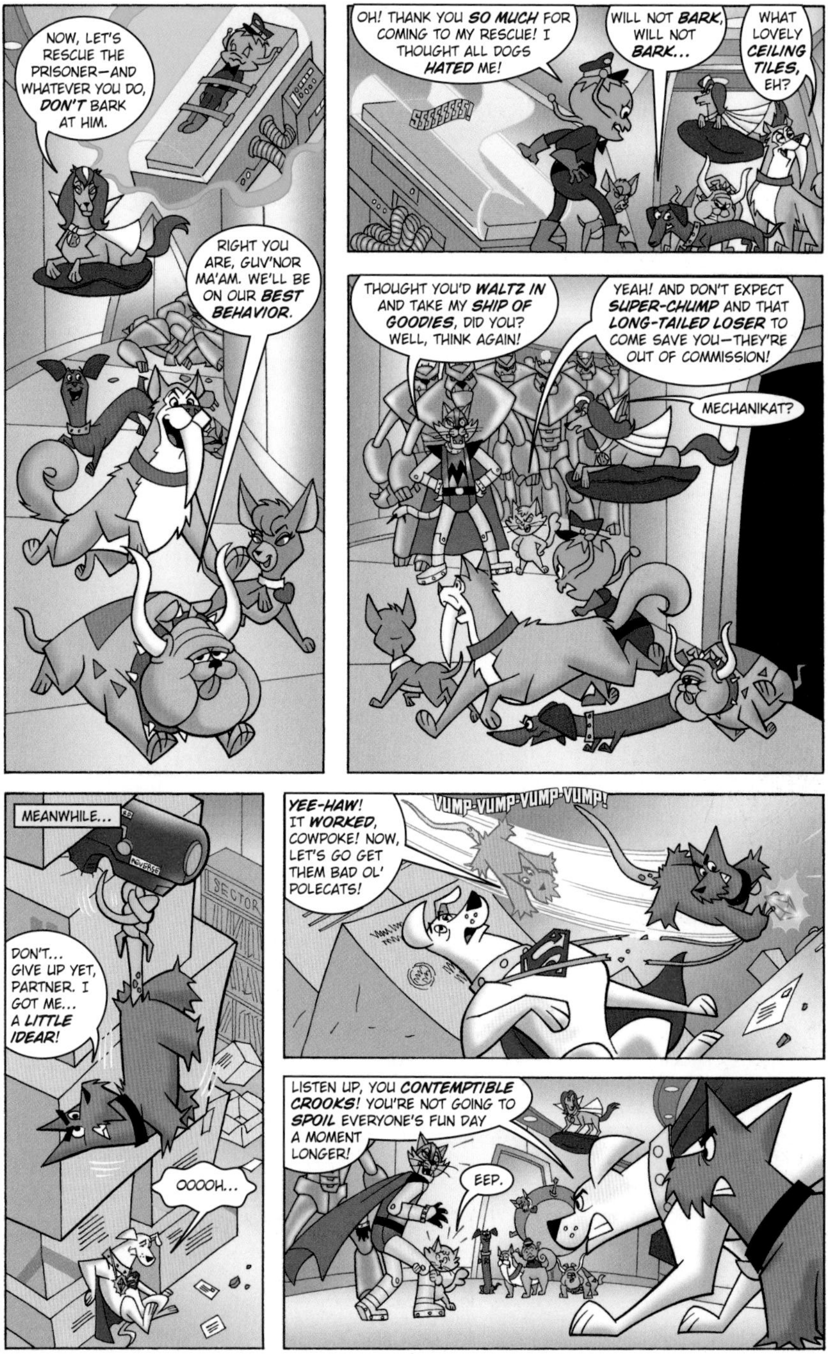
NOW, LET'S RESCUE THE PRISONER—AND WHATEVER YOU DO, ***DON'T*** BARK AT HIM.
RIGHT YOU ARE, GUV'NOR MA'AM. WE'LL BE ON OUR ***BEST BEHAVIOR***.
OH! THANK YOU ***SO MUCH*** FOR COMING TO MY RESCUE! I THOUGHT ALL DOGS ***HATED*** ME!
SSSSSSSS!
WILL NOT ***BARK***, WILL NOT ***BARK...***
WHAT LOVELY ***CEILING TILES***, EH?
THOUGHT YOU'D ***WALTZ IN*** AND TAKE MY ***SHIP OF GOODIES***, DID YOU? WELL, THINK AGAIN!
YEAH! AND DON'T EXPECT ***SUPER-CHUMP*** AND THAT ***LONG-TAILED LOSER*** TO COME SAVE YOU—THEY'RE OUT OF COMMISSION!
MECHANIKAT?
MEANWHILE...
DON'T... GIVE UP YET, PARTNER. I GOT ME... A ***LITTLE IDEAR***!
OOOOH...
YEE-HAW! IT ***WORKED***, COWPOKE! NOW, LET'S GO GET THEM BAD OL' POLECATS!
VUMP-VUMP-VUMP-VUMP!
LISTEN UP, YOU ***CONTEMPTIBLE CROOKS***! YOU'RE NOT GOING TO ***SPOIL*** EVERYONE'S FUN DAY A MOMENT LONGER!
EEP.

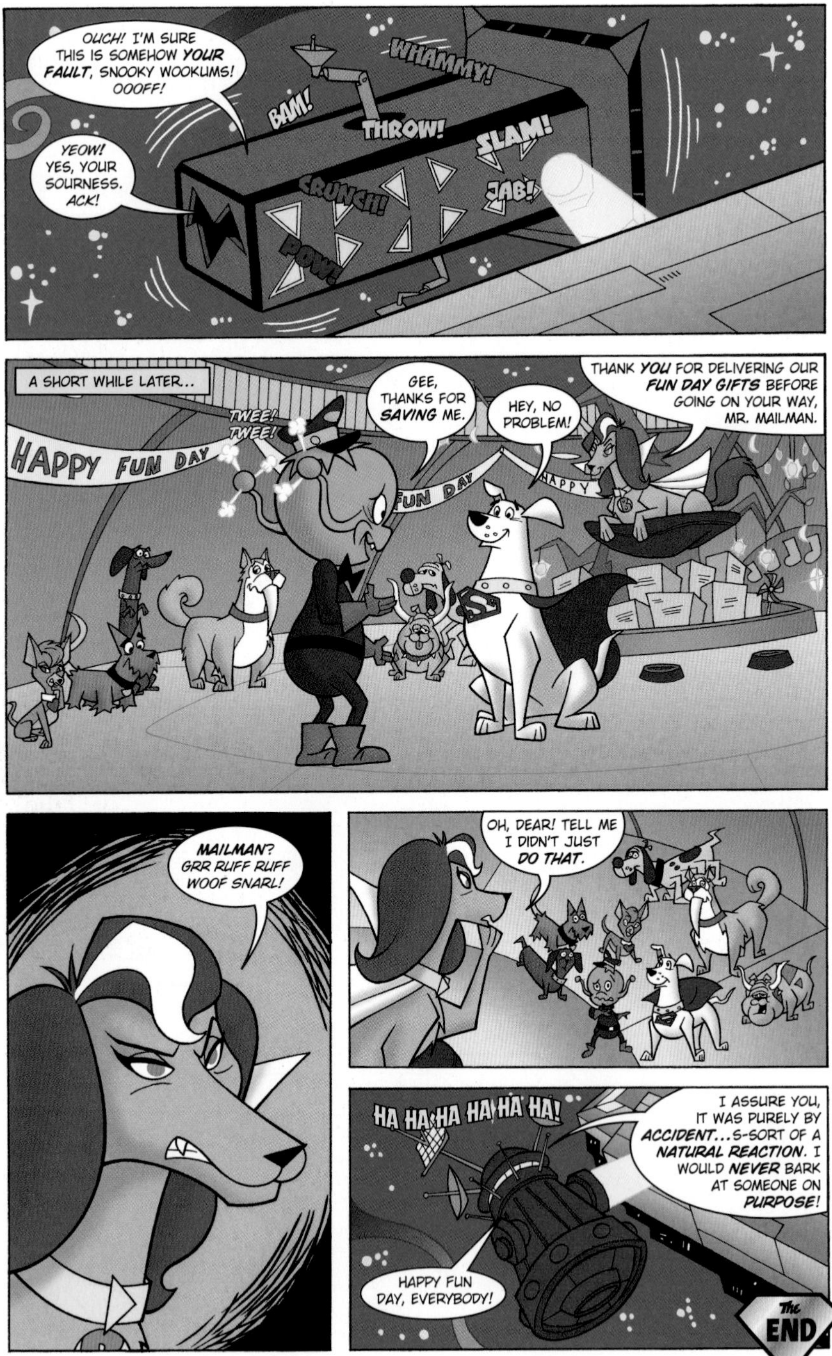

OUCH! I'M SURE THIS IS SOMEHOW YOUR FAULT, SNOOKY WOOKUMS! OOOFF!
WHAMMY!
BAM!
THROW!
SLAM!
YEOW! YES, YOUR SOURNESS. ACK!
CRUNCH!
JAB!
POW!
A SHORT WHILE LATER...
HAPPY FUN DAY
TWEE! TWEE!
GEE, THANKS FOR SAVING ME.
HEY, NO PROBLEM!
THANK YOU FOR DELIVERING OUR FUN DAY GIFTS BEFORE GOING ON YOUR WAY, MR. MAILMAN.
MAILMAN? GRR RUFF RUFF WOOF SNARL!
OH, DEAR! TELL ME I DIDN'T JUST DO THAT.
HA HA HA HA HA HA!
I ASSURE YOU, IT WAS PURELY BY ACCIDENT...S-SORT OF A NATURAL REACTION. I WOULD NEVER BARK AT SOMEONE ON PURPOSE!
HAPPY FUN DAY, EVERYBODY!
The END

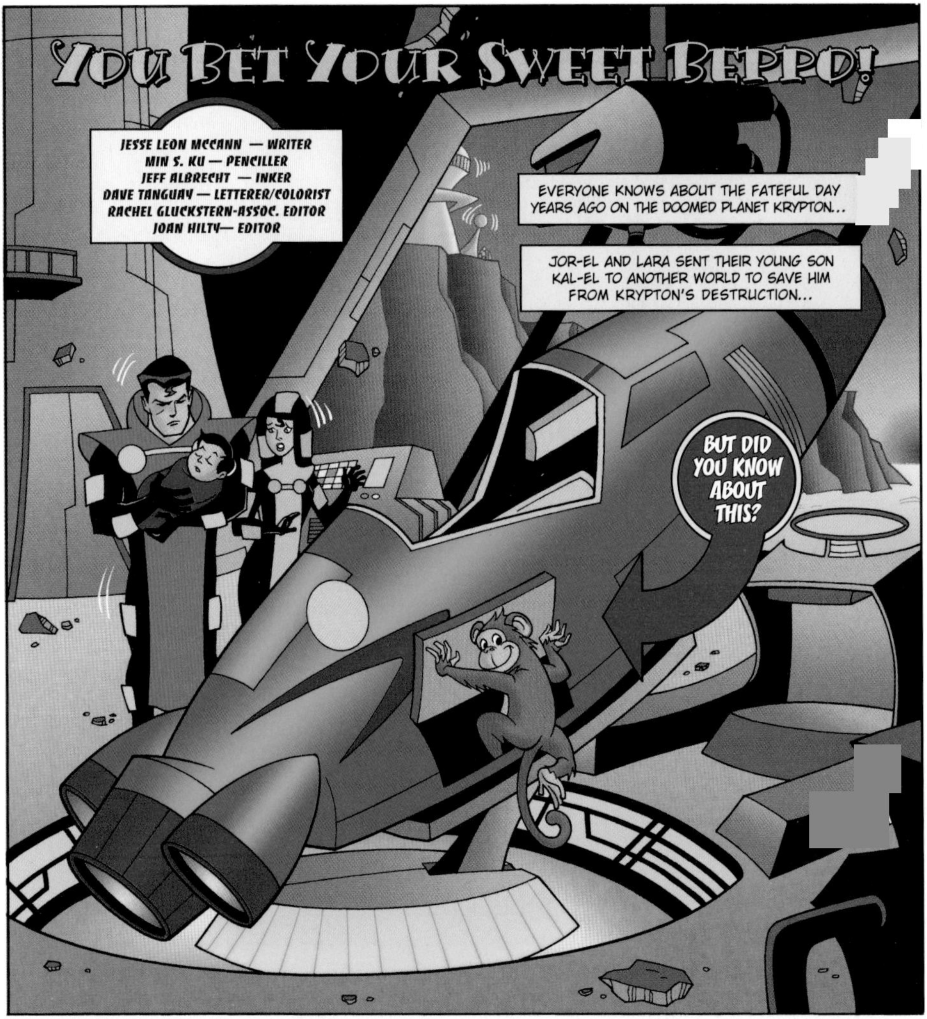
YOU BET YOUR SWEET BEPPO!
JESSE LEON MCCANN — WRITER
MIN S. KU — PENCILLER
JEFF ALBRECHT — INKER
DAVE TANGUAY — LETTERER/COLORIST
RACHEL GLUCKSTERN-ASSOC. EDITOR
JOAN HILTY— EDITOR
EVERYONE KNOWS ABOUT THE FATEFUL DAY YEARS AGO ON THE DOOMED PLANET KRYPTON...
JOR-EL AND LARA SENT THEIR YOUNG SON KAL-EL TO ANOTHER WORLD TO SAVE HIM FROM KRYPTON'S DESTRUCTION...
BUT DID YOU KNOW ABOUT THIS?

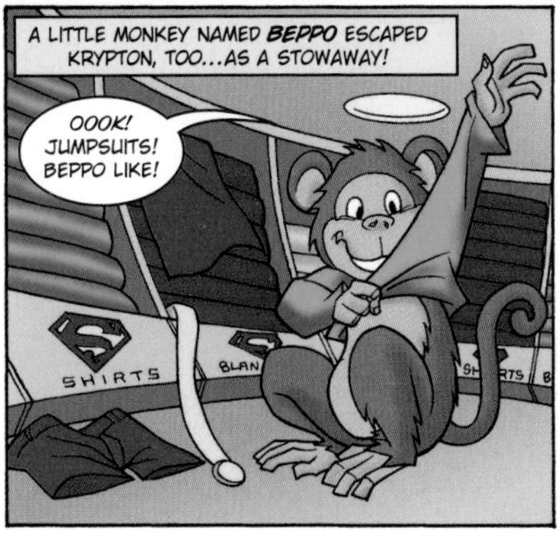
A LITTLE MONKEY NAMED *BEPPO* ESCAPED KRYPTON, TOO...AS A STOWAWAY!
OOOK! JUMPSUITS! BEPPO LIKE!
SHIRTS

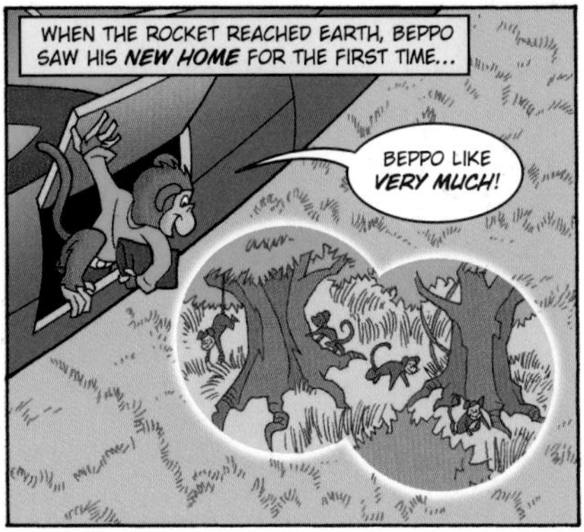
WHEN THE ROCKET REACHED EARTH, BEPPO SAW HIS *NEW HOME* FOR THE FIRST TIME...
BEPPO LIKE *VERY MUCH!*

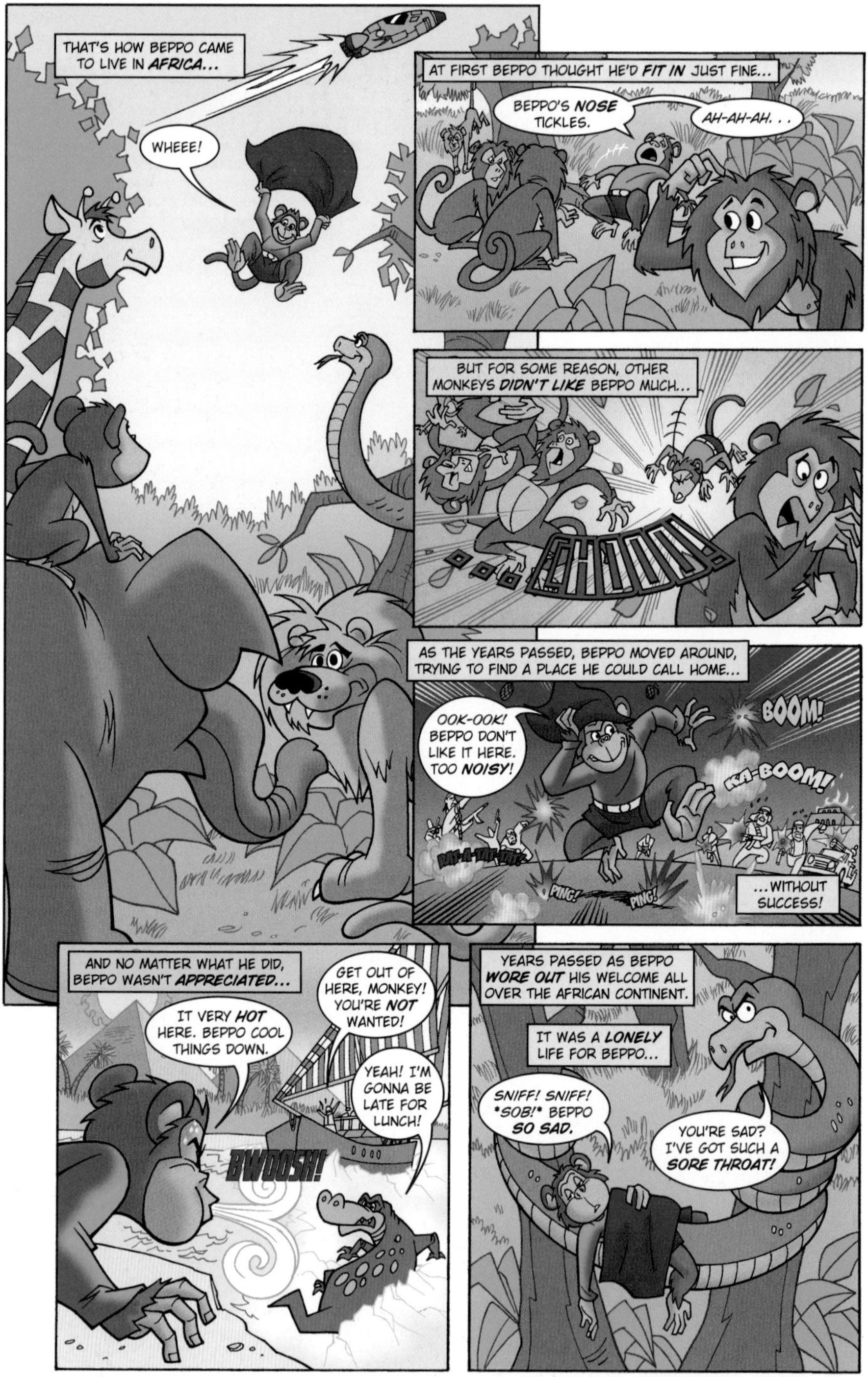

THAT'S HOW BEPPO CAME TO LIVE IN AFRICA...
WHEEE!
AT FIRST BEPPO THOUGHT HE'D FIT IN JUST FINE...
BEPPO'S NOSE TICKLES.
AH-AH-AH. . .
BUT FOR SOME REASON, OTHER MONKEYS DIDN'T LIKE BEPPO MUCH...
CHOOO!
AS THE YEARS PASSED, BEPPO MOVED AROUND, TRYING TO FIND A PLACE HE COULD CALL HOME...
OOK-OOK! BEPPO DON'T LIKE IT HERE. TOO NOISY!
BOOM!
KA-BOOM!
RAT-A-TAT-TAT!
PING!
PING!
...WITHOUT SUCCESS!
AND NO MATTER WHAT HE DID, BEPPO WASN'T APPRECIATED...
IT VERY HOT HERE. BEPPO COOL THINGS DOWN.
GET OUT OF HERE, MONKEY! YOU'RE NOT WANTED!
YEAH! I'M GONNA BE LATE FOR LUNCH!
BWOOSH!
YEARS PASSED AS BEPPO WORE OUT HIS WELCOME ALL OVER THE AFRICAN CONTINENT.
IT WAS A LONELY LIFE FOR BEPPO...
SNIFF! SNIFF! *SOB!* BEPPO SO SAD.
YOU'RE SAD? I'VE GOT SUCH A SORE THROAT!

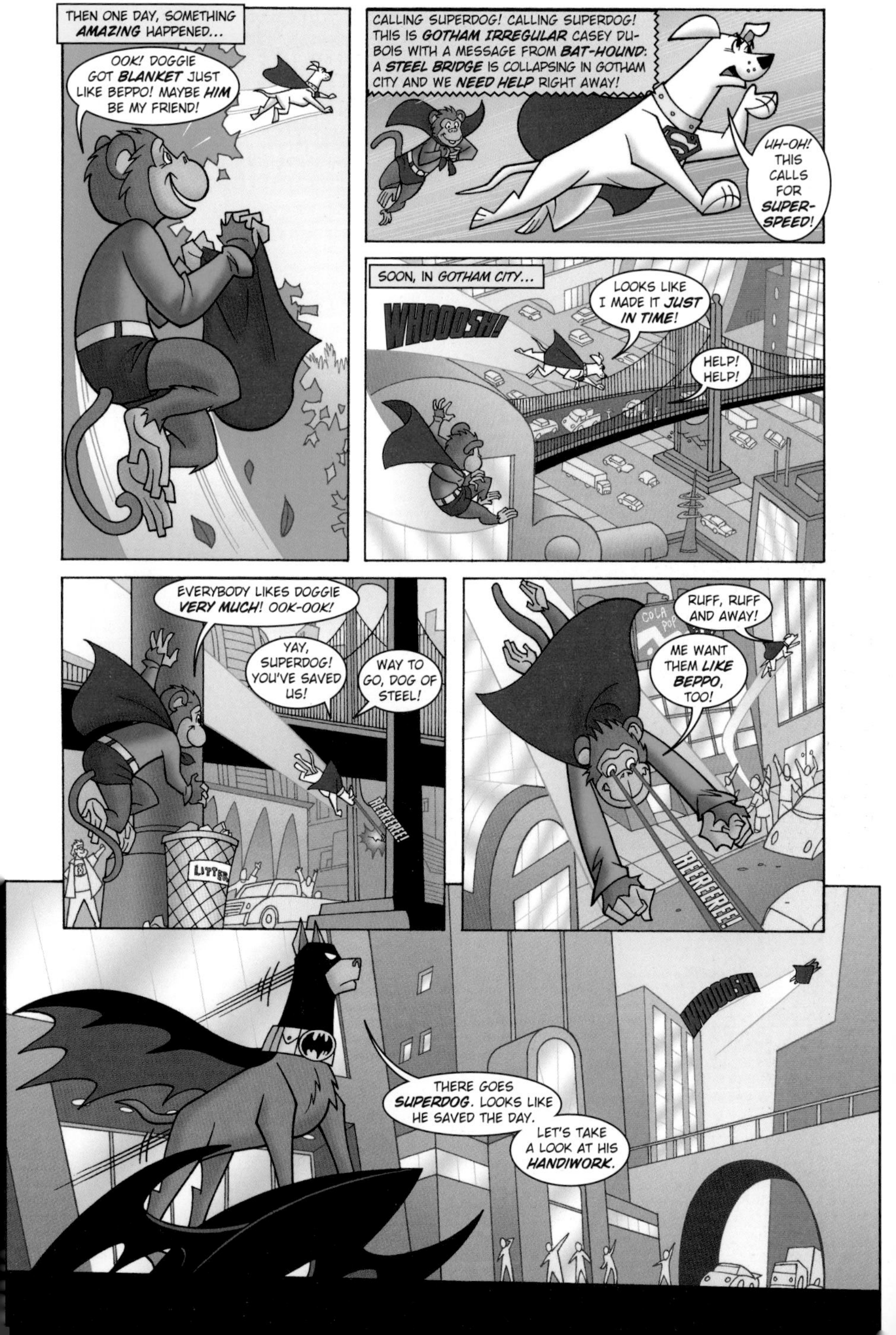
THEN ONE DAY, SOMETHING AMAZING HAPPENED...
OOK! DOGGIE GOT BLANKET JUST LIKE BEPPO! MAYBE HIM BE MY FRIEND!
CALLING SUPERDOG! CALLING SUPERDOG! THIS IS GOTHAM IRREGULAR CASEY DUBOIS WITH A MESSAGE FROM BAT-HOUND: A STEEL BRIDGE IS COLLAPSING IN GOTHAM CITY AND WE NEED HELP RIGHT AWAY!
UH-OH! THIS CALLS FOR SUPER-SPEED!
SOON, IN GOTHAM CITY...
WHOOOSH!
LOOKS LIKE I MADE IT JUST IN TIME!
HELP! HELP!
EVERYBODY LIKES DOGGIE VERY MUCH! OOK-OOK!
YAY, SUPERDOG! YOU'VE SAVED US!
WAY TO GO, DOG OF STEEL!
REEREEREE!
LITTER
RUFF, RUFF AND AWAY!
COLA POP
ME WANT THEM LIKE BEPPO, TOO!
REEREEREE!
WHOOOSH!
THERE GOES SUPERDOG. LOOKS LIKE HE SAVED THE DAY.
LET'S TAKE A LOOK AT HIS HANDIWORK.

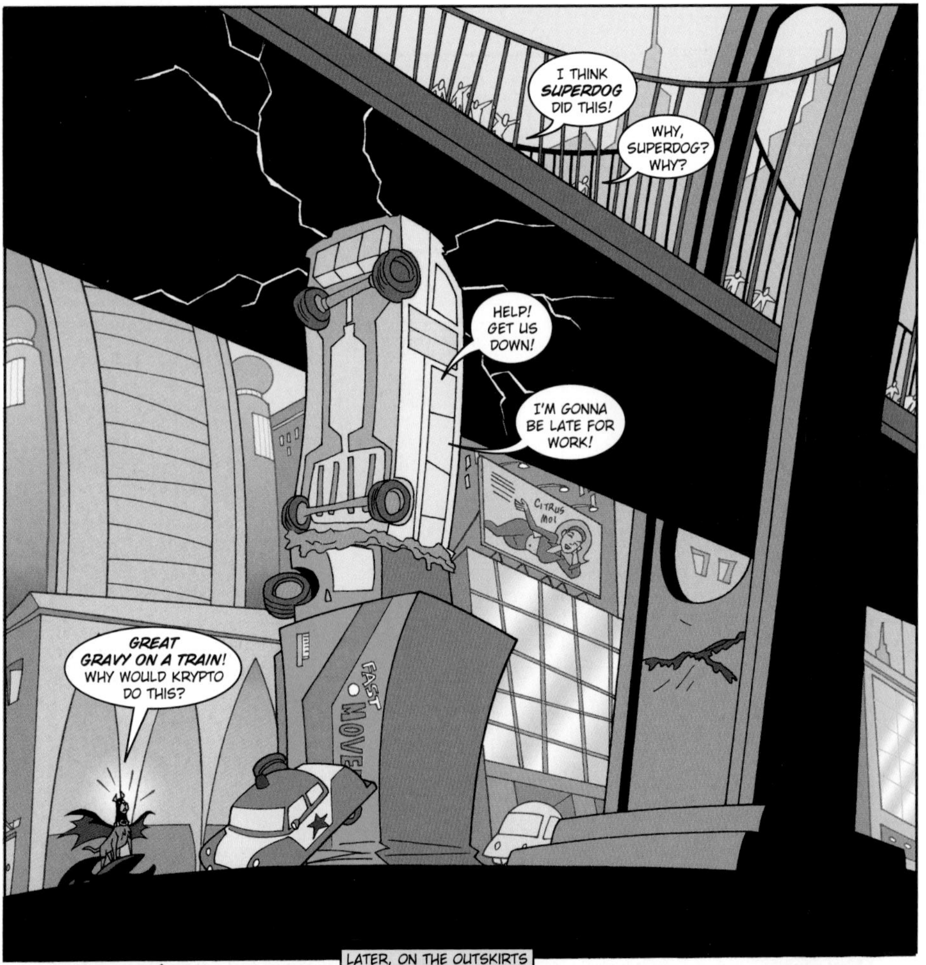
I THINK **SUPERDOG** DID THIS!
WHY, SUPERDOG? WHY?
HELP! GET US DOWN!
I'M GONNA BE LATE FOR WORK!
GREAT GRAVY ON A TRAIN! WHY WOULD KRYPTO DO THIS?

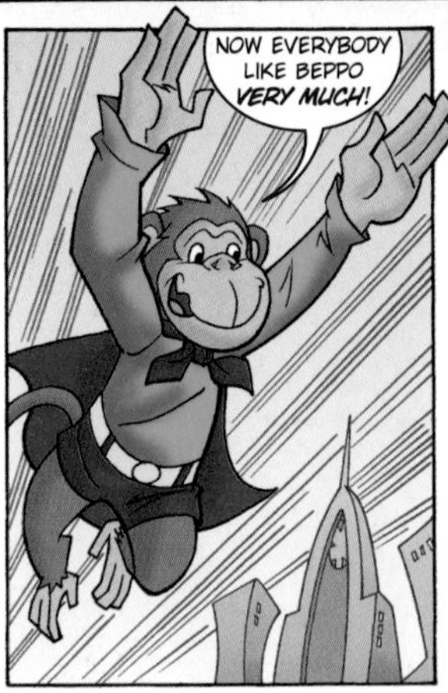
NOW EVERYBODY LIKE BEPPO ***VERY MUCH!***

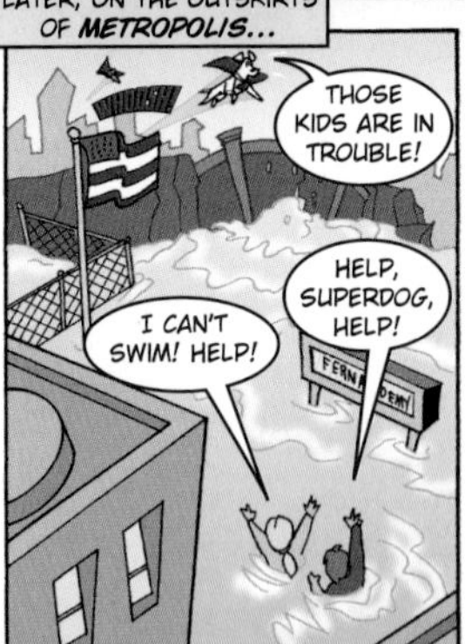
LATER, ON THE OUTSKIRTS OF ***METROPOLIS...***
THOSE KIDS ARE IN TROUBLE!
HELP, SUPERDOG, HELP!
I CAN'T SWIM! HELP!

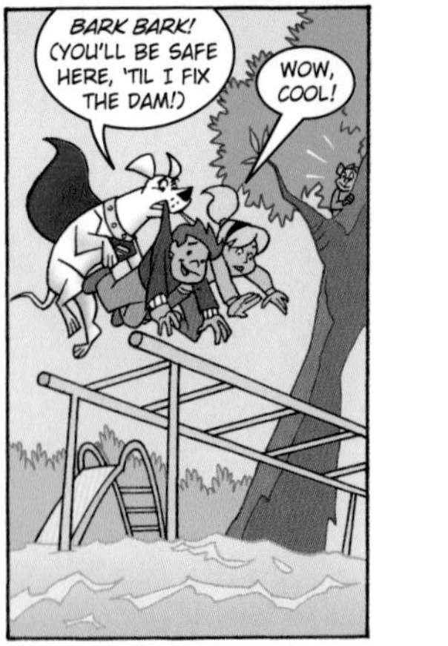
BARK BARK! (YOU'LL BE SAFE HERE, 'TIL I FIX THE DAM!)
WOW, COOL!

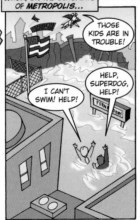

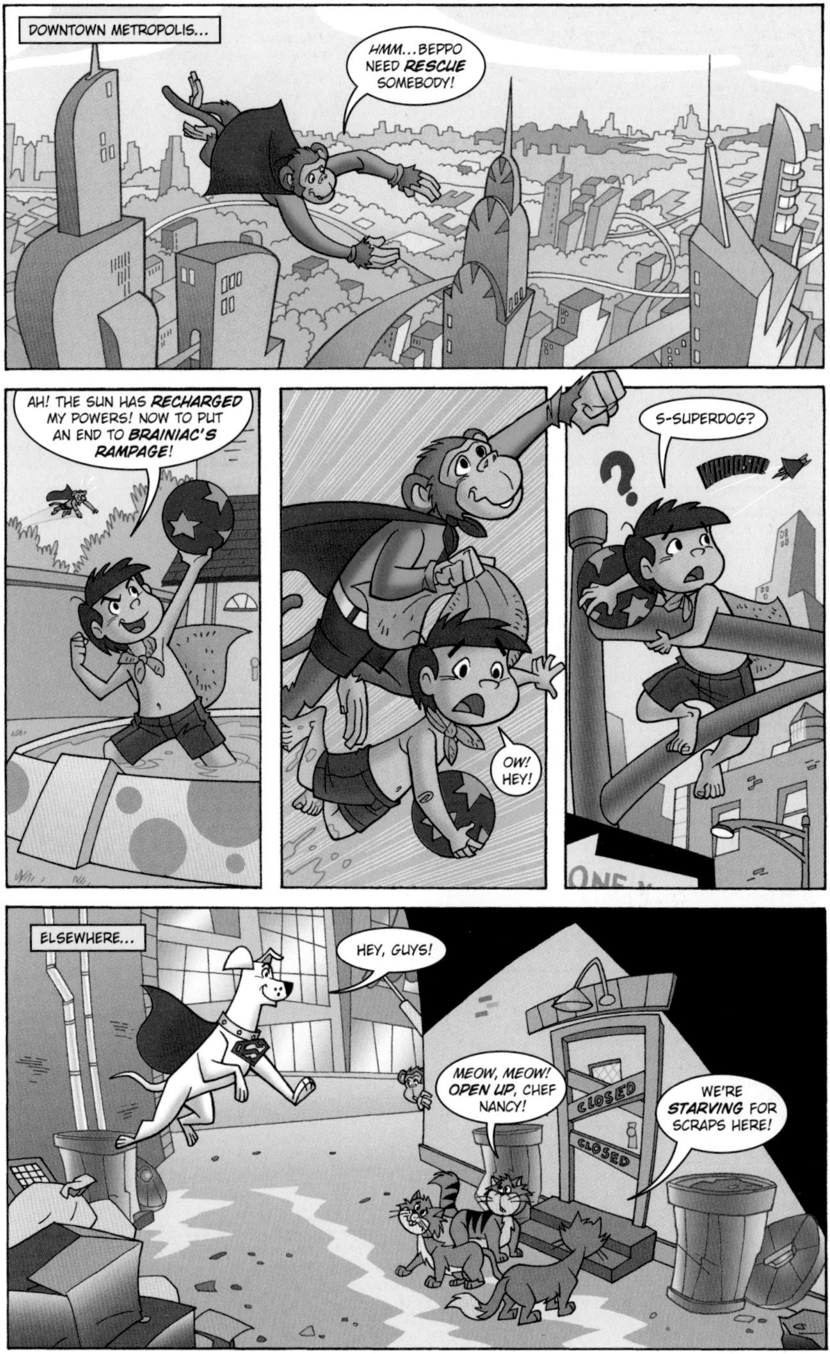
DOWNTOWN METROPOLIS...
HMM...BEPPO NEED RESCUE SOMEBODY!
AH! THE SUN HAS RECHARGED MY POWERS! NOW TO PUT AN END TO BRAINIAC'S RAMPAGE!
OW! HEY!
S-SUPERDOG?
WHOOSH!
ELSEWHERE...
HEY, GUYS!
MEOW, MEOW! OPEN UP, CHEF NANCY!
WE'RE STARVING FOR SCRAPS HERE!
CLOSED
CLOSED

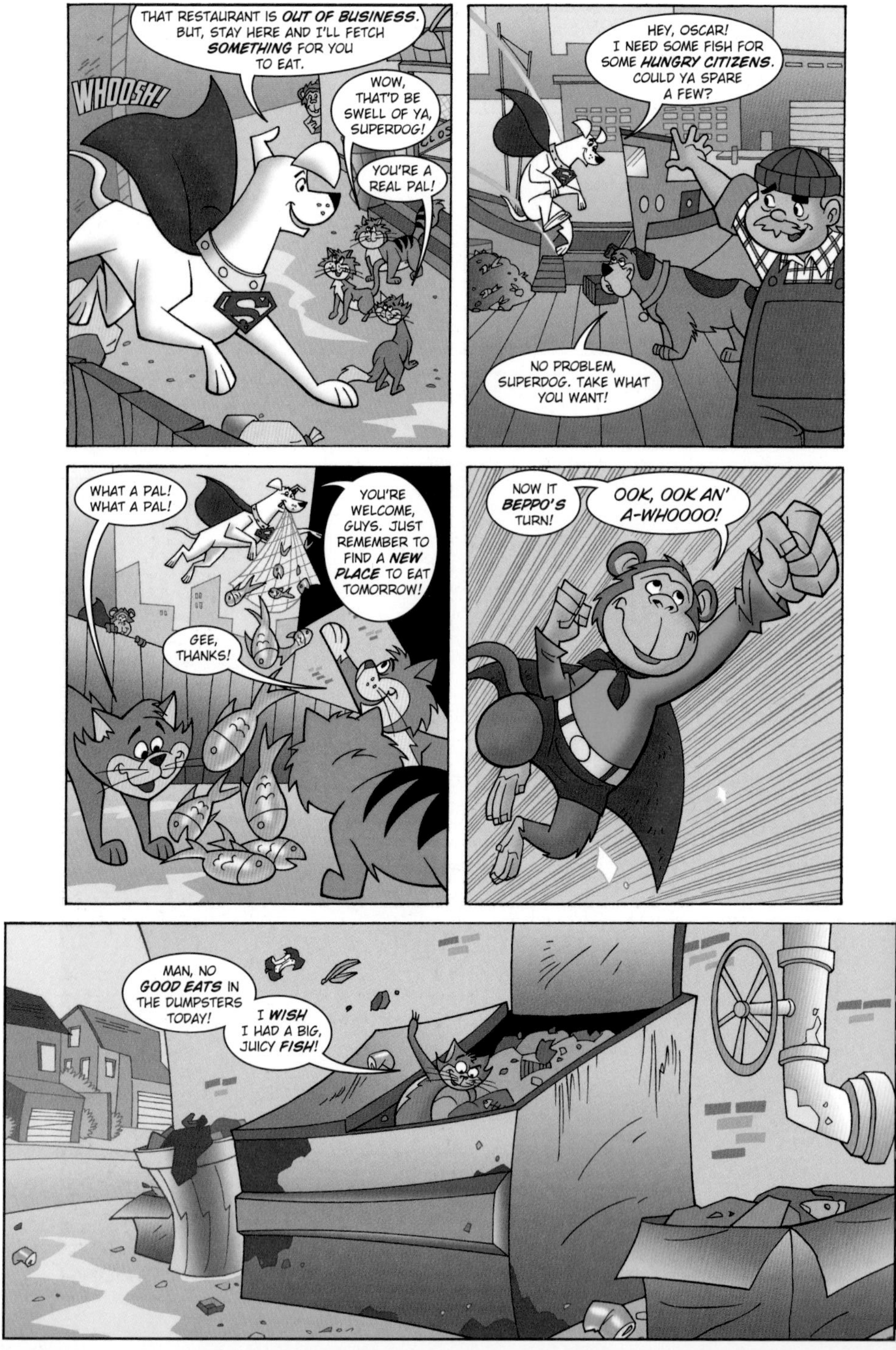

WHOOSH!
THAT RESTAURANT IS OUT OF BUSINESS. BUT, STAY HERE AND I'LL FETCH SOMETHING FOR YOU TO EAT.
WOW, THAT'D BE SWELL OF YA, SUPERDOG!
YOU'RE A REAL PAL!
HEY, OSCAR! I NEED SOME FISH FOR SOME HUNGRY CITIZENS. COULD YA SPARE A FEW?
NO PROBLEM, SUPERDOG. TAKE WHAT YOU WANT!
WHAT A PAL! WHAT A PAL!
YOU'RE WELCOME, GUYS. JUST REMEMBER TO FIND A NEW PLACE TO EAT TOMORROW!
GEE, THANKS!
NOW IT BEPPO'S TURN!
OOK, OOK AN' A-WHOOOO!
MAN, NO GOOD EATS IN THE DUMPSTERS TODAY!
I WISH I HAD A BIG, JUICY FISH!

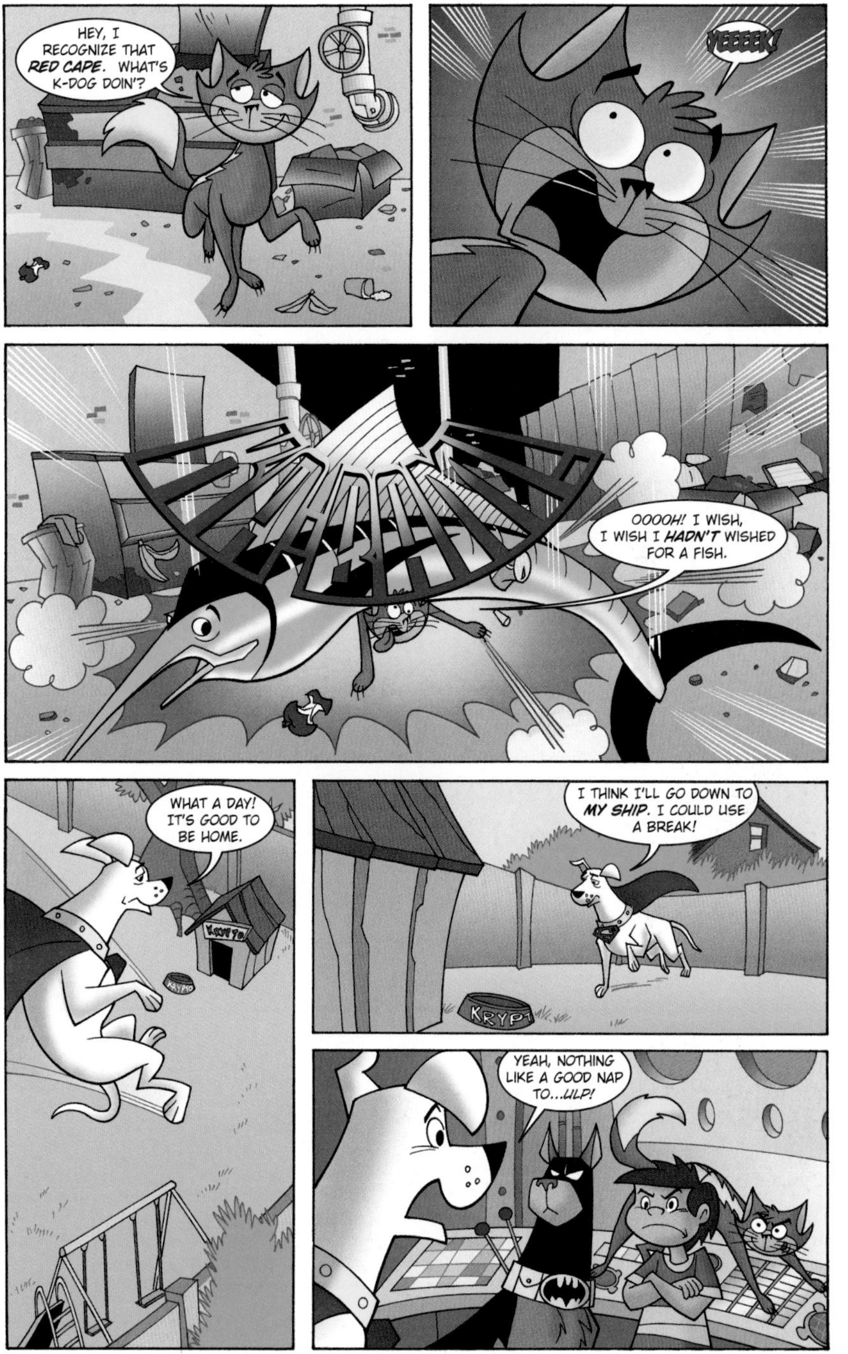

HEY, I RECOGNIZE THAT RED CAPE. WHAT'S K-DOG DOIN'?
YEEEEK!
OOOOH! I WISH, I WISH I HADN'T WISHED FOR A FISH.
WHAT A DAY! IT'S GOOD TO BE HOME.
KRYPTO
I THINK I'LL GO DOWN TO MY SHIP. I COULD USE A BREAK!
YEAH, NOTHING LIKE A GOOD NAP TO...ULP!

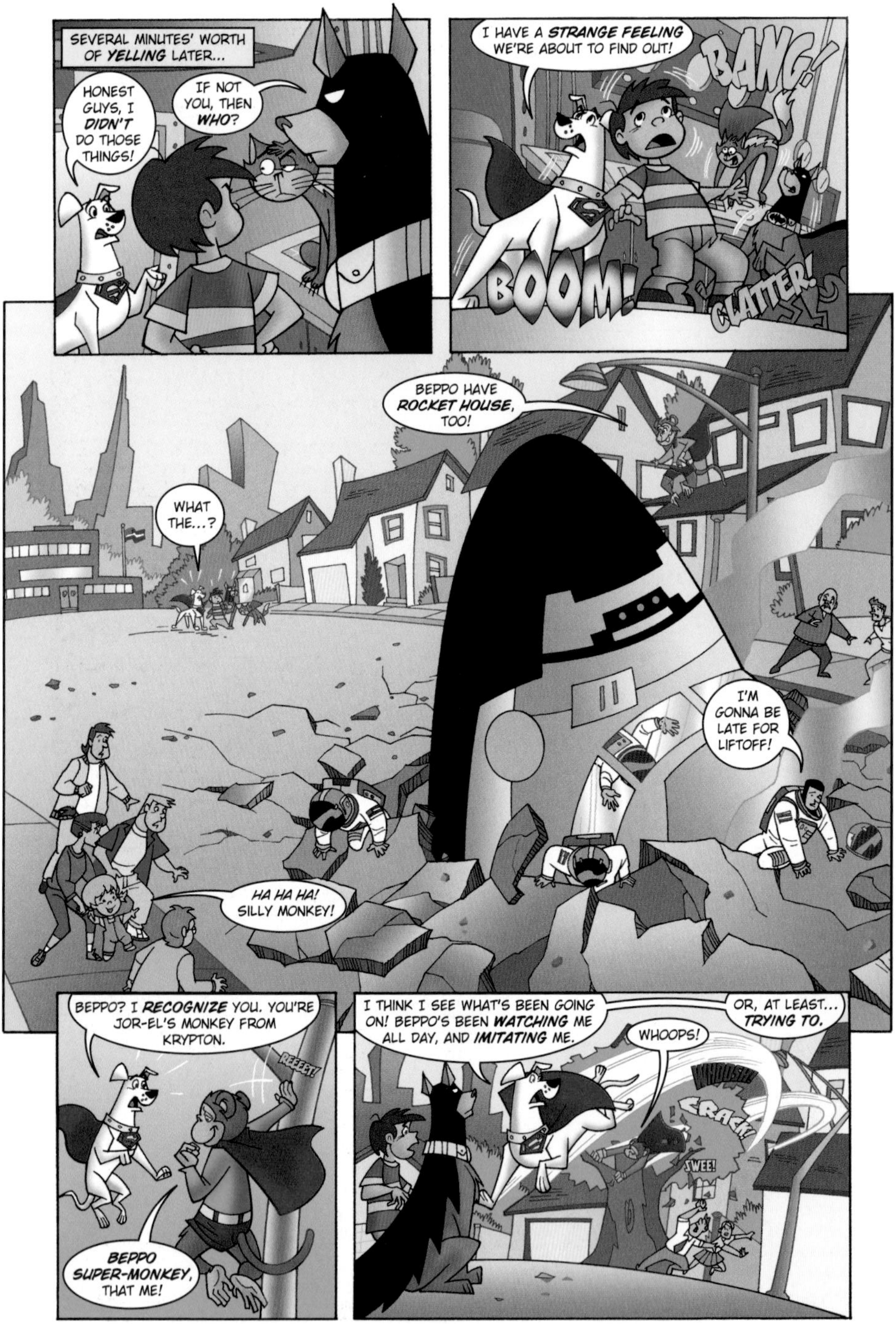
SEVERAL MINUTES' WORTH OF YELLING LATER...
HONEST GUYS, I DIDN'T DO THOSE THINGS!
IF NOT YOU, THEN WHO?
I HAVE A STRANGE FEELING WE'RE ABOUT TO FIND OUT!
BANG!
BOOM!
CLATTER!
BEPPO HAVE ROCKET HOUSE, TOO!
WHAT THE...?
I'M GONNA BE LATE FOR LIFTOFF!
HA HA HA! SILLY MONKEY!
BEPPO? I RECOGNIZE YOU. YOU'RE JOR-EL'S MONKEY FROM KRYPTON.
REEEEET!
BEPPO SUPER-MONKEY, THAT ME!
I THINK I SEE WHAT'S BEEN GOING ON! BEPPO'S BEEN WATCHING ME ALL DAY, AND IMITATING ME.
OR, AT LEAST... TRYING TO.
WHOOPS!
WHOOSH!
CRACK!
SWEE!

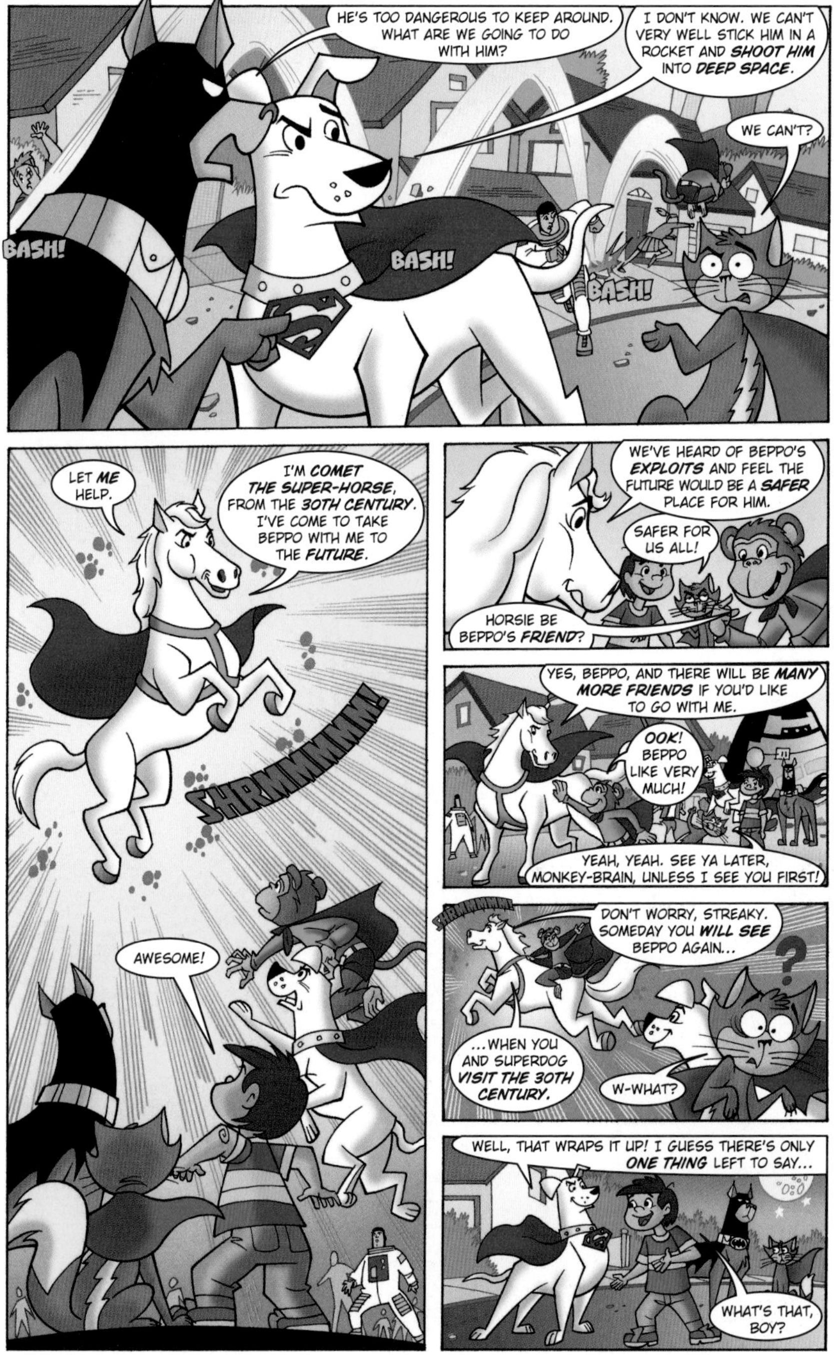
HE'S TOO DANGEROUS TO KEEP AROUND. WHAT ARE WE GOING TO DO WITH HIM?
I DON'T KNOW. WE CAN'T VERY WELL STICK HIM IN A ROCKET AND SHOOT HIM INTO DEEP SPACE.
WE CAN'T?
BASH!
BASH!
BASH!
LET ME HELP.
I'M COMET THE SUPER-HORSE, FROM THE 30TH CENTURY. I'VE COME TO TAKE BEPPO WITH ME TO THE FUTURE.
SHRMMMMM!
AWESOME!
WE'VE HEARD OF BEPPO'S EXPLOITS AND FEEL THE FUTURE WOULD BE A SAFER PLACE FOR HIM.
SAFER FOR US ALL!
HORSIE BE BEPPO'S FRIEND?
YES, BEPPO, AND THERE WILL BE MANY MORE FRIENDS IF YOU'D LIKE TO GO WITH ME.
OOK! BEPPO LIKE VERY MUCH!
YEAH, YEAH. SEE YA LATER, MONKEY-BRAIN, UNLESS I SEE YOU FIRST!
DON'T WORRY, STREAKY. SOMEDAY YOU WILL SEE BEPPO AGAIN...
?
...WHEN YOU AND SUPERDOG VISIT THE 30TH CENTURY.
W-WHAT?
WELL, THAT WRAPS IT UP! I GUESS THERE'S ONLY ONE THING LEFT TO SAY...
WHAT'S THAT, BOY?

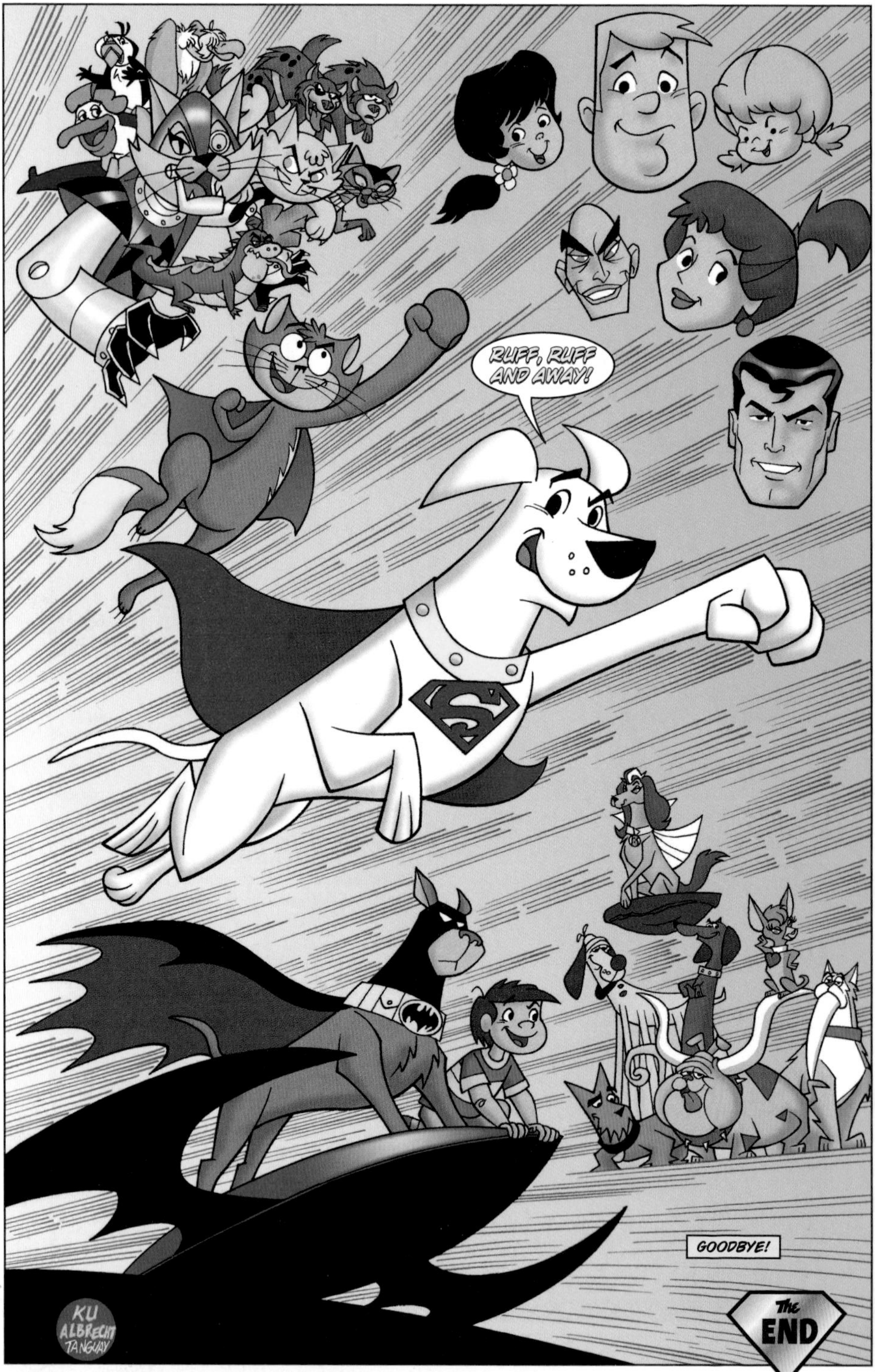
RUFF, RUFF AND AWAY!
GOODBYE!
The END
KU ALBRECHT TANGUAY

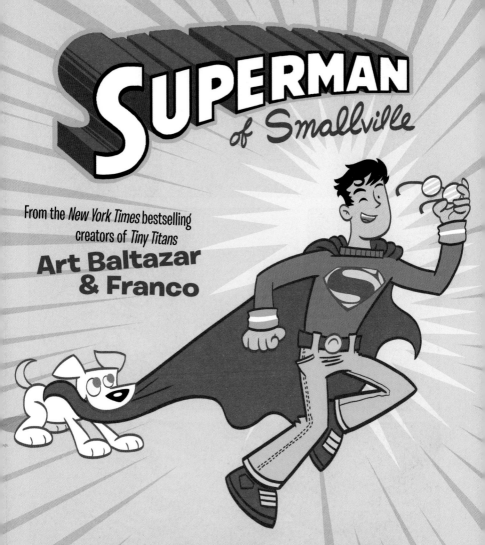

Can Superman keep Smallville from going to the dogs?

SUPERMAN
of Smallville

From the *New York Times* bestselling
creators of *Tiny Titans*
**Art Baltazar
& Franco**

From the *New York Times* bestselling creators of *Tiny Titans*
comes the hilarious story of Clark Kent as he navigates aliens,
disappearing hot dog carts, and middle school.

Clark discovers Krypto in this exclusive sneak peek!

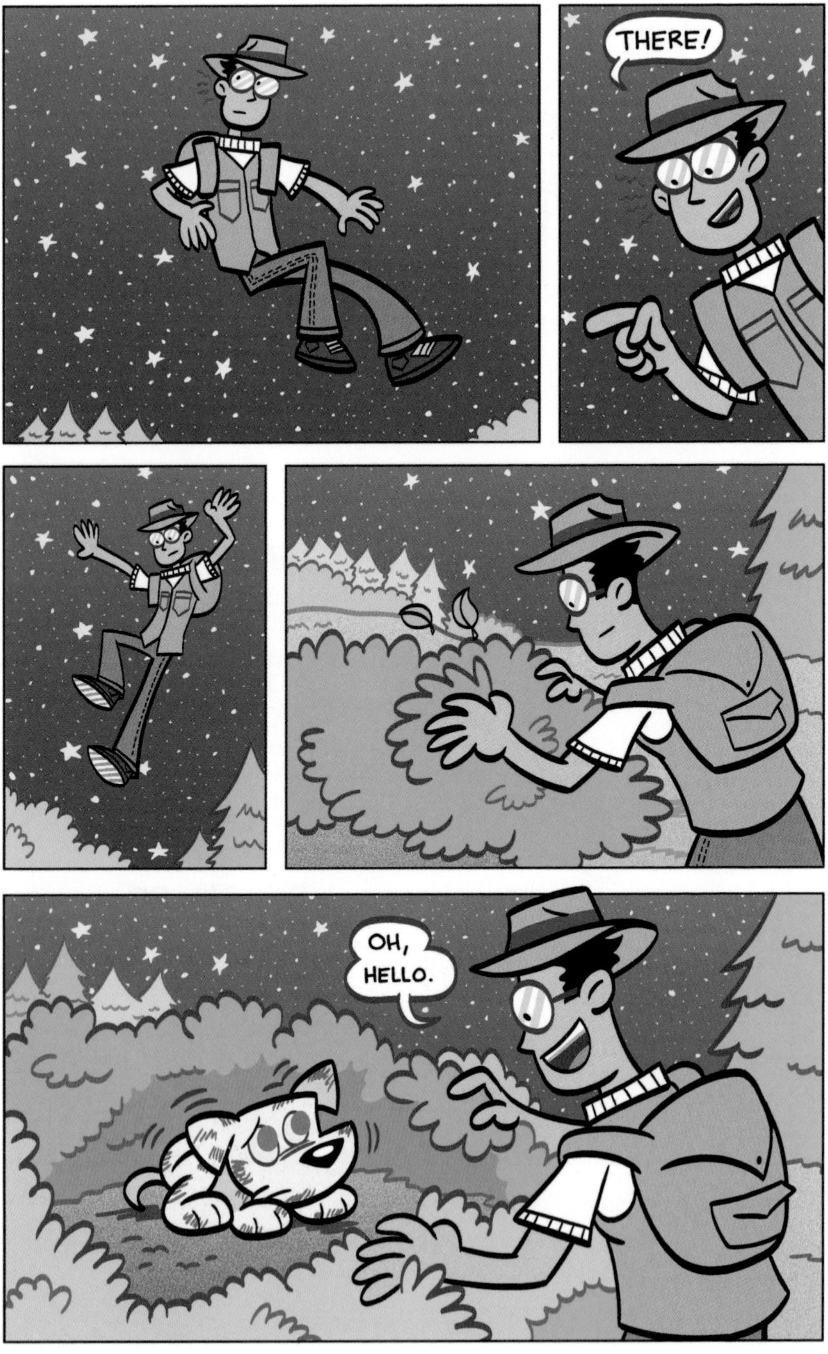
THERE!
OH, HELLO.

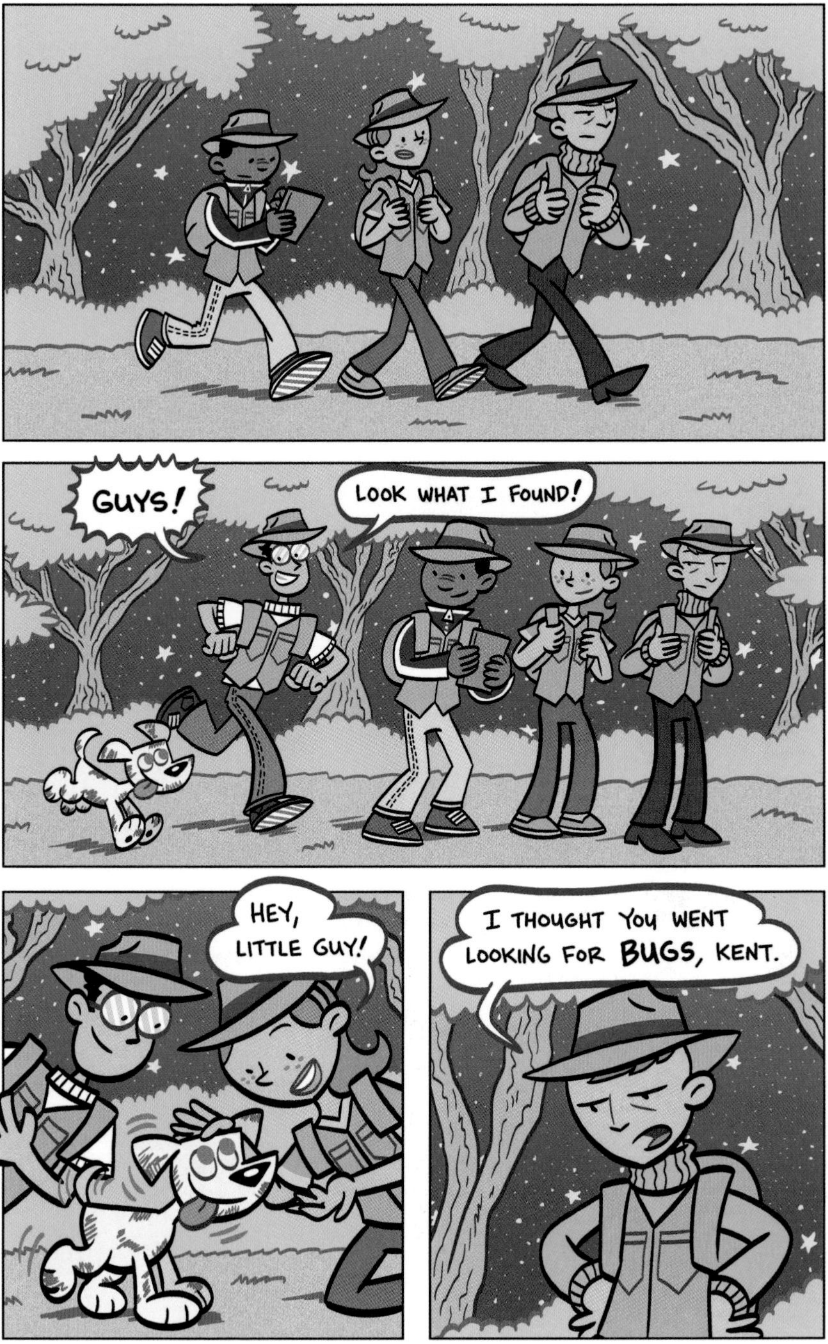
GUYS!
LOOK WHAT I FOUND!
HEY, LITTLE GUY!
I THOUGHT YOU WENT LOOKING FOR BUGS, KENT.

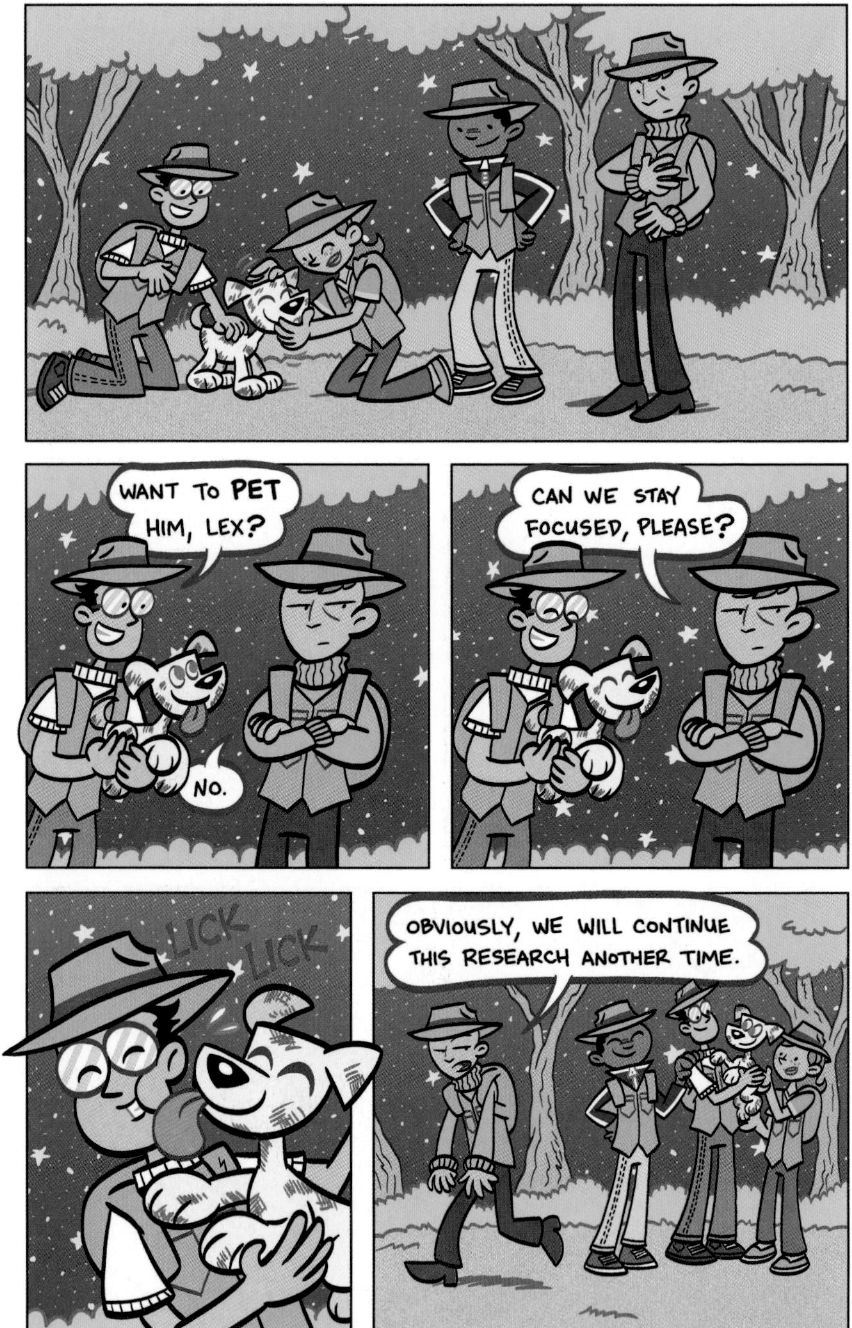
WANT TO PET HIM, LEX?
NO.
CAN WE STAY FOCUSED, PLEASE?
LICK
LICK
OBVIOUSLY, WE WILL CONTINUE THIS RESEARCH ANOTHER TIME.

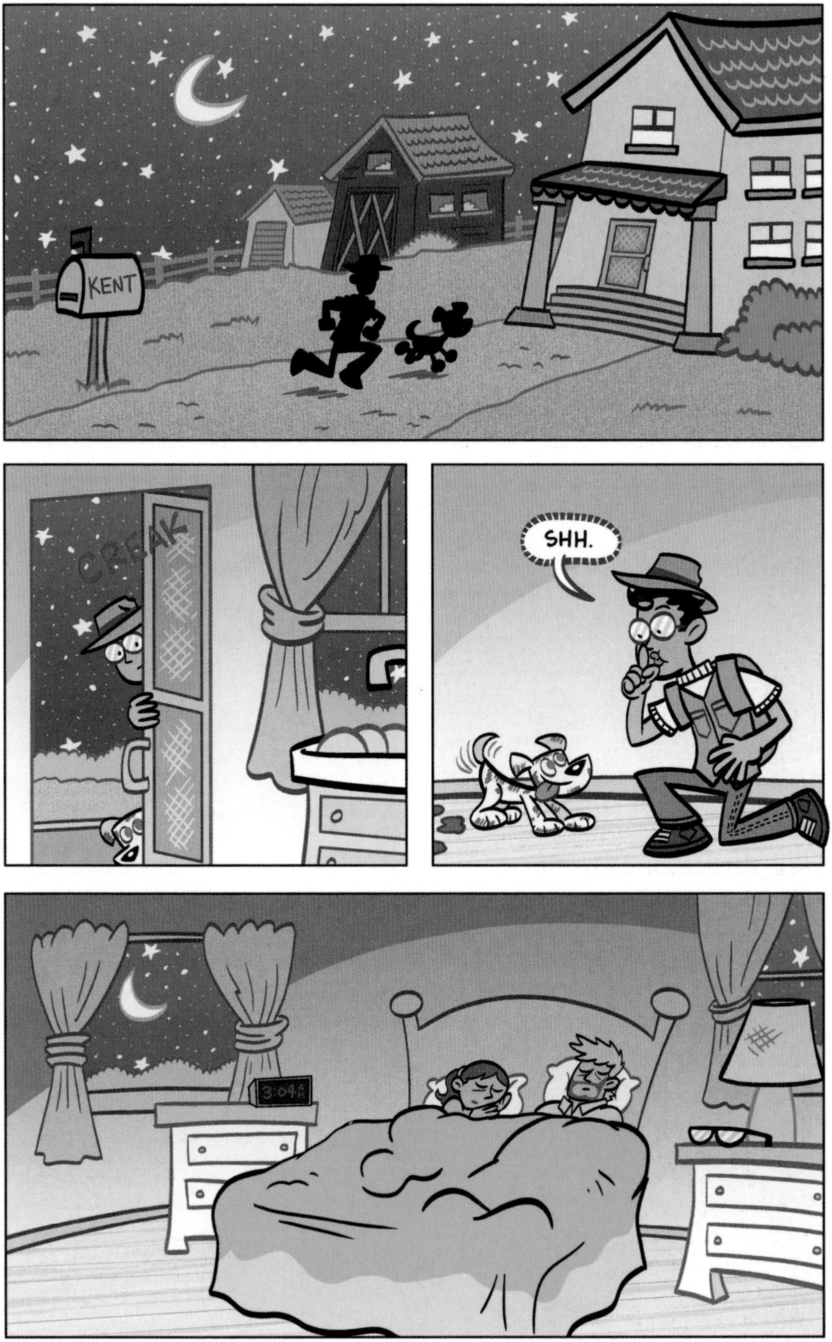
KENT
CREAK
SHH.
3:04

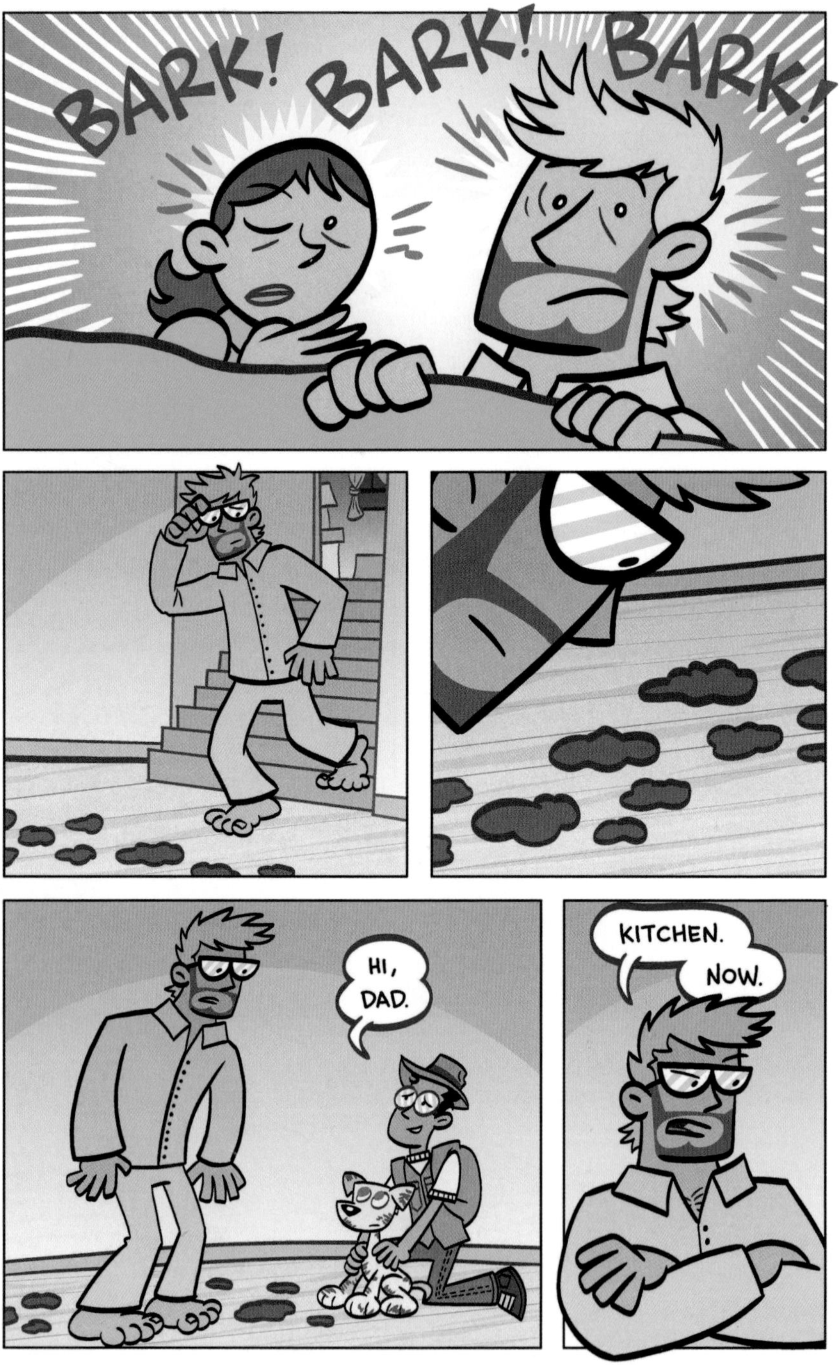
BARK! BARK! BARK!
HI, DAD.
KITCHEN. NOW.